TRAVELLING

UNRAVELLING

HarperCollins *Children's Books*

ELIZABETH NORRIS

First published in hardback in the USA by HarperCollins *Publishers Inc* in 2012
First published in Great Britain by HarperCollins *Children's Books* 2012
HarperCollins *Children's Books* is a division of HarperCollinsPublishers Lt,d
77-85 Fulham Palace Road, Hammersmith, London, W6 8JB.

The HarperCollins website address is: www.harpercollins.co.uk

1

Printed and bound in England by Clays Ltd, St Ives plc

MIX
Paper from
responsible sources
FSC® C007454

For the Js—without you, none of this would have been possible

PART ONE

The woods are lovely, dark and deep.

But I have promises to keep,

And miles to go before I sleep,

And miles to go before I sleep.

—Robert Frost

24:00:14:32

I can tell the exact moment Nick steps on the beach.

It doesn't matter that we've only been on three dates or that I wasn't his biggest fan for the last five years. It doesn't even matter that his romantic attempts to win me over this summer could be just a means to an end—better girls have been taken in by lesser guys.

But when the air changes, the temperature drops a fraction of a degree, the wind picks up, and a shot of electricity moves through the sand under my feet, I know he's here.

At least, that's what I tell Elise, since she likes to swoon over my sort-of love life and gets annoyed when she thinks I'm keeping the details to myself.

I *can* tell the exact moment Nick steps on the beach, though.

But that's just because it's sort of hard to miss seventy-eight twelve-year-olds rushing the beach.

Today I'm actually relieved to see the tidal wave of Little Leaguers descend on Torrey Pines, and I can't help but smile. Not because of them—not even because of Nick—but because their arrival signifies the end of another ten-hour shift. My last

1

dawn-to-five lifeguard shift this summer. Which is bittersweet, because I love spending my days here—there's something about the wide-open expanse of water, especially at dawn, when the only people here are the diehard surfers. But I don't love the long days or the Little League camps or the weekend warriors.

"Damn, J," Steve says as he gets out of the truck, his eyes wandering to the tendrils of my scar peeking out from under the left strap of my bathing suit. "You're bailing?"

I grab my duffel and jump from the guard stand into the sand—and ignore the urge to remind him that the scar is nothing he hasn't seen all summer. "Dude, it's all you until sundown."

Steve doesn't get the chance to say anything else. A clump of wet sand hits me in the leg, followed by a chorus of prepubescent male snickers.

"Aw, Nick. How many times I gotta tell you not to throw stuff at chicks to get their attention?" Per usual, Kevin Collins, mediocre quarterback, star shortstop, and biggest man-whore of Eastview High School stands surrounded by a half-dozen of his Little League campers. "Sorry, Janelle, but you know my man. He's got no *skillz*." He throws an arrogant smile at me because he knows he looks good enough without a shirt that most girls will forgive anything.

But I'm not most girls.

Instead I turn to his best friend. A blush and a lazy smile on his face, he's swinging his hands together nervously. Tanned skin, short black hair, almond eyes, washboard abs. If I were Elise, I might say Nick Matherson is so pretty it hurts.

Instead I say, "Hey. Happy last day of camp."

His smile widens, and something in my chest flutters a little—like it always does when he directs that smile at me.

"Thanks. They were punks today since, you know, they knew they couldn't really get in trouble. I thought I might lose my mind, but I'm just glad it's over."

I nod—he's already told me he doesn't think he'll coach or work camp again next year.

"I brought you something," Nick says, reaching into the pocket of his board shorts and extending his loose fist to me. Only he doesn't open his hand. He just waits.

"What is it?" I ask.

He shrugs. "Come here and see."

I take a hesitant step closer and reach out my hand. I'm not sure what he could bring me that would fit into his hand, but the fact that he thought of me when I wasn't around—enough to actually bring me something—makes me smile.

When I touch his wrist to turn it over, his skin is warm. I feel a tingle run through my body as I use my other hand to open his fingers.

And when I see, I can't help gasping a little. It's a hundred times better than a piece of jewelry. It's a packet of lavender seeds. Something I've wanted. Something I mentioned to him just yesterday.

"The guy I bought them from said you can plant them in a planter, not like, actually outside, if you don't want. Hopefully it will help your mom with those headaches," Nick says.

"Nick, it's perfect. Thank you," I say with a smile, and I lean in to hug him. Instead he drops his head, and our lips brush up against each other quickly, before I pull back. I work here, after all, even if it is my last day for the summer.

"I heard you had a rough save this morning," he says with a laugh. "Two grown men?"

3

"It was just a rip current," I explain, a blush creeping into my face as I give a quick rundown of the incident. As I'm talking, I glance over Nick's shoulder and see Brooke Haslen giving me her scariest death glare.

"But wait," Nick says. "Elise said both guys were, like, three bills easy."

"I had the rescue board with me. I swam out there, got them both on the board, and swam them parallel to the shore until we could get back in. It wasn't a big deal."

"Whatever, Janelle," Kevin says as he throws an arm around my shoulder. "We know you're hiding crazy guns. Think you could take me?" He flexes his biceps, which would be impressive if he weren't so cocky.

"Dude, get off her," Nick says, as he pushes Kevin. It only takes two shoves before they're full-out wrestling and punching each other in the sand. Moments like this I wonder if they share the same brain.

Before the swarm of Little Leaguers rushes over to cheer them on, I start walking toward the parking lot. I still have to pick my brother up from his best friend's house and drop him off at water polo practice, then go home, shower, and change before Nick brings me back here for the annual back-to-school bonfire.

"Janelle!" Nick shouts.

I turn around in time to see Kevin knock him over and push him face-first into the sand. Nick rolls over and punches Kevin hard in his lower back—kidney shot—and spits sand out of his mouth. "I'll pick you up around eight tonight, right?"

I nod, and a grin overtakes his face. I start to return the smile, but then Kevin is on top of him again, and they're back at it.

I turn around and catch Brooke staring at me. I lock onto

her blue eyes and refuse to look away. There was a time when I might have been the kind of girl to wilt under the disapproval of Brooke Haslen. She's seemingly everything I'm not—tall, blond, beautiful, perfect. And if this were three years ago, I might have felt guilty about the fact that Nick asked me out only a few days after he broke up with her. But not anymore.

Brooke and I stare at each other as I pass by her and her friends. It's Kate who actually breaks the glare for us. She reaches for a can of soda and leans in front of Brooke. Then she looks up—sees me—then frowns and tries to look away.

When I get to my car, I understand. Brooke's smirk. Kate's regret.

The windshield of my Jeep reads BITCH in fluorescent pink window paint. Apparently, I'll also be running through a car wash on my way to pick up Jared.

Or not. Because as I open my door and chuck the duffel into the passenger seat, I realize my tire is flat. It doesn't just need more air. It's dead flat—the rim of my tire is on the pavement.

And it's not the only one.

My other front tire is flat too.

Kate would know I have a spare in the back of the Jeep. She knows my dad wouldn't let me get my license until I'd successfully demonstrated I could change a tire, check my oil, and jump-start the car.

When your ex–best friend and the ex-girlfriend of your sort-of boyfriend call you a bitch—in neon-pink window paint—and slash your tires, the temptation to break down and cry is definitely there. My eyes sting, my body feels hot in that "I'm treading the emotional line between fury and tears" sort of way, and I'm tempted to just throw my arms out wide, look up at the sky, and scream at the top of my lungs. Only, this is hardly the first time I've felt this way. Slashing tires might be new, but the life-ruining sentiment is still the same.

And I've dealt with far bigger issues than high school mean girls.

Digging into the glove compartment for my cell, I contemplate heading back to the beach and asking Nick for help. But being a damsel in distress isn't really my thing. And I don't want Nick to make any wild guesses about how this happened—he might act like a Neanderthal sometimes, but he's actually a smart guy, and BITCH plus two flat tires equals only one possible culprit. Plus, if I go back down to the beach for help, Brooke will get the satisfaction of seeing that she got to me.

So I call AAA and explain the problem while changing into my running sneakers. It'll take them at least an hour to get here to change the tires, but no big deal, I'll be back tonight. And they'll charge the tires to the credit card, so I won't have to worry about that.

Then I start walking. This stretch of Highway 101 is wide open—just cliffs, beach, and two-lane highway. I can easily hike up the hill and run into Del Mar. It's a little more than two miles, but if I run full speed, I can probably make it in under fifteen minutes. I dial the one person who's never let me down.

Because he's Alex, he answers on the first ring. "What's up?"

"I need a favor."

"Sure."

I smile into the phone. "Can you pick Jared and me up at Chris Whitman's house? He lives in Del Mar on Stratford Court at Fourth Street."

"Of course, but what's wrong with the Jeep?" I hear him grabbing his keys.

"Flat tire. Long story." He starts to protest. "I'll tell you all about it when you get there."

"Yeah, no problem. Do you want me to pick up something on the way?"

Crap. That reminds me. I promised Jared a carne asada burrito from Roberto's. I'm not going to have time, and it would be out of Alex's way. . . . I bite my lip and close my eyes for a split second, weighing Jared's disappointment against time.

I'm about to ask Alex if he can stop at the drive-through at Cotija's, which isn't quite as good but is at least on the way, when I think I hear someone shout my name.

But it's drowned out by the screech of brakes and the grinding of metal on asphalt.

23:23:57:07

Observation skills are hardly a hereditary gene, but before I died, I would have always said I either inherited mine from my dad or honed them living with my mom.

I also would have said I was the most observant person I knew—it was why I had the most saves out of all the lifeguards at Torrey Pines.

But somehow I manage to miss the faded blue Toyota pickup until it's so close I can feel the warmth of the engine and smell the smoke of locking brakes. Until the only thing I have time to do is haphazardly throw an arm in front of my face. Because apparently I'm vain like that.

23:23:57:06

There's a second of scorching heat and a sensation of vertigo, then my heart stops, everything freezes, and suddenly I don't need to breathe. The last thing I hear is Alex saying my name, his voice raised in question.

But there's no pain. In fact, when I die—and I *know* I'm dying, I'm as certain as I've ever been about anything in my life—there's an absence of pain, a lightness almost, as if all my worries about Jared getting enough to eat, making his water polo practices, getting good grades, adjusting to high school, about my dad working himself into the ground, getting enough sleep, spending enough time with Jared, about my mom taking her medicine on time, getting out of bed before three, not noticing I dumped the last of her gin down the drain—it all just escapes.

And I'm dead.

The clichéd whole-life-flashing-before-my-eyes moment doesn't come either. Instead I see just one day. The most perfect day of my existence. Maybe the sight of it really is just my optic nerves firing as my body shuts down. But the *feeling*—that's more

9

than just my body's physiological reaction. Because I can *feel* everything I felt that day.

And there's nothing clichéd about it at all.

I see the heavy heat of the midday summer sun beat down on my mother, surrounding her like some sort of halo, her belly swollen and pregnant with Jared. Her dark olive skin gleams in the reflection of the sunlight off the sand, and a thick mess of black hair is piled in a loose bun on top of her head. She claps her hands and throws her head back, letting out wild, joyful laughter from her mouth.

I hadn't remembered she could look so beautiful—so alive.

Our discarded attempt at re-creating Cinderella's castle with sand slumps next to her, surrounded by bright pink buckets and shovels.

Love blossoms in my chest—not just my love for her, but also her love for me—and the warm peace of the feeling wraps around me like a thick blanket.

Then I see myself, a fearless three-year-old with a body board and fins, attacking the waves as if conquering them will allow me to make my mark on the world. I'm laughing and swimming. The spray of the saltwater stings my face, the roaring thunder of the swells mixing with my mother's laughter filling my ears. The smell of the ocean and Coppertone SPF 45 in my nose.

Excitement. Happiness. Peace. Perfection.

23:23:56:49

A shock of electricity rips into my chest and shoots through the rest of my body.

My perfect day at the beach fades to black. And with the blackness comes the pain, roaring to life in my bones, my muscles, every fiber of my being.

The electrical wave flies through me again, and this time my heartbeat answers. It pounds as if the strength of it can counteract the aching hollow emptiness it feels, as I'm ripped away from my memory.

"Janelle," someone whispers. "Janelle, stay with me."

Something about the voice is familiar—not necessarily the speaker, but the way it whispers my name. It reminds me of my dad and the way he used to say my name when I was little and he came home and kissed my forehead in the middle of the night. Or the way Jared used to say my name when Mom was on a rampage and he wanted me to read him Harry Potter to drown everything out.

And something deep inside me aches to hear this voice

say my name that way again.

The blackness bleeds to white, so bright it glows. Heat floods my body, and I'm on fire. It feels like the light is burning me from the inside out.

23:23:56:42

Suddenly I'm somewhere else.

My head is throbbing, like someone just took a sledgeham-mer to it. There's water—freezing-cold water—all around me, and my arms and legs feel sluggish and hard to move. Panic threatens to overtake me as I sink deeper. I open my eyes, but the salt stings them and I can't see. Even if I could swim, I don't know which way is up. My insides burn because I want to breathe. I open my mouth because I have to—even though I know I'll drown.

It's drown or let my lungs burst.

Only I know this isn't me, it's not my memory—it's someone else's. I'm just somehow along for the ride. I know because ever since I was a little kid, I could practically swim better than I could walk.

An arm wraps around me and pulls me to the surface and I see . . .

Myself.

I'm ten, wearing a pink flowered bathing suit because even though I hated pink that summer, my dad bought it for me, and he did the best he could. My wet hair, so dark it almost looks black, is swept off my face, and my chocolate-colored eyes are almost too big for my face. The sun is behind me, backlighting me—and I look like an angel.

At least, that's what this memory *feels*—that I'm an angel. Which is weird, because I can't think of a single person who would think of me that way. Not even Jared, and he loves me.

The white light rips through my body again.

And again, I see myself—*at school this time, in fifth grade, playing four-square on the playground with Kate and Alex and another boy, whose name I can't remember now. I'm laughing, the waves of my hair bouncing up and down.* And I feel . . . longing, like this memory wants nothing more than to join in. But for some reason it can't.

And again—*in sixth grade, Alex and me walking my brother to school. I reach out and ruffle Jared's hair. He swats at my hand, and I laugh.*

And again. Again. Again. And again.

The scenes of my life play out in rapid succession, as if I'm an observer to my own life.

Celebrating good grades. Perfect test scores. Reading books during recess. Swim meets and ocean swims. The breakup of my friendship with Kate. Debate competitions with Alex. Tutoring Jared and Chris in the library after school. Lifeguarding, walking on the beach with Nick.

And the emotion I feel is undoubtedly love—heart aching, chest filling, so powerful it hurts, like these are memories of someone watching me, someone whose happiest moments are when he sees me smile, and someone who aches and feels powerless and heartbroken when he knows I'm sad. Someone who loves me.

14

23:23:56:40

Blackness again.

"Stay with me," the voice says. "Janelle, stay with me."

My eyes flutter open, and through blurred vision, I see a figure leaning over me. The sun is above, silhouetting him so I can't make out any features. My whole body throbs with the rhythm of my pulse—each beat emphasizing the excruciating, ripping pain as it ebbs and flows through my body. My bones feel broken, I can barely breathe, and my heart pounds at express-train speed.

I try to move, try to see the guy above me, but I can't. Because I can't control my arms. Or my legs. In fact, I can't even *feel* my legs. For all I know, they're just gone.

"Hold on, Janelle. Hold on," he whispers. Then, "I'm sorry. This will hurt."

He moves his hand, which I just now realize had been resting palm down on my heart. It moves up to my shoulder, the warmth of his bare hand against my bare skin oddly cooling, and as his hand passes over my collarbone, I feel bones move and snap, not like they're breaking, but like they're melding back together.

"Ben!" someone shouts.

His hand flows over my arm, then reaches underneath to my back, settling on my spine. As he touches me, everything in my whole being feels like it's not just *on* fire, but like I'm seconds from spontaneous combustion.

A flash of white again, brighter than looking at the sun—I can't see anything—then this time I see myself as I must have looked only minutes ago. *Wearing my red bathing suit and matching shorts. A dusting of sand sprinkled in patches on my olive skin. Running sneakers, no socks, my brown hair pulled into a messy ponytail. My cell phone to my ear, I pause, close my eyes, and pinch the bridge of my nose like I always do when I'm debating something. And then the truck is there as if it came from nowhere, and it's hurtling toward me at breakneck speed.*

And then I can't breathe.

"Ben! We gotta go!"

Cool lips lightly touch my forehead, and the pain subsides, fading to a dull ache all over my body. My vision returns, and a pair of dark brown eyes—so dark they're almost black—hover above me. He smells like a mix of mint, sweat, and gasoline. "You're going to be all right," he says, the relief of the statement coming out in a sort of sigh as he leans back.

I try to focus, because I know I recognize him from somewhere.

"You're going to be all right," he says again, only it's not like he's trying to convince me I'm okay—it's more like he's saying it to himself . . . out of relief. His smile widens as his hand reaches out and brushes a strand of hair from my face.

Then, of all the people in the world, Elijah Palma, notorious bad boy and stoner extraordinaire, is suddenly in my face,

16

grabbing the arm of the guy in front of me.

That's when recognition sets in. Those huge brown eyes, the wavy dark hair, the tortured half smile belong to another Eastview stoner. Ben Michaels. We've gone to school together since fifth grade. I've never spoken to him. Not even once.

"Let's go!" a third voice shouts, and this one I know. Reid Suitor, who's been in my homeroom and a few of my classes since middle school. Kate had a crush on him in eighth grade, but he wasn't interested.

Elijah pulls Ben away from me, and as the two of them disappear from my line of sight, I struggle to sit up. My chest hurts with each breath I take, and my whole body feels bruised and broken. I can't help but wonder if I just imagined everything—if the truck swerved to avoid me, if Ben pulled me out of the way, or if there was even a truck at all.

But when I sit up, I see the pickup, crashed into an embankment, the front end smashed in. And in my right hand, I'm still holding my cell phone, only it's been crushed to pieces.

As if it had been run over. By a truck.

I look up to the road toward Del Mar, and I see Reid, Elijah, and Ben riding bicycles up the hill. For some reason I want Ben to look back, but he doesn't.

Then suddenly people are everywhere. Surrounding me and saying my name. I recognize Elise and a parent of one of the baseball kids. And Kevin and Nick.

I wonder how long I was dead. Because I know with absolute certainty that I was. Dead.

And I also know with absolute certainty that somehow—even though it defies any logical explanation—Ben Michaels brought me back.

17

23:23:22:29

Someone called the paramedics, probably Steve. Even though I insisted I was fine, they loaded me up in the ambulance and sent me to Scripps Green, where they ushered me straight into an ER exam room.

Nick is with me, sitting next to me, holding my hand and talking about some time when he was a little kid and he fell off his bike. His dad was trying to teach him to ride, but since his dad isn't patient or good at teaching anything, Nick fell.

I listen to him, to his story, and I try to focus on all the details—like the fact that it was a black-and-red Transformers bike his mom had bought custom-made down in Pacific Beach, and that his dad was really angry at him for falling and wanted him to get right back onto the bike. I know he's just trying to help, so I swallow down the temptation to snort and say, *You fell off your bike? I just got hit by a truck!*

It's weird, though. As he talks, I feel off—like I'm spacing out. I can't help but think of Ben Michaels hovering over me, his hands on my skin, the way he said my name. The unflinching certainty that I was dead and now I'm not—and it's because of

Ben. Somehow, he brought me back to life.

Someone squeezes my hand, so I open my eyes—when did I close them?—and Nick smiles at me. He really is beautiful, but I honestly can't remember how Nick even got here. Did he come in the ambulance with me? Or did he follow in his car?

"Janelle?" Nick asks. "Janelle, are you okay?"

He stands up and grips my hand too hard, and a wave of nausea rolls through me. He says something else, but I don't hear him.

A nurse leans over me and shines a flashlight in my eyes. She turns and says something to someone close to her—not Nick. I'm not sure where he went. The nausea turns to cramps, and I just want to curl my knees into my chest and lie alone in the dark. But when I try to do that, someone grips my legs.

People yell at each other, and the whole room sounds fuzzy until I hear Alex. I can't concentrate on who he's talking to or what he's saying, but I can tell by the cadence of his voice that it's him. I want to ask when he got here and if my brother is okay. But my mouth doesn't work, and his voice sounds farther and farther away.

My muscles uncoil and relax again, but I'm struggling to catch my breath, almost wheezing.

Something pinches my arm, and a steady warmth begins to spread through my body. Heaviness sets in. Hands let go of me, and I can't hold myself up anymore. I slump down but fight to keep my eyes open. I wonder where Alex went.

Only I must say that out loud, because then he's standing over me. "Just relax. You had a seizure, but you're fine."

"Alex." I try to grab his arm, but my hand just flops around. Because he speaks my language, he says, "Jared's fine. I took

19

him to polo and called your dad."

And then he leans down so I can whisper in his ear. "At Torrey, the Jeep . . ."

"What happened to your car?" Nick asks, his face hovering above me.

Thankfully Alex hushes him and pushes him away as I close my eyes. "I'll take care of it, don't worry."

There was something I wanted to tell him. Something important.

"Wait," I whisper before he goes away. "Alex . . . I died."

"Shh," he whispers back, and I picture him shaking his head. "You're going to be fine, Janelle. You're going to be fine."

The worst thing about coming back to life isn't, believe it or not, how physically painful it is. Don't get me wrong—even though all my bones seem to be working just fine, they feel like they were broken into tiny pieces. My body is stiff, it aches with a steady, throbbing consistency, and I'm having a hard time making it obey me the way it should.

But worse is the hollowness.

It makes sense, really. I just looked into the great expanse of nothingness, had a moment—no matter how quickly it passed—to think about what my seventeen years add up to, and the dominant emotion staring back at me now is regret.

It's not that I haven't accomplished things. It's not that the people I leave behind won't remember me. It's not even that I'm young and there was so much more I wanted to experience—so much more I wanted to do.

It's the realization that I was practically dead already.

It's that for the past I don't know how many years, I've moved through life stuffed with straw, hollow and unfeeling. Day after day passed, and I went through the motions and focused on the mundane because the significant was too hard. I had conversations about schoolwork, weather, laundry, groceries, even sports, because things like quitting swimming, losing my best friend, getting drugged at a party, watching my mother's mood swings slowly kill her, watching my father give up on her—on us—all threatened to unleash a floodgate.

I go out with a guy who, when he's being serious, is interesting and funny and sort of sweet. We get along well enough, too, but if I'm really honest with myself, I don't see a future with him. I can't even see us together when school starts, let alone see myself trying to date him long-distance or go visit him when he's in college. And I know we just started dating, but isn't that what I should be imagining if I was really into him—isn't that part of the reason why people start dating? Yet I choose to date him rather than hold out for someone I could love. Why? Because his ex-girlfriend's a bitch? Because he's pretty? Because it feels good to be liked? Because I don't want to date someone I really care about since it will hurt more when it ends? Since I'd have to *try*?

How can I ever dare to meet my own eyes again? I can't. Not even in dreams.

That night, in a drug-induced sedation, I dream my brother is crying, and instead of my dad teasing Jared to "man up" like he always does, I hear his voice, even and soothing. I can't quite catch what he's saying at first. Then Jared sniffs, and my father says, *Your sister's so tough, it's frightening. That girl will outlive us all.*

I dream about Ben Michaels hovering over me, somehow

bringing me back from the dead.

And I dream about a doctor and two nurses looking at my X-rays. They stand right near my bed, the X-rays up in the light box. One of the nurses leaves as the doctor points to something on the image.

The doctor and remaining nurse whisper to each other.

The nurse comes back, and she's brought another doctor with her. The four of them gesture to the X-ray, their voices floating through the room.

It looks like her backbone and spinal cord were completely severed and fused back together.

An old injury, maybe?

Maybe she had surgery?

Nothing in her medical history.

They sigh.

It doesn't . . . it doesn't look like an old injury . . . and even if it was . . . I'm not sure how anyone would be able to walk after an injury like that.

She's lucky she isn't paralyzed.

Lucky? It's a miracle she's even alive.

21:22:40:34

The day I'm released from the hospital my dad takes me home.

"She should rest," Dr. Abrams tells him. "Stay off her feet, no physical exertion—"

"You said she hasn't had any more seizures after the first one," my dad says.

Dr. Abrams nods and explains why it's important to keep an eye on me anyway.

To anyone else, it would look like my dad is listening respectfully and absorbing the details. I know better. He tugs on his left ear, which means he's annoyed and running low on patience. He asks specific questions that suggest more medical knowledge than he has, which means he's shown my test results and chart to someone at the Bureau, probably a medical examiner.

I don't exactly care, though, that my dad has been giving everyone in the hospital a hard time. I've got more important things to focus on. Like what the hell Ben Michaels did to me. It's just about all I've been able to think about since I woke up. I tried to have the conversation several times—where I said, "Alex, I died," and he patted me like a two-year-old and basically said,

"You don't know what you're talking about."

I roll my head to the side to look at Jared. "What's up, dude? You gonna tell me what happened to your hand?"

His right hand looks slightly bruised. I reach out, touching his knuckles. He winces. "What happened?" I whisper.

"I tried to punch Alex," Jared says with a shrug. But he at least has the decency to drop his eyes and look embarrassed. "He's fine, though."

I made Alex take self-defense classes with me the summer before sophomore year. We always joked that if a guy attacked us, Alex would duck and I would knee the guy in the balls. (There's a rumor I'm the reason Dave Kotlar only has one testicle now, but it's a total lie. I have no idea what he did to himself, but since he hasn't made any big attempts to dispel the rumors, it must be way more embarrassing than getting beat up by a girl.)

So I know if my brother—who's never been in a fight in his life—tried to throw a punch at Alex, my best friend would do what he's best at. He would duck.

"You were in the hospital, dying for all he knew, and Alex took me to *polo*."

"Um, because I asked him to. Alex is well trained."

Jared doesn't smile like I want him to.

"Jared—"

"Whatever, it doesn't matter," he huffs. "I missed anyway."

I open my mouth to try to explain, but I realize that would mean explaining my friendship with Alex, and I don't know *how* to explain something that's just always existed. He's lived two doors down from me my whole life. Once upon a time, our moms took us to playgroups together, swimming lessons, even dance classes.

But Jared knows that. What he doesn't know is that Alex has been helping me deal with our mother's illness and cover up her drinking since Jared was too young to know there was a problem. Or that our friendship has survived because Alex listens to me. Because Alex knows that supporting me means tackling obstacles my way—head-on. And I don't know how to explain that Alex is the only reason I've been able to stay sane while Dad worked and I had to be a parent—the only reason Jared has been able to *do* things like play water polo.

Which is why Alex, despite how much he would have been freaking out on the inside, would have taken Jared to polo like it was just another normal day.

But by the time I have all that sorted out in my head, Jared has started telling me about his first (half) day of school—freshman orientation.

"After the assembly and the tour, I went to my first two classes—"

"What do you have?"

He frowns at me. "Biology and ENS. But the cool part was, after I came out of ENS, Nick and Kevin were waiting for me."

Exercise Nutritional Science is a glorified gym class all freshmen have to take, but more importantly . . . "Nick and Kevin were on campus?"

Jared nods. "They brought three pizzas from Uncle Vinnie's for me and my friends, and we all sat and ate, and they told stories about their freshman year. It was awesome."

"Awesome?" I ask, even though I don't need to. Anyone getting attention from the two most popular seniors at Eastview would be glowing a little. If Nick and Kevin were here, I would hug them—even Kevin—because I want my brother to be happy more than anything. And he'll probably be over the moon all week.

"Yeah, did you know they had English together their freshman year? Nick said Kevin used to lean back in his chair all the time. And every day their teacher would say, 'Mr. Collins, don't lean back in your chair, please,' and he'd say, 'Okay,' but then he'd do it anyway."

I am not at all surprised by this story.

"And then one day when Kevin was hitting on this hot girl in his class, he leaned back just a little too far and he fell over. But it didn't matter because the girl he liked went out with him that weekend anyway."

Again, I'm not surprised.

"And Kevin said they used to jump up and touch the overhang whenever they were coming down the library steps. They'd even run, jump, hit the ledge, and then jump down the rest of the stairs, but near the end of freshman year, they both did it one time, only when they jumped, Nick fell and got a concussion."

I can easily picture Kevin and Nick jumping down the library steps and somehow managing to wipe out. "What about the rest of your classes?"

He shrugs, obviously less interested. "I have ceramics and then English with Sherwood."

I wince at the name of his English teacher. Jared will never be able to write an essay if I don't get him out of there.

"Yeah, Kevin took one look at my schedule and told me to run for the hills."

"He did?" This time I *am* surprised—in a good way.

Jared nods. "He and Nick said I should fill out a schedule

change request to be bumped into honors. So I did that before Nick drove me home."

I'm suddenly not sure whether I should be pleased or worried about the interest Nick is taking in my brother. On the one hand, I can't believe he convinced him to take an *honors* class, and I'm undoubtedly in their debt for getting Jared to actually follow directions and get out of Sherwood's class—anyone who doubts that there's something wrong with public education in this country just needs to sit in her class for a day to know—but what will happen to Jared if Nick and I break up?

"All right, J-baby, you ready?" my dad says before I can think of a way to explain that to my brother.

"I'd really prefer if you didn't call me that in public," I say as I slide out of the hospital bed and into the wheelchair they've brought for me.

My dad smiles because he knows I don't really mean it, and Jared slips in behind me, half pushing, half hopping. My back is stiff and my leg muscles are still sore, but I could feel worse—I could be dead.

Also, I'll be back at school this week. So will Ben Michaels. And I plan on figuring out exactly what happened.

"What's for dinner tonight?" Jared asks.

"Something we can get delivered," I say at the same time my dad says, "I asked Struz to pick up some Chinese."

"Sweet!" Jared says. "You think he'll get that awesome spicy kung pao chicken? I haven't had that in forever. Or, oh—call him and tell him to get the special General Tso's!"

Ryan Struzinski, aka Struz, has been working with my dad for ten years. He's in his thirties now, I think, but he's really an overgrown kid with a superhero complex. It's why he and my dad get along so well. Knowing Struz, he'll order the whole left side of the menu. "Don't worry, Jared. Something tells me we'll have enough food."

"What about egg rolls? And fortune cookies. He'd better get a shitload of them."

Jared is still running down the list of Chinese food he's hoping for—that kid can eat his way through anything—when we get outside. My dad's car is parked in the fire lane—shocking. Even less shocking is the collection of file boxes that he has to move to squeeze both Jared and my wheelchair into the backseat—no doubt because he's going to work late into the night. Just like he would any other night. Tonight he'll just have to work at home.

"You and Struz planning to Mulder and Scully it after Chinese tonight?" I ask as I slide my seat belt on. My dad has every season of *The X-Files* on DVD. When we were little, instead of Saturday morning cartoons, Jared and I had Saturday morning *X-Files* marathons.

"Dude, have you found the unit that hunts aliens yet?" Jared asks.

My dad chuckles. "Not yet, but don't worry. I won't give up. Hunting aliens is the reason I joined the FBI, after all." This is actually not a lie. Of course, the truth is that there isn't a unit that actually hunts aliens. There aren't enough creepy cases that point to aliens or unsolved paranormal mysteries to assign to even one guy in a basement.

"The truth is out there," Jared says with a laugh.

"I want to believe," I add, because that's my line. Yes, I am aware how lame we are.

"Trust no one," my dad says, trying to make his voice sound ominous.

"Believe the lie!" Jared shouts.

I let the two of them continue to volley taglines back and forth during the ride home. I jump in occasionally when there's a lull and Jared is trying to remember a good quote, but mostly I think about the same thing I've thought about the whole two days I spent lounging around the hospital. I think of Ben Michaels—of the fact that I was dead and now I'm not. Because all that *X-Files* stuff is only entertaining until it hits too close to home. Right now none of it is as strange as Ben Michaels bringing me back from the dead.

As my dad turns off the car, I gesture to the wheelchair. "We can just leave that in the car. I'm fine."

"J-baby, are you—"

"Dad. I'm fine."

Jared jumps in front of us and unlocks the front door, and my dad is about to say something when the sound of glass breaking makes all three of us freeze.

21:22:07:29

For the past nine years, my dad has been the head of the counterintelligence unit at the San Diego office of the FBI. It's ironic, really. This man who dedicates his life to the pursuit of truth, who works a nineteen-and-a-half-hour work day, who watches repeats of *The X-Files* and quotes it to his children, lives in a house where Truth always remains Unsaid.

And for almost as long as I can remember, I've learned to do the same.

My mother is bipolar. And at present, she's not exactly functioning.

When I was seven, during one of her manic episodes, she stopped taking her meds, pulled both Jared and me out of school, and drove us up the coast—at least twenty miles over the speed limit, with the windows down—all day and into the night, until we stopped at the Northern California border and got a hotel room. We stayed up late, jumped on the beds, had a popcorn fight, and laughed until our stomachs cramped.

By the next morning she'd come down and wouldn't get out of bed. We were holed up in our room at the Anchor Beach Inn in Crescent City, California, with the curtains drawn and the lights turned off, while she slept it off for two days before my dad found us and brought us home.

After that, my mom and dad fought—about her medicine, about Jared and me, about how much she slept and how much he worked, about her medication and his inability to express his feelings, about her spontaneity and his rigid schedule, about everything. They fought all the time—days, weeks, months, years. Until at some point—and I can't remember when—the fighting stopped, she started drinking herself into a self-medicating coma, and our house just fell . . . silent.

And Jared and I were on our own.

21:22:07:28

"I'll go check on her," I say, ignoring the wave of anxiety rolling through my stomach.

My dad shakes his head. "I can do it. You just—"

"I'm okay—promise," I say, giving him my best *I'm fine!* smile. "She'll want to see me anyway, and you have to bring in the boxes." I don't wait for a response. Both Jared and my dad are secretly happy to let me do the honors, even if they won't tell themselves that.

I slip into her bedroom and pull the door shut behind me, carefully enough so it doesn't make a sound as it latches. Her bedroom is cloaked in darkness. The combination of the thick shade and the heavy velour drapes pulled tightly over the picture window blocks out every speck of light, and I have to pause and let my eyes adjust. If I didn't know it was summer and the sun hadn't yet set outside, I'd think it was the middle of the night. More disturbing is the stale smell of the air—like old, wet newspaper and mold. The recorded sound of rain plays softly on repeat, and I hear her grunt as soft light floods the bathroom.

I ignore the clothes and bedsheets strewn all over the room and breathe through my mouth as I move to the bathroom.

"Mom?" I ask. I hesitate before I open the door, like I always do. Because I'm afraid of what I might see on the other side. "Are you okay?"

"Oh, fine, just fine," she answers as the faucet turns on. I let go of a breath I didn't know I was holding and push open the door.

Her wild hair is standing on end, black against the paleness of her skin. Under her T-shirt and shorts, I can see the bones sticking out at her joints in all the wrong places, and when her eyes meet mine in the mirror, I'm struck with the image of her I remembered when I was dying—and how it should be some sort of crime for God to let a woman like that turn into someone like this.

"Janelle?" she asks, fumbling with a foil packet of Advil. All the medication in our house now comes in single-serving packets. "Are you feeling better? Your father said you were sick."

I nod. "I'm fine." It's possible he told me what happened with the truck and she forgot, or it's possible he didn't tell her at all. I'm not sure which is worse, but it doesn't matter because the result is the same.

A quick glance at the broken glass in the sink—not on the floor and no blood—tells me she's fine. The thin layer of dust covering the whole bathroom tells me I need to stop avoiding this room and get in here to clean this weekend.

"My head just hurts so much." She throws a hand over her eyes to shield them from the light.

"Here, let me help you." I've barely torn open the packet when she snatches the pills from my hand and swallows them dry. "Have you eaten anything today? Struz is bringing over Chinese food."

"Great, the whole house will smell awful," she says with a snort. "It's like your father does this to me on purpose. He knows how terrible my headaches are and he knows how much strong smells bother me. And loud noises. I just need peace and quiet. I need to rest."

I flick off the bathroom light and help her back to bed.

"I just need to rest," she repeats as she gets under the covers. She looks small and fragile, like a sick child instead of my mother. "Can you get me a cold compress?"

Part of me wants to say, *Get your own compress*, but instead I nod.

Just because I died and had a moment of reflection doesn't mean anything's going to change around here.

It'll take a lot more to wake this hollow heart.

"Whoa, whoa, whoa!" Struz says, his six-foot-seven-inch wingspan flailing around the dining room table, almost knocking into both me and Jared.

I make eye contact with Alex, who's been eating his second dinner with us every night since he was old enough to think up a good excuse to walk over to our house by himself—his mom cooks only organic, vegan, and gluten-free meals. He grins at me as he goes to take a sip of his Coke, but thinks better of it. Probably because he knows what's coming. Struz has made us laugh until soda comes out of our noses many times.

Struz continues, "Jim! You gotta be kidding me. You mean you haven't done a background check or a fingerprint analysis or anything on this *Nick* character?"

Jared laughs so hard he spits some of his Chinese food back onto his plate. Alex throws his napkin at Struz's face. Dad and I shush them.

Struz dramatically wipes a hand through his hair and turns back to his captive audience. "That's just not okay. I mean, seriously!" he continues, his voice quieter now, as he gestures to the flowers Nick brought earlier. "Jared! This guy brought J-baby roses! *Pink ones!* And we don't even know who he is. What is wrong with your father?"

"Nick could be a terrorist," Alex says. He finds that way too funny.

"He could be an *alien!*" Jared laughs.

I roll my eyes.

"No, seriously," Dad says. "Let's hear something about this guy. How did he win you over?"

Batting his eyes like a cartoon character, Alex says, "He's dreamy," with a dramatic sigh.

"That better not be an imitation of me," I say.

Alex just laughs.

I look at Struz, who does his "give it to me" hand gesture, and then Dad, who also appears to be waiting for some kind of response. "Nick's smart; he works hard."

"At sports," Alex coughs.

"Don't be such an intellectual snob."

"Seriously, Alex," Struz says. "Professional athletes get a lot of play."

I ignore that comment, since Dad and I haven't really ever had the "who are you dating" conversation, and I'd prefer not to have it right now. And I'd *really* prefer not to talk about any of the guys in my life and how much "play" they are or aren't getting. Struz included. "Nick wants to play football at USC next year," I add, because something needs to be said.

"I suppose if he goes to USC, he's good enough for me," Struz says—not surprising, since that's where he went to college. "But if he goes to UCLA, you have to break up."

Jared laughs and announces that his lifelong dream is to go

to UCLA, and I break open a fortune cookie. Stuffing the cookie into my mouth, I unroll the fortune and can't help snorting a laugh.

Everyone pauses. "What's it say?" Jared asks, reaching across the table.

Instead of answering, I flick the fortune to Alex before getting up. I grab my plate and a couple of empty cartons and head into the kitchen. Just before I turn the water on, I hear Alex's voice reading my fortune. "Soon life will become more interesting."

Jared's unrestrained laughter drowns out what anyone else might be saying, and I'm glad.

I see those images of myself playing out again, watching my life pass me by. As if dying and then being resurrected weren't enough—as if anything could *become* more interesting than that.

"Just not sure if interesting will be a good or a bad thing, huh?" Alex asks when he comes through the kitchen. He hands me the dirty dishes and opens the cabinet to grab some Tupperware. Struz did order the left side of the menu, and we'll be eating Chinese for the next few days.

"I was *dead*, Alex," I repeat, because we've had this conversation already. At least six times. In the hospital. Whenever Alex made it into my room without Jared or Nick.

"J," Alex whispers, his hand falling on my arm, "I can't imagine all the shit you're feeling, but come on—you got hit by a truck, you lost consciousness, and you had seizures in the hospital."

"One seizure."

He pulls his hand back. "It wouldn't be out of the ordinary for your mind to make something up. Besides, when's the last time Ben Michaels and Elijah Palma even came to the beach?"

I can't argue with that. I'm at the beach almost every day, and I can't remember ever seeing them. Not that I would have been looking, though.

Logically, I know he's right. I've heard the Near-Death Experience stories. People seeing angels, tunnels of light, balls of energy, even God. I don't believe in that. I believe the mind is a powerful thing, and I believe people see what they want to see.

But why did *I* see Ben Michaels?

"J, did you hear what I said?"

"Hmm?"

Alex glances at the door to the dining room and lowers his voice as he sits on top of the counter and leans over my shoulder. "We should be asking about John Doe, his truck, and where the hell it came from."

I found out some of the details at the hospital. After hitting me—if it even did—the truck crashed into an embankment and the driver—still unidentified, since the license in his wallet was a fake—died on impact.

Based on the skid marks and the collision, they're betting he was flying down the hill at more than eighty miles an hour. It's no wonder I didn't see the truck coming.

But I still feel like an imposter—alive, when he's not.

"Are you listening to me?"

"What? Sorry." I turn off the water and dry my hands, making an attempt to give Alex my full attention.

"I was *saying* . . ." He draws it out, and I wave my hand to hurry him along. "I found out the truck that hit you, there's no record of it. They couldn't pull up the plates or the guy's registration in the system—no record of any of them."

"Wait, what was the fake name?"

Alex balks. "Does it matter?"

I don't have a reason that I can explain. But it does matter.

"Don't obsess over the unimportant stuff," Alex says, and I nod because the last thing I want to do is get into an argument about my tendency to overanalyze and the way it drives Alex crazy. "Nothing he had on him matched anything in the DMV database."

"What, so they're all fake?"

Alex shrugs. "I don't know. I only half heard the conversation your dad was having with the cops afterward, but when they ran the VIN and even the parts for the truck, nada."

"That's impossible. Even if somebody made fake plates and IDs—even if they stole parts from several trucks, the model numbers would still register. They'd just register to different vehicles." I shake my head. "Who would go to the trouble for an old Toyota?"

"That's the kicker," Alex says, folding his arms across his chest and leaning against the kitchen counter. When he does that, he looks weirdly like my dad. "It's not a Toyota."

"Please, are we really going to have an argument about cars again? I thought we agreed you'd stick to calc and physics and leave practical knowledge to me."

He smiles but doesn't say anything. He knows something I don't. And he's dying to share. I wave for him to continue.

"The frame of the truck is the same design as a '79 Toyota, but the engine and the vehicle paperwork, even the logo are all really different. It's actually a 1997 Velociadad."

"A what?" I turn back to the dishwasher. "I've never even heard of a car company anywhere in the world by that name."

"Which is probably why I heard your dad ask if the truck

appeared out of thin air," Alex says.

I'm not even sure what I can say about that—what can anyone?

Alex is right, of course. This *is* more important than whether Ben Michaels resurrected me or I hallucinated it. This is real, and my dad is investigating it. That automatically gives it more urgency. It's something I can handle now.

"Could someone be running a chop shop?" Alex asks. "Stealing vehicles, repackaging and reselling them as something else?"

"It's possible, but why bother with all the hassle?"

Alex just shrugs and doesn't say anything else, which means we've both reached our limit. Because I'm still pissed that he doesn't believe that I died, I add, "No theories? C'mon, they don't let just anyone into West Point."

"Don't say that out loud." Alex looks around shiftily.

I roll my eyes. "Your mother hasn't bugged my house as far as I know."

"Your dad thinks I'll be able to get in." Of course Alex will get in. He has a 4.6 GPA and he's bilingual. And my dad will write him a recommendation, since he went to West Point and graduated at the top of his class. Which is one of the reasons Alex wants to go.

Alex has gone silent, staring into space with his jaw set. I feel bad now for making him think about all the drama he'll have to deal with when he finally admits to his mother he's not going to graduate early and go to Stanford, thereby deviating from the life plan she's been outlining for him since he was conceived.

"So which one of the boxes do you think has stuff about the truck in it?" I ask, because getting back to the investigation will be the only way to make him feel better—and because I know my dad has info about the truck. It doesn't matter that the FBI doesn't allow you to investigate anything that happens to you or your family or even people you know. My dad wouldn't let a truck just appear out of thin air and hit me without investigating it.

"When I helped Jared bring them into the office, I set the lightest box in the back corner, farthest from his desk." He doesn't say anything else. He doesn't need to. We've been spying on my dad and comparing notes about his cases practically forever. We're nerds like that.

21:18:10:00

When my cell phone beeps in the middle of the night, I almost say *Whatever* and go back to sleep. A stolen Toyota—or whatever it is—is hardly worth waking up to check out.

Except for the fact that the driver is dead, when it should have been me.

I roll out of bed and fumble into the hallway. We've lived here my whole life, and I've done the get-up-in-the-middle-of-the-night stunt enough that I don't need to turn on the lights. But I curse silently as I head down the stairs and see the sliver of light coming from my dad's study. Either he and poor Struz are still working, or he's fallen asleep at his desk.

I imagine it's this way for all law-enforcement agents—long hours, sleepless nights, obsessive attention to detail, poring over case files. Every FBI agent I know has at least two cases they'll never forget and never stop thinking about, investigations they'll carry with them in the back of their minds always, for their entire lives. The one that went right. And the one that went wrong.

For my dad, the case that went right was the one that made his career.

It was more than ten years ago. It was his first case with Struz, who was a junior analyst at the time. I was too young to remember any of the details now, except the ones I heard repeated whenever he relived the story.

Ten Russian spies were discovered and arrested in Temecula, of all places. One was a Fox News reporter, popular with the public and, of course, beautiful. She ended up getting caught in a trap an undercover FBI agent set for her, and as a result all ten of them—and some guy bankrolling them in Budapest—went down. The undercover agent? My dad.

But the case that went wrong—the one still unsolved—is even older. It happened one of his first years on the job, before he got involved in counterintelligence. When my mom was pregnant with me—just after she'd found out I was a girl.

A seventeen-year-old girl—captain of the swim team, with an academic scholarship to USC, a boyfriend, friends, the perfect family, with a dog and white picket fence—went missing from her bedroom. All her possessions were untouched and in their rightful place. No forced entry, no signs of a break-in, no one heard or saw anything unusual—it was like she just . . . disappeared into thin air.

Except for a bloody partial handprint on her wall.

The files are all still on the corner of his desk. My dad reads them every night before he goes to sleep. If he even sleeps at all.

When I get to the bottom of the stairs and peek inside his office, it's empty. The boxes are all over the place, some of them open, piles of papers laid out everywhere. My dad's one of those visual/tactile learners. He's got to lay everything out, move it around, and really study it, and then answers just come to him.

Obviously, he and Struz *were* working, and on an older case, something ongoing if it has this much of a paper trail, but everything looks like he just left it and went up to bed.

Which isn't like him.

Although his oldest child did just come back from the dead. I suppose I could cut him some slack.

The "light" box that Alex strategically placed so I could snoop through it is one of the open ones. Only it doesn't have anything to do with my truck or the driver. It's an old case file from 1983, a series of deaths in California and Nevada, where the victims were killed from radiation poisoning. Deep gamma burns practically disfigured the bodies, most likely the result of some kind of nuclear exposure.

I leaf through the pages, scanning them for anything that might explain why these old files are in my dad's study. Apparently, nothing other than the actual bodies had any kind of radiation residue—as if the bodies had been dumped somewhere else after exposure.

"All the nuclear plants nearby were searched, and nothing was found amiss." I jump and drop the folders back into the box. "And the victims were never identified. Not even by dental records."

When I turn around, my dad is leaning in the doorway to the office. He's in sweatpants and an old army T-shirt—one that he doesn't quite fill out the way he used to—his tattoos peeking out from under the sleeves. The lines in his face are starting to show, and his hair is starting to gray. He wears "tired" like an old friend.

"So they just stopped investigating?"

"I've got boxes full of theories and investigation notes," he says with a shrug. "But they never found anything, and there were only three victims. After that, it seemed like just the Bureau's presence stopped whatever was happening."

This bothers me more than knowing that there are people out there who we know are guilty, but can't prove it. This is more than just a flaw in the system. Because no one figured it out. These people died alone, and they're the only ones who know how it happened—them and whoever was responsible. Someone else should know.

I'm about to say something when I see a photograph on top of a stack of papers on my dad's desk. It looks like the body of a man—I think—and I can't tell how old he is, because his body is so badly distorted by the radiation burns that he doesn't even look human.

Nausea rolls through me. This photograph isn't from the eighties. Based on the time stamp at the bottom corner, it's from last week. Six days ago.

"Don't ask," my dad says before I can open my mouth. He moves farther into the room and flips over the photograph. "You know I can't talk about active cases."

The distorted image of the dead man in the photo is burned into my retinas, and I have to blink a few times to try to see something else. And that's when I realize there was something else in the photograph—a set of numbers, written in marker on top of the picture. *29:21:33:21.*

21:18:03:54

"What are the numbers?" I ask as I reach for the photo and turn it over. For a minute I feel a sense of déjà vu, like I've seen them before. Then I realize why. They're similar to a set of numbers I saw out of the corner of my eye when I walked in, written on top of another picture—one I hadn't really looked at.

There are photos everywhere in this office. Reaching across the table, I grab a different one. This one is the body of a woman. The whole right side of her body is covered in burns that render her unrecognizable. The left side of her body looks pristine. It makes it even harder to look at her.

The numbers are there, though, in my dad's handwriting. Written in black Sharpie in the top corner of the image. *44:14:38:44*. I look back at the other set of numbers and the photograph of the dead man. The dates of the incidents on the time stamps are fifteen days apart. "It's a countdown, but to what?"

A quick look of surprise flits across my dad's face before he looks even-keeled again, and I know I've hit it right.

He shakes his head the way he does when he can't figure something out.

"You're counting down to something. I mean, what's the end date?" Because that's the bottom line—what's important. Countdowns lead to something. What and when are the important questions to answer first. The how and why will come later.

He doesn't answer. Not that I really expected him to. The fact that he hasn't shooed me back upstairs to bed yet means he's frustrated enough to forget the rules.

I set down the photograph and reach for one of the reports, skimming for numbers. I see them—*46:05:49:21*—and a reference to forty-six days only a sentence later. But I see something else too—*UIED*—before my dad remembers himself and pulls the report from my hand, placing it back on his desk.

"There's something off about this one." I have no idea what he means by "off." He's investigated thousands of cases, and there's always one keeping him up at night.

But I know what UIED means—Unidentified Improvised Explosive Device.

How a countdown factors into a UIED is relatively easy to deduce. The countdown is a timer for some kind of explosive. But what it has to do with the bodies and the radiation is well beyond me.

"Where did you find an unidentified explosive device?" I ask. "Is it a bomb?" I grab the report back from him and flip through it.

"San Diego PD followed a lead and found it in an abandoned motel room after the first crime scene two months ago. They called in the bomb squad and us."

"And?" But I'm still flipping through the report, and one line catches my eye.

So far all attempts to stop the countdown have been unsuccessful.

"This thing isn't like anything I've ever seen," my dad says, but it's clear from his quiet, distant tone that he's talking to himself. Then he sees the look on my face and adds, "The bodies and the UIED might not be connected," but I can tell he doesn't believe that.

I gesture to the countdown on the photographs. "You're keeping track of how it relates to these deaths. How does it?" He must at least think it does, if he's gone to the trouble to cross-reference them down to the second of the countdown. But even with my photographic memory and affinity for numbers, I don't see an obvious connection. "Is there some kind of pattern?" If there is, I don't see it.

My dad shakes his head, and for a minute I think he's going to tell me—to say something else about the case. But instead he nods toward the door. "Go on, go back to bed."

My skin itches—or rather, something *underneath* my skin itches—everywhere.

"You have to be exhausted, J-baby," my dad says. "Don't worry about this one. You know I'll figure it out."

I nod and leave the room, even though I'm not convinced the way I usually am.

I *was* exhausted. But now I'm not. Because I have the same feeling I did when I watched Ben Michaels ride his bike up Highway 101. Deep-seated conviction. A feeling of absolute certainty I couldn't ignore even if I wanted to.

I glance at my watch and hope being resurrected from the

dead didn't affect my ability to do math in my head. Based on the time stamps of the photographs, we're at twenty-one days, seventeen hours, thirty-nine minutes, seventeen seconds. And counting.

17:09:40:41

It's been four days, and I still haven't been able to figure out how the UIED fits in with my dad's case. I've tried to do some more snooping, but Dad has taken to locking his office when he knows I'm around and he isn't. I can't stop thinking about it, though. Those radiation burns are all I see when I close my eyes.

But the first person I see when I get out of Nick's car in Eastview's student lot is Ben Michaels.

He looks exactly like the Ben Michaels I would have pictured *before*: standing with a group of other nondescript stoners, all wearing similar dark hoodies and grungy, no-name-band T-shirts, most of them smoking something more than conventional cigarettes, some of them drinking something *more* than water from a water bottle. Elijah Palma and Reid Suitor stand in the center of the group; Ben's on the outskirts, shoulders slumped and his hands buried deep in the pockets of his baggy jeans while he half leans against some rich kid's SUV. I can't see his eyes under the mess of dark brown curls, but I wonder if he's staring back at me.

And I feel like my forehead—the exact spot where his cool

lips brushed my skin—is on fire, and I have this crazy urge to reach up and somehow wipe his touch away.

"Janelle, c'mon!"

Jared and Nick are a car's length away from me, walking toward the school. I shift my bag and follow them, ignoring Nick's raised eyebrow and the flood of heat rushing to my face.

Just like I ignore the stares from half the senior class when Nick puts his arm around my shoulder and we walk through the front gate.

Normally I'd be driving myself and getting to school early but I'm not allowed to drive. Once you have a seizure, even if it's just one, you're marked as a possible epileptic. Not that I don't get it, I do. I'm just not a fan of this rule when it applies to me.

This means I've missed two days of school. Thursday Struz took me to see a specialist. She ran some tests, and hopefully she'll clear me to drive when the results come back. And it's not like anything ever happens on the first day of school anyway.

I missed an AP diagnostic and listening to the teacher read the syllabus? Oh, too bad. Friday my mother couldn't stop throwing up, and even though I *think* she's been taking all her meds, on days when her body has a physical manifestation of her depression, someone needs to keep an eye on her. And it's not like my dad can do it.

"So, Bread Bites for lunch?" Nick asks when we're standing outside my homeroom.

"I can't," I say, thankful for a legit excuse. It's not that I don't want to hang out with him—I do. I just hate that suddenly because I was injured he's gone from goofy, immature, half-brained Nick to this skittish, hovering, insecure woodland creature who wants to attach himself to me at all times.

But Nick just looks at me, and he doesn't jump to the obvious conclusion.

"Juniors don't get off-campus lunches."

A smile sweeps over his face, and he nods. "I can get you off campus for lunch. Or we can order delivery."

And with that, the irritable, bitchy edge I've been walking around with the past few days melts away. Staying on campus for lunch as a senior is social suicide, and he's risking it for me?

"It was awesome of you to bring Jared pizza, but you don't need to worry about me like that." Not that Nick's popularity is going to suffer, but he never struck me as the kind of guy who'd forgo bullshitting with the boys to hang out with a girl. And I don't need him to do that for me.

"Don't look so surprised." He laughs as he leans in and kisses the skin just beneath my ear.

Feeling his lips against my skin, I'm a little short of breath, and the smile on his face when he pulls back is almost enough to turn me into most girls.

Until I see Reid Suitor walk past us with his head down as he ducks into our homeroom. I don't know exactly what I plan to say to him. But I know he was there when I died. He must know something.

"Gotta go," I say to Nick before following Reid. He and I have been in Dockery's homeroom since freshman year, and just like every other year, her walls are covered with old history posters—facts about US presidents, magazine collages about momentous dates or events. The only thing worse would be, of course, if the walls peeking out from behind the posters were painted something like a stifling bright orange. Oh wait, they are.

Per usual, Dockery's animated face shines through her pile of platinum-blond hair, and she's lost in a story about something embarrassing that happened to her while she was driving—seriously, *her* license should be revoked, not mine—but I wait, watching Reid, who's perfectly in my line of sight.

He's found the other two stoners in our homeroom, and the three of them are huddled together in the back corner as far away from Dockery as they can get.

I've never for the life of me understood Reid Suitor. Outwardly he doesn't look like he'd have anything in common with Ben. His jeans seem like they fit, and he's wearing a blue collared shirt and a gray V-neck sweater, which would look nerdy on most guys, but somehow it manages to look alternative on him. He's always been cute—Kate's probably still a little in love with him—and he's got these bright blue eyes, eyelashes that extend for days, and sandy brown hair. Really, he could probably be some kind of Calvin Klein model.

But more than that, I know there's a brain behind that pretty face. I had to proofread one of his essays in Honors Humanities last year—luck of the draw—and not only was his paper done, but it was actually good. Good enough that I had to struggle to edit it, which doesn't happen to me often.

"Oh, Janelle!" Dockery says, handing me my schedule. "We missed you last week. I was so sorry to hear about your accident. I'm glad you're okay!"

"Thanks," I say before glaring at Alex, who's already sitting at our usual table.

He just shrugs, like he can't understand why I wouldn't want Dockery—and thus the entire school—to know I got hit by a truck and came back from the dead. For someone so anti-drama, he's clueless about how it starts.

With a sigh, I drop my bag next to him and flop into my chair before glancing down at my schedule. Once I look at it, I'm tempted to tear it into pieces.

It's all wrong. Which is a nightmare. Because Miss Florentine, my guidance counselor, is overworked, and schedule changes are never guaranteed.

I look at my schedule again.

Earth science, American Literature, algebra, and chorus. So I'm supposed to take science for stoners, basic English, and freshman math. I wouldn't mind chorus, but I don't sing.

"Don't be overdramatic. It's not that bad," Alex says. "Just follow my schedule. I'm sure we can get you bumped into my classes."

Last resort, I could get my dad to call and complain, since that's how things actually get done around here. I cannot get through junior year in classes with freshmen and stoners. "How full are your classes?" I ask as the bell rings.

"You should be fine for Spanish, but APEL . . . ," Alex says, and I can't stifle a groan. He wrinkles his nose. "Poblete had thirty-five of us on Thursday and forty-one on Friday."

Thirty-two is supposed to be the cap on the AP English Language class. I'm doomed.

The majority of first period passes like this:

Alex goes to physics, and I head to the counseling office.

The secretary says Florentine can't possibly see me right now.

I reword my request until she changes her mind.

Florentine says my schedule can be changed, but the classes I want are full.

I reword, and she sends me to Mr. Elksen, the VP in charge

of scheduling, who can apparently override the rules.

Elksen's secretary says I'll have to come back later.

I try to reword, but she actually has a backbone.

I head to Principal Mauro's office instead to see if she'll override my schedule for me.

Her secretary says she's busy, and I'll have to come back later.

Mauro herself comes out to see what's going on.

She says I have to fill out a schedule change request form and speak to Elksen like everyone else.

It's amazing anything ever happens in this school.

I'm about to try to press my luck when the hallway double doors swing open, and Mauro stops listening and turns to see who else is interrupting her game of solitaire.

But it's security.

And Ben Michaels.

His hood is pulled over his head, shading his hair and his eyes, the white earbuds of his iPod barely visible. He has no backpack, and as if he *isn't* being escorted by two campus security guards, he just shuffles his ripped Chuck Taylors as he walks, with an ease that screams, *I don't care.*

He's just another one of those guys I can't stand here, DGAF-ing their way through life.

"Miss Tenner?"

Ben's head tips up at the sound of my name, and from underneath his hood, I can see his eyes widen in surprise for a second, before his whole body shifts, tension rolling through it.

I feel giddy with excitement, because he's right here with the answers I need. My heart beats too fast—for a second—and then I remember we're not alone.

I wish I could freeze everyone else and demand he clear up

the muddiness in my brain and explain what happened at Torrey Pines.

But since *I'm* not magical . . . that isn't possible.

I turn back to Principal Mauro. "I just really need to get my schedule fixed."

"And as I said, you'll need to go through the proper channels," she answers automatically. "There are plenty of other students with scheduling needs as well."

I want to shout at her. But I don't.

I shift, adjusting the weight of my bag on my shoulder, and turn to leave.

And almost run right into Ben. I come within centimeters of touching him, and my eyes lock onto his. Then the scent of mint, soap, and gasoline hits me, and it's like I'm on my back on the 101 looking up at him all over again. But he turns away, and we narrowly avoid any physical contact. I watch his back for a few seconds, but he doesn't turn around.

It doesn't matter. Every nerve ending in my whole body feels as if it's on fire.

17:05:07:12

I follow my messed-up schedule for the rest of the day, and each class I walk into, the teacher just looks at my name and gives me a sad look of apology. They let me sit in the back of the room and don't even give me the books. It's painful that they know I don't belong in their classes, yet here I am.

The inefficiency makes me want to throw up.

And for all Nick's flirting this morning, and all those sweet thoughts that turned me into a melty pile of mush, turns out he's still a douche bag. Sure, I told him to go to lunch without me, but he said he wouldn't.

sry babe get u off tmrw

Based on that grammatical monstrosity of a text, I know he's already off campus with Kevin, headed to Bread Bites, so I wander into the quad for lunch.

I'm walking toward the grassy area in front of the L building when some girl lets out one of those bloodcurdling screams— the scary-movie kind. My body tenses, and I swear I can see headlights in front of me, and I have this crazy desire to throw my hand up and cover my face.

But as I whirl toward the sound, the girl—Roxy Indigo, who I only know because she got a 6 percent in our ceramics class freshman year—has dissolved into hysterical laughter, while she tries, halfheartedly, to pull her denim skirt—currently bunched up around her waist, revealing a black thong—back down over her hips. After homecoming last year, word around campus was she got so drunk at the after-party that she passed out and peed herself in the back of her date's SUV.

Which reminds me that I don't have any friends here, because I've never really *wanted* any.

Except . . .

Ben Michaels is staring at me. Lounging in the shade of the theater overhang with a couple of his stoner buddies, he's only a few feet from Roxy, and once she gets her skirt readjusted, she's headed back over there.

He doesn't turn his head to look at her, even though it's obvious she's talking to him. He just watches me. And normally, this is the point where I'd roll my eyes at the creeptasticness of it all. I mean, hello, stalker much? But he's not *leering* at me. And the look on his face isn't this possessive, he-wants-to-devour-me kind of look. It's different. Almost as if he's daring me to go over there.

So I do. And as I walk toward him, I stare right back at him, letting every ounce of frustration—at my schedule, at this day, at this life I managed to create for myself—swell in my chest. Tension curls itself through my muscles, ready to unleash in his direction if he isn't straight with me.

Only then I'm standing in front of him, and I realize I haven't the slightest idea what I'm going to say.

It isn't that easy to walk up to a guy in front of his friends and say, *I'm pretty sure I died the other day and you brought me back to life. What do you have to say about that?*

Instead I look at Ben and say, "Can I talk to you for a minute?"

He shrugs.

Fabulous. "Like, somewhere else?"

Someone snickers, and I glance to the right where Reid Suitor is sitting with four other guys whose names I don't know. Reid and another guy are—no lie—chewing on pieces of grass.

"You lost, baby? Or are you looking to rebel against Daddy?"

"Wow, that's original. What eighties movie did you steal that line from?" I say, turning left to the speaker. Elijah Palma. Great. This is already going worse than I had expected. Maybe I should just tell myself Alex was right—near-death experience triggered the firing of random nerve endings in my brain, and I imagined those visions. Maybe it was a sign there really is a hell and I'm going to end up there.

Elijah shrugs. His washed-out blue eyes are so bloodshot, he looks half-dead. "Hey, I'm willing to take one for the team."

Someone punches Elijah in the shoulder and says, "Knock it off, asshole." I know without looking that it's Ben. His voice is already familiar to me, even though I've barely heard him say two words.

"Take one for the team?" I know I shouldn't be egging him on, but I can't help it. I still haven't figured out what the hell I'm going to say to Ben, so I might as well burn my frustration by picking a fight with his friend. "What team are you even on, anyway?"

And no, I have no idea how to properly trade witty insults.

59

But no one notices, because I've just implied Elijah's gay, and it doesn't matter that it wasn't particularly clever.

"I don't screw uptight virgins," he sneers, and my face floods with heat.

Reid laughs, apparently in agreement.

I want to say something back, but my voice is frozen. Elijah, Reid, Roxy, Ben—they're gone, no longer in front of me. Instead I'm fifteen again, waking up at 2:13 a.m. after I just lost my best friend, in a car parked outside Chad Brandel's house with my jeans undone and my underwear ripped.

Doubled over in hysterics, Roxy leans into Elijah, and he wraps an arm around her. They're perfect for each other.

"I said shut the fuck up, dude." Again, it's Ben.

But Elijah keeps going. "You think you're the first prude to get in some kind of accident and realize you're wasting your life away? You can't just come over here for a pity fuck and an adrenaline rush. You—"

A fist crashes into his cheekbone, and the force rocks him backward, knocking Roxy to the side. A couple other guys laugh.

And then Ben is standing in front of me, holding on to his hand and rubbing his knuckles. He jerks his head toward the L building, and we both start walking that way.

It hasn't escaped my notice that he stuck up for me. That he just punched one of his friends—a kid notorious for getting suspended at least once every few months for kicking the shit out of someone—because I'd been insulted.

The notion is a little barbaric, but I'm too flattered to care.

Ben opens the door to the first classroom and holds it for me. The lights are on, and about ten kids are eating at a table in the far corner of the room, but I don't see the teacher. There's only a note on her whiteboard that reads *Do NOT leave a mess in the microwave. Please* ☺.

"Hey, Ben," one of the girls at the back table says. "Everything okay?" Only, as she stands up, I realize she isn't a student at all. Miss Poblete is five foot nothing and probably in her late twenties, but she could easily pass for a student.

Ben nods. "Yeah, we just needed a quiet place to go over a few things." As Ben lowers himself into a sitting position on one of the tables, I wonder why he seems so comfortable here.

Poblete smiles at me and sits back down.

"Book club," Ben says.

"What?"

He nods toward Poblete and the others. "She has book club meetings every Monday. If we're quiet, they won't listen."

My cheeks warm again as I turn to look at him. There's no easy way to say any of this. "You were there, at Torrey Pines, the day I got hit by that truck," I whisper.

It's not a question, but he nods anyway. So much for Alex's theory that Ben doesn't go to the beach.

"What did you do to me?"

He looks down at his feet, dangling a few inches above the floor. He swings them lightly, nervously. "Nothing."

I shake my head even though he isn't looking at me. "No, I remember you. I remember seeing your face when I opened my eyes."

He shrugs and doesn't take his eyes off his shoes. "I checked to see if you were okay."

I don't know him at all, but I know he's lying. "But I wasn't okay."

"You—"

"Don't—" *Lie to me*, I want to say as I step closer to him. Instead I say nothing and glance toward the back of the room. No one's looking at us.

When I turn back to Ben, he's staring at me. His jaw sets into a hard line. "I'm not sure what you want me to say."

"You did something to me, something I can't explain." I pause, trying to find the right words. But I'm not sure they exist. "I . . . I *died*." I rush on before he can tell me I'm crazy. "I mean, I *felt* it. I felt myself die—my heart stopped, there was nothingness, then there was this lightness—" I stop because I'm not making any sense. "But then suddenly I was back and you were leaning over me. I couldn't move, but you did something to my back so I could, and the doctors who looked at my X-ray said my back had been broken and healed again."

I'm close enough to him now that he can't swing his legs without them hitting me.

"So, Ben Michaels, what did you do to me?"

He looks up when I say his name, and his eyes connect to mine—they're as black as an oil well. And I remember the way they looked at me *before*. "Does it matter?"

"Yes. Yes, it does."

"Why?"

"Because I need to know," I say, my voice rising uncontrollably. I take a deep breath and try to maintain my composure. Then I whisper, "Something happened to me, and I need to understand what it was."

"No, you don't," he says with a small laugh.

And even though he doesn't sound condescending, it makes me feel like he thinks I'm just a silly girl. Irrational and crazy. My fists clench at my sides, and I bite the inside of my cheek.

"You're alive now, focus on that, right?" he says.

He waits for a response, but I don't give him one. Sophomore year I tried to be a peer mediator, and they told us the best way to get people to keep talking was just to be silent. When you don't say anything, the other person is tempted to fill that silence, and you can get more out of them. I didn't make it as a peer mediator because I kept injecting my own opinions and judgments—shocking, I know—but I held on to that advice. It actually works.

And it works on Ben. He sighs and runs a hand through his hair, tugging on the ends. "If you keep focusing on what happened, when you actually die, you'll still be thinking you haven't really *done* anything."

I pull back, and a hushed gasp escapes my mouth, because it's like he was there with me when I was dying.

Is that what happened? I don't even know.

"I didn't mean that," he says, sliding off the table. "That didn't come out the way I wanted it to, I mean." He pauses to chew on the corner of his bottom lip. "Look, I saw it happen. I came over to check on you, then when other people came over too, I backed away and gave them room."

"But—"

He shakes his head. "No, I'm serious. You had a traumatic experience. I was the first person you saw when you opened your eyes."

I nod, because Alex has already said as much, and, well, it *does* make sense. The problem is that deep inside my chest, that explanation feels wooden—hollow. And even Ben's speech sounds rehearsed. I don't hear any conviction behind his words.

"Why were you at the beach?"

He smirks. "What, I can't go to the beach? It was summer."

He starts to walk away, like our conversation is over.

"I don't believe that," I say. It comes out quietly, but I know he hears me because he stops. Keeping his back to me, he just waits, and I get the impression from his posture that he's holding his breath. I believe he brought me back. I don't know how yet, but I will. I do know that right now, I believe I'm here—I'm alive—because of him. The sense of gratitude makes me dizzy and light-headed, like I need to take a deep breath.

And apparently all rational thought leaves my head and my body takes on a life of its own, because I take a step toward him, reaching out, until the tips of two of my fingers brush against his. I don't know what I'm doing, it's been forever since I just held hands with anyone, and my hand seems to tingle with the touch.

"I don't know what you want me to say," Ben says. His voice is quiet and cracks slightly at the end, as if he feels helpless, as if he wishes he had some kind of answer. And that is almost enough to make me back off and leave Ben Michaels and whatever freaky shit he's into alone. Only I'm tired of being hollow inside.

You'll still be thinking you haven't really done *anything.*

I want to feel something. I want to feel . . . alive.

And whatever he says, Ben Michaels is the reason I have the chance.

"I just . . . Thank you." And as I say it, I squeeze his hand, the level of pressure directly correlating to the depth of emotion I'm feeling—that is to say, it had to feel a little like his bones might start cracking. "Thank you."

I let go and leave him standing there. No matter how much I want to look back, I don't.

When I get home after Alex and I drop Jared off at polo, my mother is awake. And baking.

This happens sometimes, which almost makes everything worse. "Almost" because nothing beats the smell of warm bread.

"J-baby!" she calls when I open the door. "In here!"

"Here" is the kitchen. She's showered and is wearing a bright green velour jumpsuit and more eyeliner than she needs. And she's surrounded by possibly eight hundred muffins—blueberry, banana nut, bran, cornbread, chocolate chip—they're everywhere. Literally. They cover every surface in our kitchen. As does flour.

My flip-flops stick to the linoleum floor. Egg, vanilla extract, butter—I'm not sure what I'm sticking to, but I know I'm annoyed. We'll be eating muffins for every meal until we have to throw them out, and I'll be the one cleaning this up.

"How was school, baby?" she asks, turning to give me a smile and a banana nut muffin. "Here, have one, they're fabulous. I used your great-grandmother's recipe, and I got it just right. They couldn't be more perfect!"

"School's fine," I mutter as I take a bite. She's right. She did get Nana's recipe perfect, which is saying something. My dad's grandmother owned a bakery.

"Jared said your schedule was all wrong. He told me they gave you classes that were easier than his and that you'd need to get it changed. Do you have any classes with Kate? Oh, here—try this one too. I'm not sure why it isn't quite right, but they just didn't rise as well as the first batch. They taste fine, though." She hands me a flat cornbread muffin. She's forgotten that I don't like cornbread. Just like she's forgotten that Kate and I aren't friends anymore.

"I'm getting my schedule fixed," I say, taking a bite of it anyway. "I filed paperwork with Elksen and now I'm just waiting for him to get around to it."

"How is it?" she asks, nodding to the flat muffin. "I'm just not sure why they didn't rise. I could throw them out, I guess, but that would be so wasteful. I just don't know what happened. All the other batches look great."

What happened is she messed up the baking soda or baking powder, but I'm not about to point that out. "It tastes great, Mom."

She beams, and her dimples—the same as Jared's—peek out of her cheeks. Even her nose scrunches up with her smile. She looks ten years younger than she did a few days ago. I can't think of the last time she smiled like that.

I want to say something else, prolong this moment, but words fail me. And it doesn't matter. She's already turned back to the mixing bowl and begun a long explanation of why she decided to also make a batch of raspberry muffins and how they'll be different from the blueberry ones, even though she's using the same baseline recipe. I text Alex, Struz, and even Jared's water polo coach to let them know there'll be muffins on us for anyone who's interested.

And then I just listen to her talk.

It's not that I'm particularly interested in the art of baking muffins or that I don't have a ton of other things I should do. I just love how animated she looks—so opposite of yesterday and the day before and the day before that.

I have a second chance to fix all this. To try harder.

My mother offers me a spoonful of batter, but I shake my head. The problem with days like this? They're just enough to remind me what I'm missing. I don't have a mother I can talk to. I will never be able to tell my mother about Ben Michaels, that he saved me somehow, that he's denying it.

So after she finishes the raspberry batch, I grab the Clorox wipes and head to her bedroom. I throw the curtains wide, roll up the shade, and open the windows as far as I can. Once I've got some air in there and the ceiling fan is attempting to circulate it, I start picking up the clothes on the floor.

And when I'm rearranging the picture frames—putting the picture of Jared and me at Disneyland after we rode Space Mountain back on her nightstand—I see it.

My dad's laptop, plugged in, still turned on, and resting on the bed, buried in her bedspread. He has his own room. My parents stopped sleeping together forever ago. She needed her own space for peace and quiet, and frankly, if they had to stay in the same room, he never would have come home from the office.

Which means he spent the morning in here—with her.

I sit down on the bed and pull the computer into my lap, open it up, and log in. His password would be complex. To anyone *else*—even someone who knows binary code. But I can hack anything my dad has passworded. I know him too well.

As it loads, I hear my mother's singing underneath the thrum of the fan, and I can't help wondering if this is why she's awake and in a good mood. I know she'll come down from this high—she always does. But could it be this easy to pick her back up again?

Scrolling through my father's history, I open up the last files he viewed. One is a performance eval for Barclay, T. I don't know the name, so he must be a new analyst. At first it appears to be anything but average. In fact, the first part is straight-up *glowing*. A hundred percent on handgun and rifle qualifications—it means he hit dead-center on all fifty shots. His computer skills are fantastic, and his actions directly led to closing a recent investigation. Only my dad is recommending he be moved to a different unit. Apparently T. Barclay doesn't respond well to authority, and he blatantly disregarded an assignment my dad sent him on. That'll probably ruin T. Barclay's career. You can't just not do what your boss tells you to when you're in the FBI. Even when your instincts are good and you end up being right. The ends don't justify the means in a bureaucracy.

The next file is paperwork on a gang case that goes to trial later this year. Normally I'd be all over that. But the third file is the autopsy report for Torrey Pines Doe 09022012. My John Doe.

Jackpot.

This is, of course, illegal. Just looking through my dad's files could come with some pretty stiff penalties if the government found out—for me and for my dad. And even though I've been snooping through his files for a long time, my heart still races uncontrollably every time.

I glance at the bedroom door again and listen for anything out of the ordinary, but the only thing I hear—other than my own hammering heart—is my mother's off-key version of an old Whitney Houston ballad.

Taking a deep breath, I turn back to the report.

My John Doe is still unidentified. They don't even have an alleged identity next to his case file (which reduces him to the location and the date of his death). They're putting him at approximately twenty-five to forty-five years, height and weight not applicable. That, I agree with. That I understand. What I don't is what I read next. The physical examination.

FINDINGS:

01 Global burns consistent with radiation with extensive body

mutilation

02 Perimortal crush injury of right thorax

03 Head injury cannot be ruled out

What. The. Hell.

How can that even be possible? He wouldn't have been exposed to radiation on the side of the highway—or in his car, for that matter. There's no reason burns should have shown up on his skin postmortem. I'm not exactly up on medical science, but burns with extensive body mutilation are *bad*, and they tend to show up immediately. And if the crash killed him and not the burns . . . maybe that was why he was driving so fast. He could have been trying to get to a hospital. Or running from something.

Next page.

CAUSE OF DEATH:

01 Global burns

02 Perimortal crush injury, right chest

So far, the medical examiner is the only person who's signed off on the autopsy. Maybe they're getting another opinion. Not that I blame them—it seems more likely that someone switched up the bodies than that this is actually *my* John Doe.

EXTERNAL EXAMINATION:

The body is presented to the county morgue in a blue body bag
and wrapped in a white to tan sheet. The remains are those of a
Caucasian male and consist primarily of a severely burned body.
Burns are consistent with chemical burns or radiation. There is
no charring, but there is complete burning of the flesh from many
sites, massive destruction of bony tissues, and resultant profound
mutilation of the body. Soft tissues of the face, including nose, ears,
and eyes, are absent, with exposure of partially destroyed underlying
bony structures.

My stomach turns at the possible image—I get the idea— and I scroll down to try to see more.

And the smoke alarm screeches.

I jump to my feet, automatically sniffing the air for smoke. My skin itches at the possibility of burns. I shut the laptop and toss it back onto the bed before I run to the kitchen.

Thankfully, nothing is on fire.

But the muffins in the oven are burning—and smoking—and my mother is standing in the center of the room looking at a broken coffee mug, black eyeliner tears streaking down her face.

"**A**nd you're sure it was the same guy?" Alex asks.

I shake my head and take a sip of the mocha frappe I grabbed from It's a Grind, thankful I managed to get out of the house and away from my mom's latest episode. I worry a little— or sometimes a lot—about leaving her alone, but every once in a while I also just have to get away. Since Alex's house is next door, I tell myself I won't be gone long, and I won't be far in case she needs me.

Alex and I are sitting at the dining room table in his house with just about every textbook he owns spread out on the table, and he's buried in a slew of physics problems.

I can't talk to him about Ben Michaels, so I'm focusing on the accident.

"They could have mixed up the bodies . . ." There could be more than one John Doe who died in San Diego on Monday. It's less likely than people would think, but it's possible. And despite the eighty-seven different conclusions my brain latched on to the moment I started reading the autopsy, it has occurred to me that I'm supposed to be looking at evidence and letting the conclusions fall into place as a result, rather than speculating.

"But if it is him, it means he crashed because he was already dead."

Alex doesn't even glance up from his physics book. "And then you could stop being a moron and blaming yourself."

I don't want to get into that again. "Just listen to me," I say. "Three still-unidentified victims in San Diego thirty years ago, COD severe radiation poisoning. Then nothing. Now suddenly there are at least three new cases, all in the span of less than two weeks. And one of them might have died while driving." Driving the truck that killed me.

I don't say that because Alex has made it clear he thinks the whole Ben Michaels thing is in my mind. Instead I say, "Think about it. My dad's got all these case files, and now by some freak coincidence a truck hits me and the driver might be related to the same case."

This time Alex closes the book and leans back in his chair. "What do you think's causing the radiation?" he says, reaching for the espresso I brought him and lifting it to his lips. Only it's empty because he downed it the second I got here, and caffeine isn't going to magically appear just because he hopes it might.

"Sorry, I should have gotten you a double."

He shakes his head and tosses me the empty cup. "No, it's cool. Hide it before my mom comes in here and sees it." I crumple it and stick it in my purse with a smile. "So the burns?" Alex prompts.

"Right. The burns are severe—hard-core severe."

"So the obvious answer is some kind of nuclear radiation."

I shrug. "Right, but from what?"

He's chewing his lip, and I know my mission has been

73

accomplished. Alex Trechter has completely abandoned his homework. A little contraband caffeine and something interesting to distract him is all he needs. "Could it be some kind of virus?" he asks. "Like an injection of something radioactive?"

"You watch too many bad movies."

"I do not—"

"You still owe me for the two hours of my life that I lost watching *Mission Impossible 2*. I can never get those back."

He rolls his eyes. "I'm serious."

"Um, I'm serious too. What is with John Woo and those slow-motion doves?"

"Janelle, a virus would explain the late onset."

I shake my head. "Not really. And wouldn't the gamma burns manifest on the inside of the body, in the organs and body tissue?" I shiver a little at the mental image. "These burns were on his face and hands—exposed skin."

Alex shakes his head. "It could still be some kind of virus—did you get the chance to read the internal examination?" When I shake my head, he continues, "I read viral terrorism is all the rage now. And it would make sense that your dad is involved—wasn't he part of the team that investigated the viral hemorrhagic fevers two years ago in L.A.?"

"Yeah, they brought him and Struz in on that." The virus in L.A. was like Ebola. It started with low-grade headaches, but within an hour or two the symptoms progressed to a debilitating fever and muscle pain. Within twenty-four hours the major organs, digestive system, skin, eyes, and gums of those infected would break down, deteriorate, and bleed. Then they were dead. The virus was caused by a bacteria terrorists had somehow managed to insert in select toothpaste tubes that were imported from China. I know people who still use baking soda instead of real toothpaste.

As much as I want to insist that Alex is wrong, I can't. Just because I don't know *how* someone would make it work like that doesn't mean it's not possible. I mean, some kind of bioterrorism in the form of a radiation virus fits a little too easily. Easily enough that it's terrifying.

"How would someone make a late-onset virus like that?" I ask.

"J, I don't know," Alex says with a laugh. "I mean, contrary to popular belief, I'm actually not harboring a secret desire to grow up and become a bioterrorist."

"Hello, Miss Tenner, have you come to do your homework here?" Alex's mother, the formidable Annabeth Trechter, breezes into the dining room carrying a heap of folded pastel-colored towels. Despite the laundry, she looks like she just fell out of a business meeting in her skirt and suit jacket with her black hair pulled into a bun at the nape of her neck. She pauses in front of me and waits for my answer.

"No, ma'am," I say, looking down to avoid her eyes—and I'd be embarrassed about that except Annabeth Trechter is the only woman who scares my dad. And she *likes* him.

"I actually dropped by to see if I could borrow Alex's physics book when he's finished," I say. It's only half a lie. "Eastview messed up my schedule and I'm not in the right classes, so I don't have the books yet."

She turns her attention to Alex. "You've finished your reading for English and your Spanish homework?"

"Yes, ma'am."

"You have forty-three more minutes before dinner, and

afterward you'll be able to go to the Tenners' to drop off your physics book, then you'll come back promptly to study your vocabulary for the SATs."

"Janelle and I were going to—"

"No, you studied vocabulary together last night. Tonight you'll study with me."

"Yes, ma'am."

I can't help smiling at that. Alex looks right at me, and I know my expression says, *Sucks to be you*. Only then it doesn't, because suddenly his mom's attention is back on me, and I'm fighting to keep from shrinking down in my seat. I swear, she's some kind of human lie detector, and any second she's going to start berating me for keeping Alex from his real work. "How is your father?"

"He's good," I say, then force myself to elaborate. The more information you volunteer with Alex's mom, the less likely she is to think you're hiding something. "He's been up late working on a new case, but you know him. He'll solve it."

Mrs. Trechter nods. "You can go home now, Janelle. Alex will bring the book by after dinner."

"Yes, ma'am," I say as I get up from the table and grab my purse and mocha frappe. "Thank you." I turn and leave without looking back at Alex. Because we might make each other laugh. And because I know his mom is watching me leave, and she terrifies me.

Someday, I sort of hope I'm just like her.

16:09:48:02

Tuesday my schedule still hasn't been changed, but my earth science teacher hands me a pass to the library as soon as I walk in.

I flash my student ID and the pass at the librarian and settle in at one of the computers. I should try to do some of the work I'm missing in the classes I'm supposed to be in, but I check my email first. There's nothing interesting, so I open up Google, and because Alex's theory has been on my mind, I type "radiation burns."

Naturally, most of what comes up has to do with cancer patients and treatments for sunburn, which is hardly what I'm looking for. And I don't really want to check out any of the pictures, thank you.

When I try "radiation poisoning," a link for a story about the Chernobyl disaster pops up. In 1986 a nuclear power plant in Ukraine had a meltdown. It was considered the worst nuclear power plant accident in history. Twenty-eight people died that day, more than three hundred thousand people had to be evacuated to avoid the fallout, and it's estimated that almost sixty thousand were exposed and five thousand of those exposed died. And if my John Doe was one of those first twenty-eight people, his autopsy would make sense, maybe. But he wasn't. And that kind of exposure can't be solitary.

No wonder the FBI has my dad on this case.

A group of freshmen escorted by a teacher I don't know comes into the library. They're loud and awkward, and occupying the librarian's time. I'm tempted to keep reading about radiation poisoning, specifically how someone could harness radiation into some kind of viral form—if that's even possible.

But I've only got about an hour until I'll have to head out, so I pull up Eastview's intranet, log into Alex's account, and go to work downloading the notes and information I need. The librarian escorts the freshmen into one of the classrooms and begins some sort of presentation—most likely the "How to Use the Library" speech all freshmen have to sit through. I pull out my phone and make a to-do list based on the priority of the assignments.

"So your schedule sucks?"

My heart literally leaps into my throat, almost choking me, as I turn to see Ben Michaels slide into the chair next to mine. His hoodie is white today, but he wears it the same as before—over his head, pulled low enough to shield his eyes even though a few stray floppy curls of brown hair stick out. He's giving me a wry, one-sided smile.

I want to ask him a million things all over again.

But the whole clogged-throat thing keeps the words from coming, so I do the next best thing and pull my shitty schedule from my pocket and hand it to him. His schedule probably doesn't look any better, and he probably doesn't care—I know

78

that. But somehow, from the way he slumps into his seat and sighs, I think he just might understand. Or at least empathize.

He doesn't even give me time to explain. "Algebra?" He laughs. "What, do they want you to teach the class?" He shakes his head and turns to the computer in front of him.

And that's it.

I guess part of me hoped he'd say something else. Volunteer information. Start a conversation. After all, he's the one who sat down next to me. It's not like there aren't thirty other computers in here.

I wait for a second before deciding, *Screw it*. I'm going to keep asking until I get the answer I want to hear. I turn to Ben's profile and open my mouth, but pause as I realize he looks almost classically beautiful from this angle—his profile, the shape of his face—it just seems so perfect, and I'm frozen with surprise that I could see someone on campus for two years and not ever take the time to really *notice* him. He's handsome in that kind of tall, dark, mysterious, and tortured way. It's his eyes. They're brown, but they're so dark they sometimes look black. And the way he holds himself, it's like he knows and takes advantage of his bone structure, the fact that his eyes are deep set—they look shadowed. His face is almost strangely blank, and it makes him look sad, like he has some kind of tragic secret, and for some ridiculous reason I wonder what it is.

He might hide behind the dark, brooding stoner thing, but his face is actually just as perfect as Nick's or Kevin's. I can't help wondering if he gets the same kind of play.

I squelch that thought down. It's none of my business what Ben Michaels does on his own time, so I try to look away and decide what I'm going to say, but I can't seem to concentrate on my computer anymore. I want to keep staring—like if I look at him long enough, I'll unravel the enigma that is Ben Michaels.

Then I see his computer.

He has the school mainframe open and my schedule on the screen. A few keyboard shortcuts, and it's completely wiped. A blank slate.

"What are you doing?"

"Changing your schedule," he answers, as if accessing the mainframe couldn't get him expelled.

"But you can't—how'd you—"

He shrugs. "I stole the password off Florentine as a freshman. I've been fixing schedules for a couple years now."

I look around the library. No one's paying attention to us, but we aren't exactly hidden from sight, either. Anyone could glance this way and see the screen.

"Janelle," he says, and just the way he says my name—like I matter—makes me turn back to him. There's no tension lining his eyes; now they look like they could be smiling. "What classes do you want?"

Junior year is supposed to be the most important year for applying to colleges. And I *did* follow all the rules—I submitted my class requests on time, I got the paperwork signed off on. It's not my fault the schedule is all messed up.

So I tell him.

Ben clearly knows his way around the software, deftly searching for the course titles. I point to the teachers and class periods I want—and effectively match my schedule with Alex's.

When I pick Poblete's third-period class, Ben cracks a half smile. But I have a moment of panic when he tries to insert me into the class and an error message pops up to declare the class is too full.

Ben chuckles beside me—I must have gasped or something—and I realized how close we are, how much I'm leaning into him. Close enough that I can feel his body heat next to me. Close enough that I can smell the faint mixture of what I'm coming to know as pure Ben—mint, soap, and gasoline. Despite the fact that we're not actually touching, I'm leaning over his shoulder, my mouth dangerously close to his ear.

If he turned his head just a few more inches in my direction, he could kiss me.

I have no idea where that thought came from.

I lean back, shifting in my seat.

"Don't worry, I got this," Ben says, gesturing to the computer. "You think you're the first person who I needed to override to get them into Poblete's class?"

Obviously not. He enters an override code, and a class roster pops up.

"Wait," I say, reaching for him. "Don't take anyone out. That isn't fair."

"I won't," he says, but he's looking at my hand on his arm, and I pull it back, my face heating up. "I just need to manually add you in, see?" He copies and pastes my student ID into the class roster.

Which is when it hits me that he has access to EVERYTHING—even grades.

"It's so wrong, right?" he asks, as if he can read my mind. "That it's this easy to hack into the system. To steal a password?"

"How often do you do this?"

He shrugs. "I've changed schedules for a few people who were freaking out about shit, but mostly I just change a couple of friends' schedules at the beginning of each semester. Avoid the counseling office."

"Have you ever changed . . . more than schedules?"

"Like grades?" he says with a laugh. "Of course not."

I'm so relieved, I let go of the breath I hadn't realized I was holding.

"Although I think you're the first person to recognize it's the same program," he adds. "None of my friends have put that together."

"If they knew, would they ask you to do it?"

His head cocks to the side, and I can tell he's chewing on the inside of his cheek. For some reason that makes me smile.

"I don't think so. I mean, the guys who are my friends wouldn't—they know I wouldn't do it. And most of the other guys we hang out with, they don't care enough to ask." I'm tempted to tell him not to befriend any AP students because nobody cheats as much as they do, but I don't. Because technically that's me—I'm an AP student.

"What do you want last period?" Ben asks.

After I'm inserted into the right Spanish class, Ben prints my schedule and looks down, refusing to meet my eyes. My breath catches, and I wonder if he's going to say something about the accident.

"So I'm not saying you would, but usually when I do this I make the person swear they won't tell anyone."

My insides plummet. "What, you don't want eight hundred people asking you to schedule them?"

"No . . . it's not about how many people are asking," he says. "It's more about *why* they're asking, if that makes any sense. If it's 'Oh, counseling messed up my schedule and won't fix it,' okay. If it's 'I want a teacher who will let me cut class and not take attendance,' I don't want to bother."

"Honor among cheaters?" I ask. And immediately regret it, because he glances up at me and looks pained—like I've insulted him.

"It's just . . ." He sighs. "I don't always make the right decisions, and I get that." He shrugs. "But at the end of the day, I want to be able to look myself in the eyes and say I *believe* in them. I want to know I'd make each one again."

I do know. It makes so much sense, my chest aches. Right should be about conviction. For all of my condescending comments about everyone else in this school, I can't think of anything that I choose to believe in, that I choose to stand for. Except maybe Jared.

"And would you?" I ask, my voice barely above a whisper. "Would you do it again?"

Something in his face changes, and he pushes his chair back and stands up. I'm talking about more than my schedule now.

But he just shrugs. "Even I know Janelle Tenner shouldn't be in earth science and algebra. They would have fixed it for you eventually. Why not speed up the process?"

"Thanks," I say, but I don't feel it. Inside my eyes are watery and my throat is tight. A heaviness weighs down on my chest. Because that isn't at all what I wanted to hear.

I sit there for a long time after he's walked away. I replay each moment in my mind—the accident, what I saw and *felt*, almost running into him in the office, seeing him at lunch the other day, this conversation. He's not what I expected at all.

I replay it all. Over and over, like I'm trying to memorize each detail and figure it out.

Until someone touches my shoulder and I can't help but jump.

"I've been calling you," Nick says with a laugh. "Come on, let's hit off-campus for lunch."

I don't roll my eyes, even though I want to. We just went through this yesterday—how does he not remember? "Nick, I can't—"

"Don't worry. Coach is at the gate. I already talked to him, and he said he'll let you through."

He flashes me such a big smile, I instantly feel bad for thinking the worst when he's actually planned ahead.

I should be giving him a chance instead of second-guessing his motives, without looking down on him because he has different priorities than I do.

"Sure," I say, and even though I would have said it was impossible, Nick's smile gets even wider. "If you don't think either of us will get in trouble."

He holds out his hand and pulls me out of my chair—his skin warm to the touch. "I'm Teflon, baby, trouble rolls right off me."

I laugh, and this time I do roll my eyes. Because I'm not sure I'm laughing with him or at him. But of course that was his point. It's just the cheesy kind of thing he says, but somehow when he says it, it's funny—I like that he doesn't take himself too seriously.

I text Alex to see if he wants me to bring him back something, and as Nick leads me out into the parking lot, I look up to see

Elijah Palma smoking some kind of homemade cigarette and staring me down.

Only as we lock eyes does it occur to me that for someone who's allegedly a stoner, Ben Michaels didn't smell at all like smoke.

15:19:53:38

"**Y**ou're not going to believe what I found," Alex says as he slips into our library cube and slides the soundproof door shut. He's leaning back, just barely balancing the weight of what looks like six more mega hardcovers to add to the twenty-something that are piled up around me. I want to laugh at his excitement—I love when he does his "I'm determined to solve this" thing. But I don't laugh, because that's a lot more reading.

We decided to hit S&E, the science and engineering library at UCSD, because his aunt works here, which means she'll let us in and she'll report back to his mom and tell her that we're studying. And we are, just not anything school related.

"Please tell me it's something productive and not another outdated copy of *Maxim*? Just because your mom won't let you read it, doesn't mean—"

Alex ignores me and dumps his books onto our table with the rest of them. I try not to be annoyed—though I don't try too hard. Adding more books to this stack hardly seems to solve our problem. I've got everything from the 9/11 Commission Report to a Michael Crichton novel, not that any of it has turned out to be particularly helpful so far. The Crichton novel and a couple of other thrillers are pure fantasy or speculative fiction grounded in paranoia and conspiracy theory. And some of the more scientific bioterrorism books read as a sourcebook or guidebook for how to handle an outbreak. Then there are the true accounts of outbreaks of smallpox in the Soviet Union and Ebola in a Washington, DC, lab.

In other words, nothing even remotely helps me figure out how my John Doe ended up dead of radiation poisoning while he was driving a truck.

"You going to tell me what's so exciting?" I ask. My phone starts vibrating against the table, but I'm not a hundred percent sure where it is under all these freaking books.

Alex grins before leaning forward and picking up one of the thickest books and thumbing through it. "I was looking through *The Handbook of Viral Bioterrorism and Biodefense*, and I found this." He opens the book wide to page 428, where the chapter heading reads "Biological Warfare of the Future: Viral Bioengineering."

"Right now bioterrorism is based on bacterial agents," Alex says. "Category A are the worst, like anthrax—they spread easily and quickly, and could lead to a wide-scale outbreak."

"I know that. Everything we've read so far says that."

"Which is why this book is so cool. It's speculating what's next. Viral engineering isn't that far off. In fact," he adds, pushing the book toward me, "look right here. It asks whether radiation can be harnessed into a transmissible virus. And it gives a detailed explanation of what geneticists might have to do in order to come up with something that could be engineered."

He's still smiling. Which doesn't make sense, now that we've just proven finding information on how to become a bioterrorist isn't all that hard.

But I've seen this look before. It's the same look Struz and my dad get when they're close to cracking a case, like they've discovered the secrets of the universe. It makes me think Alex is doing the right thing by deviating from his mother's life plan. He doesn't want Stanford undergrad and Johns Hopkins medical. He wants West Point and the FBI—like my dad. And the thought of Alex actually working for my dad someday makes me smile.

Then it hits me.

"Wait a minute," I say. "Maybe we're coming at this from the wrong angle. Maybe it doesn't matter how the virus is being spread—someone from the CDC can figure that out. What's important is the countdown."

I stand up and push in my chair, stretching my legs. My phone vibrates again, and this time I see that it's Nick. Again.

"Let's say, for argument's sake, someone has managed to engineer a virus. Whether it's radiation poisoning or not, it's ugly and it's going to kill people. So how does picking people off one at a time—what does that have to do with the countdown?"

Alex gasps and sits up straighter. "That's how they connect!" He looks at me, and I'm tempted to prompt him to tell me, but I know better than to interrupt his train of thought. "The UIED. It's not a bomb. J, it's something that will disperse the virus. Make it airborne or make it catch fire."

A shiver moves between my shoulder blades. "But why would terrorists give the FBI a heads-up like that?"

"Because they're sociopaths? I don't know, but it makes sense. If the UIED goes off, the virus goes airborne, maybe it's some kind of chemical explosion that triggers it. And maybe the FBI got their hands on the UIED earlier than they were supposed to. Or maybe the terrorists want us to know it's coming. Think of the panic it would incite. And isn't wrecking our way of life part of the whole terrorism package?"

My phone buzzes again, and this time I pick it up and toss it carefully from hand to hand. "So with that theory, my John Doe and the other victims, they're test subjects?"

Alex shrugs. "Maybe people who pissed off the terrorist group?"

Somehow I'm not satisfied. This theory doesn't give me an identity to associate with the guy who died the same day and time that I did on Torrey Pines Road.

"J?" Alex says.

"Hmmm?"

"You think it's time we tell your dad?"

I'm about to nod. After all, it's past time we shared our theories with him. It could be totally off, and it could be something someone already thought of. Or it could be right. Or it could fall somewhere in between. Either way he needs to know. But as I'm about to say that, the door to our room slides open and Nick sticks his head in and says, "Tell her dad what?"

Inwardly, I groan. I wouldn't have told him where I was headed after school if I thought he and his other half were going to show up.

Kevin pops in behind him and pushes the door wider. "You confess your true feelings yet, Trechter?"

"Kevin, shut up," I say as I focus on Nick. "What are you doing here?"

"I've been looking for you for, like, an hour," Nick says. "Why

89

didn't you answer your phone?"

I gesture to the books. "I'm working?"

Nick picks up one of the books closest to him, and I'm tempted to take it away from him, but that'll just look more suspicious, and I don't trust him with this.

"You work too hard, J," Kevin says. Shocking that he thinks so.

Nick puts the book down and leans against the door. "I know what the problem is. You need to have fun. Come with me to Hines's place tonight."

"Alex and I are going to finish studying and then . . ."

Alex knows me well enough to know I'm looking for an excuse, so he jumps in. "We're going to watch *Tron: Legacy*."

Since this is the Lamest Excuse Ever, there's no way I can stand behind it.

"Um, no we're not. That movie is only about a tenth as good as its soundtrack."

Alex just smirks—I will totally get him back for this.

Nick says, "So it looks like you can come with me."

"It's Tuesday," I say, even though I know that to Nick this isn't an excuse. Especially not this year. His dad used to be strict about where he went—more because of sports than school—but his parents are getting divorced and he and his dad aren't speaking, which means he's been doing pretty much whatever he feels like since this summer.

"His parents are out of town until Friday."

"I can't," I say without looking at Nick. Even I'm not immune to how gorgeous he is. I know how easy it is to be charmed by those almond eyes.

"I promise I won't keep you out late," he says, holding his hand over his heart. And when I look at him, I can't help thinking of the first night we talked—really talked—this summer. He'd just found out his dad was having an affair with a girl who graduated from Eastview five years ago, and instead of getting wasted at one of the beach bonfire parties, he was just sitting by himself when I closed up the lifeguard stand and was getting ready to go home. I asked him how he was doing, and everything just poured out. We talked for three hours. About his family and their failings. About how we were afraid of disappointing people the way they disappointed us.

"I promise," Nick says again. "Scout's honor."

"You must have been a horrible Boy Scout."

"I wasn't a Boy Scout," he says, as if he can't figure out why I would say such a thing.

"Seriously. I already have an essay to write, three chapters of history to read, a shitload of physics and calc problems, plus Spanish review." I gesture to the mound of books all over the table, even though they have nothing to do with anything I've just rattled off.

He pouts. "You deserve a rest from taking care of everybody. A night of fun before diving back into the books. You didn't get to come to the bonfire."

Not that I'm disappointed about the bonfire, but I do work too hard.

"Just an hour," I say, wondering when my willpower decided to go on vacation—and when it will be back.

"Of course." Nick laughs. "I'll have you home before eleven."

"Let me pack up here," I say. "I'll meet you in the parking lot."

After Kevin and Nick leave, I look at Alex. He jams his books back into his backpack. "Maybe you should trade those crappy vintage T-shirts and ripped jeans for short skirts and tank tops. You can start hanging out with Brooke, too."

"You're the one who ruined tonight with a lame excuse. I wanted to do something else, and you came up with a movie that only has a plot in the first thirty minutes?"

"It's got great visual effects," Alex says as he goes back to shoving his stuff into his backpack, and I grab the couple of books I do want to take home with me.

"Wait," I say, reaching out to grab Alex's shoulder. "Did you call my *Great Gatsby* T-shirt crappy? I fucking love this shirt."

"Fine. Abandon me so I have to hang out with my mother," Alex says, but he's smiling again. Which is all I really needed to see.

A t twelve forty-five I give up on Nick.

An hour and forty-five minutes is my threshold—and of course he's so drunk he can't stand up without leaning on me for support. I try to take his keys but give up on those after he bellows at me that he's "just fine to drive, woman."

I get yelled at enough by my mother—someone I'm obligated to love. I don't need it from some shithead who slams two beers and then lets his friends pressure him into doing five shots of tequila in the span of an hour.

Plus, what the hell am I going to do with his keys anyway? Unlike 18 percent of my graduating class, I'm planning to not have a DUI on my record when I graduate. And since my license is already suspended because of the stupid seizure, driving really isn't an option anyway.

I should have left a half hour ago when Cecily's sister picked her up and offered me a ride, but I was still under the delusion that Nick would have an ounce of reliability. Now the problem, of course, is that Alex is asleep—not that his mom would let him out this late anyway—my mother lost her driving privileges ages ago, and Jared is too young. Both my dad's cells have gone straight to voice mail for the past half hour. And no one else is sober or worth asking for a ride. I even glanced around for Reid Suitor, since he played baseball his freshman and sophomore years and I've seen him around this crowd before. Not that I'd really want a ride from him.

I suck it up, walk out to the front porch, and call Struz.

"J-baby!" he says with his usual enthusiasm, even though he's whispering. "Whatever you need, it's gotta be quick. We're on something big tonight."

"I've got a code twenty-one," I say. My dad thought the whole FBI thing might hurt my social life when I was in junior high, so he and Struz came up with a bunch of numbered codes so I could call him from a friend's house without people thinking I was some kind of snitch. He thought it'd be hard to explain to a bunch of teenagers that counterintelligence doesn't really care about underage drinking.

Right this instant, though, I wouldn't have stopped them from coming over here and busting up this party.

"Shit." I hear rustling over the phone for a second. "Where are you?"

I give Struz the address, and he promises to send a junior agent or an analyst to come get me, then he's got to run. I want to grill him about what they're doing, but I know enough—and I respect them and their jobs enough—to let him go.

"You call for a ride?"

I turn to see Kevin in a wife beater, baggy jeans, and a sideways baseball hat. He looks ridiculous.

"What of it?"

Instead of spouting off some nonsense like I expect, he smiles

94

and thrusts his hands into his pockets. "I'll make Nick crash here if he doesn't pass out."

"Whatever, I don't care." Though that's hardly true.

"I've had a lot of practice at ganking his keys," Kevin says, and collapses into a porch chair. "I'd offer you a ride home, but . . ." He holds up a mostly empty bottle of beer.

"It's fine."

Kevin nods, and we sit in silence as the minutes tick by.

The cul-de-sac is quiet—most of the other houses have their lights off already, and not a single car turns onto the street, despite all the vibes I'm sending out into the atmosphere, hoping for headlights to appear. A breeze picks up, rustling through my hair, and I pull my hoodie over my head and fold my arms across my chest.

"It's cool that you came tonight," Kevin says suddenly, and I wonder why he even cares. "I know my man Nick fucked up and you didn't have a good time or anything, but it's cool that you came."

"I'll probably opt to stay home next time."

"I don't blame you. Some nights I'd rather just stay home and read."

I turn to face Kevin. Other than the idiotic hat, the dirty wife beater, and the jeans that are belted around his thighs, he looks perfectly serious. But I know what this is. An act, a play, because this is Kevin and he's like that.

Before he realizes what I'm doing, I snap a picture of him—beer in hand—with my cell. "If you try to hit on me again, I'll show this to Coach Stinson and he'll have you running stadium steps until baseball starts this spring," I say, because Nick once confessed their baseball coach was a stickler about drinking.

And because I'm like *that*.

But Kevin doesn't get pissed off or nervous. He just takes another sip of his beer. "Touché, Tenner. Touché." A word I didn't even think was in his vocabulary.

Apparently this month is full of surprises. No one is as dumb as I thought they were.

15:16:03:24

When the headlights of a Chevy TrailBlazer round the corner, I turn and offer Kevin a slight nod before heading down the steps.

"I'll make sure Nick doesn't drive," he says again. I look back in time to see him raise his beer bottle in a salute.

"Thanks," I say, even though I've pretty much decided I don't want Nick Matherson to be *my* responsibility—no matter how pretty he is or how many great late-night talks we had sitting on the beach. I just don't have the time or the patience.

The TrailBlazer stops at the edge of the Hineses' driveway, and even though I knew it wouldn't be Struz, I'm still disappointed when I see a dark brown head and a scruffy layer of facial hair. He's an agent I don't know, and he's on his cell, not paying any attention to me when I open the door and slide into the passenger seat.

"—and now I'm stuck playing babysitter. This is ridiculous." Nothing makes you feel uncomfortable quite like when you first meet someone who's not just talking, but complaining, about you. "Yeah, well, next time we're switching positions on this. I'm

97

not playing this angle again."

I'm tempted to say something—point out that he can start driving Any Time Now so that we can get going. I am, after all, looking forward to getting home and going to sleep, and if he's this interested in getting back to work, I'd be happy to oblige. But it's not worth it. I'm too tired to argue.

"Whatever, I gotta go," he says, glancing over at me. "Right, well, keep me on tap if you hear anything."

When he hangs up, I notice that his phone is far more high-tech than any BlackBerry I've seen. Figures. The Bureau tends to attract overgrown kids who love their gadgets.

"You Janelle Tenner?" he asks. I nod because I don't trust my voice. I tend to get irritable when someone talks about me like I'm not there. "You do realize the FBI isn't actually a drunk shuttle service, right?"

"You want to drive or keep practicing your sarcasm?"

"I could walk up there and bust all your friends for underage drinking," he says, gesturing to the house. "Bet you'd be pretty damn popular then."

I turn to face him and realize the whole goatee thing is supposed to make him look older than he is. This kid probably isn't even an agent yet—probably just some junior analyst, barely out of college and on a power trip with anyone who doesn't know better.

Well, *I* know better.

"Popularity isn't a real priority of mine," I say. "I just want to get home so I can sleep. But hey, if you've got nothing better to do, go right ahead."

He puts the car in gear and makes a U-turn in the cul-de-sac. At no point during the silent ride back to my house does he introduce himself to me—not that I care—and at no point does he ask for directions, which means I don't have to talk to him at all.

We're coming up on the Carmel Valley exit when his FBI phone rings—this one's a standard-issue BlackBerry Curve—and he answers on the second ring. "Barclay."

Oh, T. Barclay from my dad's laptop eval. So his attitude isn't just with me.

"Yes, sir," he says into the phone. "I'll be right there." Hanging up, he cuts the wheel sharply to the right and takes the exit ramp at an almost ninety-degree angle. I have to grab the "oh shit" handle to keep myself from knocking into the window. As it is, my elbow slams into the dashboard and I have to bite down on the inside of my cheek to keep from yelping.

"Where are we going?"

We take a left off the exit ramp and turn into a development. "I've got shit to do."

The neighborhood we pull into looks similar to my own. Cookie-cutter houses built of cream stucco and orange ceramic roofing. Small plots of land, barely big enough for the houses sitting on them, a couple of strategically placed shrubs and tightly trimmed lawns. But there the similarities end. Because the street we turn onto is packed. TV news vans, cop cars, a couple of ambulances, even a fire truck. Barclay slows the car to a crawl and opens his window. A perimeter has been set, and he has to wave his credentials a couple of times to get through. He even throws a glare my way, daring me to say something.

I don't. Because this looks like it might be something huge. And I don't want to risk him realizing I shouldn't be here.

We pull into the driveway of a modest house that appears to

be the center of attention, and then pull up onto the front lawn to make room for more cars. I take a deep breath as I notice my father's car parked right in front of us. I'm *here*—at the scene of a crime my father is investigating. Possibly a crime related to my John Doe. Pressing my hands together to keep them from showing any tremors, I don't realize at first that Barclay is talking to me.

"—and I don't have time to be your late-night chauffeur. So you can walk home yourself. Or you can sit in the car and wait until this is over." He's not looking at me as he talks. Instead he grabs an FBI Windbreaker and a shoulder bag from the backseat.

"It's fine." I nod. Truthfully I'm surprised he's taking this big a risk, bringing me here, a civilian and a minor. I'm sure Struz— or my dad—would have expected him to drop me at home first.

"I'll wait," I say. I'm close enough that I could probably walk home faster. God knows, we'll probably be here an hour at least, and I'm less than two miles from home. But there's no way I'm passing this up.

"Good," he says with a smirk. "If you're gonna pass out, you can lie down in the back, but try not to hurl on the leather."

What an asshole. "I'll try my best."

With that he gets out. I watch him as he walks up the lawn and disappears through the front door. Another car pulls up, and I scrunch down in my seat just far enough so that I'm not visible at first glance, but not so far that I can't see Agent Deirdre Rice's platinum-blond hair against her black blazer as she gets out of the car.

She heads around the front lawn and to the fence line. I debate going after her. She's been on my dad's squad for a long time, though she's got a family, so she doesn't hang out at my house like Struz does. But she wouldn't want me here either. So I stay put as she goes through the gate into the backyard.

I pop open the glove compartment. In a perfect world, Barclay'd have an extra badge or some kind of credentials I could pin to my hoodie and blend in—but there's nothing. He doesn't even have an extra sidearm like my father always has.

With a quick glance around, I slide out of the TrailBlazer. Zipping up the front of my hoodie, I leave the hood down and tie my hair in a low ponytail. Since we're already in front of the perimeter, I just have to act like I know what I'm doing and like I belong here. There are enough people moving in and out, most likely from some kind of joint task force, that I might be able to blend in—or at least that's what I'm telling myself.

I'm following Deirdre's footsteps toward the backyard when an SDPD uniform comes out of the gate and throws up all over the bushes just a few feet in front of me. Another uniform follows him. "Didn't I tell you not to go inside?" he says. But he looks a little pale himself, and I'd bet money he already puked his guts up.

I want to stop and listen, but that would be a dead giveaway that I don't belong here. So I keep moving, pushing past the two of them. But I still manage to hear the guy who's not throwing up say, "Seriously, man, that's the freakiest shit I've ever seen. I'm gonna have nightmares for the rest of my life."

I was right about the task force.

The backyard is teeming with San Diego PD, FBI, and maybe even the CDC. Anyone going in and out of the house is wearing a hazmat suit—hopefully whatever's in there hasn't killed Barclay—and half the people milling around the backyard are in hazmat suits too. Including my dad, who's bent over a makeshift table under a makeshift tent—where they've obviously set up some kind of base—discussing something with Deirdre and six men I don't recognize. He looks like he's arguing with them.

I walk along the fence line, getting closer but staying in the shadows. The last thing I need is for my dad to look up and recognize me. No amount of pretending I belong here would save me then.

"—after we've finished collecting all the evidence. We need to burn the house down."

"Burn it down, are you crazy? This is a family home."

"Yeah, it is. And it's been infected with God knows what. You really want to chance letting someone else catch whatever did *that* and then spread it around?"

"Of course not, but—"

I keep moving, even though they start falling out of earshot. My goal is to get around the other side of the house and then get close to the back door. I need to see what's inside that house, see what it is that has my father proposing to burn it down.

"Can I help you?"

In front of me is a guy in a cheap suit. He's in his forties, his hair slightly disheveled, his complexion pale. SDPD—most likely the detective on scene.

I tilt my head to the side and parrot the question back to him.

His eyes widen in surprise and his eyes move over me again, this time reassessing who I might be. My father has two female agents in his unit. One is Deirdre. The other, who is oh-so-conveniently on maternity leave, is—

"Special Agent Aimee Cortene," I say, offering my hand. I sound—and look—absolutely nothing like Aimee, but I'm going to fake it until someone calls me on it. "You been inside? Because that's the freakiest shit I've ever seen. I'm looking forward to burning it down. Excuse me."

Without giving him a chance to respond, I push past him and continue my path. Only, as I'm walking, the back door opens. Two hazmat suits walk out.

And behind them, before the door shuts, I see it.

I see what had that uniform puking his guts out, and I see what has my father and his team arguing to burn this place down. I have to lift my hand to my mouth to keep it closed. And that beer I drank tonight burns my esophagus the second time I swallow it down.

What used to be a man is slumped in the back hallway.

He's burned, just like the bodies in the photographs, the

radiation making him look completely unrecognizable—inhuman. Only it also looks like his skin has melted, as if it's gelatinous. And it's melting *off* his face. My eyes focus on his chin and jaw, which looks like it's become detached on the right side and unnaturally stretched on the left. His eyes are red, like they were bleeding when he died, and when I take another couple of steps to see him at a better angle, I realize it's not just his skin, but also his bones that look melted—because I can see his skeleton, and the bones look like they're dripping—like a Salvador Dalí painting come to life.

I can't stop staring. No matter how much I want to look away, to vomit and run back to the car, I'm frozen in place. Because my brain just can't process what it's seeing. There are chemical compounds that can do something like this to a body—can liquefy body tissues and *bones*—or at least I assume there are, but a body that looks like that should be something that's been dead for years or at least months, not something that happened tonight.

My hands are shaking and my pulse is too loud in my ears, loud enough that I'm afraid that the detective from before is going to hear it if he followed me.

But I still can't move.

Because what *else* is in that house? Is it worse—could anything even *be* worse?

Of course, as I'm taking it all in and staring, whatever kind of cover I thought I had going for myself is blown because Struz sees me.

"J-baby?" he says, grabbing my arm and pulling me to the fence. "What are you doing here? Where's Taylor? I sent him to get you." Struz's grip is tight enough to bruise as he pulls me out onto the front lawn on the opposite side of the house where I went in. "Janelle, I'm serious," Struz says again. "What the fuck are you doing here?"

Speaking of good old asshole Taylor Barclay, I see him over Struz's shoulder. He's obviously heard his name, and he's staring back at me, his chin lifted as if daring me to tell Struz what happened. But I'm not about to do that. Because even though he's pretending he doesn't care about authority and rules and all that, if he wants to advance *ever* he'll need to actually do something right. And having him owe me is worth the lie.

"Janelle, did Taylor bring you here?"

"Who's Taylor?" I say, crossing my arms over my chest and leaning back. "I wanted to see what was going on."

"Jesus H Christ, Janelle," Struz says, swiping a hand through his hair. "Don't blame me when you wake up in the middle of the night from the nightmares." He grabs my shoulder and starts walking me down the driveway to a police cruiser. The uniform that puked his guts out is leaning against it, still looking queasy.

Struz says a few words to him, gives him my address, and opens the back door. As I get in, I look over to where Taylor is standing, and as we make eye contact, I know he understands perfectly.

He owes me.

When my alarm goes off in the morning, I don't turn it off right away. My whole body is stiff and heavy with exhaustion. Which isn't much of a surprise. I mean, it's been less than two weeks since I got hit by a truck, and I also had about three hours of sleep.

But I need to talk to Alex about what I saw. Which means I need to get out of bed.

The alarm just keeps beeping.

And I do the same thing I do any other morning I'm tempted to turn it off and roll over. I think of my mother and the life she's slept away, and in seconds the alarm is off and I'm out of bed and digging through the pile of clothes on my dresser.

Yeah, I'm aware, normal people don't dump clean clothes in a pile on a dresser without folding them, but my dad does. It's why I try to hold on to the laundry duties for the family. It cuts down on the ironing. But whenever I get busy and fall behind, my dad takes it upon himself to try to "help." Between bumming rides, homework, and all the research Alex and I have been doing, and of course that fiasco last night—my body tries to heave when I think about it—yeah, I've been falling behind.

I throw on faded black jeans and a white Circa Survive T-shirt because they're the first things I grab. The shirt is from a concert two summers ago I didn't even go to, because the book I was reading turned out to be *crack*. And well, I chose it over the concert, because I'm like that. Alex brought me back the shirt, because, well, he's like *that*.

After giving Jared his "Dude, you've got ten minutes" warning, I'm downstairs rooting through the kitchen. I turn on the TV for background noise before I crack a couple of eggs and throw a few strips of bacon into a pan. The newscaster is talking about how the world might end from the string of natural disasters we've been having—a tsunami hit the coast of Indonesia yesterday, tornadoes are wreaking havoc across the Midwest, and apparently there was another earthquake in San Francisco during the hours I was actually asleep last night. She's dramatic about it, though, and she gets even more dramatic when she starts predicting an eruption in some dormant volcano in New Zealand. After I throw two slices of bread in the toaster, start the coffee, and pour a glass of OJ, I change the channel to MTV2, then start in on the mound of dishes in the sink. You can always tell when I've fallen down on the job because our house looks like a fraternity moved in for a few days.

Twelve minutes have passed by the time I have Jared's breakfast on the table and all the dishes either in the dishwasher or the drying rack, so I bolt back upstairs and barge into his room without knocking—he never gets out of bed unless I'm half dragging him.

"Yo," I say as I turn on every light in the room and flick open the window shades. "Time to get up."

Jared groans from under his covers, then comes his muffled, "Five more minutes."

"Your breakfast is getting cold."

That has him sluggishly sitting up as I dig into his closet, making sure all the dirty clothes are actually in the hamper and there's nothing that will stink up this room—at least not worse.

"Take this down with you," I add, laying the hamper at his feet.

"Can't I do it—"

"No," I say when I'm halfway out the door. For good measure, I lean back in to tell him he has fifteen minutes before we leave, but he's staring at my shirt.

I look down.

And see a splotchy pink stain.

Like someone who didn't know what they were doing ran the wash. Someone who washed the whites and reds together in hot water.

I look up at Jared, whose apologetic smile answers the question of which someone is at fault.

"Hey . . . ," he says, blushing. "So, I wanted to try to help, but . . ."

I look down at the shirt—it's hardly one of my favorites. I look back at Jared. He looks way too guilty. "What else did you ruin?"

He shrugs. "I might have shrunk the gray zip-up hoodie you always wear. . . ."

"Fuck, Jared!" I say without thinking. Because that *is* my favorite piece of clothing. But Jared flinches, and I immediately feel like I just kicked a kitten, so I try to relax. "Sorry. Don't worry about it."

"I just—"

"No, stop," I say with a smile. "It's not a big deal. It's just a sweatshirt after all. I'll get another one. I'm going to change, though. I'll meet you downstairs." And then, because I'm pretty sure he still feels like shit, I add, "Seriously, dude, your breakfast is getting cold."

I pull off my T-shirt as soon as I get into my room. The one thing I hate most in the world is being late, even if it's just school, and even if my teachers probably won't care. But as I'm rifling through the T-shirts on my dresser, I pause and stare at my reflection.

Correction: I stare at what's different about my reflection.

It's not the first time I've looked in a mirror since the accident. But it is the first time I paused long enough to notice that something's different.

After everything—the conversations with Alex, Ben's denials, my John Doe, and the radiation killings going around—I was willing to let the whole Ben thing go. I mean, I *had* just gotten hit by a truck; it goes without saying that my lucidity might have been in question.

Again, I *was* willing to let the Ben thing go. Because of all the other shit going on.

Now I'm not.

Because staring me right in the face is the proof I needed. Proof that I'm not crazy or overly imaginative.

I throw on a new shirt and decide exactly what I'm going to say to Ben Michaels next time I see him.

Only, finding anyone in this school is harder than it should be. Jared and I got to school late and had to head straight to homeroom, and even though I check the known stoner haunts between classes, I come up short.

In physics, I sit at a two-person lab table sandwiched between Cecily and Alex, and attempt to take notes on kinetic energy.

"These are to die for," Cecily whispers, sliding me a piece of See's candy.

"And by 'to die for' you mean?" Alex whispers back.

"To. Die. For," Cecily repeats before turning back to her notes. Her limitless energy and the way she practically bounces in her seat during a physics lecture is strangely contagious. No one can make science fun like she can. But today her enthusiasm just reminds me how exhausted I am.

The chocolate *is* good, so I can't complain too much.

But I do give up taking notes—I can't possibly pay attention to school. My mind is at war with itself. The image of that man with his face melting off his bones, the proof that I died and Ben Michaels brought me back staring me in the face this morning, and the flashes of my life replayed before my eyes. I'm going to sort this out.

Alex slides me a piece of paper.

Yo. What if the people in that house somehow got a concentrated dose of the virus? What if they were the scientists working on it? And something went wrong? What do you think??

I shake my head, because I have no idea. How could a *virus* do that to a human being—melt bones like that?

Did you talk to your dad yet?

Again, I shake my head. The first thing I'm going to do when I get home, though, is give him a call and demand he hear me out. Even though I don't think we're right. I don't know if this is viral at all. How can someone harness a virus and keep it this controlled—not that what happened in that house was controlled. At least not in the normal sense. But it was controlled enough that it didn't spread. Anything viral would take on a life of its own.

Cecily raises her hand and asks something about the difference between kinetic and potential energy, and I know I should focus on this so I don't end up behind. But I can't.

Not if in fifteen days something big is going down.

Tonight I'm going to hack my dad's computer and find out how I can get in touch with Barclay so I can call in my favor.

15:04:00:43

We're a few minutes into third period, and Poblete is handing out the reading assignment when the classroom door opens. She glances back to the door and then gestures toward me as she hands me a sheet of paper. "Mr. Michaels, glad you could finally join us. Please sit down next to Miss Tenner."

This can't be happening. I looked for him all morning, and *now* here he is. He looks relaxed, comfortable, and when he meets my eyes his lips curl into a half smile. My insides flip-flop as I watch Ben, who still doesn't have a backpack, walk toward me. I can't be surprised—the only empty chair in the classroom is on my left at my already overcrowded table.

Poblete hands me an extra paper, presumably for Ben, and continues as if she didn't just get her forty-seventh student. "Your job is to read the passage. Beware, it's a marriage proposal. Analyze the devices that the man is using to persuade, and then predict what you think the woman's response is going to be."

Ben sits down next to me, close enough that I can smell the minty soap on his skin, and I think again of the moment I came back from the dead. My throat constricts. It's ridiculous, but I'm half tempted to ask if he transferred into this class in some effort to stalk me. Though I had no luck finding him myself, so I don't know why I'm complaining that he just fell into my lap.

Of course he just fell into my lap at the same moment we've been given an AP prompt to analyze. Why is life so inconvenient?

"You have ten minutes," Poblete says. "Ready, go."

I glance at Ben and watch him as he turns his paper over and begins working. There is no way he's getting out of my sight before I talk to him. I glance at the clock—we've got eighty-five minutes before the end of the period, eighty-five minutes before I can confront him about what he did to me.

Our eyes meet for a second before he turns back to his paper, his hair flopping down to shadow his face.

Resigned to focus on this assignment and get those eighty-five minutes over with, I flip over my paper and don't recognize the passage. It's from some novel I haven't read, apparently written by Dickens.

Like Poblete said, it's a marriage proposal.

It's definitely persuasive. It begins with a romantic declaration and continues with a passionate "I'd die without you" type of speech. It's enough to make even me smile a little.

Only as I keep reading, something about it bothers me. It's like as the guy goes on he gets more and more dramatic. But buried in all the lines reiterating exactly how he would die for her (fire, water, crime, disgrace, he tries to hit all the ways possible) is this line: "what I mean is, that I am under the influence of some tremendous attraction which I have resisted in vain, and which overmasters me." Why do guys do that? Rather than just say how they feel, they act like the girl is seducing them or something. It's ridiculous.

On my right, Alice Han and Vince Le are both bent over their papers and scribbling annotations. On my left, Ben is leaning back in his chair, his passage seemingly untouched. He notices me looking at him and gives me another half smile.

I turn back to the passage and read it again.

"And stop," Poblete says. "Pencils down. Someone tell me about the passage." Hands go up around the room. "Miss Zhou, what persuasive devices is the speaker using?"

"He focuses directly on his audience—on her," Margaret begins.

"Thank you," Poblete says. "Who can tell us something else?" Several hands shoot up. "Mr. Le?"

"It's all pathos appeals—appealing to her emotions."

"Not entirely true; the first half is an emotional appeal, and the logos appeals are in the second half."

"Yeah, but that's only because this is the nineteenth century. Every guy has to say he can take care of his wife."

Poblete raises a hand, and everyone about to launch into a discussion shuts up. "We need to go back to the text," she says. "Ah, Mr. Trechter, go ahead."

I smile and glance back at Alex, who's never shied away from anything academic in his life. "Well, the opening line, 'You know what I am going to say. I love you,' gives the reader context. The woman he's talking to knows he loves her and that love, not reputation, is the basis for his declaration. He lists all the influences she has on him—she could draw him to water, to fire, to the gallows, to death. It's the ultimate romantic declaration of devotion."

And because it's Alex, I feel free to interrupt him. "But you don't think that's creepy?"

"Whatever do you mean, Miss Tenner?" Poblete asks with a smile, the only indication that I'm right.

"'You could draw me to the gallows, you could draw me to any death.' That's just like saying, 'Hey, *you* could make me commit crimes punishable by death.' That's morbid."

"You don't think it's romantic?" Ben asks.

I turn to look at him to see if he's serious, and he appears to be. "No, not at all. He says she could be the death of him—what's romantic about that?"

"He says she *could* be," Ben agrees. "Because he loves her *that* much. He's essentially confessing she has this power over him that he can't control."

"Textual evidence?" Poblete says.

Ben sighs and leans forward, the front legs of his chair coming back to the floor as he looks down at his paper. "He refers to it as the 'confusion of my thoughts, so that I am fit for nothing,' which essentially means he's so torn up over what he feels for her that he's just walking around like he has no brain."

A couple of guys in class laugh like they know the feeling. I'm pretty sure whatever is muddling their thoughts stems from an organ south of their hearts.

"But that doesn't mean he should declare that she's the death of him," I say. "The best thing about love is . . ." I stop and change tactics, because I'm not sure what the heck I'm trying to say. I'm not exactly an expert when it comes to romance. "Okay, so two people who are in love—they are who they are when they're apart, but when they're *together*, the fact that they're in love is supposed to make them better. Love and relationships are supposed to make people better."

It's one of my lamest arguments ever, and I can hear Alex

laughing at me a few rows back. I have an urge to turn around and throw my pen at him.

But Ben has an answer for even my lameness. "But he says she could draw him 'to any good—every good—with equal force.' So obviously he's thinking he would be a better guy if they were together."

"Yeah, once his feelings overmastered him and he couldn't resist in vain anymore."

"So this isn't a marriage proposal you would say yes to?" Ben says. He's giving me that half smile again. Like he already knows the answer.

I can't help but smile back. "No, it's not."

"You wouldn't want some guy confessing his love for you, and saying he'd do anything for you—even die—that wouldn't be enough for you?"

My face floods with heat again, and I can't believe *Ben Michaels* is making me feel like I'm not smart enough to argue. I think I might hate him.

"What, you want some guy to propose by putting an announcement on the Jumbotron at a baseball game or something?" Ben asks.

"Oh please, that's ridiculous. I don't want someone announcing to the whole world that he's proposing to me. It shouldn't be about the whole world—it should be about just the two of us."

"So your perfect proposal, what would it be?" Ben asks.

"Seriously?" I look at Poblete and she shrugs, obviously enjoying the real-world application. "I don't know. It would just be the two of us, and I guess I'd want him to say something honest, not overly romantic, not something that would make a great story to tell his friends. I'd just want him to lean over . . ." As I say it, I lean slightly toward Ben, close enough that I can feel the warmth of his body radiating into the empty space between us, and drop the volume of my voice. ". . . and say 'Janelle Tenner, fucking marry me.'"

A couple of people in the room gasp, probably because I just dropped the F-bomb in AP English, but Poblete laughs. "Interesting. And back to the text. What about our woman in the paragraph. What do you think she says to our speaker's proposal?"

I can't help but sigh in answer. Because I don't know. I look back at my prompt. "I want to say that she also said no. But it *is* Dickens. She probably said yes and lived out a miserable existence, because the evils of society pressured her into accepting such a ridiculous man."

Poblete nods. "Thank you. That does sound Dickensian." She looks around the room. "Anyone else care to wager a guess?"

"I agree with Janelle," Alex says. "About the response. Most of us were taken with this proposal. What's to say the recipient of the proposal wouldn't be swept up the same way? Plus, it's in the nineteenth century. Most girls didn't say no."

I turn around to smile at Alex, and he nods in response.

"Thank you." Poblete looks around the room. "Anyone else?"

No one responds.

Poblete turns back to me. No, not to me—to Ben.

"What?" he says.

"So what happens?"

He slumps down a little in his seat. "Why are you picking on me?"

"Because out of everyone in this room, I know you've actually read *Our Mutual Friend*." Her smile widens, and my chest burns slightly. I'm jealous—actually legitimately jealous. Of a teacher. Not because I think they have something going on or anything ridiculous like that. But because she knows him. Poblete *knows* Ben. She knew he was this smart, engaging, charismatic guy, who had—*has*—something to say.

Whereas I'd been fooled. Like half the rest of the population at Eastview, I'd thought Ben Michaels was a waste of life.

"Even though it's going to undercut the great argument I just staged against Janelle?" he asks. She doesn't respond, and with an exaggerated sigh, he sits up a little straighter. "She says no."

"Why?" Poblete asks.

Ben shrugs. "Like Janelle said, in the novel this guy is *obsessively* in love with her, and it kind of freaks her out."

"So if we look at this passage and compare it to the one from yesterday . . ."

While the class continues the discussion, I can't stop staring at Ben. I try to be pissed off. We just spent a good fifteen minutes arguing for the sake of debate. Even though I was right. Even though he *knew* it. But I'm not mad. I'm not even annoyed.

Because it's been a while since I lost a debate.

So when Ben looks my way, that grin on his face, I shake my head slightly and return the smile.

I have to admit, I enjoyed that. A lot.

But that doesn't mean he's going to get out of answering my questions today.

15:02:05:07

When the bell rings and people stand and start filing out of the classroom, I put my hand on Ben's arm and try to ignore the way that touching him seems strangely intimate.

"Here's the thing," I say to Ben. "I know you're lying."

He shifts his weight on his feet. And I wait until the classroom has emptied out, including Poblete, who's conveniently disappeared.

"I know you're lying," I say again. "And it's not just the usual tells—the stiffness in your upper body and the evasive eye contact and the slight change in the pitch of your voice. It's more than that. I have actual proof."

His eyes widen as he looks up at me. He's surprised, but not as much as he would be if he *hadn't* done anything.

"When I was eleven, I did the La Jolla Rough Water for the first time. It's a three-mile ocean swim from La Jolla Cove to Scripps Pier and back. I didn't finish, though. I was stung by a Portuguese man-of-war. It was a bad sting. The thing completely latched on to my shoulder and arm, and the venom was so bad, it got infected and left a weblike scar on my left shoulder."

Ben's face flushes with color, and I have the distinct impression he already knows about my scar.

I grab the neck of my T-shirt and pull it aside to expose my left shoulder, where the skin is completely smooth. The scar I've had on my left shoulder for the past six years is completely gone.

"Whatever you did, you did this, too."

PART TWO

Much madness is divinest sense

To a discerning eye;

Much sense the starkest madness

—Emily Dickinson

Ben runs a hand through his hair and then tugs on the ends, something I'm beginning to recognize whenever I seem to be making him think too hard about what he's going to say.

I fold my arms across my chest. "Whenever you're ready."

He glances up. "And what if this is one of those things that just can't be explained?"

"Don't give me that."

He takes a deep breath and cracks his knuckles. I feel light-headed and a little nauseous, because whatever he's about to say is going to be a game changer. Whatever he did to me, I was dead, and he brought me back, and that shouldn't be possible.

Ben opens his mouth, and I hold my breath waiting for him to speak.

Only he exhales and then says, "You're not going to believe me."

"Maybe you haven't heard, but a little more than a week ago, I rose from the dead. Try me."

He looks like he might deflect again, but instead he sighs. "I'm not sure I know how."

"Try."

He runs a hand through his messy brown hair again. "I saved you."

"How?"

He shrugs, and this time his voice is barely more than a whisper. "I can do things like that. I can . . . use energy to manipulate molecular structure."

"Manipulate molecular structure," I repeat slowly, and then bite the inside of my cheek to keep from saying more. If he thinks I'm just going to stand here and accept a load of crap so he can laugh about it to his friends, he's dead wrong. "Really?"

"It's hard to explain, I mean, I don't even really know the limits of what I can do. I know I can heal other people, though."

Something in the way he says that makes all the anger bleed out of me. Suddenly, I don't think he's lying. I'm looking at him and I can hear the conviction in his voice, but how can I know for sure? I don't know what to say. No matter what he tells me, I'll have no idea if this is actually the truth or if he's just making up something he thinks I want to hear.

I gesture to him. "Show me."

Ben shakes his head. "Give me your hand. It doesn't work on me."

I offer him my left hand, and a shiver runs through my chest when his hand touches mine. He turns my hand over and exposes a small cut on my thumb. I don't even know what it's from. Maybe a paper cut that was deeper than I'd thought, who knows. It's scabbed over, probably a few days from healing on its own, but Ben touches it. His fingers are warm—no, they're hot and growing hotter—and I feel a little of that heat transfer to me. It feels like heat is pouring into my thumb. Somehow it manages to be just shy of burning, but the rest of my body shivers, like it can't figure out why it's so cold in comparison.

Then my broken skin begins to knit itself together right in front of my eyes. It starts at the base of the cut and moves up, until I'm staring at clean, smooth skin, and I can't even tell where the cut was.

Holy. Crap.

I feel flushed but somehow too cold at the same time, and my eyes itch like I need to close them and rub them back into reality.

Because this can't possibly be real.

We stand there for who knows how long. I'm staring at my thumb, wondering where the scab just went and how it's possible. I don't know what Ben's thinking. But my heart is pounding so hard that my pulse is ringing in my ears, and as we stand there, Ben still holding my hand in his own, I start to feel self-conscious about my heart rate, like maybe he can hear it or sense it.

I pull my hand away, and Ben looks down at his shoes as he shifts his weight on his feet.

"How? How can you do this?"

He starts to shrug, and I just know he's about to give some line to blow me off.

"Don't bullshit me, you must have a theory." Any guy who likes to argue for the sake of debate also likes to *know* things.

Ben sighs. "I can sense chemical bonds in molecules. It's like I can feel them somehow. I have to concentrate, but I can feel when they're broken and visualize fixing those bonds until they're back together."

"So when you healed me?" I try to ignore the way my voice cracks.

"I laid a hand on your heart," he whispers. "And sensed the chemical compounds of the cells in your body that were broken or severed, and I fused them back together."

There's no swelling feeling of victory that I was right. That I knew he did something to me even though it defied all logic and reason. Instead there's a sick tightening inside my body, and it almost hurts to keep standing up straight.

"I was dead. I was, wasn't I?"

He hesitates. And my heart somehow hammers louder and harder in my chest, and this time I'm sure he *has* to be able to hear it.

"Tell me."

"Not for long," he whispers.

My whole body throbs with the beat of my pulse, like someone's fist is pushing against my skin. I feel breathless and dizzy, a little like the blood just bottomed out of my head.

"And my back was broken?"

He nods.

I believe him. And that means there's a lot more than quantum physics that I don't understand.

"What *are* you?" I ask, and then wish I'd phrased that better. It sounds like I'm asking if he's something ridiculous. Something not human.

Even though I was convinced he brought me back to life, I'm just not sure what I expected. How is something like that possible? It's not, at least not in the human scope of possible. I was so focused on getting the truth out of Ben, I didn't stop to speculate on what it meant.

I look at Ben and wait for some kind of answer.

But he shrugs. "Just a guy who's kind of a freak."

"Do people know that you can . . . can just bring people back from the dead?"

He smiles. "It's not like you're a zombie or something. I wouldn't be able to, like, reanimate a corpse or anything. It only worked because it happened so fast. Like when paramedics save someone from dying—or a hospital."

So Ben Michaels is a one-man emergency room. Some people would think that's sort of a neat trick.

"Janelle, you . . . you can't tell anyone," he murmurs.

I nod, because the logical part of me knows that makes sense, but I can't help but sway a little on my feet at the weight of this secret. I don't even like science, and my brain is already putting together a list of questions about what else "manipulating molecular structure" can do.

"Can you do more than heal people?" I ask.

Ben nods. "I can manipulate physical matter. Um . . . hold on." He looks around and then runs to Poblete's desk and grabs something. When he comes back, I see it's a number two pencil.

With two hands, he holds the pencil in his palms.

I stare at it, waiting for a movielike glow or something, but nothing happens. I look up at Ben's face—he's flushed, and a fine line of sweat covers his forehead.

"Look," he says, and I glance down in time to see the pencil disintegrating in front of my eyes.

Until it looks like a pile of sand.

I reach out to touch it—to see if it's real.

It is.

Ben Michaels is a scientific miracle.

"What else can you do? I mean, could you turn the pencil into water?"

He shakes his head. "It's not an exact science. I have to focus, sense the cells, and changing the bonds takes concentration and practice. It tires me out." He pauses. "And I can *manipulate* the molecular bonds, I can't create or destroy or even substitute them with something else."

He won't look me in the eye. His face is pale, and his movements are tense and jerky. It looks like he might be getting ready to manipulate the floor so it will swallow him whole and get him out of here.

"So you can't read minds, start fires, or turn invisible?" I ask, trying to make light of this whole . . . *thing*. "That's lame."

Ben's eyes lift to mine, and he cracks a smile.

"If the universe was going to give you superhero powers, they could have at least given you the ability to fly or something," I add, because apparently I don't know when I'm taking things too far.

He shakes his head, and his voice comes out barely above a whisper. "I'm not a superhero."

But he saved me.

I'm still trying to process everything when the door to the classroom opens and Poblete comes walking back in with a chocolate cookie and a coffee from It's a Grind. When she sees us, she actually jumps slightly. "Oh my God, you scared me to death!" she says, breaking into a laugh as she goes to her desk.

"Good thing you didn't spill the coffee," Ben says.

"There is a God, huh?" she answers with a smile before she looks back up at us, recovered from her surprise. Her expression changes. She's suddenly more serious as her gaze moves from Ben to me. "Miss Tenner, is everything all right?"

I realize too late how I must look. I can't tell if I'm flushed or pale, whether I'm breathing too hard or too shallow, but I know I'm swaying a little on my feet, and I probably have some kind of weird dazed look on my face.

I force myself to nod. "I'm fine, thank you."

She stares at me, and it takes me a second to realize she must be wondering why the hell I'm not in class, since it started probably five or ten minutes ago.

"I'm going to head to Spanish," I say, wondering when I got so *lame*. I grab my backpack and tell myself to breathe in and breathe out and put one foot in front of the other until I get outside.

"And Ben, I assume you've conveniently managed to have no class this period," Poblete says as I open the door.

"You've always been good with assumptions, Miss P," Ben says.

Pausing in the doorway, I turn back to look at him in time to see him glance at me. I don't know what he sees, but as the door shuts, I hear Poblete say, "Excellent, because I'm assuming that you're still here because you want to make photocopies and check out some books from the library for me."

And I see Ben, face flushed, jaw set, staring. There's something about his expression. I'm usually pretty good at reading people, but I can't tell if he's relieved to see me go or if he wishes we hadn't been interrupted.

15:01:01:19

After school, Alex and I drop Jared off at water polo and head back to my house. Alex's left hand rides the steady stream of wind pouring through his open window. His black hair, cut short enough that it's not really a style, barely moves—unlike mine, which is determined to whip all over the place.

I haven't told him about Ben.

Usually when I'm right, I'm all about rubbing it in Alex's face, since if I'm being honest, Alex is right more often than I am. But in Spanish, when I slid into my seat next to him and he gave me his *WTF just happened?* face, my mouth dried out and I couldn't speak. And now every time I think about telling him, I can't make myself do it.

Now that I know I was right, I don't feel vindicated or anything. I don't want to brag about it or give Alex a hard time because for once he was actually wrong. I feel strange, unsure of my movements and actions and thoughts. I feel like I'm not me. What if Ben didn't bring all of me back from the dead? Or what if I'm just not supposed to still be here?

When we pull into my driveway, I pause before I open the

door. "If I run in and grab my suit, can you drop me off at the cove?" I ask Alex.

"Why . . ."

Then he shuts up. Because he was going to ask why I would go to La Jolla Cove instead of Torrey Pines. But he already knows.

I can't go back to Torrey Pines right now—not until I figure out how my John Doe really died and how it relates to the countdown. I can't go back there and see skid marks from the truck that killed me.

Especially not today.

Torrey Pines—my beach, the one where I spent my summers, wasting my days, soaking up sun, making sand castles. That stretch of the ocean was mine—especially once I was old enough to actually make some money, and I took care of it and the people who swam there.

It was Alex's and my beach. And now it's not—not anymore.

"I'll get Struz to pick me up later."

Alex glances at me. "You okay?"

I nod, but he sees it's halfhearted.

"You don't need to take all this on yourself, you know. I'll do some research this afternoon. See what else I can find."

I lean my head back against the headrest and sigh—fifteen days isn't a long time. "So you'll drop me off?"

Because he's Alex and he'll do anything to keep from going home, he says, "Of course, J." And then when I don't move, he turns to look at me and smiles. "You did mean today, right?"

I smile and jump out of the car.

On the last day of third grade, Lesley Brandon had an end-of-the-year party. She lived in Santaluz, so she had enough space to invite our entire elementary school, and she had just about the most beautiful pool I'd ever seen—someone totally designed it to look like a pond! With a waterfall! It was awesome. I raced everyone—and won, multiple times—and then Kate and I jumped off the top of the waterfall into the deep end until Lesley's mother yelled at us.

Out of our entire elementary school, Alex was the only kid who didn't get in and swim.

It wasn't that he didn't know how, either. His mom had signed him up for one of those Mommy and Me swim classes when he was little, but he was still awkward and scared, so he sat outside the pool and just sweated.

That whole summer I made him come to the beach with me, and I taught him to swim, like really swim so that he could actually get into the pool the following year and race people, and beat them. Not me, but other people.

When I get back in the car, I look over at Alex. I can't see his eyes through his black Oakleys, but I don't need to. He's got his jaw set, and he's practically grinding his teeth, trying to think of something to say.

I want to tell him more about Ben, not so he knows I'm right—though I have to admit a part of me does want to push him and say, "I told you so!" The greater part of me, though, just wants to hear his take on this whole thing because if *thinking* I died generates reflection, actually knowing I did takes it to a whole new level. It makes me wonder if there's a reason I'm still alive, if there's a reason the world has given me a second chance at life.

Still, I can't seem to make myself form the words. It's not that I don't know what to say, it's that I don't know enough yet.

And I need Alex to believe me when I tell him this time.

15:01:00:34

The cove is right at the edge of downtown La Jolla, which means parking is a bitch. Alex pulls up near the cliffs, and right as I'm opening the door to get out, he says, "So, Ben Michaels?"

"Really? You decide you've got something you want to talk about now?" I wave to the crowds of people and cars and the general insanity around us.

Alex smiles. "Well, I was sort of waiting to let you bring it up, but since you're not going to, I thought I'd just pry it out of you."

I roll my eyes. "Right, so what about him?"

Alex shrugs. "I just never would have figured he was smart."

I can't help but smile. At least I wasn't the only person fooled. Alex is typically a nicer person than I am, so it counts for something that he had Ben pegged the same way I did.

"J?" Alex says.

"Hmm?"

He lowers his voice and makes an attempt to sound serious. "You know what I'm going to say. He kicked your ass today when it came to that excerpt. Like full-on dragged you to the gallows."

"You're the biggest dork alive," I say as I get out of the car.

"What do you expect?" Alex calls after me. "I'm half-Asian!"

I shake my head and keep going, my pace picking up as I get to the narrow steps that will lead me down the rocks to the beach. I pull my cap and goggles on, and I tuck my clothes in the crevice between a couple of hard-to-reach rocks.

And I don't look back.

Once upon a time, swimming was a stress reliever for me. Something about the rush of the water, the rhythmic movements, the absence of conversation, the pure isolation of it all—it helped quiet everything in my mind so I could focus. Swimming let me think.

Then Kate ruined that for me.

Because of her, I lost a block of time at that party freshman year. I still don't know what actually happened. Just that Kate and her new popular friends handed me a watered-down beer, and then I woke up at two a.m. in some unknown car with my jeans undone and underwear ripped. For months, I replayed every possible scenario over and over whenever I was alone. *How did I end up in that car? What ripped my underwear? Who undid my jeans?* Even swimming couldn't help me make sense of those questions. Even swimming couldn't make them right.

Lives are made of strings of moments, and every once in a while, one of those moments is pivotal and defining. It changes everything, alters you so completely that when you look back, there's a clear *before* and *after*.

Different people have different pivotal moments in their lives.

Before: Kate and I were friends, and we teased Alex about everything—even made him play Barbies with us.

After: We didn't speak.

Before: I was a swimmer. Someone who needed to be in the water every day in order to feel complete, whole, happy.

After: I couldn't bring myself to be alone, and swimming became just a sport other people did.

Before: I was naive and believed the best of people.

After: I recognized that the only person you can ever truly rely on is yourself.

Only now, getting drugged at a party isn't the most defining moment of my life. Now it's just something I survived, something I moved past and got over, maybe not completely, but enough.

Now I need to swim again—alone. And I can, because that old moment is just a shadow compared to the moment I died.

And the moment Ben Michaels brought me back.

15:00:53:01

The water is freezing when it hits my toes, my feet, and my bare legs, but I run into the water and try not to wince as the waves splash my stomach. The Pacific Ocean in September is hardly what we'd call tourist friendly. But the tourists keep coming—they're like that.

When I'm knee deep, I throw my body forward and dive in. For a second the sheer cold pounds against my head, and I feel like my brain might shut off. My eyes water slightly, but I'm already moving. My body takes over without needing to be told what to do. It remembers this. My arms reach in front of me and pull the water underneath me with each stroke, and my legs move with a steady thrum.

At the very least, in fifteen days, a bomb is going to go off. If Alex and I are right, it might spread a genetically engineered virus that will do to everyone what it did to the man in that house.

Salt water stings my dry lips as I take a breath, and I only hear waves and the even rhythm of the beating of my own heart.

I picture the man's detached jaw and wonder if dying like

that was as painful as it looked.

A wandering piece of seaweed tangles itself in my fingertips, and I almost have a heart attack and die right there. Instead I grab it and fling it somewhere without breaking stroke.

Somehow the radiation and the UIED are connected to the unidentified man whose unidentified truck killed me. Somehow they're connected to three old cases from 1983, and somehow—

Suddenly, with my pulse echoing throughout my body, the taste of salt on my tongue, and nothing but ocean surrounding me, it occurs to me that something about Ben saving me is just plain wrong. It's incredibly convenient that a guy who can manipulate molecular structure was there, at the scene of the accident, to bring me back from the dead.

Unless it wasn't just some unrelated phenomenon.

Unless it's *all* connected.

Someone who can remake skin to get rid of a scar, someone who can restart a stopped heart, someone who can meld bones back together . . .

What else is someone like that capable of?

15:00:21:24

"So are you going to tell me what the hell that was last night or what?" I say when Struz picks me up.

Only I make a mistake. The car door's open, but I'm not actually inside it yet, so he looks at me and just starts to drive. He catches me off guard, and I have to run after him for ten feet before I reach the stopped car. And sure enough, as soon as I'm an arm's length away from the door he speeds off again.

I run after him again, but this time I slow down sooner and hesitate slightly on my way to the door. When I'm two arms' lengths away, I burst forward and swing myself into the car, slamming the door shut behind me.

We're already driving when I say, "Jerk."

"You know better than to ask me about cases, Princess."

I've known Struz just about my whole life it feels like, which means I know exactly what I can ask him about and how I can do it. "I'm not asking you about a case. I'm asking you about something I saw."

Struz shakes his head. "Yeah, and you still haven't told me how you ended up past the border at the crime scene."

"Counterintelligence."

"I'm not joking—"

"Struz, neither am I! I saw that guy in the doorway, dead with his freaking face melting onto the floor. You think I don't know this isn't something to joke about?"

And then I take a deep breath and tell him almost everything. I tell him about the files I saw in my dad's study, about the UIED, about the autopsy report of my John Doe, about the theory that Alex and I came up with in the library.

I still don't tell him about Barclay bringing me to the scene. Struz isn't stupid. He totally knows how I got there. He just wants confirmation, but I'm not going to sell Barclay out, even if he is a douche bag.

And I don't tell Struz about Ben. Yet. Because I don't want Ben to be involved in this virus. Coincidences do happen even if they're unlikely, and I'm probably jumping to conclusions by even considering that.

When I finish, Struz sighs. "This is a bad one, J-baby."

And I wait, because I know there's more coming.

"We've got the UIED downtown at the Federal Building. The good news is it's not going any faster. We've still got a couple of weeks, but we've been calling in experts to look at the UIED for weeks now and nobody's come up with shit," he says, and somehow it sounds more serious coming from him than from my dad. Because Struz is almost always playful and funny. He never really gets serious. Only he is right now.

A couple of weeks . . .

"The timer just keeps counting down. Nothing we do seems to work to disable it. And none of the tests can figure out what it even is. We've started coming up with backup plans for what to do if we can't shut it off, but we can't just drive it into the desert if we're not sure what's going to happen."

"Fly it out into space?" I say, even though that's a bad sci-fi movie cliché.

Struz glances at me out of the corner of his eye, and I feel sick. Because I can tell that's something that's actually on the table.

"Is it a virus?" I ask. "The radiation?"

Again he sighs. "We're not sure. It could be. Or it could be nothing. But we have to consider every scenario so we can plan for them. We've got a theory that a virus in small doses, injected right into the bloodstream, would kill via radiation poisoning, whereas if it's induced into the atmosphere—converted to an atmospheric pathogen—it could be pumped through the air vents, for instance, and *that* might do what happened to the people in that house."

People. As in more than one, more than just that guy.

I have to take a deep breath to keep myself from throwing up all over Struz's car.

"How many people were in the house?" I ask.

"There was a family of four, all identities confirmed," Struz says, and I wonder how old the children were. I wonder if they were boys or girls, what their mother was like, what kind of job their father had, what schools they went to, what dreams they had. I wonder if they loved one another the way I love Jared.

"And the other three bodies we still haven't been able to identify."

"Wait?" I ask. "So there were three more bodies in the house?"

Struz nods.

"And you can't confirm their identities?"

140

"No, but we do know they didn't live there."

I shake my head, trying to wrap my mind around all of this.

"What?" Struz asks, giving me his sidelong glance again.

"I can't help wondering where all these unidentifiable people are coming from."

14:22:13:58

When I burn the macaroni and cheese beyond repair and drop one of my parents' nice crystal wineglasses, I admit to myself that I can't wait until tomorrow to talk to Ben. I might have a limited time frame to figure things out. Nothing can wait. My mind is running in circles, and my hands have developed a slight tremor. I have to know what he's keeping from me. I have to know if he's somehow connected to this.

Things like laundry can wait. Even if it means Jared will shrink another one of my sweatshirts.

I order a pizza and leave Jared money and a note. Alex can't get away from his mother to drive me, and I refuse to ride my bike that far, so I decide to chance having my license taken away and just drive myself. I only had that one seizure, and it was right after Ben messed with my body's *molecular structure*. A seizure as a side effect is probably getting off easy.

Alex calls as I'm driving. He's whispering, and I can barely hear him over the running water in the background—this is how he hides from his mother.

"Are you going to tell me what your obsession with Ben

Michaels is all about? I thought you were over the whole thing."

"I just need to talk to him about some stuff," I say. It's lame, even for me.

Alex says something about my obsessive personality and looking for things in people that I want to see, but I don't hear him because my phone is beeping.

As I pull it away from my ear to see who's calling, it occurs to me that maybe I shouldn't be driving with a suspended license *and* talking on my cell phone and checking my call waiting.

It's Nick.

"Alex, I gotta go," I say into the phone, more because of the whole illegal driving thing and less because of Nick. "I'll call you later."

He tells me to be careful and hangs up.

Nick is still calling on the other line, and I don't know what to do about that. So I do nothing and just let it go to voice mail. We never really had the official "we're together" talk so I don't know if we are, but it's becoming abundantly clear—if it wasn't before, and it sort of was—that I don't really want us to be "together."

He's pretty and he's got great abs, like the kind that are so toned you can sometimes see the definition through his T-shirts, and when it's just us, he's funny and charming and smart and interesting.

But he's also immature at least fifty percent of the time. It's like he's two different people. I like the thoughtful guy who listens to what I say and is sweet to my brother. I even like the guy who will make me laugh when I'm stressed out. But when he's with Kevin and his boys, he's the guy performing to a crowd, doing things just for the attention. And I don't really want to be with that guy.

Right now with everything else going on, blowing him off requires less thought and less energy. So even though it's a shitty thing to do to someone and he probably does deserve better, right now there are too many more important things I need to worry about.

Like whether I'm going to die of radiation poisoning in fourteen days.

14:21:55:36

Pacific Beach is the epitome of predictable. It's full of people who are overtanned and underdressed. And not just the MTV-type frat guys and blond chicks in their twenties; there are also all the people who *used* to be those people twenty years ago and are now leathery-skinned women who need to stop smoking and eat a burger or middle-aged hairy-chested guys with beer bellies who are still hitting on college girls, or younger. Gross.

It's also got some of the most kickass vintage shops, yoga studios, and beach cruisers in the whole city.

Kon-Tiki Motorcycles is on Garnet Avenue, PB's main street, and it's not what a normal person would expect when thinking of a place that's famous for fixing up motorcycles. It looks like you're stepping into someone's home garage instead of a professional establishment, and there aren't a ton of glitzy bikes out front or anything. Reid once told Kate that the bikes on the sidewalk aren't even the ones for sale.

I move through the front door and am greeted by cool air. I keep my hands firmly at my sides while I look for Ben. I don't need to give myself away with my giddy nervousness.

But the shop isn't that big, so it doesn't take me long to realize that Ben is nowhere in sight. Disappointment settles and twists deep inside my chest, but I keep looking anyway.

Instead I find a well-built Filipino guy in his midtwenties or so. He's sweaty, his T-shirt is stained, and he's got a set of skull rings on his fingers.

"Hi, I'm Kale, what can I do for you?" he asks with a huge smile that makes him look like a little kid. The sheer cheerfulness of his voice makes me less annoyed that he's the one in front of me instead of Ben, and I'm tempted to smile back.

"I'm looking for Ben," I say, and then clarify just in case, "Ben Michaels, he works here?"

Kale nods, though he looks a little crestfallen. "Right, I know Ben," he says. "But he left for the day."

"Seriously?" I ask, then cringe at the whine in my voice. I probably look like some clingy wannabe girlfriend.

Kale looks at the clock. "You missed him by, like, ten minutes, maybe less."

I nod and start to head to the door when it occurs to me that Kale might know something worthwhile. "Hey, so do you guys sell motorcycles here too—or just fix them up?"

Again, his whole face transforms into a huge smile. "Yes! We give lessons to new riders, too!" he says, opening his arm and gesturing for me to follow him. I do. "I can show you a great starter bike we've got." He keeps talking as he shows me over to one of the motorcycles. The price tag reads $4,075, which would be all I'd need to see if I really was interested. A dangerous toy that's going to cost me four grand? It would never happen. And my dad would probably kill me before he let me ride one anyway.

As Kale talks, I smile and nod, and as soon as he pauses to take a breath, I say, "Is this the kind of bike Ben works on?"

"Um, no," Kale says, visibly deflating like air is escaping through his pores.

But he recovers only an instant later, standing up straight and gesturing to another bike, one that even in my inexperienced eyes does look kind of awesome. "Ben did this one. He restores all the really old bikes and he does custom work on some of the racing bikes, too."

"How often does Ben work here?" People with part-time jobs aren't also into bioterrorism, or at least it seems doubtful, like selling motorcycles wouldn't fit the profile of someone genetically engineering a virus to end the world.

"Oh, he works every day after school and sometimes on Saturday and Sunday, too."

I let out a breath I didn't realize I was holding. Ben is a totally normal guy—well, except for the whole molecule thing.

"But he has a few of his own projects that he brings in too."

I can feel goose bumps raising up on my arms. "His own projects?"

Kale nods. "That kid can work on anything mechanical or anything electronic. He can fix anything." He pauses and looks me over with a smile that makes me want to punch him a little.

"What?"

He must recognize my expression, because he raises his hands in surrender and says, "Oh, nothing, it's just that I've been here five years and we've never had a chick come in and ask about Ben. I never thought I'd see the day."

"Why?" Ben doesn't strike me as the most outgoing guy I've ever come across and he's more intense than most guys, but it's not like he's unattractive. I think of him in APEL and feel myself blush. I'm sure he's had plenty of girls interested in him.

Kale shrugs. "He's one of those too-smart types always reading some weird science book or something."

So that was a bust.

I'm walking back to my car, wondering whether I should try to find out where the hell Ben lives or just wait until tomorrow, when I hear someone say, "You fucking told her!"

And it's a voice I know.

The asshole apparently isn't finished shouting. "What were you thinking?"

The voice sounds like it's coming from around the back of the shop, so I lean against one of the cars illegally parked in front of a driveway and peek down the alley. And there they are, near the back, shadowed slightly because the sun is setting. Elijah Palma. Reid Suitor.

And Ben Michaels.

Who's yelling back at Elijah. It's more of a quiet, hissing yell, though, and I'm not close enough to catch all the words. I just hear, ". . . bigger problems . . ."

Elijah: "Oh, right, like that bitch isn't going to stick her nose all up in our shit now!"

Reid says something, but he's not yelling, and I can't hear him at all. But whatever it is, it's not something Ben wants to hear.

He pushes Reid away. "We're *not* talking about Janelle."

"FUCK!" Elijah screams, kicking up rocks and punching the air—as if that ever helped anything.

Ben says something I can't make out, and I know I'm going to have to get closer to them if I want to eavesdrop.

Next to Kon-Tiki is a bar. I can go through it to the back exit and hang out there to see if I can hear them any better.

When I get to the back patio of the bar, rather than flatten myself up against the wall or do something that would obviously draw attention to myself, I sit on the edge of the railing and pull out my cell phone to pretend I'm texting.

"Aren't you hearing me?" Ben says. "We can't keep opening it. Not until we know how to keep anything else from coming through."

"We don't know that's what's happening!" Elijah says.

"I'm with Elijah on this," Reid says, and my heart is hammering. I'm not sure what they're talking about, but I don't want Reid and Elijah to be on one side and Ben to be on the other. "We need to get home."

"It's getting worse," Ben says, and there's some shuffling, as if he's the one kicking rocks now.

Elijah: "We don't know that!"

Ben: "Oh, what, you haven't noticed the creepy-ass shit that's going on around here?"

Creepy. Ass. Shit. If I were slightly less eloquent, I might describe what I saw in that house as creepy-ass shit.

"Look." Ben again. "There are too many unknowns. I've gotta figure out where the hell we're going and how to stabilize everything."

"You're too much of a pussy!" Elijah again.

I hear a sigh and there's some moving around on the rocks. Even though there's a breeze and it's only, like, eighty degrees, a drop of sweat rolls down the center of my back. I have no idea if they know about that dead family—creepy-ass shit could describe a lot of things.

"I don't know how close we are to Wave Function Collapse," Ben says.

"You don't even know if that's real," Reid says.

"It's just some fucking theory!" Elijah's scream makes me flinch.

Ben: "It might be a theory or it might not. But I'm not going to be the one testing it."

Elijah: "You—"

Ben: "No! You need me; that means we do it my way."

I'm clutching my phone and straining to hear whatever comes next, so I don't notice when someone who works at the bar comes out onto the patio. So when he looks at me and says, "Hey, you got ID?" I'm completely caught off guard.

Which means I drop the phone and almost fall backward. I grab the railing, rock back, and manage to pull myself forward, but the phone isn't so lucky. It shatters.

"Sorry, I was just waiting for a friend," I say as I hop down and pick up the phone and all but flee the scene. I've got to get out of here. I move through the bar quickly, my pulse ringing in my ears even louder than the alternative rock they've got playing.

When I exit the front of the bar, I'm out of breath, dizzy, and covered in a thin sheen of sweat from all the adrenaline.

I'm also five feet from Elijah.

"**J**anelle fucking Tenner," he says with a smile. And it's not friendly. But that's okay, I can play this game.

"Um, hey," I say, looking down like I'm planning to walk right past him, just as Ben says, "Janelle?" as if he's not sure whether I'm an apparition.

I look over at Ben slightly too long, and Elijah steps into my path, so I sort of bump into him and stiff-arm him in order to get away. "What?"

"Where you been?" Elijah says with that same creepy smile.

"If you must know, I went to Kon-Tiki to see if Ben was there, and he wasn't. I talked to Kale about buying a bike, and then I went and got a Coke," I say, trying to stick as much to researchable truth as possible.

It might be working. Elijah's looking at me, and I can tell he's trying to sort out whether I'm lying or not. It's awkward as hell and the timing sucks, but I'm not letting on that I just heard him talking about me.

"You were looking at bikes?" Ben asks, moving closer to me.

"Yeah, just for a minute," I say.

"What kind of motorcycle would you want?" Elijah says with a smirk.

"Ideally, a Ducati Streetfighter S," I say, and for a second I have no idea where that just came from. I'm pretty sure it's the motorcycle Shia LaBeouf rides in that newer *Wall Street* movie, and it's supposed to be some high-class superexpensive motorcycle.

"She's got good taste," Reid says to Ben before turning to Elijah. "I'll drive you home?" he offers.

"I'm not going home," Elijah says. "But you can drop me off at the house."

Reid nods and turns his back, walking away. Apparently I don't deserve a good-bye. Fine then.

Elijah looks at me again. "Well, I doubt you could really afford one of those today," he says. "But Kon-Tiki's got some damn fine bikes. Reid can wait. Want me to show you a few?"

I'm not fooled by his attempt to be charming. Elijah's got the strawberry-blond hair and blue eyes that make him look like he might be a reformable bad boy, but I'm pretty sure he would pull me into an alley and try to beat whatever information I had out of me, if it suited his purposes.

Or it's possible I'm exaggerating just because I think he's scum. Either way, "I'd rather Ben show me."

"Bitch," Elijah says, the smile falling off his face. He turns to Ben. "Tell me you're at least rounding third base for all this trouble."

And then he's walking away.

"Nice friends you've got," I say.

"Give me a second," Ben says, before jogging after Elijah. When he reaches him, they're still in earshot, so I don't have to inch forward like I was prepared to.

"I know how pissed off you are, and you've been my best friend for almost fifteen years, so I'm gonna forgive that," Ben says. "But if you—"

"Aw, Ben, what the fuck?"

Ben grabs Elijah by the shoulders and pushes him up against a car. "I'm serious, man. You can't talk to her like that. Get it through your fucking head."

They stand like that for a minute, Ben holding Elijah against the car, and Elijah just . . . limp. I wouldn't have expected that, and it makes me feel a little short of breath—because Ben just stuck up for me again, because Elijah's actually listening. Elijah has a reputation for fighting, and he's bigger than Ben, not taller, but more muscular, noticeably so. Yet he's not fighting back at all.

Elijah nods. "Whatever you say."

Ben backs off and drops his hands. "I don't want to have this conversation again."

"I said, whatever you fucking say." Elijah looks back in my direction, and I tip my chin. I'm not afraid of him, whether I should be or not. He smirks and turns around, stuffing his hands in his pockets and walking off into almost darkness.

I hope whatever they're involved with isn't related to bioterrorism, because I might have just made myself an enemy of Elijah Palma.

Walking back to me, Ben says, "Here, I'll show you the most basic motorcycle we've got. It's great for someone just getting into bikes."

When we're at the front of the shop with the lined-up bikes, I grab Ben's arm.

"I don't really want to learn to ride a motorcycle."

He turns to me and cues the half smile. "I figured."

"Why? Don't I seem like the motorcycle type?"

"Not really." He laughs, and for a second, I love the sound of it. Then a pang of unease moves through me, because I don't know what Ben's involved in, and that's why I'm here.

"Yeah, I'm not," I say with a shrug. "I think they're reckless and dangerous and stupid. I mean, what's the point of them, really? Why not have a car? Well, I guess if you're commuting to L.A. and you don't want to wait in traffic, it might make sense."

Why am I rambling again? Everything about Ben seems to make me lose my composure. I appear to be destined to always embarrass myself in front of him.

Ben doesn't answer. He's just standing there with a line of

motorcycles in front of him, his hand on the seat of the closest one. He's definitely waiting for me to say something.

I'm waiting for me to say something too. I should ask whether he knows about the people who died, something that's supposed to be classified. I should ask if he knows about the radiation and if he's involved, if he knows how it's happening. I should ask what the hell Wave Function Collapse is.

But instead I just blurt out, "Do you know anything about genetically altering viruses? I mean, can you do that with, you know"—I wave a hand—"what you do?"

He runs a hand through his hair and shifts his weight. "Ah . . ." He looks up at me. "I don't know anything about genetics, really. I don't know if I could do anything with viruses, though I could try, I guess. The scientific theory should be the same, since I could change the cells. Of course, I probably could do more harm than good if I messed something up, though. It would take some research. Why, do you know someone who's sick?"

"What?" It takes me a second before I realize he's misinterpreted what I'm asking. "No, no . . . it's not, never mind." He had no idea what I was talking about, not at all, which means he can't be involved with the bioterrorism or the UIED. I was just overanalyzing everything.

The relief that hits me is tangible—it's heavy, like I need to sit down and just let go of all the worry I'd been carrying around for the past few hours. I still know he's up to *something*, but he's entitled to secrets. I'm not offering up my own, either.

I have the urge to fling my arms around him and bury my face into his chest, and thinking about it, I feel a little short of breath.

"Janelle?" Ben asks. "Are you okay?"

There are a million ways I can answer that—a million things I'd have to say to answer it right. Because the answer's no. Of course I'm not okay. I came back from the dead, my dad's working on a case that might be end-of-the-world big, and even though I'm relieved Ben's not involved, I'm not at all closer to solving anything.

I still need to know what he's not telling me. I need to know exactly what happened and what else he's up to. And how he's managed to get under my skin.

Instead of answering him, I ask, "Is what I saw real?" My voice cracks a little under the weight of the question. And it's not until I ask that I realize how much this has been bothering me. Because the first part of my theory was right—I did come back to life—and now I desperately need to know whether those visions I saw of myself were real too.

"What you saw?" Ben asks, his face flushing. "What did you see?"

I'm not sure I can answer. I want those things to be real so badly my tongue sticks in my mouth.

I'm somewhere else. Everything is black. My head is throbbing, like someone just took a sledgehammer to it. There's water— freezing-cold water—all around me, and my arms and legs are sluggish and unmoving. Panic threatens to overtake me as I sink deeper. I open my eyes, but the salt stings them and I can't see. Even if I could swim, I don't know which way is up. My insides burn because I want to breathe. I open my mouth because I have to— even though I know I'll drown.

It's drown or let my lungs burst.

An arm wraps around me and pulls me to the surface and I see . . .

Myself.

I'm ten, wearing a pink flowered bathing suit because even though I hated pink that summer, my dad bought it for me, and he did the best he could. The sun is behind me, backlighting me—and I look like an angel.

I take a deep breath and tell him. Because I need to know. Because whatever else Ben Michaels is involved with—whoever the real Ben Michaels is—I want my presence in this life to have mattered to *someone.*

"I felt like I was drowning, but then someone reached in, grabbed me, and pulled me up." I pause because this is the part that sounds ridiculous and unbelievable. "Only the person who pulled me out was *me*, when I was, like, ten."

He flinches and takes a step back. And his voice is strained, like he's choking the words out. "That was me," he says, running a hand through his hair. "I almost drowned when I was a kid. A girl pulled me out of the ocean and saved me."

He takes a deep breath, and a short laugh escapes his mouth. "It was you."

14:21:11:21

I don't remember that. At all. As a kid, I swam better than I walked. I saved things all the time from the ocean, kids who got knocked over because the waves were too powerful, a golden retriever that had gone after a tennis ball, some guy's envelope of money (yeah, that one was weird). Sometimes I even tried to save people who didn't need any help. I was sort of on a mission.

But one of those times, I saved Ben. I saved him from drowning. If I hadn't . . .

The enormity of that twists in my chest. By saving me from the truck, he was returning the favor.

"So if I saw that?" I ask.

"You saw, ah, my memories of you. Things I was thinking about when I was, you know."

"Healing me?" I say.

He nods and looks away. I know he's embarrassed because we both know I don't have substantial memories of him—at least not before the crash—and I'm not going to insult him by pretending I do. I mean, I do remember that day. I remember that bathing suit, that morning and afternoon, and I remember grabbing a kid who looked like he'd just given up. I even remember how he coughed up water and almost threw up on me.

But I don't remember it being *Ben*.

He remembers everything about me—details I wouldn't have even remembered about those moments—and the way I looked through his eyes . . .

"And the way it felt?" I whisper, as if that might soften the blow of embarrassment I'm about to deal. "Is that how you were feeling—how you *feel*—about me?"

A breeze comes off the ocean, and my skin feels strangely empty and open as he gives an almost imperceptible nod. Then he backs away from me like he's going to put an end to this discussion, and I feel like the most manipulative bitch in the world. Why couldn't I have just said thank you?

"Ben," I say, a little too loudly and a little too panicky. He pauses, and the look on his face is just so tortured—so James Dean in *Rebel Without a Cause*—that I want to hug him. Desperately. I want to hold on to him and feel those things I felt when I woke up in his arms. Because it's intoxicating to feel like I matter for *me*—and not for the mundane things I do like cleaning the house or making dinner.

But he's uncomfortable, and despite the fact that we shared this intimate connection—for lack of a better term—I don't actually *know* him.

Even though now I want to.

This guy who dresses like a stoner and tries to fade into the background, even though he's intelligent and full of opinions. Even though he knows how to debate for the fun of it. This guy who steals a password to hack into the school's mainframe and change schedules, but has an honor code about it and hasn't ever changed his grades. This guy who I saved from drowning in the ocean and has never let go of that. I want to know who Ben Michaels really is.

And I want to do something that doesn't cheapen my gratitude. You can't just shake hands with someone who saved your life and then trusted you with a secret their life could potentially depend on.

Reaching out, I grab his hand and intertwine my fingers with his. And I move into his space until we're not even an inch from each other. Laying my forehead on his chest, I take a deep breath and feel his whole body relax, as if tension is rolling off his body in waves.

I was always that kid who loved the smell of gasoline.

His free hand comes up, and his fingers slip through my hair before his hand settles between my shoulder blades.

"Ben," I say into his shirt.

"Janelle," he whispers back, and I can feel his mouth against my hair. I can feel him smile.

I tilt my face up to look at him, to take in the strong lines of his face, the deep-set darkness of his eyes, the way his brown hair flops into his face. And wonder how I didn't see that he was right in front of me this whole time.

But as I take him in, my gaze falls on his lips, and I'm hyperaware of how close they are to mine. The air between us has a tactile quality, like it's been magnetized. And we're frozen in this spot, surrounded by the audible sounds of our breathing and the inaudible pounding of my heart.

"I'm alive," I whisper, because without him I'd be dead, but even more than that, I feel more alive in this moment than I have in a long time. I lift my gaze up to his eyes, and he's looking at me.

For a second, I think he'll kiss me—or I'll kiss him.

Instead he takes a step back and shoves his hands in his pockets. "I have to get home," he says.

Face flushed and trying to ignore the heavy disappointment in my chest, I nod. "Yeah, me too." And I almost ask what Wave Function Collapse is, but I can't bring myself to do it.

Because if Ben *is* involved in something, I'm smart enough to know that I shouldn't tip my hand without having some kind of leverage.

14:20:15:50

When I get home, I have another missed call from Nick and a couple of random texts asking what I'm up to and could I make it to another party tonight, really just for an hour this time. And I'm not sure what to say, other than no.

But I can't ignore him—or the fact that I just almost kissed another guy in the street in front of Kon-Tiki Motorcycles in Pacific Beach—forever. So I text back.

not tonight. talk to you tomorrow.

Now I just have to figure out what I'm going to *say* to him tomorrow, since I'm not sure about that.

Only not right now, because when I get inside, I hear voices coming from my dad's office.

"We've only got fourteen days before this thing goes off, and you're telling me we're no closer to knowing what it will do than we were over a month ago when PD found it?" It's my dad asking.

"What about the suspect?" says a female voice—Deirdre.

163

"No one's had any luck tracking down the guy," a male voice says.

"It's like all traces of him vanished." That's Struz.

"He could be one of the unidentified bodies, for all we know." It's the guy's voice, and this time I recognize it.

Without thinking, I start walking toward them. And they must hear me, because as soon as they come into view, I have a split second where I recognize Deirdre, my dad, and my good old friend Taylor Barclay standing around my dad's desk, and then I see Struz shutting the door in my face.

I stand there for a second, but they've lowered their voices, and I can't even hear muffled words. I don't want to go up to my room, because if they raise their voices or open the door later, I want to hear what they're saying.

Jared is playing *World of Warcraft*—shocking. "Did you get enough to eat?" I ask, peeking my head into the family room. If he was more observant, I'd ask him if he heard any of what they were talking about in Dad's office, but he's sitting at the computer with his headset on and the volume too high. Some days I swear I dream to a Warcraft soundtrack.

Instead of answering, he says to himself, "Why are frost mages still ridiculous? Seriously."

"Jared?" I repeat, because sometimes when he plays video games, he also ignores people.

"I had some pizza when I got home," he says without tearing his eyes away from the screen.

"And?" Since he still hasn't answered the question.

"It was good," he says. "But I'm kind of hungry again."

I glance at the door to the study and try to will it open. But nothing. I look at Jared again. "Did you finish your homework?"

By the way his fingers pause for a second and he falters, I know the answer is no. "Pause it, dude."

"It doesn't pause," he says with a roll of his eyes, but he looks over at me. "Can you make some of that mushroom risotto?"

"That'll take too long, but I can make you some fried rice, and I think we have shrimp in the freezer? But you have to come do homework in the kitchen."

He nods, and I head to the kitchen, knowing he'll follow me, because one of the best things about Jared is that he'll do just about anything—even homework—for food.

"Nick and Kevin think I should try out for baseball this spring," Jared says as he sits down at the kitchen table.

I turn around. Jared is awesome at water polo; he made the JV team this year, and he's one of their best players. He hasn't played baseball on a team since he was twelve. But I don't say anything, because something along the lines of "Who cares what they think?" probably isn't what he wants to hear.

"But I really want to train for polo. Do you think Nick and Kevin will be disappointed?"

"Dude, of course they'll be disappointed. You're awesome, but they aren't going to be mad or anything. Just tell them the truth. They'll get that." Jared nods and opens his mouth to say something else, but I stop him. "Read *Of Mice and Men*. At this rate we're going to be hanging out waiting for you to read your pages all night."

He mutters something about how little he likes the book, and since it wasn't one of my favorites either, I keep my comments to myself.

My dad's study isn't in my line of sight, so periodically I pause in my stirring and leave the kitchen under the guise of "getting something," and I try to hear more of what's going on in there. But each time, I come up with nothing.

Jared and I are both eating when the door to my dad's study opens, and the four of them make their way into the kitchen.

Deirdre's blond hair is pulled into a messy pile on top of her head, and the dark lines under her eyes make her look like she hasn't had a good night's sleep in days. I wonder if it's all the testosterone at work, or if it's more than that—worse than that.

She smiles at me anyway, and it doesn't look forced. "Hey, guys, how are you doing?"

"Good. Do you want some?" I ask, gesturing to the pan on the stove. I'm desperate to ask about the UIED and the case, but I can't. Because I'm not supposed to know anything, and they all think I know less than I really do.

"Yes!" Struz says, pushing past her. He looks like he always does, like an overgrown kid, enthusiastic and too tall. "Barclay, you want some of this?" But he doesn't give anyone time to say anything else. He's shoveling the rice into four bowls and passing them out.

My dad says, "J-baby, what would we do without you?" and then he looks at Jared. "The best-laid plans of mice and men!"

"Would be better if it had aliens in it," Jared says.

"Thanks, but I'm heading out," Deirdre says, as she winks at me.

"Excellent, more for us," Struz says, dumping the contents of her bowl into his.

"Think about what schools you want to visit during spring break, J," Deirdre says. "I might be able to convince my boss to give me those days off so we can do a college tour." She elbows my dad, who just laughs, then she drops her voice to a whisper.

"Some girl bonding might be in order."

I nod, even though I can't even begin to think about college. And then I almost laugh. Because a few weeks ago, that's all I was thinking about—where I would go. Now I'm worried the world won't last that long.

Struz passes a bowl of fried rice to my dad. "James, I bet you could get some extra cash by renting J-baby out to people. She could cook for them, maybe clean up around the house a little. She seems pretty good at that kind of stuff."

I snort.

"What, you don't think so?" Struz says.

My dad slides an arm around me. "She's too good to us," he says with a squeeze. "And it's more than the cooking and cleaning."

"Wow," Barclay says, his mouth still full of fried rice. "This is really good."

"Don't look so surprised." I almost add that he's a jerk, but my dad is right there, so I let it go. Tonight I have more important things to solve than Barclay's attitude.

I lie awake thinking more about Nick. Most nights recently, I've lain awake thinking about Ben Michaels, coming back from the dead, my dad's case, and the UIED. But right now I have to focus on what I can solve.

I remember the night Nick told me how betrayed he felt by his dad. We were at Torrey—almost all of our talks were at Torrey after my shifts. But there was no bonfire that night, no reason for Nick to actually come to the beach, and Kevin was nowhere in sight.

We walked, the wet sand cold under our bare feet, as we moved side by side down the beach. We joked a little, and a couple of times he bumped his shoulder into mine, and then he opened up and told me how torn up he was about stuff going on with his family.

Sure, his dad hadn't cheated on *him*, but his dad was so hard on him all the time, he always demanded perfection, then he went and messed up their family. And I got that. Because I love my parents, but they still manage to let me down.

One on one, we connected. Moments like that, I thought I

really might like him. A lot.

But when I'm around Ben, I can see what the difference is. And it's huge.

Even one on one, *I* never really opened up to Nick. I never told him too many details about my mother; I never introduced him to my dad. I talked about Jared a little, but most of what I said was superficial. And Nick either wasn't observant enough or was too selfish to ask. So even though he likes me, I don't feel like he knows me at all. Not really.

I know that's not Nick's fault—it's mine. But the fact that I didn't want to talk to him, that means something.

And I don't know Ben, but I want to. I want to know him, and I want him to know me.

No matter what I decide to feel about Ben, I need to break up with Nick. It's just not fair to lead him on like this. Not when I'm spending most of my time thinking about another guy.

Which means I know what I need to do.

14:06:56:32

Near the end of first period, I ignore the urge to go home and go to bed, and I try to convince myself that I'm doing the right thing and I have nothing to feel guilty about. So what if I almost kissed Ben last night? I didn't actually kiss him, and Nick and I never really said we were "together," and I'm about to break up with him, and I don't actually know he hasn't been having drunk hookups at parties I don't go to. Except of course, if he hooked up with anyone else, Brooke would make sure that news made its way to me.

I slip out of class early and walk to the front of campus and wait for Nick in the shade under the overhang.

I'm going to be short and concise, tell him he's awesome, but I'm just not interested. That's harsh, but I'm not going to give him some "It's not you, it's me" cliché, and I'm not going to lie and say I need time by myself or that we'd be better as friends.

Nick sees me waiting for him. He and Kevin are together, coming out of the gym—they have weight lifting together.

When he sees me a smile overtakes his face. I can see it from here.

"J!" Kevin shouts, and the two of them continue their walk to the front entrance, where they'll pass right by me.

My heart pounds harder in my chest, and I feel sick to my stomach. A text message would have been less stressful.

"We're going to head to It's a Grind and get coffee," Nick says, when they've almost reached me. "Want to come with us? I think we can get you off."

I shake my head. "Actually, can I talk to you a minute before you leave?"

"Sure," Nick says at the same time Kevin says, "Want to walk and talk? We still wanna beat the crowd, babe."

"Then go start the car," I say without looking at him.

Kevin smirks. "Good luck, dude."

"Look, J, I'm really sorry about the other night," Nick says as soon as Kevin's out of earshot. "I don't know what I was thinking—well, I mean, I wasn't thinking, and it won't happen again. . . ."

My plan is completely out the window. I don't know how to break up with an apology.

But then the G building lets out and I see Alex come out of our calculus classroom, and on the other side of the building, Elijah and Ben come out of another class. I wish I was there with Alex so that I could run into Ben.

"Look, Nick, I don't think we're right for each other. Any girl on this campus would forgive you, but—"

Nick looks away. "But you're not any girl, are you?"

I sigh. "No, I'm not, and I just don't think this is working for me."

He nods but doesn't face me. "Is this because of the other night?"

"A little," I say because that's the truth. "I just don't feel like we're good together. I'd say we should just be friends, but . . ."

That does get him to look back at me. The smile on his face is sad and forced. "We were never really friends in the first place."

I nod.

We stand there awkwardly. He doesn't say anything and I don't say anything, and around us the noise of students getting out of class just gets louder. Until a car horn honks, and I hear Kevin shout, "Let's go, dude! What's the holdup?"

"So I'll see you around?" Nick says.

I let out a breath. I feel bad that it's come down to this. "Yeah, around."

As he walks off, I'm relieved that it's done. It feels right. And I realize I'm ridiculously happy.

Ten days ago, I should have died. But I didn't. I'm alive. I have so much to live for. And this time I'm going to do it right.

14:04:29:51

"**S**o," Mr. Hubley says as he tosses a piece of chalk and catches it—he's the only teacher at Eastview who refuses to convert to whiteboards. "What is the ultimate goal of today's lab?"

Next to me, Cecily's hand shoots into the air—shocking.

This time Hubley doesn't even ask if "anyone other than Cee" wants to wager a guess. He just nods at her.

"Of course, the goal is to observe and participate in an actual projectile word problem, but it's also to see the differences in height and distance that an object will travel based on the angle of the projectile it creates and the force—"

The door to the classroom opens, and for a second I think I stop breathing.

Because Ben is there in the doorway.

Something in my chest flutters a little as he moves into the room and extends a piece of paper to Hubley. He looks around the room. Our eyes meet, and he offers me a half smile that I can't help returning with a full one.

"It's awfully late for a schedule change," Hubley is saying. "You'll have a lot of work to catch up on." Ben doesn't react to that, so Hubley just shrugs and looks at the rest of us. "Well, double up and grab your materials and let's head to the soccer fields."

Everyone stands up at once, grabbing their papers, notebooks, and lab supplies. I don't take my eyes off Ben as I get my own stuff, and I must be sort of in a daze, because when I'm reaching for my pumpkin—approximately one kilogram in weight—Cecily grabs my arm and snaps a finger in front of my face.

"Alex will do that. Let's go get a good spot." As she talks, she grabs my arm and pulls me away from our table, then lowers her voice. "And by a good spot, I mean one where we can keep watch on wherever Ben Michaels is. I, for one, want to know what he's doing suddenly transferring into our class. And because I know you've got a thing for him."

Except Ben waits for us, standing by the doorway and smiling at me.

"Any advice for me?" he asks when we reach him. For some reason, I have no idea what to say.

"Yes," Cecily answers. "Do all the reading and don't fall asleep in class. Take notes and then read them over each night before you do the homework."

"I meant, got any advice on getting Janelle away from Alex."

My face heats up, and I bite my bottom lip to keep from looking too excited. "You can join the three of us."

"What? No," Cecily says. "Alex, Janelle, and I are a triumvirate. And by triumvirate, I mean not just anyone can break us up."

"Cee, he has to have a partner," I say, trying to extricate myself from her, but she tightens her grip.

"You'll have to pass a test so we can see if you're worthy," she says.

Ben glances at me, and something must be wrong with me because I have the urge to burst into giggles—and I don't *ever* giggle. "I accept."

"That's a mistake," Alex says, coming up behind us. "Here, first challenge. Carry all this."

"These too," Cecily says, grabbing my notebook and handing all of our things over to Ben.

And he does. He takes all four pumpkins, the measuring tape, the stopwatch, the slingshot, and all three of our notebooks, and he walks with us as we cross campus.

I try to absorb every answer as Cecily grills him on everything from his favorite color ("blue") and movie ("*Donnie Darko*") to what he thinks about aliens ("we can't be alone, not with all the other planets, solar systems"). I want to remember exactly what he says.

"You know this might be the longest ninety minutes of your life," I say when we finally get to the soccer fields and Cecily takes a break to argue with Alex about exactly how we should set everything up.

Ben leans over, his mouth close to my ear, and says, "I hope so," and then he heads over to Cecily and Alex. "So what exactly are we doing with all this stuff?"

"Essentially we're slingshotting pumpkins," Cecily says. "We have to measure the angle of the projectile, the distance, and of course the time for each shot. That will allow us to also determine the height and effectively draw a graph of each projectile."

"Awesome. Let's get started."

"Cee, did you know Ben rides a motorcycle?" Alex says, and I want to hit him.

Cecily frowns. "You know, I'm not sure you're smart enough

to wreck the triumvirate. I mean, we can't be a triumvirate with a tagalong. We'll have to graduate to some kind of higher power if we take on someone else."

"Because I like motorcycles, I'm not smart enough?" Ben laughs. "But we could be a tetrarchy."

"Motorcycles are dangerous," she says with a roll of her eyes.

"True, but they're freeing," Ben says. "When the wind is on you like that, you can smell everything. You feel everything with a thousand times more significance." Our eyes connect again. "But I appreciate people who think motorcycles are dangerous and less practical than cars."

I'm not sure if he's saying that because I said it last night or if it's a coincidence, but I smile anyway.

Cecily puts her hands on her hips. "Okay, I have one more question, and it's the most important one."

"Maybe we should actually do the lab?" I say, even though this is just as fun.

Ben rubs his hands together like he's getting ready. "Hit me."

And with complete seriousness, she asks, "Who's your favorite superhero?"

Ben steps back like he's been wounded. "That's it?" He laughs. "That's all you got? That's easy. Wonder Woman."

"Wonder Woman? Why her?"

He looks at me this time when he answers. "I've always liked female superheroes best. A girl saving a guy is hot."

I think of pulling him out of the water when we were younger—of saving him—and I feel like I need to sit down. For the best possible reason.

"Then there's her costume," Alex adds.

"Yeah, I wasn't forgetting that."

"Here, come help me, you can be the shooter," Alex says.

"No, Alex, I'm the shooter," Cecily says. "Ben can help you hold the slingshot, and Janelle can be the timer. And yes, this means you're with us, on a trial basis only."

"I'll be on my best behavior." Ben grins.

As I'm grabbing the stopwatch, Cecily turns to me and whispers, "So we totally know what you have to be for Halloween now."

And then she's back to being the general and ordering us around. When we're in position, with Alex and Ben each holding one end of the slingshot three feet off the ground, Cecily pulling the slingshot and pumpkin four feet back, and me off to the side with a stopwatch, I count to three. Cecily releases the pumpkin and sends it soaring.

"Alex, measuring tape!" she says, before she runs after it.

Ben and I stand there for a second, watching them, and then he says, "What are you doing after school?"

"Just the usual, homework and stuff."

He swipes a hand through his hair. "You want to grab something to eat tonight, maybe?"

I can't imagine much that would be more perfect.

14:00:01:13

Ben shows up at my house with Reid's 4Runner—and looking like he raided Reid's wardrobe. In a polo shirt and jeans, he probably looks nicer than I do, since I'm still wearing the same jeans and T-shirt combo I've been in all day.

"Who are you and what did you do with Ben?" I ask, even though I love it. He shrugs, and I'm worried I embarrassed him, so I add, "You look nice."

He smiles like he doesn't necessarily believe me, and as he walks me to the car and opens my door, I have a second to wonder if this isn't the best idea. He seems stiff and tense, and I'm not that great at putting people at ease, and I don't even know him that well. Plus, I just broke up with Nick.

But I want to know Ben Michaels.

As I get into the car, he looks like he might say something but then he doesn't, and the awkwardness during the ride seems to stretch out in front of us as we pull out of my driveway and get on the 56 heading west. Ben doesn't say anything; he just keeps his eyes on the road and fidgets in his seat.

The car smells like Mexican food and I'm starving, and I'm

not sure what else to say, so I say that.

And it must be the right thing to say, because Ben glances over at me with a smile and asks, "Best place to get Mexican food?"

"Roberto's. No contest." The California burritos are to die for. My dad started taking Jared and me there when we were younger. We'd go every time something good happened. I think I've celebrated every major accomplishment in my life—swimming or school-related—with a California burrito from Roberto's.

Ben smiles. He doesn't say why he asked or what his plan is, but his whole body seems to relax into the seat.

"Tell me something about you—something I don't know," I add, because that's what I want. I might as well cut to the chase.

"When I was fourteen, I got a paper route and woke up every day at four thirty in the morning to get all the papers out. I bought an old 1954 Harley-Davidson Flathead from a junkyard for twenty dollars, then I spent two years working that paper route, so I could spend the money restoring it."

"So is that the motorcycle you have now?"

Ben shakes his head. "That's how I got a job at Kon-Tiki. I sold them the bike for five grand, and they turned around and sold it for eight and offered me a job."

The amount of hard work, dedication, and patience it must have taken to restore a bike from a junkyard is mind-blowing. And then to know enough to sell it to a restoration shop and impress them enough to get a job offer. I'm not surprised. This fits the new image I have of Ben—even if it is different from the one I used to have.

I ask a few more questions about motorcycles—not because

I'm all that interested in them, but because I like the way Ben smiles when he talks about them. When he tells me about the 1917 Indian he sold for more than twenty thousand dollars, he goes on this whole tangent and tells me everything I could have ever wanted to know about them.

I've always found passionate people sort of infectious, though, and he sucks me right in, so by the time he's finished talking about it, I almost want to at least see an Indian motorcycle. At this rate, I don't think it'll take Ben long to convince me to ride one.

And then I notice where we are. We're driving south through Ocean Beach. "Where are we going?" I ask, interrupting Ben's story.

"We're almost there," he says, and we both fall silent. As I stare out the window, Ben turns onto Sunset Cliffs Boulevard. The road runs right up against the cliffs, and it feels like we're only inches from the edge, inches from going over and tumbling down to the ocean. Something in my chest swells, because I know exactly where we're going. We pass the parking lot we'd use if we were going to try to head down to the beach like normal people—because Sunset Cliffs is one of the hardest beaches to get to.

Some of the cliffs literally drop straight down to the water, and the city actually put stairs in at the one place where there's beach to use. In some of the good surf spots you can see paths that have worn down from people heading the same way over the years. But there are mile-long—or more—stretches where you'd have to use rock-climbing equipment or be insane in order to get down to the water.

When we pass Point Loma Boulevard, Ben pulls off into a

small dirt lot along the edge of the cliffs and parks the 4Runner in one of the empty spots. From the angle we're parked, if the car accidentally shifted into drive, we would roll off the end of the earth. Looking straight ahead, all I can see is clear blue ocean.

Ben looks over at me. "There's a blanket in the backseat behind you. You pick a spot where you want to sit down, and I'll grab the food."

I find a flat spot and stare blankly off into the distance—the richness of the colors, the feel of the heat on my skin, there's nowhere more perfect he could have taken me.

When Ben comes over, I can smell the food, and he doesn't need to tell me what it is—it's from Roberto's. I take the bag from him and peek inside. It's my favorite. Burritos, chips, and guacamole. I look up and stare at him for a second, and I want to ask how he knew this was my favorite, but I'm at a loss for words.

"Come on," Ben says, nodding toward the ocean, and we climb over the guardrail. I spread the blanket near the edge of a flat cliff overlooking the ocean—it's as close as I could get without worrying about taking a wrong step and sliding to a rocky death.

As I sit down, Ben tosses me a can of grape soda, and I wonder how he could possibly know how much I used to love this stuff. He must see it on my face, because he smiles and looks down. "You must have had grape soda every day for lunch in sixth grade."

"How do you know that?" I laugh.

"We were in the same history class, right before lunch."

"No, we weren't." I would remember that.

"Mrs. Zaragosa, sixth-grade history," Ben says. "You sat in the last row two seats from the front. I sat in the third row, all the way at the back. Sometimes you would get hungry and eat your lunch in class."

I remember *that*, and I feel like a moron for not knowing he was in my class. "Your memory is scary good."

He blushes. "Only when it comes to you."

Off to the left, in the middle of the ocean, there's a big rock that's its own island, a landing spot for the seagulls, and I watch them as they fly in, land, and squawk at one another before taking off. Ben leans into me, the heat of his body keeping me warm as the wind picks up off the ocean. Below us, there are only rocks and white water crashing against them. The sun is starting its descent, and it hangs like a huge golden globe near the edge of the water, casting red, orange, pink, and purple streaks in the sky.

It feels like we're the only two people in the world, and for a minute I let myself forget about everything else.

We sit next to each other, shoulder to shoulder, the sun setting in front of us, eating my favorite food in the world, and I just know—this is why I have a second chance. This is why I came back from the dead—so I could really feel alive.

"This might be the coolest thing you could have done for me," I say, bumping my shoulder into Ben's.

His fingertips brush over the back of my hand until his whole hand covers mine and gives it a light squeeze.

Tearing my eyes away from the sky, I look at Ben. His floppy brown curls are falling into his face, shading his eyes, but I can see the look on his face, like he's laughing at himself.

"What?"

He shakes his head. "I almost just drove us to the movies."

He's lying. I can see it in his face. He might have thought

about it, especially when he was all tense in the car, but he knows me too well to just take me to a movie.

I smile, and that's all it takes. He leans forward and our lips touch, and it's like his lips were made to fit around mine.

His arms tighten around me, and I reach up to the back of his neck and pull him into me. Our lips part, our tongues touch, and I taste him until a sigh escapes with my breath.

Ben pulls back just a fraction of an inch so our foreheads are touching, and his lips smile against mine.

"This was perfect," I whisper.

He closes his eyes, and his voice is quiet, like the words are simply being exhaled. "It was better than perfect."

13:22:45:41

I'm still thinking about the way Ben's lips tasted as he turns the car onto my street.

I can't stop smiling.

And every time I look over at him, I notice he's smiling too.

Yes, I am completely aware that I've suddenly morphed into one of *those girls*. I don't care.

But as he's about to pull into my driveway, I reach out and put a hand on his arm. "Stop here," I say, trying not to sound like anything is wrong.

Struz's TrailBlazer is behind my Jeep. They're the only two cars in the driveway.

The smile falls off my face, and the warmth in my body is gone. I shiver a little as I open the passenger-side door. Something's wrong. I can feel it.

Ben acts like he's about to turn the car off and walk me up to the door, but I shake my head. "I think something's wrong."

"What?" he asks. "I'll come in with you."

I shake my head again and look at him. I try not to worry about whatever is going to come next and just remember how awesome this day was—this *whole* day. "We should do this again."

He leans across the car and as his lips brush against mine, he whispers, "Definitely."

It's not until I get out of the car that I realize Struz is standing on our doorstep, one arm raised as if he's been knocking, but his palm is flat against the door like he's tired and supporting himself.

I feel short of breath, but I turn and wave at Ben as he drives away. Then I look back at Struz and my house, and will myself to walk up the driveway.

All the lights in the house are on. Every single one. Our windows are lit up enough that they could illuminate the whole street.

"Elaine!" Struz calls to my mother. "Please open the door."

He turns when I'm only about five feet from the porch, and I can see his eyes are bloodshot, like he's been crying. Sadness and relief wash over his face in a weird mixture, and then he pulls himself together, stands up straight, and takes a deep breath.

"J-baby, unlock the door for me?" he says. "Your mom locked me out."

On any normal night, I would. I would roll my eyes and we would exchange looks and sighs that said we didn't know what to do about her.

But this isn't a normal evening. Something is very wrong.

I hold my keys tightly in my fist. "What happened?"

"J, this is important," Struz says. "She's been freaking out for at least twenty minutes."

"What happened?" I repeat.

"Jared is in there with her," Struz says, and that almost makes me lunge for the door and fumble with my keys. I've managed to keep Jared away from most of her episodes. But I'm not going to let Struz play me like that.

"Why isn't Jared at Chris's house? They had an English project. . . ."

"I picked him up and brought him home," Struz says. But he doesn't tell me why.

"If you want me to unlock the door, you tell me what happened, or we stand out here all night."

Struz looks away from me, and not at anything in particular, and then he looks back, and his eyes are watering. "It's your dad. Earlier today he went to investigate a lead on his own, I'm not sure what. . . ."

My voice shakes when it comes out. "And he's not back?"

As soon as I say the words, I realize how wrong they are. I can see in Struz's face that it's worse than that, and a cold feeling of dread settles deep in my chest and begins to spread outward, its tendrils reaching out, squeezing the air from my lungs.

"San Diego PD found his body a couple hours ago in one of the canyons behind Park Village."

13:22:43:57

His body.

San Diego PD found his body.

He's dead. My dad is dead.

As I'm trying to process that, I'm struck with the most ridiculous thought.

We've done the same thing for Jared's birthday every year. He invites his friends over, and Struz and my dad play baseball or football with them, and then my dad barbecues ribs, chicken, and hot dogs.

Next month when I have fourteen teenage boys in our house, who will grill the food?

And then I feel absurd because who cares about that? My dad is dead. I'm never going to come home to find our garage door wide open again. I'm never going to wake up to a phone call at two a.m. from him, apologizing for missing dinner and asking if he should bring home ice cream to make up for it. I'm never going to wake up for school and find him passed out in his work clothes at the desk in his study.

The weight of that knowledge sucks all the air out of my

body, and I reach out until Struz catches my hand and steadies me. I bend slightly at the waist, leaning forward in some instinctive attempt to protect my organs from physical pain even though it won't help.

My dad is dead.

"J-baby."

"J, it's going to be okay."

Struz is talking to me. I force myself to gulp down as much air as I can and straighten up. But something is ripping me apart from the inside out, because this isn't right. This isn't supposed to be happening.

It has to be some awful nightmare and in a minute I'll wake up and go tell my dad about it and he'll laugh because he's going to die an old man in his sleep long after Jared and I have moved out of the house and gotten families of our own. Because the job is never going to claim him—not like that.

San Diego PD found his body. . . .

"We'll figure it out," Struz says, his hand on my back.

I pull away, thinking suddenly of the *way* my dad died. The corners of my vision are blackening. I feel a little like I might pass out. Someone killed him. "Do you know who did it?"

"Not yet, but we will," Struz says. I see the determination in his eyes, and I want to believe him. He won't just sit on this. Neither will the other agents in my dad's squad. Even if it goes cold it'll be the case that sits on Struz's desk, the one he looks at every night before he goes to bed until he figures it out or until he dies. Whichever comes first.

But that doesn't make the weight that's pressing down on my chest let up. "Maybe it's a mistake," I say, even though I know it's not. "What lead was he chasing up? What the hell was he doing in the canyons behind Park Village?"

It really doesn't make much sense. Cops patrol the canyons behind Park Village because it's this crazy huge housing development and kids always hang out there and get drunk or smoke weed. The only time my dad ever went out there was when I was a sophomore and this kid a year ahead of me threatened to bring a gun to school and didn't show up for homeroom the next day. The teachers locked us down and called the police. Alex's mom heard about it and called my dad. He and a couple of his agents dropped everything and went searching for the kid. They found him in the canyons.

They hadn't needed to; it was a suicide. Not like this.

Thinking about that—about a case and the death of *someone else*—helps keep me grounded, helps me focus on what's important at this second, and I look at Struz straight-on to make sure I can gauge his reaction as I ask, "Was his body dumped there?"

Struz sets his jaw and doesn't answer, but he doesn't need to. He's trying to stay composed, but I can see how angry he is, and I know I'm on the right track. My own anger burns in my chest before spreading through my veins to the rest of my body, and my fingertips itch with the urge to break something. Or someone.

The real question is what was my dad doing and who was he

meeting in Park Village?

The dull throbbing of the car keys digging into my palm makes me realize I've been clenching my fists. I believe Struz. I know he'll work forever to figure this out. I know because so will I.

The sound of something breaking inside the house brings me back to the immediate problem. My mother. "Did you tell her?"

"She's his wife," Struz says, and he doesn't need to say that he told her, he doesn't need to say that it was probably a mistake to do it before I was home, and he doesn't need to say he wasn't thinking clearly.

For once, I'm not mad. I take a deep breath and think about how I can use this to my advantage. Because in the next few days—or weeks or months or even years—while the FBI scrambles to solve the loss of one of their own, I don't want to just sit on my hands and wait for them to give me a few pieces of the information I'm entitled to know.

"I'm sorry, J-baby," Struz whispers, and I know the apology covers everything—from what's going on with my mother behind this door to the fact that my father is gone, to everything in between.

I nod and move toward the door, taking my time as I find the right key and make sure it actually fits into the lock. I look at Struz and hope he's preoccupied enough, and that this is enough of the truth that he won't catch me when I lie, "You take care of her, and I'll take care of Jared."

He just nods.

"The Xanax are in her bedroom. Give her two. That'll put her to sleep." Which is true, but if she's well into an episode it'll take him everything he's got to get her back into her bedroom and force her to take the pills.

Which will give me enough time.

I take a deep breath and turn the key.

The inside of my house is only a step away from a scene from *The Exorcist*. The end table in the foyer is overturned, its lamp in pieces. Pizza sauce and some kind of liquid are splattered on the walls.

"Jared!" I call immediately.

In the kitchen, there are shattered pieces of porcelain everywhere. A half-eaten pizza is on the tiled floor, and a two-liter bottle of Coke lies on its side, liquid still seeping out and making a puddle on the floor.

Jared is standing wide-eyed and frozen in the center of the kitchen, watching as my mother pulls dishes from the good china cabinet—her wedding china—and throws them as hard as she can at the floor. As a bowl hits the tile and shatters, Jared flinches, the only evidence he hasn't gone completely into shock.

"Jared!" I say again, moving into the doorway of the kitchen. I step on a piece of glass and it cracks under my shoe. Jared's eyes flick to me before they move back to our mother, who has a few small cuts on her face and arms, obviously from pieces of the broken dishes and glass that have ricocheted off the floor.

Struz pushes past me into the kitchen, yelling at my mother to "stop" and "calm down." Instead she turns on him, throwing the dishes at him.

"Jared, come with me now!" I say, snapping my fingers at him.

This time he rushes toward me and throws his arms around me. I stumble under his weight. We're about the same height now, and he outweighs me by at least fifteen pounds.

For a moment, I just hug him back. He's crying, and I stagger to move us both away from the kitchen and close to Dad's study. "Is it true?" Jared keeps asking.

When we're almost to the study, I push Jared off me, grab him by the shoulders, and give him a quick shake. "Jared!"

His eyes focus on me.

"This is really important," I say. "I need you to do exactly what I say. Exactly."

He nods.

"I need you to run up to my room and get my swimming backpack, the big one, and I need you to bring it to me, here in Dad's office, and then I need you to go upstairs to your room and stay there until Struz calms Mom down."

"But—"

"You cannot breathe a word of this to Struz. There's something I have to do, but I need you to be strong for me. Can you do that?"

He nods.

"Okay," I say, and turn to the study as Jared runs toward the stairs. I hate doing this to him, I hate that I'm about to make him lock himself in his room and wait for me to get back, make him deal with this alone.

But I have to.

If I'd died that day at Torrey, my dad would have moved heaven and earth in order to know everything about what happened.

He was doing that anyway, even though he thought I walked away without a scratch.

Only I don't have the same resources. Once the FBI comes in and cleans out everything that had to do with my father's work,

I won't have any of the information I need. Which means I need to move now, and take care of Jared later.

In my father's study, I move immediately to his desk. Swallowing down the lump in my throat, I pick up the files that are open, obviously the last ones he looked at last night. I close them and begin piling them on the desk. Then I grab all the ones in the immediate vicinity, ones that look like he might have looked at them in the last few days.

And Jared is back with the exact bag I was thinking of. "Hold it steady," I say as I dump the files into the bag.

I unplug the laptop and dump it and the power cord in the bag as well, and Jared says, "Why are you taking Dad's case files?"

"Because this is what killed him," I say before I can stop to think how to soften it. But when I look at Jared, he just nods. He's keeping it together. My chest expands with pride and love. He's my brother and we're cut from the same cloth—there's something of our dad in both of us.

"Go to your room and stay there," I say to Jared, moving around him so we can get out of the study before Struz realizes what we're doing. On a whim, I grab the case file of the girl who disappeared all those years ago, the case he never solved, and stick it in the bag. It was important to him, and I'm just not ready for the Bureau to swoop in and take it away. "I promise I'll be back in a couple of hours."

"Where are you going?" Jared asks.

"It's better that you don't know," I say, pushing him out of the study and toward the stairs. "Let's go."

Struz and my mother are still arguing in the kitchen. I hear him call out to me, and for a moment I feel a twinge of guilt that I'm doing this to him, leaving him to sort her out, but I push the guilt away and run up the stairs right behind Jared.

"Stay in your room," I say again. "I promise I'll be back tonight."

Jared nods and does what I say, and I'm glad he's the kind of brother who respects his sister. Then I go to my dad's room. Unlike his study, it's neat and orderly, a throwback to his army days. I'm glad, because this makes it easier.

The files on his nightstand are important—they must be, since he would have looked at them right before getting into bed—so I grab them and throw them into the bag.

In the walk-in closet, I push his suits around until I find the safe. The key code is eight digits, my birthday. I key it in—03241995—and pull the lever.

Inside is a .40-caliber Glock 22. It's the same issue as the one he got his fourth week at Quantico. My dad carried a Sig Sauer P226 and a Glock 27 for backup, but this gun is the one he taught me how to handle and shoot for my tenth birthday. We used to go to the shooting range once every couple of weeks when I was younger.

The gun is heavy in my hands, like I've suddenly recognized the significance of it, the fact that this could be the same model that killed my dad—if he was even shot.

I don't even know how he died. Whether he saw it coming or if he was caught by surprise. Whether he died instantly or if he had time to think of what he was leaving behind.

My throat constricts, and I remind myself that I'm wasting time. I check the gun—it's not loaded—before I tuck it into the bag, then I grab the box of bullets, the two file folders, and my father's passport and put them in there as well. I'll see what they are later.

"Janelle, where are you?" Struz calls from downstairs, and I zip the bag and put it on my back.

I open the door to the hallway and see Struz coming up the stairs.

So I guess the front door is out. There's no way he *won't* figure out what I'm doing. Pushing the door shut, I lock it and weigh my options.

One of the windows will put me on the roof of the garage. I move that way, throw open the window, and as I'm struggling with the screen, I hear Struz knocking on Jared's door. "You guys okay?" he calls.

Jared's voice is muffled, so I don't hear what he's saying, but it's very possible he'll sell me out without realizing it.

The screen is cheap, and the frame finally bends under my hands. I push it out and watch as it tumbles onto the roof, then slides down into the grass.

"J, are you in here?" Struz says, and the doorknob to my dad's bedroom twists a little. The lock holds, but only because Struz isn't trying to bust in here yet. As soon as he makes the attempt, I'm sure it'll give way. "Janelle, open this door!"

Which means I have to move. Now.

Taking a deep breath, I climb out, one leg at a time, holding on to the window frame as if my life depends on it. I test the shingles with the toe of my sneaker, and when I don't slip or slide, I go ahead and put my weight on them.

I hold my arms out wide for balance and move carefully to the edge of the roof. The driveway is on the right, and the side yard is on the left. If I take off in the Jeep, all Struz needs is to make a phone call, and any cop in the area will be ready to pull it over. But discarded thoughtlessly in our neighbor's yard is a gold beach cruiser with a purple leather seat. On a bike I could take back roads and cut through people's yards.

As I get to the left edge of the roof, I hear Struz break open the door, and I don't even have time to look down and think about how far the grass is from here. I just jump.

Legs shoulder-width apart, even, not quite straight, relaxed, ready to give when they hit grass.

My landing is almost perfect, and even though my left ankle turns and pain shoots up my leg, it's as good as I could ask for. The weight of the backpack hurts my balance and I pitch forward to my knees, but I'm up again before I can think about it, moving toward my neighbor's yard and that gold bike.

Pain stabs my left foot every time I put weight on it, but I try to ignore it as I hop-run to the bike. If it was broken, it would feel worse.

The bike is perfect, maybe a little big for me, but definitely something I can ride. I hop on and start pedaling.

I think I hear someone call my name—Struz, or maybe even Jared—but I don't turn back. I was interested in the case before because it involved me and my John Doe. But now it's different. I wouldn't have thought it possible, but the stakes are even higher now.

Because now this case has taken something from me.

13:22:07:19

I'm out of my neighborhood before I realize I don't actually have a plan when it comes to *where* I'm going.

Alex picks up on the first ring. "What's going on at your house? My mom's been calling for at least the last five minutes."

"It's a long story," I say. I'll tell him in a minute. First I need him to think for me. "If I have a backpack full of things I want to keep from the FBI, where can I hide them?"

There's a pause on the other line.

"I just need an answer."

"Couldn't you have asked this in person rather than over a phone line?"

"Alex. I don't have a lot of time, especially for one of your conspiracy theories," I say, and I hate how harsh my voice sounds. "Can you think for me for a second? I need to know where to go. It would just be to keep something there for a few days." Until I have a better idea of what I'm doing.

"You could keep stuff here, obviously, but that'd be the first place your dad would look if he knew you were keeping something from him," he says, and my eyes water at the mention of my dad. "What about Kate's? Your dad and Struz might not know the details, but they know you had a falling-out and haven't spoken. And her new house has that pool apartment that nobody ever uses. Her mom keeps the key under the mat."

Kate's house is the last place I want to go, but he has a point. I'm already heading toward Santaluz.

"J, are you going to tell me what's going on?"

"My dad is dead," I say, because maybe if I keep saying it, I'll get used to the idea. "San Diego PD found his body in a canyon behind Park Village."

I hear Alex suck in a breath, and suddenly I need to see him.

"Can you pick me up at Kate's? I'll tell you everything when you get there."

"Of course," he says, his voice hoarse. "I'll see you in five minutes."

I hang up without saying anything else, because I don't trust either of us to get the words out.

Kate, Alex, and I all grew up together, only three houses apart—until the summer before freshman year, when Kate's parents bought the "new" house in Santaluz and they moved. She already knew Brooke and Lesley because the three of them played volleyball together and Kate was likely going to make varsity, even as a freshman, but once she moved into their neighborhood, I could see her change.

Even before the party, even before she drugged me for their approval, she had chosen them over Alex and me. She'd started dressing like them, hanging out with them at the country club instead of going to the beach with me.

That's what bothers me most about that night: I should have seen it coming.

I knew she'd changed, and I had a moment when I thought, *I should just go home and play* World of Warcraft *with Jared or watch a lame action movie with Alex,* but I stayed. And when Kate gave me that beer, I wanted our friendship to be the same as it had always been. So I did my part to hold on to the past.

I drank it.

13:21:48:38

A lex's car is parked on the street when I get to Kate's.
Her house is this sprawling monstrosity—peach stucco with a three-car garage, a wraparound balcony, desert-style landscaping that probably cost way more than it looks like it should, and a pretty intense pool. With the accompanying pool house that looks like a mini version of the real thing.

By the time I reach his car, Alex is already out, shutting the door. I drop the bike on the grass, and we have our arms wrapped around each other in the same motion. He's breathing hard, and his body shakes as it holds on to mine.

My dad is dead.

We cling to each other as it sinks in. "Are you sure?" Alex asks, because like me he can't believe it's possible.

I nod. "My dad is dead." I take a deep breath. "And we have thirteen days to figure out what happened."

I have to get this bag stowed away and then I have to figure out my next step. "Come on, let's break into the pool house and get out of here," I say as I pull away.

Alex turns away so he can wipe his eyes and save face, and we move through the yard to the pool house. He's right and the key is under the mat, easy for the taking, though I'm not surprised. Kate's mom is chronically forgetful. She's always losing her keys and her purse and everything else that isn't attached to something. When they lived a few doors down from us, we had an extra set of her house and car keys in case she lost them.

And she did. A lot.

Alex is also right about the fact that no one uses the pool house. It makes me wonder if the two of them are still talking.

The whole place is dark and untouched, and there's a light layer of dust on everything. Given that it's only September, you'd think this place would look a little more lived in.

"Where should we put it?" I say as I look around. Even though the place isn't lived in, it still looks like a room that just fell out of *Vogue Living*.

"Here," Alex says, reaching for the backpack. "I think I have an idea." I slip it off and hand it to him, only to have him ask, "What the hell do you have in here that's so heavy?"

I'm not sure if it's the gun, the laptop, or all the files, but I assume it's better if he doesn't know.

"I'll tell you later."

He nods, and he must know what I mean, because he doesn't ask again. Instead we move through the pool house to the back bedroom. There's a king-size bed and a matching dresser and desk set, and then a huge walk-in closet.

Inside is every outfit Kate ever wore as a child. Boxes of baby clothes, dance recital and Halloween costumes.

Alex moves a couple of boxes around and ignores the ruffly lace from Kate's *Swan Lake* dance costume from second grade— yeah, it was hideous to watch seven-year-olds attempt that.

But when he emerges from the dance costumes, the backpack is behind them, and we pile the boxes back up. If you don't know they're sticking out a few more inches than the rest of them, you'd never be able to tell.

And that works for me.

"What now?" Alex says as we're leaving.

"Now I have to go home before Struz has a task force out looking for me." And I suppose I should come up with some story about what I took from the office and where the hell I went. I'll have to admit to taking the gun and everything in the safe. Struz would try my and Jared's birthdays first, even if he doesn't already know the code.

Alex nods and locks up the pool house again, sliding the key back under the mat.

"Do you know any of the details?" he asks.

I shake my head.

Alex reaches over and squeezes my hand before letting go. "We'll find them out," he says, and his voice has the same determined edge Struz had to his when we were standing on my porch.

I nod, not trusting my ability to form words, and I notice the curtains of the dining room window in Kate's house are open wide and someone blond is standing there watching us.

The noise that comes out of my mouth is neither intelligible nor anything close to English, but it's enough for Alex to realize there's something I need him to pay attention to, and he looks toward the house.

I know the moment he sees her, because his body tenses. She didn't do anything malicious to him; she just stopped acknowledging his existence, and I'm not sure which is worse.

He turns to me, and his voice has a hard edge to it. "I'll take care of it."

"You're going to go talk to her?" Like that will solve anything. She'll probably call the FBI out of spite.

"I'm going to get her off our backs," he says, already moving toward her house. He tosses me the keys. "Here, get the bike in the car. I'll drive you home when I get back."

I have the urge to kick something, but my ankle still hurts a little, and I doubt hurting the other one would really help.

It's when I get the bike in the car and slide into the passenger seat that the memories press down and threaten to strangle me. For a minute I can't move. I can't even shut the door. I'm paralyzed by the knowledge that my dad is gone. He's just ceased to exist.

My body jerks as my mind decides it can no longer use the focus of some other task to keep from breaking down.

He's gone.

The tears come, and I have to hold a hand over my mouth to keep from letting loose some kind of wail. My face is too hot, my nose runs, my whole body convulses and shakes, and I lean forward, resting my forehead against the warm leather of the dashboard.

Gone. Completely. He's not here anymore. And nothing will ever bring him back.

13:21:35:17

My mom wasn't always crazy. Or at least she was only as crazy as the average twentysomething girl in love with an older guy just back from serving in the Gulf War.

Bipolar is the kind of disorder that's late onset. You don't realize you have it until you crack. And most people crack somewhere between age eighteen and thirty.

My mother was twenty-seven.

It was after Jared was born. She spiraled down into this insane depression, and the first doctor my dad took her to thought it was because of the pregnancy. Maybe it was. But she didn't get out of bed for months. And when she ultimately did, she was different. Different enough that even I could recognize it.

While she was in bed, my dad tried to play the good husband and father—and he did. He made us dinner every night—we ate every different kind of pasta he could find. And every night, as he laid Jared down to sleep in his crib, we would go into my bedroom with the baby monitor and he would read to me.

But the children's books I had bored him. So he read *Ender's Game* by Orson Scott Card. And he read the whole Ender series.

Some nights when it was early and Jared was still awake, we'd all pile into my bed and read until baby Jared fell asleep.

When my dad finally finished after months of reading, he closed the last Ender book and asked what we should read tomorrow.

"*Ender*!" I said.

"But J-baby, that's the end."

I shook my head. "Read it again."

Thus began my obsessive personality. It's all gone downhill from there.

I was three.

10:07:01:31

The funeral is closed casket. And outdoors.

It's warm and typical San Diego weather—about eighty—but the marine layer set in last night, so it's overcast. Not a speck of sunlight anywhere.

"I overheard a couple of guys talking," Alex says, his voice breaking as he comes to stand next to me. He's in a black suit and the jacket is a little too big. He looks like one of those kids who dresses up in his dad's clothing. My dad would be teasing him about it if he were here—my eyes burn at the thought.

After a few deep breaths, Alex squares his shoulders and steadies himself. "It sounds like he was shot three times. Once in the arm and twice in the chest."

I nod and flick my eyes to the sky so I don't lose it right here in front of everyone. I don't tell Alex now isn't the time for me to talk about this, because everyone I know is struggling to get through this however we can. This is how Alex is dealing with the loss—he's hurting and he's focusing on what happened as a coping mechanism. I get that. It's what my dad would be doing.

I've been going back and forth between taking care of Jared

and trying to make sure none of the arrangements fall apart.

But every once in a while, the emotion seeps in, and right now at his funeral I don't know if I can keep myself together.

Once in the arm and twice in the chest.

He probably died within seconds.

Alex opens his mouth, and I have a split second to wonder if I'd piss him off and hurt his feelings by telling him to just shut up about it, but I don't have to. He closes his mouth again, his gaze falling over my shoulder.

Cecily stands there. Dressed in all black, her shoulder-length milky-blond hair and light blue eyes make her look like a character out of a fairy tale. She comes up next to me, and she doesn't say she's sorry for my loss or that she knows how I feel or that my dad was a great man. Instead she just looks up into my eyes and says, "This sucks."

I remember that I've heard Cecily lives with her aunt and uncle, that her mother died a few years ago before she moved to San Diego.

I nod because it does suck. In fact it sucks so much and yet no one—except Cecily—actually says that, and I have this ridiculous urge now to just scream as loud as I can. To announce to the world how I really feel about all this. That it sucks. That it's not fair. That I'm not ready to say good-bye.

The three of us stand there for a few minutes while several other people come over to offer me their condolences, and before she leaves, Cecily just squeezes my hand.

When she's gone, Alex is staring at me. It takes me a moment to figure out why, but then I remember what we were talking about before Cecily came over, and I say, "Let's compare notes tomorrow?"

He nods, and I notice how glassy his eyes are. I put a hand on his shoulder. "Are you okay?"

Alex looks away, half laughing, half snorting. "You shouldn't have to worry about comforting me. He's your dad."

I lean into Alex, a hug without an embrace. "I shared him with you a little," I whisper. "You're allowed to be devastated."

Because the truth is my dad was like another parent to Alex, or at least like the cool uncle or something. His dad works a lot and his mother is, well, his mother. If I were Alex, I would have loved my dad too.

I move to take my place front and center, standing next to my mother, who has to stay seated because she's so full of drugs she's practically catatonic, and Jared, who's been only slightly more than a zombie since I found him in the kitchen four days ago. Tears leak from my eyes, even though I'm putting all my energy into being the strong one, into not thinking about it, into keeping myself together.

Because my father is a war veteran, the service has full military honors, complete with the flag-draped coffin and seven armed service members who will each shoot their rifle three times and a bugler who will play "Taps" when it's all over.

And because he's been a pretty visible and upstanding member of our community, everyone I've ever met in my entire life is here. Classmates and their parents, my dad's entire team, neighbors, relatives, swim coaches, even some of my teachers, they're all here. And then there are the people I don't know too.

I try to be glad that this many people will remember him, that he made a difference in this many lives—that he mattered. Those things were important to him, and I try to focus on that.

But even the good things hurt.

211

Like someone is holding me down, pressing something heavy against my chest.

Because I shouldn't have to be *trying* at all.

Kate and her parents are here, too. She had the nerve to come talk to me when she first arrived and tell me she was so, *so* sorry for my loss. I took one look at her bloodshot eyes and tearstained makeup and had to keep myself from punching her.

When the ceremony starts I try to pay attention, to look at the faces of the soldiers honoring my dad for the commitment and service he put in twenty years ago, before I was born. For some reason it bothers me that they don't know him any more than what they might have heard from someone here—how hard he worked and how many hours he put into his job. That they don't know him like I do. They don't know the only thing he could cook was pasta, or that he thought everything emotional could be solved with chocolate ice cream, or that he'd memorized half of the dialogue in *The X-Files*, or that his favorite novel was *Of Men and Monsters* by William Tenn, or that he always bought tickets to San Diego Comic-Con even though he didn't get to go half the time because something would come up at work.

Or that Jared and I loved him.

The wind picks up and whips my hair around, and I have to pull it back to keep it from getting into my eyes. I glance over at Jared and the lifeless way he's standing. I don't think he's cried yet, and I'm not sure what to do about that, but I know letting him follow my own attempt to deal with the grief isn't a good idea.

I wonder if Ben can heal people who are emotionally stalled, if there's some way to reorganize molecules so people don't feel sad or empty inside anymore.

Somehow I doubt it.

As if thinking about him conjured him into existence, when I look back at the coffin draped with the American flag, I see Ben, the concern written on his face somehow different from everyone else's pity. It makes me wish he was closer, or that the service hadn't started yet, that I could feel him next to me. But he's next to Elijah, standing with Reid and his parents. They're standing respectfully among the crowd, like everyone else.

But all three of them are looking at me.

10:06:23:12

A US Army lieutenant general who apparently served with my dad right out of basic brings us the folded American flag and hands it to me.

My eyes sting and my vision blurs.

I look up at the sky when they lower the casket into the ground. There's just something a little too final about it.

I can't watch.

S truz corners me on the way to the car. "Janelle."

I hate that he uses my full name. "Struz."

"J, I need those files you took from your dad's study," he says.

"What files?" I ask, even though my heart throbs that I'm putting him through more hell. He's obviously feeling beat up and lost without my dad—his hair looks like he hasn't brushed it in days, his suit is wrinkled, and his tie is crooked. He needs a wife, but by now he's probably too absorbed with work and weighed down by responsibilities to find one.

"I don't know what you took," he admits. "But I know you, and I know you took *something*, and I need you to bring it back."

I nod, because I know he's right. Who do I think I am, pretending that I can run around like Jack Bauer and try to solve a case that the FBI is working on? After all, the FBI has a thousand times more resources than I do. What was I even thinking by taking them?

I'm about to offer up the files and tell Struz they're in the closet of Kate's pool house when out of the corner of my eye, I see Barclay. And I remember he owes me. With everything else going on with Ben and then my dad, I'd forgotten about Taylor Barclay.

"J?" Struz says, bringing my attention back to him.

This time I don't think about how hard this is for him too. This time I think about how much he's kept from me because I "don't need to know."

"Maybe when you deign to tell me the details about my father's death, maybe then those mysterious missing files will turn up." And I don't even try to keep the bite from my voice.

It's bullshit that no one will tell me anything—that I have to ask Alex to spy on people at the funeral in order to find out the details.

I'll just do my own digging first. I'll get the information out of Barclay. I don't think Ben's involved, but I'll find out what he isn't telling me, just to make sure. And then I'll tell Struz everything.

Struz sighs, and his shoulders sag a little. He hasn't given up—he's not like that—but he is giving it a rest. "What are you going to do?"

"I'm going to take my mother and brother home and attempt to take care of them, and then I might get really drunk," I say, forgetting for a second that Struz isn't just a family friend, he's also a law-enforcement officer.

"Christ, Janelle, that's not going to solve anything," he says, thinking I'm serious. "What are you think—"

I grab his arm, about to give some snarky response, but as I catch what he says—*What are you thinking*—what comes out of my mouth is different. It's shameful and something I haven't admitted to a soul. And it's true.

216

"I was so mad at him."

Struz stops thinking about whatever he was going to say next and turns to me. "Your father?"

I understand the shock and disbelief in his voice. My father is—*was*—a great man. He loved us and he loved his job, and anyone would be lucky to have him touch their life.

I don't trust my voice, so I just nod as the tears sting my eyes. I don't understand how I have any more tears to cry. When will my eyes just dry up?

Struz loved my father almost as much as I did. So he can't keep himself from asking, "Why?"

The guilt and the shame are choking me so much I can barely get the words out, and my voice is no more than a whisper. "He never made the one decision we needed him to."

I turn and look at my mother, whose expression still hasn't changed, and Struz follows my line of vision. He must get it immediately, because he opens his mouth, obviously to defend my dad. And why not? There are so many excuses. I've made them all for him too.

But now he's gone, and I can't make them anymore. "I needed him . . ."

"J-baby," Struz whispers, reaching for me, but I take a step back and shake my head.

"I needed him to take care of her so that I didn't have to do it." The tears are completely out of my control now, pouring down my face in streams so powerful I can't see more than a few inches in front of me.

This time, Struz is faster and more demanding. He pulls me into a hug. My whole body gives itself up to sorrow at that moment, and I'm shaking and trying to suck down too much air at one time. My whole body feels numb, to the point where I don't feel like I have limbs anymore. I'm just a floating head, an outpouring of emotion, a heart that doesn't seem to know how to beat regularly anymore.

10:05:48:45

Minutes pass, and I manage to swim out of the black hole of my grief, only to realize that Struz is still petting my hair and whispering that it will be okay.

I shake my head, gulp down a few swallows of air, wipe the tears and snot from my face, and ignore how pathetic my voice sounds. "I don't think I can forgive him for leaving me here. How will anything ever be okay again?"

Struz doesn't have an answer for me, though, so we head back to my house to eat the food everyone's brought over and accept more condolences.

Never mind that everything in that house is a glaring beacon that my father is gone.

After the last well-wisher leaves, I really do have the desire to just forget this awful day.

So we go to Chad Brandel's party.

"Don't fidget so much," I tell Alex as I hand him a beer. "Just relax. Try to enjoy yourself."

He just shakes his head. His mom thinks we're at the library doing the work we missed at school today. "I still don't know why you even wanted to come. We could be watching *The Mummy* at my house right now."

I shrug. "Maybe I think it would be a crime to let you graduate without going to one high school party. You know I'm charitable like that."

"I don't have much desire to be social," he says, but I ignore him.

Chad Brandel doesn't follow anyone's schedule but his own, so I try not to be offended that he doesn't cancel his annual back-to-school party when it ends up being the same night as my dad's funeral.

After all, he's throwing a party on a Monday night. Who

knows where his parents are or if they're even out of town? He's a fifth-year senior and has only two classes—and one of them is ceramics.

The blaring techno hits its chorus and repeats, *"This time, baby, I'll be bulletproof"* all around us. The truth is I don't know why I wanted to come tonight. I hadn't been planning on it, but I couldn't spend another moment in my house watching my mother sleep and Struz play *World of Warcraft* with Jared. And maybe getting drunk, and forgetting how messed up everything is, is exactly what I need.

The first person to come up to me is Ben. He puts a hand on my shoulder and squeezes lightly. "How are you?"

I desperately want to lean into him, but I know as soon as I do I'll start to cry, and I need to be done with all the tears. "I think I could use a drink," I say, and I feel bad, because from the look on his face that's obviously not at all what he expected.

But he recovers easily and says, "Come on, I know where the beers are."

A few days ago, he took me on a more-than-perfect date. We should be reveling in that—smiling and blushing, feeling like we have a secret because we've just shared something other people can't be a part of.

But my dad is dead now.

As we're walking, a hand grabs my arm. "Janelle, can I talk to you?"

"Nope," I say without looking back. I don't need to see her to recognize Kate's voice.

"It's important," she calls after me.

"*That's* shocking." Everything Kate wants is important.

Of course the irony isn't lost on me. It was, after all, Chad

Brandel's house where we had our falling-out. This time I don't plan to end up in some unidentified car. That's why I brought Alex to watch out for me.

I move through the throng of people, even though I don't really know where I'm going anymore. I've lost Ben somehow, but it's probably for the best. He might reconsider how he feels about me with the mood I'm in tonight. I ignore the murmurs of condolences, since they're the last thing I want to hear right now.

At some point, after Alex has abandoned me for Kate, who's talking his ear off somewhere else, I sit down on the sofa with another beer even though the first few haven't done anything to make me forget, and I find myself next to Reid, who's apparently drinking away a few sorrows of his own.

He's sitting on the couch alone except for the slew of empty beer bottles in front of him, and I realize as I sit down next to him that it's the first time I've ever seen him by himself. Unlike Elijah or Ben, he does have other friends. I think he even dated some girl for, like, all of last year or something.

"What's up?" I ask.

He lifts his chin, which I think is a version of hello.

"Why'd you ever want to come back to this place?" he asks, slurring his words.

I look over at Reid, not sure I understand the hostility dripping off them. His Heineken is at his lips, and he's not looking at me, even though I'm the only person he could have been talking to.

"What do you mean?"

"After what happened."

My throat constricts, and I remember waking up in that old

222

Honda Civic that smelled like gym socks. I'd never felt so dirty in my life.

Only that can't be what he's referring to, because no one knows that. No one.

Except whoever did it.

Reid was never in my pool of suspects—not even close. It's like I'm about to overheat, my heart pumping overtime, while the rest of my body is just frozen.

Reid glances over at me. "Elijah and Chad aren't friends by any stretch, but he was here. Elijah pretty much goes where he wants to, invite or not. Ben and I didn't come. I mean, who'd invite *us*, you know? But Elijah called Ben when you showed up. Janelle Tenner at a party like that—he had to rub it in. Ben came to my house and we 'borrowed' my dad's car. We had to come."

My heart feels like it's sinking, bottoming out, and I'm going numb and cold. This is the moment I've been waiting two years for, and now I don't feel ready.

He pauses to gulp down the rest of his beer, then reaches for another one and twists off the top. "You're like gravity to Ben— his own personal gravitational force. He revolves around *you*. It's been that way ever since we got here."

I'm about to ask him what the hell he's talking about, but Reid keeps going. "Only when we got to the party, we couldn't find you anywhere. We were about to leave when we heard Chris Santios spouting off about how Sam Hines had you in the back room."

My mouth dries out, the noise of the party—the voices, the music, everything—all falls away, and every beat of my heart is a drum pounding in my ear.

"We didn't know what was really going on, but it didn't

matter to Ben. It was like he knew—*he just fucking knew*—something wasn't right, and Elijah tried to stop him, but he just shot through the party to that back room, tackled Sam, and started beating the shit out of him."

Sam Hines.

"Elijah tried to grab Ben and pull him back," Reid continues. "We were sure Ben'd kill him—and then all Sam's friends jumped in, and it was Elijah and Ben against half the fucking football team. I grabbed you and went out the window and stuck you in the backseat of my dad's car—because Ben would have wanted that—and then I went back to help them."

Reid's dad's car.

My stomach twists into a knot. I press the palm of my hand to my chest to keep myself from gagging, as my insides turn themselves inside out and upside down. The black hole I'd shoved deep into a cold corner of my heart feels like it's suddenly eating its way out, and if I don't get up, it might explode.

"You were gone when we got out. . . ." Reid seems to realize I've stood up, and he reaches for me. "You didn't know?"

I can't even be bothered to shake my head in response, but it looks like the question was rhetorical anyway. "Elijah and Ben put three of them in the hospital," Reid says. "If the cops hadn't showed up, Ben probably would have killed Sam."

Something behind my eyes is burning, and I'm struggling to remember to keep breathing.

I vaguely remember hearing something during my post-party depression about a fight that got Elijah Palma, Ben Michaels, and Reid Suitor suspended for ten days. Something about Sam Hines, Brian Svetter, and Chris Santios getting beat up badly enough that they ended up in the hospital.

224

Every kickboxing class, every stroke during an ocean swim, every time my feet hit the sand when I was running, all those moments well up inside me, and I straighten my back and take a long, ragged inhale, trying to steady myself.

I turn away. Walking with purpose. Heading straight for the beer pong tables.

"Janelle, you okay?"

I walk right past Alex, ignoring the way he calls after me.

My fingernails are biting into the palms of my hands, and I only have eyes for the beer pong tables, which means I almost run straight into Brooke, who says, "Go home, bitch, no one invited you," but I'm past the point of caring. When I go to move around her, she steps in my way, and I just push her hard enough that she loses her balance and backsteps into Lesley. I don't even slow down when I plow past Kate—Kate, without whom I never would have been at that party. With my right hand, I swipe a half-empty bottle of Bud Light that's been abandoned on a table, and then I'm standing right in front of Sam Hines.

Sam Hines, backup quarterback of the football team, senior class vice president, Lesley Brandon's boyfriend, and would-be rapist.

Nick is on the other side of him, and when he sees me, that smile that used to make me smile back lights up his face. Now it makes me feel sick to my stomach, like bugs are crawling all over me, like I want to vomit all over myself. I can't help hating that he can be friends with these guys.

"J!" he shouts, and moves as if he's going to give me a hug.

But Sam is in his way, and he turns to me, his eyes raking up my body, lingering on my chest. "Hey, Janelle," he slurs.

And he's so preoccupied with checking me out, he doesn't

have a chance to see the beer bottle slam into the side of his face until it's far too late. He loses his balance immediately, and as he falls, I wind up and slam my foot into his balls.

Nick just stands there, staring at me, with his mouth hanging open and his eyes wide.

I want to slap him, to scream at him, to ask how the hell he could be friends with someone like Sam. And I know he couldn't know what Sam did to me—I know he's better than that—but I think I'll still always look at him differently now. Because he'll forever be connected to one of the worst moments of my life.

I open my mouth to say something to him when a strong hand grips my arm and pulls me backward.

I struggle for a second as I'm pulled into someone's arms, until I feel the warmth of his chest behind me and the faint underlying smell of motor oil. I relax, but the venom doesn't leave my voice when I look down at Sam. "If you ever come near me again, so help me God, I'll kill you."

And then Ben is turning me in his arms, and just as I'm sagging and my legs are about to give out, he's lifting me off the ground, curling me into his chest, and carrying me. Elijah and Reid are on either side of him, and I can hear Alex talking to one of them, demanding to know what the hell is going on.

"**H**ow could you not have told me!" I scream at Ben when the five of us are alone and cutting through the soccer fields on the way back to my house.

Ben sticks his hands in his pockets and shrugs, eyes looking down.

"Do you realize I've had no idea what happened that night—for years!"

"Give it a rest, Janelle," Elijah says, grabbing my arm and turning me around. Ben takes a step toward him, but Elijah just laughs. "Dude, I think she can take care of herself." Then he looks at me. "What did you want Ben or any of us to say to you?"

"What's wrong with the truth?"

"Okay," Elijah says. "How about this? Hey, Girl I've Never Met or Talked To, my friend Ben has a thing for you, so he went apeshit when he heard Sam Hines might be having sex with you, and he beat the shit out of him, we all got into a fight, and the cops came and broke shit up, and you weren't where we left you, so we weren't really sure what that meant." He spreads his arms out wide. "How's that? Feel fucking better?"

"You could probably soften that a little," Alex says.

No one says anything, then Reid starts laughing.

Ben pushes him, and he says, "What? He's right."

They're both right, I guess. But I am too. I needed to know what happened. I shouldn't have had to wait like this. Of course, things could have been worse.

Alex looks at me and tilts his head in the direction of my house, and I turn to Elijah and offer him my hand. "Thanks."

His eyes narrow. "For what?"

"For beating the shit out of them for me."

"I aim to please." He snorts as a smile breaks across his face, and he reaches out and shakes my hand. "You know, Tenner, I might not like you that much, but I sure as hell respect you after that number you did on Hines tonight."

I turn to Reid, but he's so drunk he's looking a little like he might hurl, and I doubt he's going to remember much from tonight. Then I turn to Ben.

"Janelle, I'm sorry, I—"

I shake my head. "Let's talk about it tomorrow."

And as Alex and I move to walk away, Ben reaches out and squeezes my hand, and neither one of us lets go as we move in opposite directions, until the last possible moment.

That's one mystery solved. The mystery I never told my dad about. Guilt squeezes its way inside my chest and just throbs there. It was the only secret I ever kept from him. At least, the only important one.

"You okay?" Alex asks.

I glance over at him. He's flushed, but he looks relieved. This secret was a weight on him. And he bore it for me, because I needed him to.

I nod, even though things are far from okay. Because this time Alex needs me to. I can't keep asking him to pull me back from the cliff, and he shouldn't have to keep worrying that I'm going to fall.

I wake up hung over and a little depressed and decide I deserve a day off from school. Jared isn't hung over, but he decides to follow my lead and I let him. We lie on the couch most of the morning, watching the first season of *The X-Files*.

Which is exactly where I am when the doorbell rings.

I look at Jared and he looks at me. "I think the *older* sibling has to get the door," he says.

"Shocking," I say as I get up off the couch and go to the front door.

It's Kate.

By the way she's dressed, she's obviously just cutting class and not taking the day off, and even though I'm tempted to shut the door in her face and go back to the couch, I lean into the doorway and ask, "Are you lost?"

"No," she says, shaking her head, and despite how put together she looks, underneath all the makeup, I can see how glassy her eyes are. "J, I'm so sorry about your dad."

"I am too, but you're the last person I want to talk about him with," I say.

She opens her mouth to respond and then closes it. "Look, I had to talk to you," she says, and I must be in a charitable mood because I wave a hand for her to continue. "I didn't know."

"Didn't know what?"

"I didn't know the beer had been roofied until after the party," she says. "Brooke gave it to me to give to you and said it would liven you up, and—"

"And what? Kate, even if you didn't know before, you knew after." I shake my head. "Sorry, you're not going to get absolution from me. You chose your friends, you have to live with it."

She opens her mouth and looks like she might start pleading with me, but then her face changes. It sets, and I see the hard line of her jaw. "Fine. How long are you going to be keeping shit at my pool house?"

"I'll have my shit out of there by the end of the day," I say, this time not holding back when I want to slam the door in her face.

I grab my cell phone and call Alex. He's in class, so it goes to voice mail, but he calls me back a few minutes later.

"Meet me at the UCSD library after school again?" I say when I answer. I have a renewed sense of purpose now.

"Why, what's up?" he asks.

"Because if we were right about the bioterrorism angle, we have nine days before our own faces might be melting off."

We sit in our soundproof cube, poring over my dad's hard-copy files and his laptop for two hours. I try not to think about Ben, about last night, or about anything but this case. I need to figure it out, for my dad. But we're ready to give up.

And then I find something.

It's pure luck, but while I'm trying to root through my dad's email, someone replies to him. And it's exactly what I need to see.

"Alex . . . ," I breathe.

He leans over to look at the laptop and the brand-new email. It's from a G. Lickenbrock with the Department of Homeland Security.

James,

After we spoke last Friday, I put a trace on all the credit cards we had associated with Mike Cooper. This morning we got a hit on one of them. Two charges—at Unique Pawnbrokers

(3039 University Ave.) and Mira Mesa Pool
(8251 Mira Mesa Blvd.). When you bring the
bastard in, call me.

G

"A pawnshop and a pool store?" Alex asks.

I feel sick to my stomach. Because I know exactly what
you can buy at a pawnshop and a pool supply store if you're a
bioterrorist. "Pawnshops sell guns and bullets," I say to Alex.
"And pool supply stores sell chemicals."

He nods. "Should have seen that coming."

Mike Cooper is our first solid lead. Whoever he is, my dad
was interested in him, which means he could be important.

But it's more than that. My dad organized his emails with
preset filters so important ones came in already labeled. This
new email is labeled **MULDER**. And I'm betting if I follow this
one back to the folder, I'll find more emails about the case.

Alex rolls his eyes. He's never been an *X-Files* fan. "What do
the other ones say?"

I scroll down to last Friday, which G from Homeland Security referenced, and I find a thread of emails between the two
of them, beginning with the first one my dad sent to G. The
subject is **PERSON OF INTEREST.**

I open up the first email and skim it quickly. My dad cuts to
the chase right away. He's attaching a picture of a guy who's a
person of interest in a case. He can't identify the guy in any of
his databases; could Homeland Security do Facial Recognition
and let him know if they find anything?

I click on the attachment.

"Is that him?" Alex asks.

I shake my head. "I don't know yet, but look at this," I say, clicking to the next email, while we wait for the picture to download. My dad didn't just send this email to G and Homeland Security. He literally sent hundreds of emails out to various counterintelligence agents and other agency contacts in different cities. Every email says the same thing—it all revolves around this one guy.

Alex leans in when the picture finishes loading. It's grainy and black and white, and it looks like it might be a still shot from a security camera outside of a gas station. It looks like there's a black Honda Accord and a gas pump in the background. But I wouldn't be able to tell which gas station unless I was standing wherever this camera is, taking in everything at the same angle— and maybe not even then.

The guy himself is more distinguishable. He's male, white, and probably between five feet nine and six feet two. He looks like he's in his mid- to late thirties, still fit with broad shoulders, brown hair that's cropped close to his head, and no facial hair. He has the look of someone who's former or current military. Unfortunately, I can't tell if he has any tattoos or piercings from the picture.

"Great, so he looks pretty average. Shouldn't be hard to find him," Alex says. "What's Lickenbrock say?"

Agent G. Lickenbrock from Homeland Security had replied less than an hour after my dad's original email.

James Tenner,

Haven't talked to you since that stint out in L.A.

234

and you can't even ask how I've been. I'd say
I'm surprised. . . .

The guy in your picture: alias Mike Cooper,
real identity unknown. The case file's attached,
call me if you want details.

G

"The case file is from 2010 regarding the deaths of two
people, identities unconfirmed, as well as a missing person,
suspected dead, where Mike Cooper, age thirty-six, was their main
suspect. Until he went off the grid before they could gather enough
evidence to take him into custody. When I open the picture on
Cooper's driver's license, I'm staring at the same guy as the one in
my dad's grainy gas station picture. There's no mistaking it.

Now we have a more identifiable picture.

"Do you have the backup drive?" Alex hands it to me
before I've even finished the sentence, and I plug it in and start
downloading all these emails and the files on this guy. "Are there
color printers here?"

"Probably, but J—"

"We need to print a nice copy of this picture and go over to
the pool supply store and the pawnshop. We might be able to get
someone who remembers talking to Mike Cooper," I say. "And
we should keep an eye on the gas stations between those two
stores. With all three of them in a similar area, it's likely that he's
living or staying somewhere nearby."

"Janelle."

I glance up at Alex and stifle a groan. He's wearing his serious face, and whatever he's about to say, it's going to be delivered in the form of a lecture.

"We should go to Struz with this," he says.

I shake my head. I'm not ready to go to Struz with anything.

"I'm serious," Alex continues. "You found a lot more than I thought we would today, and I'm not saying you don't know what you're doing. You're good at this, but . . ."

"But what, Alex?"

"We're in over our heads, you have to know that. We don't even really know what the UIED is."

I do know that. We don't even know what we're looking for. I might be ignoring it, but I do know. It's more than just the fact that I don't have credentials or access to an FBI database. It would be easier, sure. I could walk into Mira Mesa Pool, throw my ID on the counter, and demand to see exactly what alias Mike Cooper bought. But would that really solve anything?

We might be looking at the end of the world—the end of existence—and I'm running around playing teen detective.

"So I give all this to Struz, and then what?"

"I don't know," Alex says. "Maybe he'd investigate it?"

"Thanks for that—I mean, then what for us?" I ask, pulling my hair back into a ponytail. "Think about it, Alex, do you really just want to sit around and watch the clock count down? I can't do that."

Because that's the truth. If something big is coming, I can't just sit and wait for it. I need to be doing something active to stop it.

Alex nods. "Okay, but if we're going to do this, you have to at least make sure that Struz and the FBI have found these leads too."

"I'm sure they have someone going through my dad's emails," I say, because it's true, though a part of me just dreads any phone call to Struz that's going to clue him in to what we're doing. I know he'll be mad that I'm "playing FBI," that he'll want me to let him take care of it, and that he'll pretend he doesn't understand why I can't.

"But you know your dad better than anyone else."

He has a point. "Fine. I'll call, but you find the color printer for this picture."

"Yes, drill sergeant," Alex says, grabbing the backup drive.

I pick up my cell phone and dial Struz.

And hope we've found everything useful on this laptop and in my dad's email, because as soon as Struz realizes I have it, those passwords will get wiped.

09:00:52:06

I doubt the guy in the pool supply store believed my story about my boss sending me to buy chemicals and forgetting which ones I was supposed to get, but he told me anyway.

Mike Cooper bought several gallons of two different kinds of chlorine.

I buy the smallest size of each one, since he at least played along with my lie. I probably know a few people who have a pool, and I can donate it to them.

As he rings me up, he says, "Make sure you don't mix them. These are two different kinds of chlorine, and they explode when mixed. You could end up blind, or worse."

I have less luck at the pawnshop.

That is to say: none.

Not only is the guy unwilling to buy my bullshit story, he threatens to call the cops unless we leave. I don't actually think he'll do it, but I'm not willing to call his bluff either.

"Friendly guy," Alex says when we get in the car. "Maybe we'll have better luck on our gas station scavenger hunt."

"That implies we're looking for something at the gas station. We're just looking for the *right* gas station."

Alex shrugs, and we pull out of the parking lot onto University Avenue. "Hey, think that guy from the pawnshop could be in on it?"

"I doubt it," I say with a yawn. I haven't slept through the night since I came home and found Struz on the doorstep. "He seemed more like he was just an irritable guy tired of taking shit than a terrorist."

Alex laughs for a few seconds before his face sobers. "But really, J, how do we know what a terrorist looks like?"

The obvious answer: We don't.

For some reason I decide to bargain with Struz when he shows up at the house this time. Probably because trying to keep him out of the house didn't work, and now I don't have any other options.

"Where's the laptop, J?" he asks.

"What will you give me for it?"

"I'm serious, the director has been riding my ass about how you managed to hack in," he says. "I could arrest you."

I hold out my arms as if I'm ready to be led away. Struz wouldn't arrest me.

"I can go through this whole house and turn it upside down, is that what you want?"

"Now, see, that's the right question," I say, dropping my hands at my sides. "Because what I want is to know details about my dad's death, and if you can give them to me, I might be able to find my dad's laptop."

"This isn't up for debate—"

"Janelle, who is it?" my mother says, and both Struz and I jump at the sound of her voice. She's always in the back of my mind, but sometimes I forget that she's not always at one extreme or the other.

"Elaine, it's me. It's Ryan," he says.

My mother comes into view, wearing a tank top and a pair of my father's pajama pants. If it's possible, it looks like she's lost weight since my dad died.

"Hi, Ryan, are you going to stay for dinner?" she asks, but she doesn't wait for his answer. Instead she turns to me and says, "I was thinking burgers on the grill, and maybe corn on the cob would be nice. Do we have that?"

"Yeah, I think we still have some from the last time I ran to Wiedners. If not, I can always get more."

She nods and heads into the kitchen.

We both wait for a second before Struz folds his arms across his chest. "Where were we?"

"You're welcome to turn the house upside down," I say. "I can assure you, there's no laptop here."

"I can search Alex's house too. You—"

"Can you? Without a warrant? Have you met Annabeth Trechter?"

From the other room my mom yells, "You don't have to stand in the doorway, Ryan. Even though James isn't here, you're always welcome in our house."

Struz breaks into a smile and swipes a hand back and forth, ruffling his hair. "You've thought of everything, haven't you, J-baby?" Then he looks me directly in the eye. I have a split second to be afraid of what he's going to say, and then he says it. "You're just like him."

My whole face tingles, and I clench my jaw to keep it from quivering, but I can't stop my eyes from watering.

241

Because actually I haven't thought of everything. Even if I am just like him. The laptop is in the Jeep, which is currently unlocked in my driveway, but I don't tell Struz that. "I just want to know the details."

Sighing, Struz nods to the kitchen, because keeping an eye on my mom is a good idea. I follow him. My mother is rooting through the fridge, and I assume she'll tell me if she doesn't have everything she wants.

Struz drops into a kitchen chair and gestures for me to do the same.

I do.

He deliberately takes his time emptying his pockets and laying his car keys, cell phone, and pack of Marlboros on the table. I'm tempted to give him hell about the fact that he's smoking again, since it took him three tries to quit a couple of years ago, but I figure he deserves a break.

Struz keeps his voice low, but I'm not worried about my mom hearing. She might be lucid right now, but she's not exactly interested in what we're doing. "He'd been investigating a couple of leads on his own—you know how he is. He told me he was heading out to Park Village to check something out around lunchtime."

"I know all this." I add, "And I know he took one in the arm and two in the chest."

Struz doesn't seem surprised. "We haven't found the exact crime scene—his body was dumped in the canyons. He was either set up and walked into a trap or he misjudged whoever killed him."

I want to deny it and say my dad wouldn't have done either of those things. Instead I ask, "Why?"

242

"There's nothing to suggest he ever drew his gun," Struz says, his voice shaking slightly on the last word.

I let that digest for a minute, because that doesn't seem like my dad at all. True, he wasn't the kind of guy who rushed into situations guns blazing, but he was smart and he'd been doing this job for years.

Maybe he thought he was meeting a friend? It's possible, though I don't know where alias Mike Cooper fits into that.

I stand up and try to clear my head. "Have there been any more bodies?"

Struz rubs his temples. "Not since two days ago, when we found one in Ocean Beach, in a phone booth that I swear is straight out of the seventies."

"The phone booth?"

He shakes his head and reaches for the cigarettes, but I lean forward and bat them out of the way. "Not in this house."

Struz smiles—that's what my dad used to say whenever he tried to smoke here. "J, I shit you not, I don't drive around much in OB, but on every canvass, people swore up and down they'd never seen that phone booth."

"So where did it come from?"

He gives an exaggerated shrug, which looks a little cartoonish since he's so tall, and I want to press him more, but he's jittery and obviously on edge, and I get the sense he's worried that we're running out of time.

"I'll procure you the laptop, as I seem to remember now where it is," I say.

Struz nods and stands up, thinking he's won, but as soon as he turns his back, I grab the cigarettes and his cell phone and take them with me. While I retrieve the laptop—and not the files—I scroll through his contacts and find Barclay's number, then repeat it to myself over and over again while I break each one of Struz's cigarettes in half and put them back in the pack.

Number memorized and cigarettes broken, I head back into the house. I lay all three on the table, and Struz turns to see me do it. And groans as he notices the cigarettes aren't in the same place as before.

"Please tell me you left me at least one," he says.

"Will you stay here for a few hours and watch this while I run out?" I gesture toward the meal my mother seems to be planning.

He nods. "Yeah, sure, I can do that."

I grab my keys and head for the door. Because I have to put those files somewhere else before Struz realizes exactly what I have.

And maybe because I want an excuse to see him, I'm thinking I can ask Ben to hide them for me.

08:18:56:47

I drive aimlessly through Rancho Peñasquitos for about ten minutes before heading to Ben's. I'll talk to him about everything that happened when we were freshmen—if there's anything even left to talk about. And then I'll confront him about what he hasn't been telling me about the accident. Coming off the whole "you didn't tell me the truth before" conversation, I think he'll confess whatever he's got going on.

At least, I'm hoping he will.

And it might be nothing. Maybe Elijah is growing weed in his basement or something. I wouldn't exactly put it past him.

Then I'll figure out where I can keep the files. If I sort things out with Ben, keeping them at his house makes a lot of sense. Struz doesn't even know who he is.

But I don't have Ben's phone number, and it takes Alex those ten minutes to get me an address up on Black Mountain Road, north of school and no phone number. I'll just show up unannounced—apparently, I'm like that.

When I do, I knock on the door, wearing the backpack on both shoulders, hoping it will pass to unobservant parents as a school bag. But a little girl who's about eight answers the door. She's fair-skinned with bright red hair, and she looks so little like Ben that for a minute I wonder if I have the wrong house.

"Hey, is your brother or your parents here?" I ask in my best dealing-with-little-children voice, which isn't that good at all.

"I don't have a brother and my parents are dead," she says.

My pulse throbs more forcefully throughout my body, and the word "dead" seems to echo between us.

Then I see a woman in her forties, who looks a lot like she could be a mother, coming toward us out of the kitchen.

"Cassie," she scolds. "How many times have I told you to be respectful?"

"You're not my mother," Cassie says, her voice pitched close to a yell, before she turns and runs up the stairs.

The woman—Mrs. Michaels?—looks at me. "I'm sorry about that. Cassie's new to foster care, and she hasn't quite adjusted. How can I help you?"

"I was wondering if Ben was here? I have a couple homework questions I was hoping he could help me with," I manage to spit out, though I want to ask her if Ben is in foster care too. I feel stupid and hurt that I didn't know that. Not even a week ago, I told myself I wanted to know him better. I'm embarrassed at how self-absorbed I must be to not know something this basic yet important about his life. And I can't help wishing he'd told me.

"Oh sure," she says, opening the door wider and pointing me in the right direction. "He and his friends are downstairs."

Most houses in California don't have basements—or at least most of the ones that I've been in—so I find them unnaturally creepy.

I suppress a shudder as I shut the door behind me and begin the descent into a cooler, damper, and darker room than the rest of the house. But I make it only two steps when I recognize Ben's voice over the alternative music.

"Eli, people are dead," he says.

That stops my forward movement, and I suck in a breath. I didn't expect to hear something like that.

People are dead.

This guy, whose lips fit perfectly against mine, who makes me feel warm and short of breath whenever he smiles at me, he knows *people are dead*.

I crouch where I am, steady my balance, and slow my breathing so they don't know I'm here before I'm ready for them to know.

"I thought we established that it's not your fault," Elijah says. "You didn't fucking kill them."

"No, I didn't mean to kill them. That doesn't mean it's not my fault."

"Ben, we don't know if you're responsible," Reid says.

"What do you mean, 'we don't know'?" Elijah says. "We *know* he's not responsible."

"I'm just saying that correlation doesn't mean causation. Unless you actually found some link between them—"

"What the fuck does that even mean? Stop throwing scientific terms at us," Elijah says. "Ben, none of this was your fault."

"The whole thing was my fault," Ben says. "We wouldn't be here, we wouldn't be dealing with any of this if it wasn't for me."

"That's not fucking true—"

"It doesn't matter. This isn't a school science experiment. It's people. Lives," Ben says, his voice rising. "I told you I'm done until I figure out how to do it without hurting anyone."

"But we're still fucking here!" Elijah yells, and there's a crash of things, possibly heavy things, falling and possibly breaking.

My heart rate spikes. I can feel each pulse in the tips of my fingers, and I'm too warm. Sweat is beading at the back of my neck.

"He's right, we've—"

"You think I want to be here any more than you do?" Ben says. "But did you see the burns on those bodies? They didn't even look human. I'm not going to do that to more people."

Bodies. Burns. *They didn't even look human.*

08:18:50:33

Air leaves my lungs. Blood stops moving in my veins. And for a minute, it feels like life itself just got sucked out of this room. My vision is blurry, like I can't focus on anything, and the only thing I can hear is white noise.

I look up, my eyes watering, and open my mouth, hoping I won't suffocate from shock.

And then the earth starts spinning again. Life un-pauses, and the world around me rushes back in.

From the sounds of their voices, when I get to the bottom of the stairs, they'll be to my left—all three of them. Each of them outweighs me and could easily take me down if it came to hand-to-hand combat. And I still don't know what kind of freaky shit Ben can do.

But I can't listen anymore.

Carefully, I slide the backpack off my back and retrieve the Glock 22. And I take a deep breath, hoping I can remember everything my father ever told me about advancing on a potentially hostile target.

I'll have the element of surprise on my side—and a gun.

Assuming there isn't another person down there and there aren't a bunch of assault rifles hanging on the wall—or something worse—I should have the upper hand.

Bodies. Burns. *They didn't even look human.*

It's too obvious. I know exactly what they're talking about. And it's about time, because I know everything else.

08:18:48:53

I don't rush in. Instead I go slowly, each step matching my even breaths and the steady pounding of my heart. I hold the Glock with two hands, arms straight out but slightly bent at the elbows—relaxed but secure.

When I get to the bottom of the stairs, I point the gun in their direction and say, "Get your hands up!" Then I absorb the details. All three of them are somewhere between five and seven feet away from me, and the unfinished basement offers a few household items as potential weapons, but nothing that will get me from a distance. "Hands up, right now," I add, trying not to pay attention to how hard my hands want to shake.

"Again? You've gotta be fucking kidding me," Elijah says, throwing his arms out wide, though I don't think for a second he's serious.

Reid has his arms up, but he's looking to Elijah for cues. "I told you she heard us."

Ben is the only one who doesn't listen right away. And at first glance I think he's planning to try to talk me out of something, but when I get a closer look at his face, I can see his eyes look

251

pained. He opens his mouth as if he's going to say something, but nothing comes out.

I train the gun back on Elijah, and he smiles at me. "What's your plan, Tenner?"

What's my plan—that's a good question. I don't entirely have one, but I do know that I need to stay calm and in control.

There isn't a gun rack on the wall. In fact there's not much of anything down here. An old tattered carpet, an end table with a tiny TV and a small stereo, a shelf of books and DVDs, most of which are scattered on the floor along with the shards of what might have been a vase, and a worn, tan-colored couch that's sagging in the middle.

I nod toward the couch. "Sit down."

As they move, I circle around, making sure to keep my distance. If I get close enough for Elijah to reach out and go for the gun, it's all over.

"Janelle," Ben says, his voice hoarse.

"Don't." My own voice is harsher than I intended. It has to be. I can't for a second let them see weakness, and right now any potential feelings I have for Ben are just that.

Elijah turns. "You really know how to use that thing?" he asks, taking a step forward. "I don't know if you have it in you."

This is it.

I take a step forward too—still with enough distance—and look down the sights of the barrel to stare him dead in the eyes. I summon all the anger and frustration that have been following me around for the past few days, and I let them pour out. "My dad was a decorated war veteran and the head of counterintelligence for the San Diego office of the FBI. Now he's dead. You think I don't have it in me? I think that's a big gamble you don't want to take."

It's not the response Elijah expected. He believes me, and as he backs away I can see it in his eyes.

When all three of them are on the couch, I lean against the wall across from them, steadying myself before my arms begin to shake. And then I take a deep breath.

"Keep your hands where I can see them," I say, nodding to Reid, who then folds them in his lap. "Now I don't care who tells me what, but I want to know everything—the bodies, the radiation burns, and your part in it."

"And if we don't know what you're talking about?" Elijah asks.

That would be a shame, since I just played my hand. If they don't tell me anything, I've lost.

Instead I say, "I'm not leaving here until I know what you're hiding." And I don't have to fake the desperation. My eyes flick to Ben. "I need to know."

My voice shakes on the last word. I need to know what the hell they're into. My dad is dead, and I'm going to solve that, and a couple of stoner punks from my high school aren't going to get in the way—even if they are more than I thought they were.

"I need to know," I say again, steadying the gun.

All that follows is the music, the sound of my pulse in my ears, and my own ragged breathing.

Then Elijah stands up. "Fuck this, she's not going to shoot us."

I don't wait for him to finish. I'm talking over him. "You have no idea what I'm capable—"

We both talk over each other, and I'm not sure what's going to happen next. I just know that I'm hyperaware of the air filling my lungs, and the way my hands are starting to feel slick with sweat.

But I don't know what else Elijah says, because Ben jumps up and yells, "Stop!"

He's loud enough that we do. We both shut up and turn to glance at him.

When his hands rake through his hair and grab onto the ends, I know I've gotten through and that the wall of secrecy is about to break down—or at least, a few more bricks are going to come loose.

"This isn't easy. Are you sure you want to know?" he asks.

"You can't be fucking serious!" Elijah says.

Ben turns on him. "I told you we'd do things my way. Just sit down and shut up."

For a moment, looking at the two of them—two guys who have obviously been friends forever—a twinge of guilt worms its way through my insides. I've gotten in so over my head.

But whatever Elijah's objections are, he throws himself onto the couch with a dramatic sigh.

"You're just going to let him tell her?" Reid says, and the way he says it—like I don't even deserve a second of their time—makes me want to punch him.

Elijah says nothing, and I look at Ben, this guy with deep-set eyes I can't read, who surprises and challenges me, and at the same time makes me weak in the knees. I swallow down the sick feeling of betrayal—whatever his involvement in this is, this is about more than him keeping secrets from me.

People are dead—my father is dead. And we're eight days from the crazy-ass countdown to whatever it is.

"Yes," I answer, keeping my voice even. "Everything. I want

to know what you know."

Ben takes a deep breath, his face lined with worry. "Elijah, Reid, and I. We're not from around here."

"Not from around here?" I'm not sure what that means or how it plays into what they know about the radiation. "All three of you—where are you from?"

"Somewhere else."

"Wow, thanks for the specifics," I say. "Care to be less vague?"

Ben wipes a hand over his face and pinches the bridge of his nose. "We're from another universe."

"Another universe?" I'm doing that thing again where I repeat things I hear—like I'm either a moron or hard of hearing. So I clarify. "What do you mean by 'another universe'?"

"Like another fucking world," Elijah says.

I don't know what I expected. But it wasn't this.

08:18:40:32

"We were born in a universe like this one, but . . . different," Ben says.

"So you're saying you're an alien?" My voice sounds incredulous.

"No." Ben shakes his head with a smile, but then he shrugs. "Well, maybe. We weren't born here on *this* earth, but we're human—like you." He pauses. "Seriously, I checked in a science lab in middle school."

That sounds like him.

"And we didn't come through space or anything like that. We came from an alternate universe through some kind of wormhole."

I'm trying to wrap my mind around that, but I still don't know what it *means*. Sure I've seen plenty of bad sci-fi movies, but that stuff is supposed to be fake—as in, not actually possible. Maybe the three of them have done too many drugs.

"That's ridiculous," I say, because I need to say something. I can't just believe this at face value. "Travel through wormholes is impossible—it violates every natural law of physics."

"I thought so too. We all did," he says, waving at Elijah and Reid. "We didn't grow up believing in this shit, trust me." Ben takes a deep breath and a few steps toward me. "Okay, so the theory of metaverse says there isn't one universe, but rather—many. A multiverse. There could be hundreds or thousands of different universes. This is one. We're actually from one of those other universes."

"I still don't buy it." They could be making this up to avoid telling me what's really going on. "If it's true, prove it."

"Prove it?" Ben asks. Then he shakes his head. "I can't, I—"

Elijah makes a disgusted noise. "You've seen what Ben can do—you're alive because of it—isn't that enough proof for you?"

I look at Ben, and he nods. "The things I can do, it's because I'm—because we're—from somewhere else."

I ignore the groan that comes from Reid's direction and plow forward. "And Reid and Elijah—they can do the things you can do?"

He shakes his head, and I breathe a little easier. "No, I mean, sort of. They can, but not like me."

Not exactly the vote of confidence I wanted.

Ben fidgets, and I want to jump in and ask what the hell he means, but I force myself to wait.

"Reid can manipulate molecular structure like I can, but he doesn't concentrate or something, and it only works sometimes. And Elijah can only seem to do anything when he's really emotional. Partly because he drinks too much."

"Whatever, I can concentrate just fine," Reid throws in.

Wow. I'm not sure what to say to that.

I bring my hands together to keep them from shaking. "Okay, so let's say I go with this. If you're from a parallel world, does that mean you each have a double who lives here?" I ask. The thought of two Elijah Palmas on one earth might make me hurl.

"No," Ben says. "I mean, I suppose there could be alternate versions of each of us in different universes, but who knows? I've never seen another me, or another one of them." He points to Reid and Elijah. "Within a multiverse, all the different universes, they're not necessarily parallel, though the technology in some of them would be similar. And same with the structure of cities and other things. One theory is that all the universes started parallel, but when different people in the different universes made different choices, things grew outward differently. And now the differences are limitless."

"Yeah, I've heard the theory."

"Right," Ben says. "So technically we could have doubles on some of the worlds, but it's actually pretty unlikely. And if we have doubles here, we've never met them."

I take a deep breath. As much as I want to call bullshit, I *have* seen what Ben can do, and I already know there's a lot about the world—or worlds—out there that I don't understand.

"Okay, so you're from another world, what else?"

"So each world," Ben says, his voice sounding strained. "They're supposed to be completely independent of one another, you know?"

Reid says, "Crossing over has ill effects."

"Ill effects . . . ," I say, turning back to Ben. "Like turning into someone who can bring people back from the dead."

A bitter laugh comes from Elijah. "So you are more than just book smart."

"But it's more than just that," Ben says. "Crossing over . . .

we were lucky. Lately, anyone who's crossed over has ended up dead."

Ended up dead. Crossed over. Unidentified people.

This shouldn't make sense—it shouldn't fit.

But it does.

"From radiation poisoning," I whisper.

Ben nods and looks down at his feet. "Not a good way to go."

"Wait," I continue. My body feels cold and weak now that the adrenaline has fled. If I believe them—*if*—then I'm in even more over my head than I'd thought. I don't know how I'll ever make sense of this case if it's this far outside my scope of understanding. "How did you cross over?"

All three of them look at me, and I'd be an idiot to not notice how much Elijah and Reid don't want Ben to tell me.

But he will.

I can see it in his eyes—he wants me to know.

Ben asks me to put down the gun. I don't want to. I know it can't protect me from anything I'm about to hear, and I feel light-headed and a little sick to my stomach. But I remind myself it's not even loaded—my dad always said never to point a loaded gun at someone unless you plan on pulling the trigger, and Elijah was right. No matter what happened, I wasn't going to shoot anyone.

I put the gun on the table.

And Ben tells me everything.

This is how it happened:

Ben and Reid have birthdays less than a week apart. When they were turning ten, Ben's mom and Reid's dad, who both worked together in a government-funded lab, decided to throw them a joint birthday party.

Elijah came.

The party was at Reid's house. They played games, ate cake, opened presents, and had a video-game tournament. It should have been perfect.

Only once Elijah got knocked out of the tournament, he was bored. He wanted to play something else, and Reid was pretty sure there were some old games down in the basement. Ben and another boy went with them.

There *were* board games in the basement, but nothing exciting. But there was more than that. There was a locked door.

And once Elijah discovered the locked door, he had to know what was behind it.

It was Reid's father's home lab. It was where he kept all his failed experiments—the ones the government wasn't funding anymore, but he wasn't ready to let go.

Between the four of them, they managed to pick the lock.

They found weird-looking laser guns that didn't actually shoot, a computer with some kind of card game, and a table full of different multicolored liquid chemicals. And they found something that looked like a helmet made of different wires that all hooked up to a mini television. The other boy tried it on, and Elijah turned on the TV and pressed several buttons to see what it did. The TV just showed white noise, but the helmet gave the boy a shock and made his hair stand on end.

Which was funny. Funny enough that Elijah wanted to try. Then Reid, and finally Ben. They took turns making their hair stand on end and laughing at one another. Until Elijah declared he was thirsty and ready for something new.

Reid grabbed some kind of weird juice from the lab-room fridge, and they all split it. It tasted bitter and strange and somehow it made them even more thirsty. They drank it until it was gone, then started to head upstairs.

Only on the way, Ben found something half-covered and discarded in a corner. It looked like an engine. He called the others over and began inspecting it. At first it wouldn't start. But that didn't stop them. Reid found what looked like his father's notes, and each of the four boys looked through a few of the pages. Ben fooled with the engine while Reid read random comments, until eventually Elijah had enough, and he reached in and pressed two of the open wires in the ignition together, and it flared to life.

The motor connected to a laser beam, and a huge liquid circle manifested itself in the air. Right in front of them. Double their height, and even though it looked black inside, it rippled, like waves, and cold air emanated from it. Elijah dared someone to touch it, but no one would. So they started daring one another, then shoving one another.

Until Ben tripped.

Elijah tried to grab him, but they both fell into the circle. And Reid dove in after them. They're all pretty sure the fourth boy stayed behind, but they don't know. They just know they never saw him again.

And then they were underwater—in the ocean. Reid and Elijah swam to the surface and then to shore, but Ben seemed to flounder. He knew how to swim. But somehow he just couldn't. He hit his head on something and flailed around, trying to figure out which way was up, until he realized he was going to drown.

Then a girl he thought at first was an angel—me—reached in and saved him. And I pulled him to the surface.

For the past seven years, the three of them have been trying to piece together exactly what happened and figure out a way to get back home. They had three pages of Reid's father's notes on the machine that opened the portal. It explained what he wanted the machine to do—open a wormhole to another dimension. It had a diagram of the machine, so they had an idea of what they needed to create a new one. But they were missing so much. Even with his notes, it was impossible to get all the parts they needed to replicate it. So they read everything they could find on string theory, quantum physics, and wormholes, and they kept trying.

Six months ago Ben and Elijah got into a fight. Elijah tried to use his powers on Ben—he tried to cut Ben by breaking apart the molecules in his body, destroying them instead of healing— but Ben fought back, and when their powers combined, they accidentally had a breakthrough—they opened a small, unstable portal that flickered and disappeared. But they instantly recognized what it was. How could they ever forget what a portal looked like?

Fight forgotten, they worked together with Reid and changed the molecules of the air in front of them. And they opened another portal. Just like every other aspect of their abilities, it was a matter of concentrating—and practicing. But how could they know if it was the right portal—the one that would take them home? They couldn't.

They still don't.

They've opened hundreds of portals in the past six months. At first they could only do it when two or all three of them were concentrating on it together, though now Ben can do it alone. But they're no closer to getting home. There are possibly thousands of Earths—they have no way to know where they'll end up this time if they go through.

And now, it's worse. Twice when Ben's opened a portal, he's accidentally brought someone through, and they've died. Of radiation poisoning.

The first body they thought was a freak accident. Ben waited a few weeks before opening another portal, and that time it was fine. He even opened several more without any problems. Elijah tried to convince them to go through one. If it wasn't their world, they knew how to open the portals now. They'd just keep opening them until they made their way home.

Of course, they didn't know how many universes there were—which meant who knew how long it would take them to get home. So Ben convinced him to wait.

The second body was worse.

As I'm waiting for Ben to keep going, I'm struck with a realization that makes me want to throw up. I was right to question whether Ben was dangerous. More than right. Ben, Reid, Elijah—all three of them are dangerous. It doesn't even matter that I have a gun.

Anyone who can cause a heart to restart like Ben did for me—anyone who can do that can also cause a heart to stop.

If the cops hadn't showed up, Ben probably would have killed him. Reid said that to me. It hadn't occurred to me at the time to think exactly *how* Ben would have killed Sam. But I get it now.

"I thought we should try to replicate opening the portal as close as we could to where we came through," Ben says.

"But it's not like we could go out to the middle of the fucking ocean," Elijah adds.

I feel sick. I can't stop thinking of all the bodies. Burned from radiation beyond recognition. The family in that house.

"There's that empty land across from Torrey Pines Beach," Ben continues. He looks like he's forcing himself to keep going—his jaw is tight, and he won't look me in the eyes. "It was the closest we could get without being seen. So I started to open a portal there, but almost immediately something came barreling through."

My heart pounds.

"What?" I ask, my voice barely a whisper.

"A pickup truck," Ben says.

"Fucking full speed too," Elijah adds.

My John Doe in his 1997 Velociadad. And there I was, in the wrong place at the wrong moment.

08:18:29:47

"I stopped after that," Ben says.

For some reason I look at Elijah. It's not that I trust him to tell me the truth more than Ben. I just know he won't soften anything.

He shrugs. "He did."

"I'm not going to open any more portals until we can figure out how to get everything working," Ben adds. "It's more than just knowing where we're going. I'm not sure what we did back then. I'm not sure why we could come through the portal then, but now it's killing people. I need to know how we can get back through without it killing us."

I nod, because that makes sense. As much as any of this makes sense.

I look at Ben's face, but his eyes are downcast, and I can't make him look at me. Seven years. He's been here, bouncing around foster homes for seven years. I can't imagine what that must have been like—especially when he was just a kid. He must have been so scared. *And alone. And homesick.* My chest aches with a hollowness that reminds me of my own loss, and my throat feels tight.

My fingers are shaking, so to cover it up, I start cracking my knuckles, and I think of how this changes what I know.

"But what about the other bodies?"

"What other bodies?" Ben asks.

"Stay here," I say before I run up to grab the backpack. I call Alex and tell him to figure out how to escape his mom and get over here. He starts to argue, but when I tell him we were wrong about the virus and I've found a game-changer, he shuts up, and I know he'll get out of his house even if he has to climb through a window.

Then I head back downstairs. I open up all the files and pass them around, and this time it's my turn. I tell them everything. The unidentified bodies my dad's unit was investigating, the house that had to be burned down in case there were any residual effects, the unidentified improvised explosive device the FBI found. Which of course they want to know more about. I give them my speculation, because it's all I've got.

I even tell them about Alex's and my theory about the virus and alias Mike Cooper and the emails Dad got about him.

Alex shows up somewhere in the middle of my explanation and sits down. He doesn't ask any questions, but at one point, I turn to him and give an ultra-abbreviated version of the whole other-universe thing. It comes across a little crazy, something like *All three of them are from some kind of alternate universe, not a parallel world, but something like that. They've been trying to get home and accidentally bringing people through from another universe. Those people are the ones dying of radiation.*

I say this like I totally believe it, but Alex still calls bullshit. "You can't believe this," he says to me. "This is crazy."

I open my mouth to explain more, but Ben says, "Alex, here," and he grabs a glass of water and sets it in front of us. He holds on to the base of the glass and stares at it.

"What am I supposed to be watching?" Alex says. Then his eyes widen, and I can tell he sees it. The water just turned into air. "How did you . . . ?"

"We went through the portal, and when we did, it somehow changed our bodies' molecular structure or our chemical makeup or something." Ben runs a hand through his hair. "And now I can change the molecular structure of other things."

"It's how he healed me," I whisper.

Alex swivels his head and stares at me for a second, but I drop my eyes. I should have told him before this.

"Believe it now?" Elijah asks.

"No." Alex shakes his head. "But I'm willing to listen."

Which is when I realize we're going to at least operate like this makes some kind of sense.

"Someone else must still be opening portals," Ben says when I finish giving him the details of the case.

"Like who?" I can't help but laugh at the idea. "How many people out there are running around trying to open a portal and cross over?"

"It's my dad," Elijah says. His smile reaches his eyes, and I realize it might be the first time I've ever seen him really happy. He looks five years younger, ten years less jaded. He's almost cute like this.

"Your dad?" Alex asks. "Why would your dad be opening portals?"

"My dad—my real dad," he clarifies. "He's in government, sort of like the president here, only we don't have limits on the number of terms. He's been running the country since before I was born. I know he's looking for us."

"We don't know that," Ben says quietly, and I get the impression this is an argument they've had before.

"What if one of the portals you opened *was* the right one?" Elijah continues. "And what if they know where we are now? They could be trying to open a portal to get us back."

"Or it could be Mike Cooper, or whoever he really is," Alex says.

"It could be anyone—or any*thing*," Ben says, standing up. He paces around the room. "For all we know, the portals might be opening on their own and bringing people through. We could be approaching Wave Function Collapse."

Elijah shakes his head. "Why do you have to be such a dickwad? I told you that's just a theory. We don't even know if it's real."

Ben swears under his breath. "All of this is real—we're living proof it's real!"

"Wait!" I grab Ben's hand and give it a squeeze. "Somebody explain to me, what is Wave Function Collapse?"

"In theory," Reid says, "universes are supposed to stay separate. And each breach, each time two universes connect and cross—which would happen for three kids to get dumped from one universe into another—they move closer together. Until they eventually collide."

"Collide?" I repeat, because my mind is speculating what that means, and—well, I hope I'm wrong.

But I'm not.

"Destroy each other," Ben whispers.

"Wave Function Collapse?"

Ben nods. "That's what we think it means."

"Could that be the countdown?" Alex asks. I look at him. I can't vocalize any of my thoughts—I can't even put my thoughts into words. I was relieved at first when I realized this wasn't a virus. But now I think maybe this—whatever *this* is—is worse.

"What if the UIED that the FBI has . . . ," Alex says. "What if it's not a bomb or something that will release a virus or anything else? Struz told you they couldn't disarm it. Maybe it's because it can't *be* disarmed. What if the UIED is counting down to Wave Function Collapse?"

Ben's eyes meet mine, and he says, "Then we have . . ."

"Eight days."

He nods. "We have eight days to figure out how to stop it before it destroys this world—and us."

08:17:42:19

Eight days means we have to work together. It's a tenuous alliance based only on how Ben and I seem to feel about each other, even though we haven't really articulated those feelings.

I trust Alex, I have feelings for Ben—and I want to trust him—though I doubt I'd expose my back to Reid and Elijah. But they're all I've got at this point. If I take this to the FBI without some kind of proof, Struz wouldn't believe me. My dad probably wouldn't have either, and it makes me think. Because this is another secret that matters—would I have kept it from him? Even with so much at stake?

But I try not to think about it too hard. Because what if I'd gone to him with this and he didn't believe me?

When Alex, Reid, and Elijah leave to go talk quantum physics, Ben looks at me. "How much do you hate me right now?"

"Not at all." And it's true.

He shakes his head. "I'm a terrible person. I've killed people. I almost killed you. I might have brought about the end of the world."

"I know." I do know, and I still can't find any blame to pin on him. "But you've been in a terrible position, and those deaths, they were accidents." I bite my lip because even though it's true, I wish I could think of something better to say. But I'm not about to lie to him, either. I'm not like that—and Ben deserves better.

We sit silently next to each other, and between us, there's this—this feeling, this electrical charge, and warmth moves through me. But I have so many questions, I barely know where to start. The weight of those secrets he, Elijah, and Reid have been carrying around—I can't fathom what that must be like. And I already wanted to know everything about him, so I start where this all began. "What was your family like? At home."

Ben gives me a half smile and stares off into the distance. "My mom was a scientist. She worked for Elijah's dad, and my dad worked in sales. He traveled a lot, and he always felt like he had to prove how good he was at fixing things around the house, because my mom was actually better.

"One time, the toaster broke, and he insisted he could fix it." Ben laughs. "He even took the whole thing apart and tried to put it back together. My brother and I sat around the kitchen table and just watched him work on it for hours."

"Did he fix it?" I ask.

Ben shakes his head. "You couldn't even get it to hold the bread down when he was done with it. My mom bought another one that was identical the next day, and we just pretended my dad fixed it."

I try to imagine that, and I can't—at least not with my own parents. "Is your brother older or younger?"

"Derek's two years older," Ben says, and his voice cracks slightly. "He's the one who got me into cars and motorcycles. We had these miniature car kits. They were like toys, but you built a car that was about two feet long from scratch and it was real, like with an engine and everything. But they were really expensive, so when my mom bought Derek a new kit, she used to make him let me work on it with him. Then we'd take turns with the remote, racing the car down our street. We chased the dog a lot."

He takes a deep breath. "Hope, she was this pit bull Derek adopted from a shelter. She had this reddish-gold-colored fur and superintelligent eyes and more energy than even Derek and me. Every game we played included chasing her. She loved it."

I laugh, thinking of a remote-control car chasing a dog around.

"You know what the worst part is?" Ben asks, his eyes bloodshot and watery. "I can't remember what they look like. I mean, I think I can. I have a vague idea of them. I remember my mom was wearing a pink blouse at the birthday party. And Derek was wearing a T-shirt with some kind of cartoon robot on it. But I can't remember their faces."

I don't even think. I just grab him and pull him into me and wrap my arms around him. Because I can't imagine anything worse than that.

"Sometimes I even start to second-guess my memories, or I mix them up, like I can't remember what happened there and what happened here," he whispers into my hair.

I put my hands on the sides of his face, and I turn him so we're nose to nose, our foreheads touching. We're both breathing heavily, and I wonder what he's thinking. If his heart is beating so fast it's ready to explode out of his skin. If he's glad that truck came barreling through from another universe and hit me because it brought us together. If he realizes the smell of mint, soap, and gasoline now drives me crazy—in the best possible way.

"You're my anchor," he whispers, and I can feel his breath against my lips. "You were the first thing I saw when I got here. You pulled me out of the water, and I knew that we'd be okay. Even if we were stuck here."

The memory—vision—of me, backlit by the sun, pulling a boy—Ben—out of the water.

What if I hadn't been in that exact spot? I press my forehead against his—closer—because at this moment, he's the only thing that seems to make sense anymore.

I lean forward and kiss him.

He kisses me back.

And I feel like I'm on fire and my insides are exploding. Only this time, it's amazing.

"S top," Ben whispers against my lips. "Janelle, stop."

But his hands don't leave my body—his fingers press tightly into my skin as he holds my hips and lower back in place, tightly against him. His lips are back on mine, his tongue in my mouth.

As I nibble on his bottom lip, he moans and jerks me against him tighter.

Then abruptly, he pushes me away.

"Stop."

I'm left gasping for air, my body aching with the loss of him next to me.

"Stop, Janelle, we can't."

"We can't?" I ask with a laugh to cover up the gnawing feeling of rejection eating my insides. "Because it seems pretty obvious that actually we *can*. It seems to me like we were doing just fine."

"We can't be together. I mean, I want to, and I thought we could, but with all of . . . this . . ." He waves a hand. "We're from different worlds—literally. And look what's happening. People are dying. I have to focus on fixing that."

275

I don't say anything—because I just stare at him. This can't possibly make sense.

Ben shakes his head. "You shouldn't have broken up with Nick for me."

"What?" Hot rage flows through me, and I curl my hands into fists. "I didn't break up with Nick *for you*. That had nothing to do with you."

"Wait, that's not what I meant. I—"

"Then what? Did I misinterpret something? Did you not mean what you just said to me?"

"No, of course not." Ben takes a step toward me, but then backpedals and reaches up and grabs his hair with both hands. "But that's not the point. How I feel, that doesn't matter, because we can't be together."

"Why?"

"I can't do this," he says. "I can't be this close to you after wanting it so long, only to have it all ripped away."

"What are you talking about?"

He closes his eyes, and his voice comes out strained and barely above a whisper. "Janelle, we all might die in eight days, but even if we don't, I'm . . . I'm not from here." His eyes flick open again, and his face looks pained. "Don't you get what that means?"

I don't say anything.

Ben reaches out and grabs my shoulders. "I've spent every waking moment of the past seven years trying to get back home."

"Back . . . ," I say, and I can't get anything else out, because of course I know that. All the experiments, the quantum physics, the open portals, and the bodies coming through. "Home to your universe. You're leaving."

Ben nods.

"But when?"

"It doesn't matter," he answers. "Whether it's tomorrow, the next day, or seven days from now, or ever. My goal is always going to be to get home."

Home. For him, it's a place I don't belong.

08:15:56:47

"**W**here the hell have you been?" Struz says when I open the front door to my house and slip inside.

My heart rate skyrockets and I lean against the door for a second, reminding myself that I left the backpack at Ben's, and the approaching interrogation is more about the fact that I'm coming in at one in the morning on a school night.

"You scared the shit out of me," I say.

"Damn straight," Struz answers. He's in the kitchen, putting dishes away from the dishwasher. "You gonna tell me now where the hell you've been? And don't even say Alex's. I saw his car pull in almost an hour ago."

"Did you hear his mother yelling from here?" I ask with a laugh.

"As a matter of fact I did, but answer the question."

"I was up at a friend's house on Black Mountain Road," I say. I'm not exactly lying to him. I'm just withholding some of the truth. "Alex was there for a while too. We were talking about physics."

"Next time, could it occur to you to call, maybe, and let me know?" he says, and I instantly feel guilty. I just did to Struz

278

what my dad used to do to us all the time.

"You're right, I should have called." I nod.

"Okay, well, now that I made you feel bad, I have something for you."

I love that he's like that. "What is it?"

He pulls something from his pocket—square and black—and immediately my eyes water, because I know it's my dad's wallet. The one I bought him for Christmas a few years ago. The leather is already starting to wear, but he wouldn't buy a new one, because this was the one I'd given him.

"Thank you," I say, forcing the words through the tightness in my throat. I know my mother was fine when I left, but I still feel compelled to ask, "How did tonight go?"

Struz shakes his head. "It was a quiet night. She's sleeping now, I guess. She took some food into her room but I don't know if she ate anything."

I nod and turn to head up the stairs. "Good night, Struz," I call, knowing he'll either crash on the couch or let himself out, depending on how tired he is and how early he has to get up in the morning.

In my room, I throw my purse on my dresser, kick off my shoes, and fall into bed. I'll change my clothes tomorrow. I open up the wallet and pull out everything that's inside. There's a picture of Jared and me from Comic-Con three years ago, a twenty-dollar bill, my dad's driver's license, a couple of credit cards, a gift card to Target, and a slip of paper with the numbers 3278 on it. I want that to be a clue, but I know it's probably his locker number at the gym.

Even though I know he's probably asleep and that it'll go straight to voice mail, I call the number for Barclay's FBI phone and listen to it ring. I need information, and I'm hoping he can get it for me without asking too many questions. He doesn't care about me like Struz does, which means he won't be worrying about what I'm up to. When the generic voice mail picks up, I leave a message, asking him to call me back tomorrow. I even tell him we need to meet, exchange information.

As I'm hanging up, there's a knock on my door.

Instinctively I throw the phone down and leap off the bed, wondering if whoever's knocking just heard me leave that message.

I crack open the door, and Struz is there. He's got his sweatshirt on and his car keys in his hand.

"What's up?" I ask, trying to pretend he didn't almost just catch me calling an analyst so I could illegally involve myself in a federal investigation.

"I just want to say . . ." He coughs into his hand and shifts uncomfortably. "You know you can come to me, with whatever you're into?"

"Of course," I say, probably too quickly for it to be believable.

I start to shut the door again, but then his hand comes out and stops me. My heart beats faster. What does he think I'm into—what does he know?

I almost tell him. I almost let Ben's seven-year secret just pour out of my mouth, but I can't do it. Even if Struz did believe me, I don't know how the FBI would really help. I know someone like Elijah isn't going to talk to them.

Instead I just look up at Struz and wait.

He clears his throat. "Whatever you're doing with the backup gun and the files that were in your dad's safe, be careful."

I nod, but I can't help but wonder why so many people seem to have so much trust in me to do the right thing.

I hope I don't let them down.

08:05:46:15

Barclay calls me back when I'm at lunch. I see his name on my caller ID and practically jump up from my seat next to Cecily and answer the phone.

"It's Janelle," I say, because *hello* seems just a little too social for the two of us.

"What do you need, Tenner?" he asks. "I only do designated-driver runs after midnight."

"I'm sure most girls find your humor tantalizing. But actually I was hoping you'd meet me after work," I say, trying not to let my voice show how desperate I am for him to agree. "I have some information about a case that I think would be of interest to you, and I have some questions."

"You think you're going to get me to give you information?" he asks with a laugh.

"I know I will," I say. "After all, I know you violated a direct order and brought a civilian—and minor—to a crime scene that's been kept under wraps."

"I'll just get a slap on the wrist from Struz."

"Maybe, but what will happen to you if this gets leaked to the press?" I say, even though I'm not a hundred percent sure where that threat is coming from. Too many bad Mafia movies? "I'm sure they'd be shocked and appalled to hear how traumatized I am."

Barclay must be trying to digest that, because he doesn't say anything.

"I have information for you too, you know," I offer. I don't want to scare him off too much.

"Information?" he asks. "What could you possibly have?"

"Just all my dad's files."

I swear I can hear the intake of breath through the phone.

"All right," Barclay says. "I get off around five. Where do you want to meet?"

I tell him the address of the Chili's in Mira Mesa, the location Alex and I agreed on. I'll get information from Barclay, and Alex and Ben will drive around and compare gas stations to the photo my dad had of alias Mike Cooper.

When I hang up, I head back to my table. Alex is eating with Cecily and a few friends—people we've had classes with the past two years. They're still talking about the upcoming calculus test and whether we'll be prepared for the AP test in May—the same thing they were talking about when I got up. They have no idea how little that will matter if the world ends.

I pretend to listen, but glance around the quad, looking for Ben.

He and Elijah are in their usual spot on the grass, with girls like Roxy and Alicia, and laughing loudly.

Ben looks casually disinterested, the way he always does, and for some reason this time I feel insanely jealous and wish he were eating lunch with me.

"So Ben Michaels . . . ," Cecily says suddenly, and when I turn back to our table, she's smiling at me.

A couple of people laugh, like they're waiting to be let in on some joke, but Cecily just keeps looking at me with her big smile. "He *is* cute," she giggles.

I shrug. "If you like that mysterious bad boy kind of thing."

She smiles wider and looks in Ben and Elijah's direction. "I do, actually."

"I'm not sure I understand the whole allure of the bad boy," Alex says. "Frankly, I've always thought the intelligent and hardworking valedictorian type should be more appealing."

"Oh, Alex, how little you understand girls," I say with a laugh.

Cecily turns back to us. "Ben Michaels seems pretty damn smart in physics. I seem to recall a recent lab where he told one of those intelligent and hardworking valedictorian types what he was doing wrong."

Alex nods. "I suppose this means I need a new wardrobe."

Which springboards an entirely too long conversation about what Cecily would do to make over Alex in order to make him look like a bad boy.

My eyes wander back to Ben.

Until Alex bumps my shoulder.

"What?" I say, turning my attention to him.

He nods his head at something, but he's terrible at it, and I have no idea what direction he actually wants me to look.

After a few seconds of me blankly staring, he rolls his eyes. "Kate," he says. "She's eating lunch by herself?"

I turn to look at the tables by the gym where Kate and her friends always eat, and sure enough, Alex is right. Kate is eating at a table by herself, while the girls she always eats with are several tables away. As I'm watching, Brooke gets up from her table and practically bounces over to Kate and says something.

But Kate just shakes her head and looks down until Brooke walks away.

"I wonder what that's all about," Alex says.

"Does it matter?" I ask, turning back to my food. And wishing it didn't.

"So you're now more than halfway through the novel," Poblete says, "and you just hit a major turning point. Based on your reading last night, what new revelation have we learned about Gatsby?"

I should be relieved to be in school. It's the only time of the day I can actually forget about the countdown, alternate universes, and alias Mike Cooper and pretend to be normal. Except when I realize how behind I am, how little I know about what's going on in class, panic wells up in my chest, because with everything else going on, I didn't do my reading last night, or the night before.

But apparently Poblete has radar for that. "Ms. Tenner, give us one new thing we learned about Gatsby."

Right when I'm about to just bite the big one and admit I've got no idea what she's talking about, I see Ben tap his notebook a few times.

Everything Gatsby's done has been for Daisy.

Thankfully, I have read *The Great Gatsby* before. I actually love the tragedy of the story, but I'm not entirely sure how far we're supposed to be in the book. So I go for Ben's answer and add my own two cents about Gatsby doing everything from throwing elaborate parties to getting his neighbor's grass cut, and having a hundred different shirts. Sure enough, after I give my answer, she says, "Thank you, Ms. Tenner."

"Now Ms. Zhou had previously claimed that Daisy was just an innocent victim of her terrible husband. What do we think of her now, after this chapter?"

I look over at Ben, half-thankful he just saved me, half-mortified he had to. When this is all over, I need to get my priorities straight.

"Now," Poblete says, "let's look at some of the language Fitzgerald uses in chapters four and five. What are some quotes you annotated that would point to Fitzgerald using Gatsby as an example of the withering American Dream?"

"Didn't you read this, like, two years ago?" Ben whispers to me, his breath warm in my ear.

I stiffen and look over at him. I wonder how he knows that—he must read the question on my face, because he leans in again. "Not many people at this school sit out on the quad during lunch and read. Even fewer alternate between *The Great Gatsby* and Harry Potter."

"Harry Potter is a classic," I whisper back.

"What's your favorite book, if you had to pick one?"

"*The Electric Church* by Jeff Somers," I say without hesitation. "If I had to pick one—it's this crazy science fiction noir, and the main character is badass. And it's different, nothing else quite like it."

"If we get through all this, I want to borrow it."

I'm about to make that a deal and ask what *his* favorite book is, but Poblete says, "Mr. Michaels, please stop asking Ms. Tenner to marry you and pay attention."

My face flushes with heat and I look back at my notes, but Ben just laughs. "Why are you bent on ruining all my shots at getting a date?"

I'd love it if the floor could swallow me up right about now. Because I can't help thinking about our date and how Ben says we can't be together, which means we won't ever have another one. It makes me feel a little like someone's cutting me open.

"Not all your shots, just the ones infringing on my class time," she says, and then she's back to Gatsby.

At least for a second. Because the next thing I know, I feel dizzy and nauseous, like I'm about to be sick. And I realize it's because the ground beneath my feet is moving.

The floor shakes, the walls rattle, and the tables and chairs dance around. Everything moves right and then left and right again, and I feel like someone's jerking me side to side. Poblete stumbles and falls into the wall. For a minute, we all just sit there, shocked that the whole classroom appears as if it might collapse around us.

Someone behind me says, "Holy shit, are we having an earthquake?"

And then Poblete is yelling for everyone to get on the floor under the tables, like we've been taught to do every year since we were in preschool. This is California. We knew what to do in an earthquake before we even understood what it was.

I push my chair back and get under my table, trying to focus on the fact that this is okay, this is normal, it's just an earthquake. Only I look over and this time I'm the one trying to help Ben. He just sits sort of dazed in his seat, and I can picture the windows blowing out and a chunk of glass hurtling at his face. The thought makes me feel even more sick to my stomach, and I reach up and pull him by one of his arms, tugging him out of his chair and onto the floor.

And the ground keeps shaking, harder and faster, like we're on some kind of crazy theme park ride, and I realize we haven't hit the worst of it yet. It's hard to breathe, like air is catching on something in my throat, and I'm starting to feel disoriented, like I don't know how to keep my head above the rest of my body.

My whole body feels like it's vibrating, like I have no control over my own skin. Books and backpacks fall off the tables and chairs and bounce around on the floor. I try to grab the leg of the table to steady myself, but that only emphasizes how much it's jerking around. I feel like I'm on a roller coaster gone wrong— like we're about to run right off the tracks.

Pictures fall off the walls, sparks fly from Poblete's computer, the lights go out, the windows break, glass rains down on the tabletops, and someone screams.

And then it takes me a second to realize it's over—that my hands and body are still shaking, but the ground has in fact stopped.

It's only when it's quiet that I realize how loud the earthquake was—like thunder, only coming from beneath the earth, like the earth was screaming, letting loose some kind of roar.

Now I can hear my own heart beating, and I reach over to grab Ben's wrist, listening to the steady thrum of his pulse against my fingers. I can hear all forty of us breathing and the quiet sobs of someone behind me. And then the PA system crackles and I hear Mauro's voice. "This is a Code White," she says. *Earthquake.* "Lock down your classrooms, this is a Code White."

And then it's quiet again, and we're left with the sounds of our breathing and the smell of fried circuits.

"Is everyone okay?" Poblete asks. A chorus of shaky affirmative replies echoes through the room. "Ms. Crowley, you okay back there?"

"Just dandy. I banged the shit out of my knee, but I'll live."

"Please do. Any blood?"

"Nope, just hurts like a bitch."

"Well, that is at least promising. Ms. Desjardins, are you hurt?" Poblete asks.

It's Alex who answers for her—she's crying too hard. "Maddy's fine. Just scared, but she's starting to calm down."

"Good. Good." Poblete gets up and moves to her desk. "Stay where you are, in case there are any aftershocks. I'm going to try to check in with admin."

Murmurs move through the room, everyone asking one another, "Are you okay?" or giving some brief description of what they thought was happening when it first started, or even telling stories about other earthquakes they lived through.

"I hit Poblete in the face freshman year," Ben says out of the blue.

"What?" He can't possibly be serious.

But he nods. "It was still, like, the first or second month of school, and I was dealing with a lot of anger issues. We'd figured out what happened, and I knew what we had to do in order to get back home, but I couldn't figure out *how* to do it. And the whole thing was my fault. I was the one who tripped."

"Please, it didn't sound like it was anyone's fault."

He shakes his head. "No, it was my fault. But school seemed like such a waste then. I was spending every waking moment reading about what people here considered pseudoscience, and no one would teach me the things I wanted to know. Plus, the home I was in then was pretty bad, and Reid and I were going through a phase where we hated each other."

"Reid?" I ask with a laugh. Elijah seems more hateable to me.

Ben nods and offers me a small half smile. "I never actually liked him much—as a kid, I mean. Our parents were friends, so we had to be friends. Then we got here and we became close, you know, but he adjusted so easily. I hated him a little because of it.

"So I acted like a jackass a lot. I didn't get into that many fights, that was always Elijah's thing, but I talked out in class, corrected teachers when they messed up, just made myself a general nuisance. I pissed Poblete off daily. I'd come into homeroom late, no one would ever excuse my absences, I'd swear for no reason, move her shit around, whatever. One time I even lifted her classroom keys so I could check out the faculty bathrooms."

"Why were you so lame?" I laugh.

Ben shrugs. "I could tell she'd get pissed at me. But then the next day when I'd come in, it was like a clean slate. She never stayed mad."

"Not even after you hit her in the face?"

He shakes his head. "I was being an idiot, and I had grabbed her yardstick and was carrying it around. Twice she told me to put it away, but I swung it at someone's water bottle cap, like it was a baseball bat. And the cap nailed her right in the face, like, an inch under her eye."

I bite my lip to keep from laughing, and Ben smiles.

"She told me not to let the door hit me on the way out and kicked me out of class, and I stood outside, sure that I was done. She was going to tell admin, and since I'd already been in trouble plenty I'd get suspended or expelled. My foster parents at the time were already threatening to send me to a group home. So after homeroom ended, I went back into class and apologized, and I meant it. She had this red welt on her face from where the cap had hit her. I felt terrible. But after my apology, she just looked at me and asked what I wanted.

"No one had ever asked me that," Ben whispers. "So I told her about metaverse theory and everything I wanted to learn. She went to college at Duke, and they used to have a parapsychology department. She got me in touch with a retired professor who got me in touch with a couple other people, and that's how I started to put it together."

"So Poblete is one of the reasons you ultimately figured it out?"

"Yeah," Ben says, but the laugh that comes out is bitter. "She'd just love to know that she's one of the reasons I've been opening portals to another universe, one of the reasons people are dead, one of the reasons we just got hit with probably the worst earthquake San Diego has ever seen."

My throat tightens. I hadn't thought of all that. "You can't know—"

"Have you ever felt an earthquake like that?" he asks, and then he shakes his head. "It's not a coincidence. When we were sitting there, I thought that was it, it was over."

Which explains why he didn't move to get under the table.

I feel sick to my stomach, like I might not be able to stop my body from spasming and expelling the lunch I just had. Because the enormity of it feels like it's squeezing my insides—my heart, my lungs, my stomach, my *soul*.

Because Ben is right. I've never felt an earthquake like that. And I've lived here my whole life.

08:03:09:40

The earthquake was an 8.1 on the Richter scale.

The biggest earthquake to hit San Diego. Ever. In fact, it's the biggest to ever hit California.

The known death toll is already at least two hundred people. And rising.

My cell phone service is out, and I can't call Jared to make sure he's okay, but according to the PA announcements, there's been nothing but a few minor injuries from broken glass or things falling on people.

They start evacuating the school by classroom, and when we're finally allowed to get up and leave, I grab my stuff and bolt out the door, relieved to finally get some air. Only when I get outside, I'm struck by how serious this is. There are downed palm trees everywhere, and the quad is covered with palm fronds. The front of the library has cracks going up the walls, and the fountain at the front of school is just a pile of broken stones.

I don't stop moving until I'm in the girls' bathroom, standing over a toilet. I haven't even caught my breath, and I'm bracing myself with a hand on the stall and vomiting.

Until there's nothing left, and I'm just dry heaving.

My eyes water and tears leak out of the corners of my eyes, my nose is running, and drops of sweat slide down my side, even though I'm freezing cold.

This is real. Alternate universes. Portals to other worlds. Universes colliding and destroying each other.

My shoulders shake, and I feel myself starting to lose it.

"Janelle?" Ben's voice calls. "Are you in here?"

I don't answer. Instead I hold a hand over my face and try to smother the crying.

"Are you okay?" Ben asks, and this time his voice is closer. I'm pretty sure he's actually in the bathroom with me.

I hold my breath and wipe at my face with the back of my hand, before opening the bathroom stall.

"I just need a minute," I say to him. "I'll meet you outside."

"Hey," he says, reaching out to me. "Don't be upset."

But he doesn't tell me it will all be okay. Because he can't. And apparently Ben Michaels isn't the kind of guy who lies to people. Even if it's just to make them feel better.

"How can you say that when the world might end in eight days?" I ask, wiping my eyes one more time.

"We just need to focus on what we can do," Ben says. "We have to find out who's opening the portals and stop them. Then we'll have more time, and we can go from there."

"Oh, piece of cake," I say, rolling my eyes. "Maybe we should give up, just recognize that the next eight days will be our last, and I don't know, live them to the fullest or something."

He gives me a half smile and pulls me into him. "That doesn't sound like you."

I lean into his arms and wonder why nothing has ever felt

this good before. Which is my only excuse for the words that come out of my mouth next. "If all we have is eight days, why can't we be together, even if it's just for a few days?"

"It would be too hard. I wouldn't be able to handle leaving you." His breath tickles my hair, and I wrap my arms tighter around him and try to memorize the exact feel of his body against mine.

"If our worlds collide, that will be the least of your problems."

He nods against me. "I just can't."

"But why?" I need him. I need this. I need something good in my life, something worth holding on to, worth fighting for, some reason not to lie down and say, "Wave Function Collapse, come get me."

"Janelle, your dad . . ."

And he pulls away.

"It's my fault he's dead. I killed him."

It's like I'm stuck outside—like the world has just tilted off balance, like a wall of bulletproof glass has just shot up in between us so that even though we're separated by only inches, we're a world away.

My mouth dry, I can't form words. In fact, all my senses have just turned off. My ears refuse to hear Ben's words. My skin can no longer feel the heat. My nerve endings are all dead.

I'm finally broken—more broken than I was days ago when my body lay dead on the side of the road by Torrey Pines Beach.

Broken. There's no other way to describe it. My insides are cracking apart, imploding. Nothing can give me life again—nothing can make me whole. Not even Ben.

This is Just Too Much.

I can't breathe. I can't even stand right.

But when he reaches for me again, I *can* jerk away.

Part of me wants to go back to the beach that day and go get Nick. Instead of playing Independent Woman, I could have just been Helpless Female and I never would have gotten hit by that truck. I never would have let Ben Michaels into my life. A part of me even wishes that Ben had just left me there to die after the truck hit me. What good has rising from the ashes of death and being resurrected even done me? My father is dead, Jared is devastated, and my mother needs to be committed. And the one good thing in my life—Ben—is actually the tipping point, the reason everything fell apart.

Part of me even wishes I'd never pulled him out of the ocean that day to begin with. None of this would have happened, then.

Or would it have happened anyway?

"What do you mean?" I ask, forcing the words through.

"I shouldn't be here." Ben's voice breaks on the last word.

"But you didn't kill him?"

"Not physically, no, but it's my fault he's dead." He turns away.

The relief that washes over me is a palpable thing, like a cool ocean breeze or a shot of pure oxygen. I can suddenly breathe normally again. Of course Ben didn't kill my dad.

"Don't you get it? Every moment that I spend in this universe, every minute, every second, is *wrong*. I'm altering the course of events in a world where I'm not even supposed to exist."

"Ben Michaels, changing the world. Awfully self-important, don't you think?" Even though I know exactly what he means, I can't help myself. Mostly because I *want* him to belong here. With me. Because it wouldn't feel so right when his arms are around me if he wasn't supposed to exist here.

296

Ben laughs bitterly. "I wish I were. I wish I were." He pauses in his pacing and sits down on the couch before burying his face in his hands. "Butterfly effect: A seemingly insignificant incident can cause an infinite chain of events. Think of what a significant incident does."

"Your existence isn't what killed my dad. A person killed him, and—"

"I'm not supposed to be here. I don't belong here." He looks up. "Those people who died in that earthquake, that's on me. All of this is on me."

"You don't know that's what this is!" I swallow and make an effort to lower my voice. "Chaos is the natural state of life. You can't control chaos. You can't control life—and you know it. You're here now. You've been here for seven years. Fucking deal with it."

"But just my being here could mean everyone is going to die."

"You don't know that!" I scream. Not because I don't believe it. I see what he's thinking. I get it. I don't even know what we're arguing about anymore, just that I need to scream at him, and then kiss him until I'm not scared anymore.

Of course the logical part of me worries he's right. But there's another part of me that's dead convinced he's wrong. Because there's another option. "What's to say you coming through the portal and ending up here wasn't what was meant to happen in the first place? What if you didn't belong *there*?"

Because the truth of it is I can't imagine a world that says Ben doesn't belong with *me*.

08:00:01:38

The weirdest thing I notice after the earthquake is that there's water everywhere. Streets and sidewalks are awash with water that got shaken out of nearby swimming pools. Everywhere you look, you can't see more than a handful of feet in front of you because of the combination of smoke from nearby fires and the layer of dust that's just hanging in the air. Some buildings look pristine, like nothing happened, and then others—maybe ones right next to them—have their roofs caved in, or their garage taken out by a tree.

I'm getting out of Alex's car when Ben leans forward and says, "Maybe you shouldn't go alone. Should someone sit in another booth or up at the bar to keep an eye out?"

"This isn't some undercover cop show," I say as I shift my swimming backpack on my shoulders. "From my interactions with him, Barclay seems like a jerk, but he's still one of the good guys."

Ben looks at Alex, like he's not sure he should take my opinion without male corroboration, but thankfully, Alex knows who his real friend is, and nods. "She'll be fine."

I slam the door without waiting to hear what one of them will say next. Jared is safely at a friend's house for the next three hours, and Struz is dealing with fallout from the earthquake. Mission Valley, where the 5 and the 163 all meet the 8, suffered the most damage. Reports are coming in about the death toll climbing, and the beach towns are supposed to get hit extra hard too once the aftershocks start rolling in. Right now the biggest concern is whether the quake will create a tsunami. The news is predicting a couple of thousand deaths and billions of dollars' worth of property damage.

Chili's in Mira Mesa is closed, of course, but luckily for me, Whole Foods is still open, and Barclay agreed to meet me there instead.

Apparently Barclay is sort of a slacker, so he didn't cancel on me to go put in time helping emergency responders, like Struz did.

Power is out all over the city, and the fact that Whole Foods is dimly lit gives this meeting a sort of sinister, illegal feel that makes me shiver a little. That and the fact that every housewife within a ten-mile radius is here now or has been here already, rushing through the aisles, fighting over canned goods and bottled water and anything else that won't go bad. Things they left—like economy-size packages of paper towels and crates of oranges—are overturned and strewn in the aisles. It looks like a tornado went through here.

I step over some discarded and smushed fruit and head toward the café, where I'm supposed to meet Barclay.

Alex, Ben, and Elijah all have the photo of alias Mike Cooper, and they're going to attempt to drive around and figure out which gas station it is—but who knows how far they'll get with all the traffic. Despite my objections, Alex and Ben are working together on all the gas stations north of University, Elijah is on his own on the south side, and Reid is apparently stuck at home with his parents.

Barclay's already waiting for me with a beer and a slice of pizza. "So Tenner, what've you got for this meet-up?" he asks as I slide into the seat across from him.

It looks like he's the only one in the seated café.

I guess most people are taking the whole "go home and stay home" thing seriously.

"My questions first," I say, sliding the picture of alias Mike Cooper across the table. "Can you find this guy for me? He sometimes goes by the alias Mike Cooper."

Barclay glances at the picture and shrugs. "What do you want with him?"

I debate explaining what I found on my dad's computer, but if he doesn't already know how alias Mike Cooper factors into the case, I don't want to tell him. Barclay strikes me as the kind of guy who'd be likely to find Cooper and not tell me—just go for the glory and take all the credit himself. And he can have the credit, but unless the FBI is ready to jump forward leaps and bounds with what we know about science, it's not going to do us much good in the scheme of things.

Instead I say, "I just want to talk to him."

Barclay looks at the photo again. "He looks a little old for you. Is this about drugs?"

I roll my eyes. "Stop being such a dipshit. Can you do it?"

"Of course I can, but what do I get?"

"These are the files my dad had for the current case you guys are working," I say, opening the backpack and retrieving them.

I've already been through them forward, backward, and upside down, and there's nothing here I haven't seen yet. But I've made copies of everything just in case.

"Case files? I have access to these at the office."

"I doubt that." Dealing with Struz would have been easier if I thought he'd believe me—and keep me in the loop. "This is everything, plus all my dad's notes. But if you don't want them, I'll just keep them."

"No, I'll look at them." He's trying to keep up the nonchalant act, but I can see in his eyes how much he wants them. When he reaches for them, I pull back.

"And you'll find alias Mike Cooper for me?"

"I said I would," Barclay says. "C'mon, give 'em up." When I do, he adds, "You should quit the whole junior-investigating thing, though, and leave this stuff to the people who know what they're doing."

"You appear to be doing a bang-up job so far," I say, because I just can't deal with his condescending attitude. "Do you have any idea what did that to the people in that house—"

"I told you to stay in the car, there was no reason you had to see that—"

"—how to shut off that countdown?"

He stops talking over me and reaches out and grabs my arm. His voice is low, serious, and a little frightening. "What do you know about the countdown?"

07:23:29:17

Gone is the arrogance and condescension, almost like he flipped a switch, and I realize I'm meeting Taylor Barclay, FBI agent, for the first time. Before this I was just dealing with a jerk who underestimated my intelligence and dismissed me, but this guy, with the tight grip on my arm and the fierce determination on his face—this is a guy I don't want to mess with.

I try to jerk my arm out of his grip, but he holds steady and pulls me across the table so I'm closer to him. "I said, what do you know about the countdown?"

"It's in the files," I hiss back at him. "A UIED with a countdown. No one knows how to disarm it. My dad thought it was connected somehow to the bodies."

He lets go of my arm, and I pull it away from him and lean back as Barclay starts to flip through the files. I'm tempted to say something about his unnecessary use of force, but I don't. Instead I sit still and quiet and try not to let on how much my arm hurts from the way he grabbed it.

I knew what I was getting into when I decided I wanted to play with the big boys.

I'm trying to think of something to say to him, some way to right the scales of control again, so I'm the one with the upper hand, when I have that sick feeling again, and there's a quick jerk beneath me, like a car just ran into the building.

Barclay's beer falls off the table and shatters on the floor. A collection of screams go up through the store, and I hear a rumbling—products shaking and vibrating against the floor.

"Shit," I say. It's an aftershock. Not as strong as the earthquake this morning, but it doesn't matter. It's just emphasizing the fact that this is a colossal waste of time. I think of Jared, and I know I should be with him, or at least be around when he gets home, to make sure he's okay.

I look down and grab my backpack, pulling a twenty out of my wallet for the food. Any more conversation with Barclay is a waste of time. "This is a sign," I mutter to myself.

Apparently, a little too loud. "A sign of what?" Barclay asks.

"The apocalypse."

The asshole laughs. "The *apocalypse* apocalypse? Like four horsemen, pestilence, all that?"

And because I'm frustrated and I hate how helpless I feel—like I'm wasting what are potentially the last precious moments of my life sitting here with one of the biggest jerks I've ever met—I just tell him the truth. "I was thinking two universes colliding and effectively destroying each other. How about that?"

And then I get up and walk out. I need to go. I'll wait at home for Jared. Hopefully Alex has had better luck.

It takes me about fifteen minutes to walk home, but when I'm there I find a package in front of the door. It must have been delivered before the earthquake.

It's addressed to my dad.

My legs feel like Jell-O, and I just have to sit down. So I do—right there on the worn WELCOME TO EARTH mat that my dad bought forever ago. I hold the box, and for a second I don't know if I'm actually going to open it. Not because it's technically illegal to open mail that doesn't belong to you, but because I'm not sure I want to know what's inside.

But I only hold on to it for a second. Because I have to know.

Using my keys to cut through the tape seems to take forever, and the only thing I can hear is the ripping of cardboard as I pull it open.

When I see what's inside, I realize I've been holding my breath, and I lean my head back against the door with a thud and close my eyes to keep from crying. It's for Jared. It's a *Firefly* poster, signed by each of the cast members. The inscription at the top reads "To Jared." And then Nathan Fillion's signature is at the bottom. It's perfect.

My dad has—had—an eBay addiction. Sometimes the strangest things showed up on our doorstep because he'd been mildly interested in something listed for a penny, and then he'd gotten so caught up in winning the bidding war that we had some ridiculous toy from the 1980s that cost over a hundred dollars.

I don't know how much this poster was, but I know it's a Christmas present. It doesn't matter that it's only September. My dad never rushed out to buy presents on Christmas Eve. He bought us presents year round and stored them in odd places we'd never think to look. It made opening presents that morning that much more exciting, because each present came with a story—where he found it, how long he'd had it, where it had been hiding.

It occurs to me now that we're not going to have that this year.

I take a deep breath and try to wipe the emotions away from my eyes. Because I wonder how long I'll be finding random Christmas presents he stashed all over the house. And I wonder if it will feel this devastating each time.

Another deep breath and I get up and put the keys in the door. When I get inside, I drop the backpack and the *Firefly* paraphernalia next to the door—not much chance of Struz dropping in until this whole earthquake thing is more under control—and head for the kitchen.

And the hits just keep coming.

07:23:12:54

My mother is sitting at the kitchen table, wearing my father's FBI sweatpants and his West Point sweatshirt. She has an empty mug in front of her and a bag of Earl Grey on the table.

"Did you want some tea?" I ask, because Earl Grey has always been her favorite. She used to brew it every morning when I was little.

Only when I get closer, I realize there's something wrong with her hands.

They're red and swollen.

I can't help thinking of the unidentified bodies burned beyond recognition from radiation poisoning.

Her hands aren't like that, but they're burned.

"What happened?" I rush toward her. She doesn't respond, just holds her hands out to me, and I look at them without touching them. Maybe second-degree burns. Maybe third.

I grab her, pulling her out of the kitchen chair and over to the sink, and I turn on the water and push her hands underneath the stream.

The steel teapot is in the sink, and I glance to the right and notice one of the burners of the stove is still on. Like she started to make herself tea and somehow it went terribly wrong.

"Stay right here," I tell her as I reach for the phone.

I could be a good daughter, treat the burns with aloe vera, wrap them up, and put her back to bed, but this is my limit. I can't watch her all the time and make sure she doesn't hurt herself, and I certainly can't do it for the next few days. Not if I'm also trying to stop this countdown and figure out who killed my dad.

So I tell myself, these are her hands, and if they don't heal right, anything she wants to do in the future—painting, baking, playing the piano—will be a nightmare. I call 911. Then we sit at the kitchen table, the two of us, for ninety-seven minutes before the ambulance actually shows up.

If I have any luck, the fact that they're probably overrun dealing with injuries will mean she'll be there longer, and I'll have a night or two to not worry about her. My chest tightens with guilt—part of me can't believe this is what's crossing my mind. But a bigger part of me is just relieved. And tired.

And worried about everything else.

"**Y**ou're sure it's the same guy?" I say, looking at the blurry picture of the back of a guy's head on Elijah's phone. I try to keep my voice down because Jared is upstairs in his room, hopefully sleeping.

"Of course it's fucking him," Elijah says, reaching for the phone, but I hold on to it, pulling away and looking at it as closely as possible.

The guy could be the same height and build as alias Mike Cooper, and he's got that high and tight military haircut, but really it could be anybody. It just so happens he's walking into a Staybridge Suites close to both the pawnshop and the pool supply store on University Avenue.

I'm not sure whether it's good luck that Elijah just happened to see him and take a picture or it's us trying too hard to put the pieces together.

I guess it'll depend on whether or not this is really the guy.

Alex takes the phone from me and hands it back to Elijah. "Okay, assuming it really is him, what's the next play here?"

"You mean we're not going to just send Janelle after him with a gun, demanding answers?" Elijah asks.

"You're hilarious," I say, even though our options are running pretty thin at this point. We can't just ask him if he's opening portals to another universe. But I can't run in there with a gun, because who knows who this guy is and what I'd need to do to scare him into talking.

"Maybe this is the point where we should go to Struz," Alex says.

"We're not going to the FBI," Reid says at the same time Elijah says, "Fuck, no!"

"Let's stake him out," Ben offers.

I shake my head. "We don't have time to follow him around and try to catch him in the act. And even if we did, what would that do? We'd still be in the same position we are now. With no authority."

"I don't mean stake him out and try to catch him in the act," Ben says. "We stake him out for a day at the most, figure out which hotel room is his, wait until he leaves—"

"And then we go in and toss that shit and see what he's hiding," Elijah says. "I like it! Call your people, I'll call my people, we'll both say we're staying at Reid's tonight, we'll grab some shit from the house, and we'll check him out."

"Wait a minute," I say, because I'm not sure about this plan— and I am sure we shouldn't be rushing into anything.

"This is a bad idea," Alex says, looking at me. And I can tell from the look that this is an argument we're going to have later.

"We're not going to the FBI," Reid reiterates.

"Yeah, I got that, I'm just trying to make sure there isn't another option better than breaking into a potential terrorist's hotel room. How will you even know what you're looking for?"

My eyes meet Ben's, and he shrugs.

"If he's opening portals, he'll have some of the same things I'd have. But at least this way we can find out who he really is and get more information." I don't like the idea, but I don't exactly have a better one, either. "If he's not our guy, whatever information we get, you can turn over to the FBI," Ben offers, as some kind of truce.

I look at Alex, who asks, "How are you going to get into his room?"

"What, you think this'll be the first hotel room I've broken into?" Elijah laughs.

"Right," Alex says. "And please tell me you have something better than some half-baked movie-inspired plan. Calling room service for every room and trying to keep an eye on who opens the door isn't exactly an effective method of finding out which room he's in."

Elijah doesn't even dignify that with a reply. He just keeps laughing.

"A hotel like Staybridge Suites doesn't have room service," Ben says.

"What he was trying to ask was if you guys have a plan," I say, because I'd like to know what that plan is, if possible.

Elijah shrugs and gets up from the table. "Of course we have a plan. Don't worry your pretty little head, I'll make sure to keep Ben safe." Then he laughs, and Reid and Ben both follow him out. I watch Ben leaving, hoping he'll look back, hoping we can at least acknowledge the discussion we had after the earthquake, but he doesn't.

"I gotta get home," Alex says, packing up his stuff. "And for the record, I'm going to say again, I think this is a bad idea."

"I know." Because I do.

"We should go to Struz," Alex says.

"He won't believe us," I say.

"We're seven days from something big—whether it's a terrorist attack, worlds colliding, or something we haven't even thought of. We'll make him believe."

I shake my head. "We'll give them a day, and then if I still don't have a better plan, I'll go to Struz."

Alex leaves, and I can tell by how loudly he slams the door that he's pissed off. And then I'm alone, with copies of my father's case files and too much that I don't understand.

I grab the folder with the crime-scene photos from the house. There's nothing in there that I want to see ever again, but that's all the more reason I should look at them one more time. I don't want to have missed something just because I'm being squeamish.

The first picture is the one of the man slumped in the back hallway. I skip that one because the image of it has been burned into my retinas.

His eyes are red, like they were bleeding when he died, and when I take another couple of steps to see him at a better angle, I see it's not just his skin, but also his bones that look melted—because I can see his skeleton, and the bones look like they're dripping—like this is some kind of Salvador Dalí painting come to life.

I take a deep breath, refocus, and flip to the picture of the body in the kitchen. Based on her clothes—pants, a blouse, a cardigan, and an apron—I wonder if she's the wife of the guy I saw, the woman who lived in this house. She has her hand around a frying pan, only her hand and the handle of the pan look like they've melted together, almost to the point you can't tell where one ends and one begins. The skin from her face is all but gone, and she looks like just a misshapen melted skeleton from that angle.

I have to look away. Up at the ceiling or something—just away from that image. I know the trick is that I have to stop thinking of her as a person, and just focus on the fact that this is a case, and I'm trying to solve it. That's how agents who work on cases like this don't go insane. Their brain has to separate the horror of the crime from the humanity of the victim.

I can't seem to do it. I just keep wondering what she was doing with the frying pan—cooking, washing the dishes, what?

In the grand scheme of things, I guess that says something about me, that I'm not a sociopath or whatever, which is great, except . . .

I need to be able to do this. I need to look at these pictures for clues instead of getting so hung up on who these people were. Because this is one piece of the case that doesn't seem to quite fit with everything Ben has told me. Even if someone else is opening up the portals, even if we're only seven days now from Wave Function Collapse, there's no explanation for what happened at this house.

I turn back to the picture in time to jump when I feel a hand on my shoulder. "What are you looking at?"

I leap to my feet, pushing Jared back in the process, and scramble to turn all the pictures over and shut the files so he doesn't have to see any of that.

"God, I was just asking," he says as he turns to leave the room.

"No, Jared, it's not that I don't want you to see," I say, following him into the living room. I opt to go for partial truth on this. "It's one of Dad's cases, the one he was working on when

312

he died. I'm trying to figure some of it out, that's all."

"Why can't I help?" he asks, folding his arms across his chest. "You think I don't want to help figure out how he died?"

"No, it's not that. I know you do, it's just . . ."

"Just what? That I'm too young? That I don't know anything? What?"

I shake my head, even though it is that he's too young. "Jared, *I'm* too young for this. Trust me, I don't know anything either. But I still have to try."

"Then why can't I try too?"

I don't have an answer for that, and he sees it on my face and shakes his head. Then he turns around and leaves me here with these nauseating pictures I don't understand.

And I let him.

06:01:10:48

L ife is supposed to have returned to normal.

It's Friday. School started back up today—but only about half the student body actually showed. Jared tried halfheartedly to get me to let him stay home, but the truth is, during aftershocks, we're probably safer at school than we are in the house.

"How can they suspend people for something that happens when there's no school?" Jared says, as Alex pulls into the pool's parking lot. They've been talking about why half the football team was walking around looking beat up today—apparently part of life returning to normal is that a bunch of guys decided to get into a brawl over a few traded insults. "It's bullshit."

"We're living in a social world these days," Alex says. "Next thing you know we'll have no freedoms and it'll be like *Total Recall* or *Enemy of the State*."

"Oh my God, stop with the bad action movies."

"Hey, I liked *Enemy of the State*," Jared says, opening his door. Then he looks at me. "Will you come pick me up tonight?"

"Maybe," I say. "If it's not me, I'll call Struz and ask him to do it."

Jared frowns, and I'm overcome with guilt. "Okay," he says, shutting the door behind him.

Both Alex and I are silent as we watch Jared head down the steps and into the gate, and then we're driving again, pulling back onto the street, heading home, and the silence seems to stretch miles between us.

It's not like I don't know what he's mad about—I do. He wants me to go to the FBI with the information about the alternate universes. Alex knows the silent treatment is the easiest way to make me give in to whatever he thinks is best, but this time is different. The stakes are higher.

Finally I can't stand it anymore. "Please tell me you have something better than a bad Arnold movie planned for tonight."

"Don't do that," he says.

"What?"

"Act like everything's just fine and we can joke around like we always do."

"Alex, I've told you," I say with a sigh. "I can't tell Struz. He's not going to believe me anyway."

"Why not?" Alex says.

"You didn't believe me at first either."

"At first," Alex says. "But I do now—or at least I'm willing to consider it an option. Struz will be too."

I shake my head. "This is too *weird*, Alex. This is stuff that shouldn't be possible. Alternate worlds. It's crazy."

And that's a big part of it. What's going on—what I've chosen to believe—is crazy. I don't want Struz to think I've cracked under the loss of my dad and the pressure of taking care of my family. Not when mental disorders run in my family.

"You need to tell him," Alex says again.

"I can't. Not yet."

"That's bullshit, J," he says back. "We're sitting on this huge secret, and it doesn't make any sense for us to be running around playing junior detective when the FBI doesn't know what the hell is going on. They have resources and we have nothing!"

"You didn't seem to mind playing junior detective when we thought it was a virus," I say. I don't add that he also didn't mind when it was just me and him.

What I don't say doesn't matter. I've pissed him off enough. I feel the brakes grinding together before I realize he's decided to pull over and stop the car. The tires squeal and the car jerks to a stop, and Alex turns around to face me. "Six days," he says. "Six days!"

"Don't you think I know that?" I yell back.

"Look, when we thought it was a virus, we were planning to tell your dad the theories as they came up, just like we always do," he says, his voice slightly more even, though no less tense. "And this is completely different. We stumbled on something way too big for us, and as far as we know, the FBI doesn't even think it's in the realm of possibility. You need to tell Struz."

"We've had this argument before," I say. "Nothing is going to change if we have it again."

"No, that's not good enough. I just sat back and did nothing when you got roofied and didn't want to tell your dad because it was your decision to make, but I'm not—"

"What does that have to do with anything?"

"I'm just saying, this is bigger than you."

"Again, you think I don't know that? Even if Struz did believe me," I say, trying to force myself to calm down, "how is he going to actually help us? The FBI will bring Ben, Elijah, and Reid in for questioning, which would actually waste more time."

"Is that what this is about?" Alex laughs, only it's filled with bitterness. "You don't want to turn Ben in? I don't care what you feel for him, J, for all we know he hasn't told us everything, and by protecting him, you could just—"

"It would end up being counterproductive!" I lean toward Alex. "If Ben, Elijah, and Reid are the only ones who understand alternate universes, we need them. Locking them up and questioning them could be the worst thing for us."

Alex shakes his head. "Why do you even believe them?"

"What?"

"Why do you even believe them?" he asks again. "Seriously, three random stoners? Sure, they're not as bad as we thought they were, but still, you don't even know them."

"You said you believed them," I say, even though I know that's not what Alex wants to hear. He wants to hear he's right— because he would be, except I do feel like I know Ben.

"I said the alternate universe theory works," Alex corrects me. "It fits, and yeah, I guess I could believe them about that, but why do we believe they're not the ones opening the portals anymore? Their motivation still hasn't changed."

"People were dying. Ben wouldn't—"

"How do you know that? Because you think he's hot? C'mon—"

"This is crap," I say, unbuckling my seat belt. "I can't even talk to you. Not when you're not going to listen to anything I say."

"Seriously?" Alex says. "Seriously. I always listen to what you say. How can you even—"

"You didn't believe me when I told you I'd died!"

Neither one of us has any response to that. I don't because I didn't realize until this moment I was still upset about it, and Alex doesn't because he didn't, either. Only now that I've said it, I'm furious. My hands curl into fists, and I feel like my whole body is shaking under the weight of my anger.

"I told you," I say. "I told you I died and you passed it off as my optic nerves firing, like I was just some crazy idiot girl."

"That is not at all—" He's shaking his head.

"Of course you don't believe Ben. You didn't even believe *me*, even though you've known me forever. You don't believe anything."

I'm suddenly too hot to be in the car. I swing the door open and get out.

And as I'm slamming the door shut, I hear Alex say, "I always believe you!"

"Not when it matters!" I yell back, even if it isn't completely true.

Then I stalk off down the road.

Alex tries to drive alongside me for a few minutes, but when I give him the finger, he throws up his arms and hits the gas.

I watch as his car gets smaller and smaller until it finally disappears, and when it does, I have the urge to sit down and cry a little. And with everything going on, I don't quite have the strength to resist it. So I do.

05:23:51:24

Without thinking about it, I show up at the Staybridge. Reid's blue 4Runner is easy to spot now, because it also throws into sharp relief how wrong everything went for Ben and Elijah. All three of them went into the foster-care system on the same day, and through the luck of the draw, Reid found a family that took him in and adopted him and gave him things—like a nice car. And Ben and Elijah got shuffled from home to home.

I'm sick thinking about it.

Ben must see me coming, because he opens the passenger door and gets out. "Is everything okay?"

I nod, despite the fact that my eyes feel a little watery, and my throat constricts as I think about the way I just left things with Alex. I don't want to tell him that, though, so I try for the most honest answer I can give. "I just can't sit at my house and wait anymore."

Ben nods once like he understands, and Reid gets out of the car. "I'll check on Elijah." Then he looks at me and back at Ben. "You should sit in the driver's seat. Just in case."

And then Reid is gone, walking around to the back of the

hotel, and Ben is moving around the car to the driver's side. I slide into the passenger seat and shut the door. Even with the back windows open, the inside of the car is hot and sticky, and my shoes step on a week's worth of potato-chip wrappers, making them crunch.

"Please tell me you've had some real food," I say, looking over at Ben.

A smile starts to curl his lips, but he doesn't look at me.

"If you could eat anything right now, what would it be?" I ask.

"Steak," he says without hesitation. "A huge piece of steak, medium rare, and mashed potatoes."

"Oh my God, testosterone overload," I say.

"Does that mean you weren't offering to make dinner?" He laughs.

"I might have offered to spring for a pizza."

"My mom made the best steak and mashed potatoes," he says quietly. "It's what we ate on all our birthdays."

I'm about to say something else when someone—a man—comes out the front door of the Staybridge. Ben and I both sit up, and he grabs something from the center console and leans forward, lifting it to his eyes.

Binoculars. And ones that look like they must be pretty expensive.

Ben hands them to me, and I look through. As soon as I manage to find the guy walking out of the Staybridge, I know it's not our guy. Alias Mike Cooper has probably fifty pounds of muscle on this guy.

I give Ben the binoculars and lean back in the seat. "Where's Elijah?" I ask.

"We've been taking turns watching the two exits. Two of us will stay in the car and watch the front exit, and one of us will hang out by the back exit in case he comes out that way."

"Just out in the open?"

Ben shakes his head. "There's some trees and bushes back there."

"So you've been hiding out in the shrubbery in the middle of the night?"

He smiles again. "Yeah, it's not really as glamorous or exciting as Elijah had imagined. This guy is pretty damn boring."

Speak of the devil. Elijah turns the corner of the hotel and starts jogging toward us.

"He would do anything for me," Ben says as we watch him. "He always has. He's like my version of Alex."

That hurts, since Alex and I are currently not talking, but Ben doesn't know that, so I just nod and keep watching Elijah. Alex puts up with all my shit and misanthropic tendencies. I suppose I should be able to understand why Ben puts up with Elijah.

When Elijah reaches us, he opens Ben's door and says, "Get out."

"You're sending me somewhere already?" Ben says. "Reid just got back."

Elijah shakes his head. "That dickwad spends too much time jerking off. Go inside to the third floor and see if Suspect Zero is still in his room."

Ben groans a little, but he gets out of the car and Elijah gets in instead.

"Wait, what are you going to do? You can't just knock on his door," I say.

"Sure he can," Elijah says, pulling the door shut before Ben has a chance to answer. Then he says, "Relax, it's been two days since we first pulled the fire alarm."

That's how they found out what room alias Mike Cooper is in. Each one of them took a floor, Elijah pulled the fire alarm, and then they each pretended to be just another aimless hotel guest walking around and going, "What happened? Is there really a fire?" Not exactly science, but it worked.

"It hasn't quite been two days, actually. Besides, a fire alarm every two days, even for a dump like this, is excessive," I say.

Elijah shrugs. "Ben probably won't do that anyway. He'll listen at the door, try to hear if the fucking guy is still watching TV, and he can always make a hole in the door or the wall or something and peek through."

That doesn't sound stealthy, and I almost say it, but Elijah must see my face, because he just laughs. "Relax, Tenner, it would be a tiny hole, and he probably won't do that anyway. You act like we've never spied on people before."

I don't say anything else. I'm not exactly excited about sitting in the car alone with Elijah.

As if he can read my mind, he says, "I don't care that you don't like me."

"That lack of caring is mutual."

He smirks at that but doesn't say anything else. We watch as a woman and two small children come out of the Staybridge and head toward the In-N-Out across the street.

"Don't fuck with his head, either."

"Save it," I say. "Whatever happens between me and Ben isn't any of your business."

"Oh, but it is." Elijah turns and looks at me this time. "Because nothing is going to stop me from getting home. Nothing. Not this fucking guy, not Wave Function Collapse, and certainly not you. We're all getting home."

"Right, even if it kills innocent people. Trust me, I think I understand your commitment to the cause."

"You don't understand shit. He got plenty of those portals open without bringing anyone through, and he can do it. He can fix the portals, figure out where we're going, and get us home. I know he can." Only I have the sense Elijah is trying to convince himself and not me.

Which I might have been tempted to say if his phone didn't ring.

"What?" Elijah says as he answers it. "Shit, we'll be right there."

He hangs up and starts the car, and I reach around to pull my seat belt on as I ask, "Where are we going?"

"Call Ben," Elijah says. "Suspect Zero is leaving out the back right now."

"So where are we going?" But I open up my phone and dial Ben.

"Tell him to break in and toss the room but to keep his phone on. We'll call when he's coming back." When Ben answers, I repeat Elijah's instructions, even though my heart is racing and I feel a little light-headed about the fact that I just told the guy I like to break into a hotel room.

"We're following this guy. If he's opening portals, I want to know how he can fucking help us get home." Elijah pulls over and we pick up Reid, who gets into the back and makes the entire car reek of cigarettes.

"He's in the blue Ford F-150," Reid says. "Remember to stay

a car's length behind him."

Elijah doesn't acknowledge Reid's instruction, but I watch as the Ford turns onto University Avenue and as Elijah waits for two cars to pass before he turns onto the road as well.

I'm not sure how, but this stakeout just turned into a chase.

05:23:41:48

I realize where we're going as soon as I see the Ford F-150 turn into the residential neighborhood. "What the hell is he doing *here?*" Reid mutters as we follow him.

"Circle around," I tell Elijah. "Pass him when he stops. Two streets down, make a right, then you can make your next two rights, and we'll be able to see him from the street."

He glances at me, and I say, "This is where the portal dropped three people and melted everyone inside."

Elijah's eyes widen with surprise, and he turns back to look at Reid. Some sort of information passes in that look, but I'm not sure what it is, and then Elijah does what I said, passing the Ford F-150 just as alias Mike Cooper is getting out of the car.

It is him—the guy from my father's grainy gas station photo. He looks like he's in his thirties, and he's definitely military. Seeing him in person, it's not just the haircut, but his posture, the way he carries himself, his movements—it all says military.

As we're passing him, I take note of the bulges in his

clothes—his left ankle and the small of his back—that's where he's carrying his guns.

I wonder if he's some kind of spy, a navy SEAL turned CIA operative or something. If he does know something about the portals and the radiation burns, he must be working for someone. The thought is a rock in the pit of my stomach. If this guy is just muscle, we're a long way from figuring out who's opening portals and how we can prevent Wave Function Collapse. Alex might have been right. Even if alias Mike Cooper is just a mercenary, this is even bigger than I'd expected.

When we park, I make us all scrunch down in our seats so it's not obvious we're spying on him. We're at the corner, across the street from where that house used to be, and alias Mike Cooper is standing on the scorched earth with his back to us, but I don't want to take any chances.

After about half a minute of silence, Reid says, "What's he doing?"

"How the fuck should I know?" Elijah says.

Alias Mike Cooper squats and reaches down to the ground. "It looks like he's checking out the dirt." Which makes no sense at all. What *is* he doing?

"Let's get out of here," Reid says. "We'll have more luck helping Ben with checking out the room."

"Don't be such a pussy. We need to call him when he's leaving and—"

"Get down, he's getting up," I say as alias Mike Cooper stands up and starts walking the backyard fence line. He's going the same direction I went when I was here that night, and once I realize that, I can't help but shiver.

"This fucking guy," Elijah says, and then he looks at me.

"Should one of us get out and get a closer look?"

"Are you kidding? He'd see us for sure. How would you explain that away?"

Elijah looks back at Reid, and out of the corner of my eye, I'm sure I see Reid shake his head slightly.

I'm ready to ask them what the heck they're hiding from me, when another car pulls up in front of the house. A car I recognize.

It's a TrailBlazer. Specifically, it's Barclay's TrailBlazer, and I have a moment to wonder if it was stolen from him before the door opens and he gets out.

"Who the hell is that?" Elijah asks, looking at me.

"Doesn't he work for the FBI?" Reid asks, sliding farther down in his seat.

"The fucking FBI," Elijah says, glaring at me, and I know they're both going to be even more dead against involving Struz now.

Barclay walks slowly but with purpose as he approaches alias Mike Cooper. He must have taken the information I gave him, found alias Mike Cooper, and made the connection himself, and now Barclay is going to arrest him and crack the case. I want to be angry with the arrogant prick for not telling me whatever it is he's found, but I only feel relief.

"How are we going to get any information from him now?" Elijah says.

"I can probably get info out of Struz," I say. Or Barclay, even though I don't say it. Again, he'll owe me since this bust will make his career. He'll probably get a promotion in a few months and become a full agent.

"You better not say anything about us," Reid says. "I don't

want the FBI knocking on my door."

"How'd this FBI guy even find our Suspect Zero?" Elijah asks. "Did you fucking tell him?"

I feel giddy and light-headed, and I'm sure a smile has just taken up permanent residence on my face. This was actually the perfect solution for me. The FBI knows now. I can go to Struz, confess everything, and they already have the bad guy.

Only as I watch them, it's as if everything is happening in slow motion. "Wait."

Elijah and Reid drop whatever argument they were about to launch at me and turn to the windows, and the three of us watch Barclay talk to alias Mike Cooper.

It doesn't look like an interrogation.

It looks like they're chatting.

Like they might be friends.

05:18:13:34

When I get home that night, after we fill Ben in on the meeting alias Mike Cooper had with Barclay and he fills us in on the fact that he found nothing out of the ordinary at the hotel room—*nothing*—I open the front door to find Jared playing video games and eating more pizza and Struz on the phone in the kitchen.

The house is a mess. Struz has actually tried to pick up after himself and Jared. He just hasn't done a great job, because there are still three people eating and at least pseudo-inhabiting this house, and no one's actually cleaning it.

I check on Jared first. He's playing *World of Warcraft* again, not really a game I get in any capacity even though I play with him sometimes, but he's addicted. "How was polo?" I ask.

Jared shrugs in response.

"Did you get enough to eat?"

He nods, and when I reach down to tousle his hair, he shrugs me off. "I'm fine."

"Okay, let me know if you need anything," I say, because I just can't do another fight today. I'll have it out with Jared tomorrow. When I have a better idea of what I might say.

I head back into the kitchen, thinking about Ben. He did make a conscious effort to carefully go through the room so alias Mike Cooper wouldn't know anyone had been there.

"Look, Barclay, did you meet with him today?" Struz says, and I freeze where I am and slowly back out of the kitchen, while Struz's back is turned. "Good. No, that's good."

Struz couldn't possibly be talking about alias Mike Cooper—unless Barclay *was* there to interrogate him and we just misjudged it. We were far away.

"All right," Struz says. "Well, get it done. I'll see you tomorrow."

Get what done? I want to ask, but I can't make my body move, I can't make my lips open, and I certainly can't make words come out.

I can't possibly believe Struz is somehow involved—I just can't.

Except ever since Ben brought me back to life, no one is who I thought they were.

Which means I can't tell Struz about what's going on—not yet—because the only thing I know anymore is that I don't know who to trust.

04:00:00:00

A day passes and nothing changes.

I help Jared with homework and clean the house like everything is fine, only this time it isn't an escape, because Ben is all I can think about no matter where I am. I check my phone for texts from him or Elijah every couple of minutes.

We requested a psych consult, and my mother's still in the hospital—she's just been moved to the psychiatric ward.

Jared's decided the best way to convince me he's not too young is to give me the silent treatment.

Elijah swears they'll find out more about alias Mike Cooper next time.

I give him and Ben more time—and then more time. And still more time.

Because I don't have another plan.

When I tried to apologize, Alex declared himself out until we call Struz and get people who know what they're doing involved. And he's not going to speak to me until then either.

I still don't know how the house fits with everything else.

And I'm still not a single step closer to figuring out what to do to stop this countdown.

Which means I've become obsessed with it—as if watching it tick might somehow make it slow down or at least not feel like it's speeding up.

Which is why at 5:10 p.m. on Sunday evening, I know the exact moment four days to Wave Function Collapse becomes three.

03:23:59:59.

03:08:20:00

After checking up on my mother, I come home to a quiet house. Jared is still asleep. And still mad at me for the other night, for not telling him anything, for not treating him like an adult, for locking myself in Dad's home office, for breaking up with Nick of all things—for everything.

I check my phone for a text from Ben, but there's nothing. I debate texting him to see what's going on, but I know he'd tell me if there was news.

I clean up the kitchen. We're almost out of dishes—not that it matters much, since Struz and Jared seem like they're happy to live out of pizza boxes. I take out the trash and the recyclables before they both start encroaching on our living space, and then I open the fridge to see what's inside that's salvageable.

In the back of the fridge, I find a Tupperware of spaghetti with red sauce, obviously a batch my father made and then forgot about. From the way it smells, it might be a month old. He always cooked too much pasta—we usually had enough for at least two more people. He never learned how much was enough. And he always forgot about leftovers.

But holding the cold Tupperware container in my hand, I don't care about the smell. I just wish I hadn't always complained so much about the fact that he cooked the same thing over and over again and that I hadn't yelled at him so much about putting food in the fridge and forgetting about it.

That all seems so insignificant now.

And that makes me think of Jared. If I'm looking at what could be the end of the world, I'm not about to let my brother be mad at me in the middle of it.

It's not that I'm giving up—not even for a second—but I'm looking at it with a heavy dose of realism. We're stalled. We don't know how to stop Wave Function Collapse. And if the world really ends, I need Jared and me to be on good terms.

There's only one thing left for me to resort to.

Bribery.

From my mother's email address, I email both of our homeroom teachers and excuse us for the day. I let Jared sleep until nine forty-five, and then I wake him up with waffles and ice cream. I actually wouldn't have let him sleep so long except our waffle iron is archaic and it totally burned my first attempt.

He doesn't ask what's up, because he's still giving me the silent treatment, but I know he wants to—which is important.

"Here," I say when he's finished. I hand him the video game Alex's dad brought home yesterday. Anything Jared-related has managed to remain unaffected by his whole not-talking-to-me thing. The game is wrapped in funny snowman wrapping paper, because when he was in preschool, Jared had a thing for snowmen.

"What is it?" The first three words he's said to me in days.

I shrug like I don't know.

He gives me a skeptical look but rips into it anyway, his whole face lighting up as he realizes what it is. "Shit! How'd you get this? It's not gonna be released for at least another month!"

"I called in a favor," I say. "I know people, you know." More like Alex's dad knows people, but whatever.

"This is awesome," Jared whispers. "Seriously, Janelle, so cool."

"Good, now before you think I'm just going to let you cut school and get you an advance copy of a video game every time you're mad at me, get dressed. We have things to do."

He looks crestfallen, and those big puppy eyes almost make me change my mind. "I can't start playing now?"

"Later tonight." *Like when I'm absorbed in the case again and you need something to do.* Only I don't say that, because I know Jared, and being *that* truthful might ruin his excitement about the bribery gift.

"Where are we going?" Jared asks.

"Disneyland."

I leave the room, because we both need a minute to digest why the hell I just decided that.

After all, the last time we went to Disney, Mom had just gotten out of her third stint in a mental hospital and Dad actually took vacation days and left his FBI cell at home.

It's one of my top five moments. The only top five moment with all of us together.

On the car ride home, Dad held Mom's hand, Jared fell asleep with the stuffed animal our dad won at one of those shooting games, and at the end of the night when I was almost asleep, my mom came into my room, stroked my hair, and told me how she was proud of me.

I'm sure she's said it other times.

But that's the only time I remember.

Despite everything going on, Disney manages to make me feel like I'm ten again.

It feels like we've somehow managed to transport ourselves outside of the real world, and it's easier not to think of real-world problems. The smell of popcorn and funnel cake, the bright colors, the balloons, and little kids on vacation laughing and screaming, it's happiness, and it's everywhere.

Jared and I get giggly over everything. We gorge ourselves on chili bread bowls from Golden Horseshoe and then Mickey Mouse ice cream from one of the street carts, and wait in line for Space Mountain and the Tower of Terror twice, though since it's mid-September and we just had a horrendous earthquake, we don't have to wait too long. We catch the Jedi Training show and even the end-of-the-night parade and the fireworks at Sleeping Beauty Castle. At one point, after fooling around with all the characters in costume, we almost get thrown out because Jared tackles Goofy to the ground.

It's the perfect day.

Not because of any one specific thing we do, but because it's just me and Jared. We're together, we're happy and laughing, we're not thinking about school or our parents or even what's coming next. We're not thinking at all. We're just moving from one ride to the next.

We're only living for each moment as it happens.

And knowing I might die in less than a week—for real this

time—that perfection means everything.

Because Jared is the most important person in my life. Now and always.

And if I died today, my perfect moment wouldn't be my mother and me at the beach. Not anymore.

It would be this.

On the way home, Jared is leaning back in his seat, his eyes closed. I think he's asleep until he asks, "So what'll happen to us now, anyway?"

I keep my eyes on the road. "What do you mean?" *Please don't be what I think.*

"Now that Dad . . . and with Mom . . ."

"Try not to worry about it," I say automatically. Even though it sounds lame. Even though there are a million better things— truer things—I could say. But I can't.

"Is Mom going to be in the hospital for a while?"

I hope so, but I can't tell him that. Instead I say, "Maybe," and hope he changes direction.

But he doesn't. "We're not going to get put in foster care or anything, are we?"

"No," I say, even though I don't really know. I think between Struz and the money I've got in my name, I'll be old enough that the court will let Jared stay with me. Suing for emancipation is just another thing I've been putting off until after . . .

Jared is still looking at me, but I can't get anything other than clichés through the lump in my throat. "We've still got each other."

"No, it's not that," Jared says. "I guess . . . I mean, I miss Dad, I do. But sometimes it doesn't feel real, because he was never around, you know? He was always working, so it doesn't feel like he's really gone."

I have to swallow a few times before I can trust myself to get the words out. "I know," I say. Because I do. Sometimes I forget Dad isn't just at work. "I still wake up in the middle of the night thinking he's going to come home any minute, or I check my phone to make sure he didn't call to tell me he can't find his house keys."

Jared laughs. "I still look for the *X-Files* notes, you know, the Post-its with quotes that he used to put on the fridge sometimes when he was in the middle of a case?"

I nod, trying to ignore the way my eyes are starting to burn.

"How long do you think it will feel like that?"

I would never trade what I have with Jared. Ever. But there are moments—like this one right now—where I feel like I was thrown into parenting him, and I resent my parents, both of them, for dumping this on me. I don't have all the answers. Not for Jared and not for myself.

"On some level, probably for a long time," I say. "Maybe even forever."

Jared nods and looks at his lap. "I feel . . . I don't know. I just . . . I don't feel sad enough about it." He whispers the last part, as if he's ashamed.

My throat constricts again, and my breath hitches. "I know how you feel," I say, because I don't want him to feel guilty. Only it's not true. I don't know how he feels. Not at all.

Because every time I forget that my dad is really gone, and then I realize he *is*, I feel devastated all over again—like I'm losing him all over again. I even miss the bad cooking, the terrible B movies on the Syfy channel, the lame jokes, the stunts he used to pull to embarrass me. I especially miss the faces he'd make when he got phone calls from Alex's mom, about nothing in particular, just her wanting to feel in the know about his job, while at the same time checking up on me and making sure I wasn't being a bad influence on her son.

But when Jared was younger, before we both gave up on Mom, Dad and I moved heaven and earth to keep him from seeing her at her worst. We both kept him an arm's length from that. The only problem is, of course, that Dad coped by working more, and I coped by taking care of Jared. Which means Dad pushed Jared an arm's length away too—essentially he pushed Jared to me.

For the past fourteen years, I've been pretty much the only parent Jared has known.

02:15:19:49

After Jared's asleep, I sit at the kitchen table and stare into space. I don't even think, I just try to absorb some of the peace from the quiet house.

And then the phone rings.

"If I'd known you'd leave us for an earthquake," I say when I answer.

"Not now," Struz says, and his tone makes me sit up straighter. Whatever he's called about, it's serious. I'm about to ask if everything's okay, but then he three-names me. "Janelle Eileen Tenner, I'm going to ask you something, and I need you to give me the straight-up, no-nonsense, absolute truth on the answer."

"Done." Because whatever he asks, if it's important I'll tell him anything.

"Were you at the Federal Building downtown today?"

"No," I say, and then, because that might not be enough, I add, "I took Jared to Disneyland."

"And you didn't open up the safe in your father's office?"

"No." I didn't even know there was a safe in his office, but of course I'd love to get in there now.

The other end of the phone is silent, and I wait for Struz to speak, listening to the empty house and the sound of the steady rain outside, while a feeling of dread settles between my shoulder blades and begins to radiate outward.

"You're not lying to me," he says, but it isn't a question. He knows I'm telling the truth.

I answer anyway. "No. What's missing?"

He doesn't answer me. Instead I hear him mutter to someone wherever he is, and then he sighs into the phone. "I won't make it back there tonight, but I'll come by the house to check on you tomorrow."

"Okay." I want to say something else, but I don't even know what.

"And whatever you've been doing on this case, Janelle, you need to stop. Shut it down."

"Why?" I ask. "What happened?"

But it doesn't matter, because he's already hung up.

I stand up and move over to the copies of the case files I still have spread out on the dining room table, wondering if that was my moment where I should have admitted there's more to this thing than he knows. I pick up the stack of my dad's notes about alias Mike Cooper—and the notes I've added from Elijah and Ben stalking him—and start reading through them again to see if I can somehow see something new. Alex is right—it's ridiculous to suggest I can make sense of it when my dad's entire team at the FBI has more resources, manpower, and experience, and they're coming up empty. But I'm still driven to try. Because I don't know exactly how Barclay fits into this thing.

And because if I don't focus on solving this case, I'll have to focus on how lost I feel without my dad around.

Two days, Ben, alternate universes, Wave Function Collapse, alias Mike Cooper, the house, radiation poisoning, and my father—dead. There has to be something else I haven't seen yet.

I look at the receipt for the different kinds of chlorine I bought at the pool supply store. If alias Mike Cooper wasn't actually going to use these for some kind of bomb, what was he going to do?

I doubt he was really planning to use them to clean pools. So what other uses are there for chlorine? I grab a pen and a scrap of paper and write them down.

> water purification
> disinfectant
> baseline for a number of chemicals *
> dry-cleaning
> medicines

I think it's also used in manufacturing to make things, everything from temperature-resistant nonstick Teflon on frying pans to components of cars, and a lot of other stuff, which means this is going to require more research and probably not get me anywhere.

When I put the pen down and look back at the table, I have that hyperaware feeling again, like someone's watching me. I try to ignore it. It's after two a.m., and I don't hear anything to suggest Jared is awake. I get up, move a load of wet clothes from the washer to the dryer, grab a glass of water, and come back to the table. I need to try to solve this. We're running out of time.

But the feeling stays with me, giving me goose bumps.

And when I look up, my eyes go directly to the window and

my blood stops moving for a second, because Ben is standing under the back porch light in the pouring rain, his hair soaking wet, flattened on his head, rivulets of water streaming down his face into his eyes.

I put my hand to my chest and listen for a heartbeat and as I do, it comes back double the pace, double the strength, and I wonder if Ben is real. Or if going without seeing him for a whole two days was too hard for my subconscious. The rain just accentuates the darkness of his hair and eyes, and I imagine his lips tinged blue from the chill.

I must be dreaming.

How is it possible to go years and never speak to someone, never notice them, not once, and then suddenly think about them all the time? Even when you know nothing will—nothing *can*—ever happen between you?

Without realizing it, I've stood up and taken a step toward him, and I hold my hand out, pressing it to the window. Ben mirrors my movements, and I know he must be my imagination, that I must be asleep at the table and dreaming this, because everything else in my mind just falls away, fades out, and there's just the thundering sound of the rain outside, the pounding of my heart reverberating through my veins, echoing in my ears, and the warmth of his hand on the glass.

I see his chest rise and fall, like he's breathing heavily; wisps of warm air fog the window, and I realize I'm breathing just as hard.

My fingers tense, and I wish I had more control over this dream, that I could just will away the glass between us and feel his skin touching mine.

Then I notice his mouth moving. I look closer, focus on what he's trying to tell me. And I realize this can't be a dream. Because the Ben of my imagination wouldn't be standing in the rain outside my dining room with red-rimmed eyes like he'd been crying, asking if he can come inside.

When I open the back door, he's there in front of me. But the dreamlike illusion is gone because he's shivering so hard his whole body shakes, and I can see now the rain only managed to wash away some of his tears. I suddenly feel so cold, *I* start to shiver too, and I have to clench my jaw to keep my teeth from chattering.

"What happened?" I ask as I pull him inside and shut the door.

His head drops. "I'm so sorry," he whispers. "I didn't have anywhere to go."

"You can always come here," I say as I reach my arms around him, pulling him to me. Water soaks the front of my clothes, but I don't care because this is Ben, and we're both freezing, and despite the secrets between us, I would do anything for him.

His arms hesitate at first, but then he presses his cheek against mine, and as his body sags, his resistance fades. His arms encircle me, his hands entwining in my hair.

"It's okay," I whisper into his ear, even though I don't really know that. I know this is bad. Whatever drove him to come to my house *has* to be bad.

We stand like that for a while, just clutching each other. And the heat from his body contrasts with the chill of our wet clothes. Our breathing and heartbeats speed up in sync until the pounding of my pulse and the rise and fall of my chest are loud enough they drown out even the sound of the rain.

There's a fierce tension in our bodies, as if any movement,

any shift would release the coiled springs of our bodies.

I break away despite the physical ache that sets in. "Come on. Let's get you into different clothes." I try to ignore how ragged my voice sounds, and hope he doesn't pick up on it.

Focusing on the task at hand, I grab the zipper of his hoodie and start sliding it downward. But before I can get to the bottom, Ben steps into me again. His hand touches my neck, and his forehead leans against mine. His face feels feverish, and he's breathing hard—a fluttering goes through my chest. Because I want him. More than I've ever wanted anything in my life— I want Ben.

His hand tilts my chin up. I close my eyes. His breath is warm against my skin. Our noses brush against each other. I hold my breath. Before he kisses me, I can feel how close we are, like the nerve endings in my body are so sensitive they've extended inches outward, and the electricity between us charges the space between. Ben hesitates, and I wonder if he's changed his mind. I open my eyes to check.

And then his lips touch mine.

They're soft and smooth, and they taste salty from his tears. And then he opens his mouth, our tongues touch, I taste mint, and his other hand slides around my waist, settling on my back. My mouth opens wider, and I don't know if I'll ever get enough of him.

And his hand at my back pushes me into him. Hard.

There's no space between our bodies anymore, and all thought turns to frenzy.

Our lips are pressed together, our tongues moving, exploring. There's biting and sucking, and I don't have time to think about what I'm doing. Our hands are all over each other, gripping and pulling as if we can get any closer without merging into the same person.

When I back into the dryer, I realize he's been slowly pushing me. And then his hands slide down my back and he grabs my ass and lifts me up so I'm sitting on top of the dryer, the steady hum of vibration underneath me.

Out of surprise, our lips break, and Ben kisses his way across my jawline. He stands between my legs, and without thinking, I wrap them around him and pull him closer. His kisses trail from my ear down my neck, and a moaning sigh escapes my lips, mingling with my panting breaths.

I reach down for that zipper again because I need to put my hands on his skin, and his kisses move back up my neck.

When the zipper snaps open, Ben pauses, his breath hot in my ear. "Janelle Tenner," he whispers. "I fucking love you."

A smile breaks over my face, because even though it's not the romantic declaration of most girls' dreams, it's *so* Ben to remember something meaningful I said, even if it was in front of Alex and forty of our classmates on a day that feels like forever ago—it's so perfectly Ben.

I can't help it. I grab his face and cover his lips with mine. And then I slip my hands under the hoodie and over his shoulders, down his arms, pulling it off. He shrugs out of it without resistance.

"Janelle—"

I kiss him harder this time, and he sighs into my mouth.

His hands slip under my shirt and touch skin, and my heart hammers a mile a minute, like it might just start beating so hard it will break from my chest and exist outside my body.

I reach between us and press my palm against his chest to feel his heartbeat—to see if it's beating as hard as mine.

And it is.

But my hand—

My hand sticks awkwardly to his shirt.

That's when I open my eyes, look down. And see all the blood.

"**O**h my God." My hands are all over him. Only this time the franticness is completely different. Because now that I've noticed it, I can see the blood is *everywhere*. And with this much blood, his injuries have to be extensive.

When did I become such a hormone-crazed psycho? Ben comes to my house in the middle of the night, obviously upset, and I practically jump him. And in his weakened-by-blood-loss state, he doesn't fight me. If he ends up dying because I was turned on, I might shoot myself.

Something grabs my head and tilts my face upward, and I realize it's Ben's hands. He's forcing me to look at him and saying my name.

"Janelle, it's not my blood."

And I'm not sure how that's supposed to make this any better.

Okay, actually that does make it better. If someone had to lose this much blood I'd rather it not be Ben, but of course it begs the question, "Then whose blood is it?"

He doesn't answer right away, and that crazy, heart-pounding fear I had just moments ago morphs into the kind of fury that makes people do things so regretful and so rash that their mind makes them forget. If he doesn't tell me in the next ten seconds, I might strangle him.

I back up to avoid throttling him. I can't possibly keep my voice from shaking. "Whose. Blood. Is. It?"

Ben refuses to meet my eyes. "Elijah's."

"And?!" I've never been Elijah's biggest fan, but the fact that Ben isn't jumping in to offer an explanation or at least some information freaks me out. "Is he okay? What the hell happened?"

"I don't know," Ben says. He looks down at the blood, and for a second I wonder if Elijah is the bad guy, and if Ben found out and did this to him. But when he looks up at me, I know the guilt on his face would look different than it does. "I tried to heal him. But whatever I can do, it's like it didn't work on him, it's like he was immune."

"Where is he now?"

"I called 911. Waited for the ambulance."

I take a deep breath. If Elijah is in the hospital, there's nothing we can do for him. He's already got people helping him.

I turn on the light. "Take off your shirt," I say, grabbing one of my dad's old clean T-shirts from the to-donate pile. "Put this on."

He hesitates for a second, and the anger I feel melts away. I'm not sure why he came to my house. I'm not sure what possessed him to make out with me while his clothes were still stained with his best friend's blood. But he's here. And from the look on his face, he needs me. Yet he's still thinking of me and of everything I'm going through.

I nod, and he switches shirts, and I feel like something's wrong with me because I can't keep myself from thinking of the way his arms felt around me just a moment ago.

I throw his bloody shirt and his hoodie into the wash and bring him into the kitchen.

"All right, tell me what happened, and try to tell me fast, because I don't exactly have the most patience in the world."

"All three of us were at the Staybridge watching Suspect Zero. He finally left a couple hours ago, and we used a card to break into the room. That part was easy.

"This time we tossed the whole room, and we didn't really bother to be careful. It's just gotten to the point where we need to find *something* we can use, and I don't care whether he knew we'd been there or not."

I have to interrupt at this point, because I need to know.

"Did you find anything?" I don't say what else I'm thinking, which is *Please don't let this be an enormous waste of time* and *a mission that ended with Elijah in the hospital.*

Ben nods and reaches into his back pocket. "From what we found, it looks like his real name is Eric Brandt." The wallet he retrieves looks reminiscent of the one my dad carried with his FBI credentials in it.

I grab it and flip it open, examining the ID. The picture definitely identifies him as alias Mike Cooper/Suspect Zero or whatever we want to call him. And sure enough, the name under the ID reads ERIC BRANDT, INTERVERSE AGENCY, #340578.

"What does it mean?"

"I have no idea," Ben says. "I was hoping maybe you'd heard of that agency."

I shake my head. Not that I know all of the different agencies in the intelligence community, but this doesn't ring any bells to me. "I'll ask Struz."

Ben groans, leans back in his chair, balancing on its back two legs, and folds his hands behind his head. "We found that in the hotel safe. I managed to . . . manipulate it open. Most of the other stuff in the room just made him look like a guy who's been living out of the Staybridge for the past several months."

"How'd Elijah's blood get all over you?" I ask, since that's one of the most important things going on here.

"Eric Brandt came home," Ben says, leaning forward so all four legs of the chair land back on the ground. "Reid was supposed to be looking out for him, and I don't know what he was doing, but he was doing a shitty job. Brandt came back and found us in his room. He took aim at me because I was the one with his ID." Ben hesitates and shakes his head, and when his voice comes out this time, I can see that he's fighting to keep it even. "Elijah tried to grab me and pull me out of the way, but he got shot. Then Reid came back into the room, and he and I both went after Brandt. I wasn't worried about Elijah, because I figured I'd just heal him. I've done it before. . . ."

"How did you guys get away?"

"Elijah got up and got himself out of there, and between Reid and me, it was two on one. . . ."

My mouth dries out, and I fight the urge to take a step back. For a second I remember Reid saying, *Ben had Sam Hines within an inch of his life. If the cops hadn't showed up, Ben probably would have killed him*, and I'm worried they killed our only lead.

"Brandt was beat up enough that he wasn't about to come after us," Ben says instead, and I let out a breath I didn't know I was holding. "Elijah got us into a neighborhood cul-de-sac before he had to pull over. We were going to ditch Reid's car and call it in as stolen, just in case the guy had spotted it, and that's when I tried to heal Elijah."

He shakes his head and leans over so I can't see his eyes. "But I couldn't. I tried everything and it just didn't work. And I could feel whatever it is inside me, it was working on my end, but it just didn't *do* anything."

"You couldn't heal him?" I ask.

"No, it's like I couldn't sense those molecules at all."

"We'll figure it out," I say, because what else do you tell someone whose superhero powers suddenly stop working?

"So I called 911 and stayed with him while Reid took the car and was going to ditch it somewhere, and then when the ambulance was around the corner, I left and came here." He looks up. "I figured they'd ask questions."

I nod because he's right, and then I do what I've been doing all week. I try to think of what all this means. And I just don't know. "What about the chemicals?"

Ben shakes his head. "We couldn't find them anywhere."

I feel cold all over, because that could mean there *is* a bomb somewhere, or it could mean anything. Maybe he was just some undercover operative posing as a guy starting his own dry-cleaning business. Though something makes me doubt that.

Ben shivers next to me, and I realize his jeans are still wet from the rain outside. Whatever's going on, we're not actually going to solve this right now, this minute. "Come on," I say, standing up and pulling him with me. "You should get cleaned up. I'll get you some dry pants, and you can spend the night here. We'll figure it out in the morning."

I don't add the "or we'll die trying" part, since that's pretty much understood.

02:14:04:13

I put Ben in my dad's bedroom with a pile of fresh sheets, and when I'm safely back in my own room, I call Struz.

And get voice mail.

I'm tempted to leave a message, except I'm worried he'll take it the wrong way. He's working on something that's obviously got his mind wrapped in a knot, and I don't want him to freak out. He'll see that I called, and he'll call me back.

When I hang up the phone, I get into bed—I'm going to have to will myself to get any sleep tonight, and I'll probably have bad dreams. The house, my dad, earthquakes, getting hit by that truck, Ben—they all sort of meld together in my nightmares. Might as well add Elijah getting shot to them.

I'm reaching over to turn off the light when there's a knock on the door.

I don't move right away. It's either Ben or Jared. And I'm not sure which one I'd rather it be.

Normally, I'd easily say I'd rather it be Ben knocking on my bedroom door than my brother—except I'm mortified about how desperate I must have seemed when he got here.

I slide out of bed and go to the door.

It's Ben.

"Hey," he says, not meeting my eyes.

"You okay?" I ask, opening the door wider, so he can come inside rather than loiter in my hallway.

He does. And then he looks around as I shut the door. Obviously taking in the details of my room. It's standard—posters of indie bands on the wall, a few pictures of me and Alex and me and Jared, a stuffed bear, two bookshelves overflowing with books, a dresser with some clothes piled on top of it.

Finally his eyes come back to me. "I made a mistake," Ben says.

"What? What's wrong?"

"With you—I mean, with us," he whispers, and I swear for a second my heart stops beating. "I made a mistake."

I force myself to breathe normally, but I feel dizzy and light-headed and I want to just throw my arms around him. "What do you mean?"

He runs a hand through his floppy hair. "It's just you—you're perfect."

I can't help but laugh at that. "Not quite."

"No, you are," he says, reaching out to grab one of my hands. Our fingers intertwine, and those dark, deep-set eyes look straight into mine. "You're strong and smart, and you never put yourself first. You don't let anything get in your way, and you're beautiful."

My breath catches, because there isn't a single thing I could have wanted to hear more than that.

He shakes his head. "When you didn't know me, it was easy to just focus on getting home, but now we're running out of time. We've got less than three days, and you're right here and even more perfect than I imagined."

"I haven't tumbled short of your dreams?" I ask with a laugh.

He gives me a half smile, recognizing the *Gatsby* reference. "Not at all."

But I still don't know what that means for us. "Then what's the problem?"

"What if we do solve this? I'll have to leave," he says, squeezing my hand. "I'll have to go home. My family, I haven't seen them in ten years, and everything I've done since then has been aimed at getting back to them."

I nod. Because I know this. But he's thinking too far ahead. Even if we live through these next two days, who knows if he ever will get home? And who knows if something else wouldn't tear us apart anyway? But I can't say either of those things out loud.

"I'm not going to make you choose," I say, the words sticking in my throat because I know he'd have to. And I know I'd lose.

"But if we're together," Ben whispers, as if he's afraid to say it out loud, "how will I ever leave you?"

"If it ever comes to that—I won't ask you to stay."

He nods and pulls me into him, wrapping his arms around me and burying his face in my hair. "God, you smell so good."

"I just don't want to always regret this—that I felt this way about you and you felt this way about me, and we just lost it because we were afraid of the future," I say into his chest.

I feel him nodding into me. "I know."

We hold on to each other, and I feel the steady pounding of his heart against my body. I don't know if this is what love feels like, but I know I would do anything for him. Anything.

Ben pulls back and puts his hands on the sides of my face, and kisses me. Lightly. Quickly. Just once, and I feel empty and hollow and a little like I want to scream, because that kiss feels like good-bye.

But then he sucks in a breath and closes his eyes. And with only an inch separating our lips, he says, "There are only two things I can remember wanting. To go home. And you."

"Ben," I whisper against his lips. "I'm here now. Right now. And right now, I want you too."

"Janelle?" There's a knock at the door. "Did you oversleep or are we cutting again?"

Jared.

I open my eyes and remember Ben's arms are around me.

"Janelle?"

And Jared is right outside my room. Extricating myself from Ben's arms, I glance over at the clock and see that it's 7:05. School starts in less than a half hour.

"I'm up. I'll be right out!" I call, before shaking Ben.

He just groans.

"Hey, get your ass out of my bed and somewhere not in sight so I can open the door." His eyes open. "I'm serious. I'm not about to try to explain to Jared that we didn't actually sleep together and what you're doing in my bed."

Ben smiles a half-sleepy, half-purely-guy smile. "We did just sleep together."

"You know what I mean," I hiss. "I'm not about to have the 'I did not just have sex with that boy' talk with my little brother."

He smiles again, but this time he slides out of bed and onto the floor so the bed is hiding him from Jared, and I get out of bed and go to the door.

"I can't even remember the last time you overslept," Jared says when I open the door.

"Yeah, I know," I say, herding him away from my bedroom and down the stairs. "I'm actually not feeling that great," I lie. "I think I might stay home. But I'll get you some food if you call Alex and see if he's left yet." He probably has, but he'll probably also turn around and come back.

It takes a sesame bagel with cream cheese and five dollars to buy lunch, plus promising Alex that I plan to tell Struz what's really going on, to get Jared out the door, but I do it. And I try to do it without smiling like an idiot the whole time—which means I have to *not* think about the fact that Ben's upstairs on the floor of my bedroom.

When he comes downstairs after Alex's car has pulled out of the driveway, I'm paralyzed for a second. I'm sure he's about to say that last night was the mistake, that we have to go back to ignoring how we feel about each other, that he's scared.

But he doesn't. He hugs me and kisses me once. No, twice. Before he says, "I have to go home and check in with my foster parents and call Reid."

I nod. "What hospital is Elijah at? I'll call and see if I can get an update."

"I think they would have taken him to Scripps," Ben says, his face tight.

"I'm sure he'll be okay," I say, even though I don't know that. "I'll call Struz and ask him about the Interverse Agency, and then you, Reid, and I should meet up and figure out what we're going to do next."

Ben nods and looks away. "There's something else about last night that I haven't told you yet."

Blood burns in my head, but my whole body feels too cold. "What?"

Ben squeezes my hand. "In the safe, with the ID, Eric Brandt had a couple of files. I didn't have time to grab them because that was when he came in, but I saw them." He pauses, and I can't will myself to breathe until he keeps going. "They were files about your dad and Ryan Struzinski—Struz, right?"

I nod, but I can't speak. Files on my dad. And Struz. I want to ask what else was in the safe, was this guy following them around, keeping tabs on their schedule, what?

"I think you should tell Struz everything. I don't know what else we can do about it, but they could at least detain this guy and try to figure something out," he says.

I let out the breath I was holding and gasp a little, trying to refill my lungs. The headache I didn't realize I had is suddenly gone, and I could cry with relief. Because he's right. Alex has *been* right this whole time. I need someone to take this off my shoulders. But it was Ben's secret, and . . .

"They might detain *you*," I say.

He nods and then gives a shrug. "We're running out of time."

We sit in silence for a second, and then Ben pulls me into his arms and hugs me again, even more tightly this time. "I think, based on the files," he says, and I don't need to hear the end to know what he's thinking.

It's already occurred to me.

Eric Brandt may have killed my dad.

02:09:31:38

When Ben leaves, I call Struz again. And this time I leave a message. "It's Janelle. I think we should talk. I have some information—not about whatever was in the safe. I don't know anything about that. But I do have information I think you need. Call me when you get this." And then I add, "But don't worry. I'm fine," because I don't want him to jump to conclusions.

As I'm hanging up, the doorbell rings.

I look around, trying to figure out what Ben forgot, but nothing jumps out at me, so I just open the door and figure I'll let him come in and grab it. And hopefully steal one more kiss before he leaves.

But it isn't Ben on my doorstep.

It's Barclay. Only he's shaved his facial hair, and he seems young, almost boyish. Except for the look on his face—that's determined, and a little terrifying.

"Hey," I start to say, but he shoulders his way past me and inside the house, shutting the door behind him.

"We need to talk." This is serious Barclay—Agent Barclay—and I resist the urge to touch the light bruises on my arm, left over from where he grabbed me the other day.

He's not wearing standard FBI uniform—instead of a suit and tie, he's wearing a black jacket, a fitted gray T-shirt, black cargo pants, and military-style black boots. From the bulk in his jacket and pants, I can tell he's packing at least two weapons, one on his right ankle and one in a holster under his left arm. This means he's right-handed.

"Did you find out who that guy is?" I ask, even though I'm pretty sure that's not why he's here. In fact, I know that's not why he's here.

I don't know why he is. But I know it's not good.

Humans have precious few instincts, but that's because we don't listen to them. We let logic and knowledge get in the way. My dad always said that when instincts are at war with something society has taught you, listen to your instincts first and ask questions later. Logic tells me Barclay is a good guy. Struz trusts him, my dad trusted him enough to bring him into our house, but he knows Brandt, and the fight-or-flight instinct I have right now is so strong, I'm practically twitching to get away from him.

Biting the inside of my cheek, I fold my arms across my chest and position myself between him and my dad's office—where the gun is. Barclay is stronger, faster, and a better shot than I am, or at least that's a safe assumption. But we're half a room from the study, and if I get a jump start on him, I might be able to get in there, shut and lock the door, then grab the gun and get behind reasonable cover before he can stop me.

Might.

With this last resort in the back of my mind, I take a deep breath. And then I stand my ground.

I refuse to be afraid of an overconfident jerk like Taylor Barclay.

"I underestimated you," Barclay says with a nod. "I thought you were just some spoiled kid who was going to end up being a waste of my time."

"I'm glad to see you got over yourself," I say with a roll of my eyes. No one would say I can't do bored and bitchy like a champ. "Please tell me this isn't your version of an apology."

He flashes me a smile and shakes his head. "I'm onto you. I know this is an act." He gestures to the kitchen. "You should sit down."

But I don't want to do that, because that'll put me farther away from the gun.

Only I screw up. I glance toward the study and Barclay catches me. He's better than I would have thought.

"Is that where your dad's gun is?" he asks. "I'm surprised Struz let you keep it, though maybe not that surprised. He's not quite as strict with you as he should be—though neither was your dad." He takes a few steps back, putting at least three feet of distance between us, and I almost ask him why he'd bring up my dad. But I need to keep a cool head. If I can't go for the study, I could probably get to the front door and outside, where there might be witnesses, before he gets to me.

"What do you want?" I ask, because I'm ready for him to cut to the chase.

"Who told you about alternate universes?" he asks.

"Physics class."

He smiles, and it should be nice. He's an attractive guy. Only it's the kind of smile that screams, *I'm about to win*. I've seen that smile in enough of the movies Alex makes me watch, right before the villains deliver their diabolical monologues. Only something tells me Barclay isn't the kind of guy to make such a lame action-movie mistake.

"You're a good liar, probably good at reading people too," he says. "If we had more time, I might actually kind of respect you. But here's the thing—you're right."

I'm not sure what to say, so I just wait for him to keep going.

"We don't have time for you to bullshit me, because this world is about to collide with another one, and life as you know it? Over." He takes a step toward me. "I've been following you, and I need to know which of those guys you're hanging out with is the one who told you about alternate universes."

He takes another step toward me, and this time I can't stand my ground. This time, I take a step back.

"I'm not going to tell you anything. No matter what." And I mean it. I don't know what he's capable of—but I won't let him be capable of making me talk.

He pauses, and I can see that he's thinking. Then he changes tactics, shrugging out of his jacket and letting it fall to the floor. In addition to the gun, there's a holster for some kind of long knife.

"Here's the deal, Tenner. I'll be honest with you, and then you'll be honest with me. An information trade. You should respect that. So here's the truth: I'm not an FBI analyst."

Which means the question is, Who is Taylor Barclay?

02:09:22:03

This is where things get weird:

Ben was right when he told me there's a multiverse.

He just didn't have all the facts.

The multiverse is bigger than I ever could have imagined. Hundreds of thousands of alternate Earths with varying technologies, structures, cities, civilizations—even life-forms.

I obviously come from this one, *my* Earth. Ben comes from a different one.

Taylor Barclay is a guy who comes from a third one that's more technologically advanced. The one that's named itself Prima.

Somewhere along the line in history, several universes, including Prima's, realized they weren't alone—that there were other alternate universes. They developed the capabilities and technology for travel between them. But because it was dangerous, with possible catastrophic consequences, Prima instituted laws about interverse travel.

And they policed it with a group called IA, the Interverse Agency.

Interverse agents have metal necklaces they wear with an electronic charge that allows them to travel through the activated portals, and they take vitamins and injections to keep themselves safe from the radiation.

They also have quantum chargers, digital handhelds like cell phones, which activate and open portals. A quantum charger can pinpoint universes, like a navigation system, so they know where they're going. But it does more than that. It stabilizes the portals.

Because that's what Ben has been doing wrong: He's been opening portals, but his portals have been unstable, and that instability is why they were bringing people and things from other universes over here when he opened them. It's also why it's been bringing this world closer to Wave Function Collapse. And consequently, why the portals attracted attention from IA.

Taylor Barclay isn't an analyst for the FBI. He's an agent for IA.

So is Eric Brandt. They're part of a small task force that's been sent to this universe to find out who or what is causing the disturbances. And to put an end to it.

"**A**nd if you can't?"

"Can't what?" Barclay asks.

"Figure it out, put an end to it?" I say. "As in, what happens if you fail?"

Barclay looks at me, and any humor or arrogance leaves his face. "Tenner, we don't fail. We have a fail-safe device."

"A fail-safe?"

"Of course." He laughs. "You think this is the first time someone in one universe has been fucking everything up?"

I'm not sure what to say to that.

Barclay sighs. "Okay here's an example. Before I was born, two universes actually declared war on each other, but casualties kept spilling over. People were traveling through other separate universes to stage attacks. Sometimes people in those universes got killed or sucked into the fighting. Too many portals were opening, and it started having adverse effects on the universes between them. Earthquakes, floods. IA had to step in."

Earthquakes, floods. Like what's been happening here. "What did they do?" I whisper.

He shrugs like it's no big deal. "They destroyed them."

02:09:11:37

He says it so matter-of-factly, like two worlds being destroyed is commonplace—and maybe it is to him. But it makes me feel like the walls are closing in on me.

I wave a hand for him to continue, and he sighs. "The goal is to keep from letting two universes collide and destroy each other, because in addition to the lives lost, it would have rippling effects and potentially affect the stability of interverse travel and life in other universes."

And I know what he's not saying. Because the concept of the "greater good" is universal—or multiversal or whatever.

If they can't stop the universes from colliding, the fail-safe is going to be to go ahead and destroy one. The one that's the problem—mine.

Oh my God. "That's what the UIED is for," I whisper. I feel like I'm choking and someone punched me in the stomach at the same time. I'm looking at The End. And there might not be a thing I can do about it.

"The Oppenheimer," he says with a quick nod. He must see the surprise on my face, because he shrugs. "We had an

Oppenheimer too. He just discovered a different kind of bomb. A more powerful one. It's—"

"The destroyer of worlds, I get the significance," I say. My eyes are leaking, because Barclay and his IA task force are planning to destroy my universe in two days. Even if we can manage to hold off Wave Function Collapse, some higher-up on a universe light-years away—or whatever—is going to decide our fate. Nothing I do is going to matter.

"It's the only way to preserve the stability of other universes," Barclay whispers.

"I hope you're not trying to make me feel better."

He shakes his head. "Look, the FBI wasn't supposed to find the Oppenheimer. I brought it here as a fail-safe, but I fucked up. Eric and I came over to investigate deaths from suspected un-stabilized activity. The first crime scene we were at, it took us longer than it should have. We had to rush out of there. Police traced me back to my hotel, and I had to bolt. The Oppenheimer was in my room. I had to infiltrate the FBI to get it back."

"You've got it now?" I ask. "How?"

Barclay nods. "I knew where your dad was keeping it, but I didn't have the clearance. Until you gave me the files. I managed to swipe it from his safe yesterday."

His safe. No wonder Struz is freaked. The UIED is missing.

"Look, I've got it now, but you were right that day at the café. That earthquake was a sign, and there will be more. More destruction before it's all over. According to command, I've got a little more than forty-nine hours to arrest or kill whoever's responsible, or I'm leaving the Oppenheimer somewhere safe and going home."

"You could just disable it. You could—"

"Didn't you hear what I just said? The earthquake was only the beginning. This world is starting to crumble. Haven't you been paying attention to the tornadoes, the flooding, the hurricanes? It's getting out of control. When two worlds collide, the ripples affect every world around them. There are thousands of different universes. And they'll all get hit with earthquakes, tsunamis, all the stuff happening here now. Millions of people will die. You want that on your conscience?"

I don't say anything. I don't have to.

Barclay nods. "I certainly don't want it on mine, and I don't want to be stuck here when the world ends."

"And if you do find out who's opening the portals and stop them?" Since that's the point.

"I'll disarm the Oppenheimer and go home."

I breathe a little easier at that idea. That is what I want.

"Did you kill my dad?" I ask, even though the answer won't change anything.

He shakes his head. "I liked your dad. He was onto us—at least onto Eric—but I would have brought him in before killing him. Besides, I'm only authorized to kill whoever's destabilizing worlds."

"Did Eric kill him?"

He shakes his head.

"You're sure? I deserve to know."

"You do. But you're looking in the wrong place. I don't know who killed him, but it wasn't Eric."

I don't know what else to do. So I sit down on the floor, and I tell him.

I don't use names, and I try to avoid telling him personal details. But I give him the facts.

A couple of kids from an alternate universe stumbled on a failed experiment, only they accidentally made it work—they opened a portal and fell through. And then couldn't get back.

So now they've been trying to get home. They just didn't know what they were doing.

"And they made it?" Barclay asks, pulling out his quantum charger, which apparently also doubles as some kind of advanced smartphone. I remember it from his car. It looks like a Game Boy. "They must have taken hydrochloradneum or the radiation would have burned them up."

"Hydro what?"

"Hydrochloradneum," he explains as he uses the touch screen on his charger. I try to watch and memorize what he's doing in case I ever need to work one. "It's a chemical compound that can be produced as a bright yellow liquid or a powder. It looks a little like Gatorade. It hasn't yet been discovered in this world, but among other things, it nullifies the effects of radiation."

Hydrochloradneum. That must be why Brandt bought the chemicals—he was mixing this compound. "Does it have any . . . side effects?" I ask, because that's good to know. But also because I'm thinking of Ben and his superpowers.

"Of course," he says without looking up. "It changes the body's chemical makeup. In concentrated or high doses right before interverse travel, the effects can be catastrophic. I know a guy who can walk through walls, which would be fine except half the time he can't pick up his cup of coffee because his hand goes right through it. Ah, here it is," he says, showing me the screen of the charger, though he's careful to hold on to it. There's what looks like a satellite picture of Earth with a lot of numbers and symbols around it.

"I don't know what I'm looking at," I admit.

"Earth number 19317," he says, pulling the charger back and tapping the screen. Whatever it is, it loads faster than my iPhone. "Lorraine Michaels and Malcolm Suitor discovered hydrochloradneum in late 2002, though no one discovered the advanced benefits of it until about five years later.

"And it looks like each of them lost a son in 2005," he adds. "Three boys disappeared, and the one remaining witness described a shimmering black hole swallowing them up. Like a portal."

Barclay looks at me, and I nod. There's no sense lying to him about them. He already knows. And he's their ticket home.

"It was a huge case. A lot of media attention is involved when the son of a world leader goes missing."

I wonder if Elijah was right. If his dad is looking for them.

"They're not opening portals anymore," I say. "They stopped when they realized they didn't know what they were doing."

Barclay gives me what can only be described as an absolutely pitying look. "You're smarter than that," he says, tucking the charger away in his pocket. "Think about this. You saw what happened in that house. You know what does that? An unstable portal that's about ten times too big, and out of control. It brought three people over and swallowed up that house and killed everyone inside. You were there.

"And you know what else unstable portals do? They cause earthquakes, tsunamis, and all sorts of other natural disasters, because they start to cause the universe to shift unnaturally. So I need to know who's opening them."

"I don't know!"

"Is it the one who was here this morning?" He shakes his

head and grabs his jacket. "Whatever you feel for him, don't let it get in the way of what the laws of physics tell you."

"No, Barclay, I swear." I grab his arm. If I can't convince him Ben isn't opening the portals anymore, I know he'll kill him. "Please, you need to listen to me."

"No, Tenner, you listen to me. They lied to you. They haven't stopped opening the portals. And I have to stop them before they do it again. Or you'll all be dead."

He shakes me off his arm and walks out the door.

Stop them.

I know what he really means is, kill them.

When I get to Ben's house, Barclay's car is already there. I park the Jeep haphazardly on the side of the road and run up the driveway. My heart is pounding, and I try not to let myself wonder if it's too late. The door is unlocked, so I let myself in and race through the kitchen and down into the basement, where I can hear them arguing.

At the sound of Ben's voice, I gasp from relief.

I'm halfway down the basement stairs before I regain my wits and stop right before Ben and Barclay are visible.

"Tenner, I know you're up there!" Barclay calls.

Because I made so much damn noise on my way in. And because I'm breathing so hard I'm wheezing.

From what I can see—not much—Barclay is standing in almost the same place I stood when I was here. He has a gun on Ben, and Ben is backed up against the couch with his arms up.

My whole body is hammering with the beat of my pulse.

"I haven't opened a portal in weeks," Ben says.

"You seriously expect me to believe that?" Barclay says.

I can't listen to any more. I have to do something.

So I do.

And it's probably the most reckless thing I've ever done.

I come down a few more steps, swing over the railing, and throw myself off the steps at Barclay. I land on his back, knocking him off balance as I essentially tackle him to the ground like some kind of psychotic linebacker.

And it hurts. One of my knees hits concrete and I cry out from the pain, and then I can't breathe, because Barclay's elbow just went into my stomach and knocked the wind out of me.

But I don't need to breathe to reach for the gun. I pull at his right hand, grabbing his fingers and pulling him back. He screams, and I'm pretty sure I just broke his ring finger.

Then his left hand reaches over his shoulder, grabbing a fistful of my hair, and he's pulling me back, and suddenly Ben is there. He punches Barclay in the face, and the sound of his fist connecting with those bones makes a sickening crunch. And I already feel nauseated.

But Barclay lets go of my hair to go after Ben, and head throbbing, body protesting with each move, I manage to twist the gun from him and roll away and to my feet. I open my mouth to tell Ben to grab Taylor's other gun, but I'm too out of breath.

It's not a gun I'm familiar with. It looks similar to a normal handgun, but it's a little bigger, heavier in my hand, like it's weighted down with liquid. I don't even know if it shoots real bullets or something else.

But I train it on Barclay.

Only Barclay's not on the floor.

His nose bleeding and right ring finger broken and bent at an awkward angle, he's just pulled the gun from his ankle holster. And he has it pointed at Ben.

And Ben has his hands up.

"This gun has liquid hydrochloradneum bullets. They go through tactical vests, which is why we use them. But for you, it means you won't be able to heal any injuries from them," Barclay says, and I'm not sure who he's talking to, me or Ben.

"If I shoot you, I doubt Ben is going to want to heal you," I say, even though I know we need him to disarm the Oppenheimer.

"Fuck, Tenner! This doesn't involve you."

"How do you figure? My world is about to end, and you think it doesn't involve me?" Seems like I've found my voice now. "And if it involves Ben, it involves me. I told you, it's not him."

"There's evidence in his garage that says otherwise." Barclay spits blood onto the floor.

I almost ask what, but then I remember Ben telling me about that half-built replica of Reid's dad's machine.

"Hear him out," I say. Because I'd really like to avoid people dying if we can help it. And while I'm a good shot, and Barclay is only a few feet from me, I've never used a weapon like this before. And chances are, even if I shoot Barclay, Ben will end up dead.

"I don't want to shoot you, but I will," I say.

Barclay sends me a glance that tells me he's come to the same conclusion that I just did, and he's not about to pretend that I'm fooling anyone with false bravado.

"Two people are dead because of me," Ben says. "That's on me, and I'll own that. If you need to shoot me or take me in, go ahead, but I'm not the one opening portals. Not anymore."

But Barclay doesn't answer. Instead he addresses me. "This is his fault. Your world is about to end, and it's his fault. The damage he's done, it might even be irreparable."

My eyes burn. I know he could be lying to me, but I also

know it might be the truth. I might die in two days no matter what happens to Ben.

I try to take a deep breath, but I can't seem to get enough air. "You don't know that!"

"I'll bring you back with me—you and your brother," Barclay says. "It's against the rules, but I can make a case for it. Eric will back me up. I'll keep you alive."

For a second, I think of Jared and wonder if Barclay really would save him. But I shake my head. I don't know what is coming or how we'll survive it—or if—but I'm not about to trade Ben's life for mine. I'm not like that.

"It's his fault your father is dead."

"No, he had nothing to do with that," I say. I already heard Ben's confession, and I know he's wrong. "Someone shot my father. That's why he's dead. It was a bullet. It wasn't Ben."

"Are you sure?" Barclay asks.

The only sounds in the basement are the ticking of an old clock and our own heavy breathing.

"Janelle, I told you everything," Ben says. "You know I stopped when I realized what we were doing."

"It isn't Ben," I say. "You can't pin this all on him."

Barclay refocuses on Ben. "Then who is it?"

"I don't know!" Ben shouts back. "Don't you think I've been racking my brain for days? But no one else knows the science, and it's not me!"

"Then it has to be you. If no one else knows the science, it's you."

I see Barclay's logic. If I didn't believe Ben, I'd think he was lying too. And I wish I knew something to say, but I don't. Which means . . .

I focus on the gun in my hand. It's just a gun. It has a trigger like any other gun I've shot. I only have one chance, and it has to count. I slow down my breathing, five seconds per inhale, hold for five, and then a five-second exhale. I let everything else just Fade A w a y.

And I ask myself if I can live with killing a man.

With Barclay in my sights, holding the gun on Ben, the answer is easier than maybe it should be.

Barclay is yelling at him, "You violated the laws of physics— you don't think there are consequences to that?"

And right as I'm about to pull the trigger, the walls rattle, and the earth opens up beneath my feet.

02:08:30:29

The basement stairs collapse, and a combination of dirt, concrete, and wood from the frame of the house begins to fall on top of us. Cracks in the cement floor of the basement sprout and race across the room.

I'm jerked into the wall. Hard. And the gun gets knocked from my hand.

Then the violence of the quake doubles and I'm thrown upward—my whole body airborne—and then to the ground. I hold out an arm to break my fall, but when I hit the floor, I hear something in my wrist crack. Pain shoots up my arm and into my shoulder. I can't help letting out a yelp from the impact.

A piece of wood—maybe from the stairs, but who knows— falls on me, slamming into my hip, and I try to curl myself into a ball to protect my organs. I have a split second to wonder if this is really it. If I won't even have those extra two days.

But then Ben is there, falling on top of me, shielding me with his body.

Still the earthquake rages on.

There's a high-pitched electronic noise, something that smells and feels like the thickness in the air right before it rains, and Barclay is grabbing Ben and yanking me up into his arms.

"Let's go!" he shouts, and then he's pulling us both into a black hole.

02:08:30:00

The summer Jared was three, all he would eat was hot dogs—hot dogs made on a charcoal grill. We tried to offer him other stuff. Odds were, he'd get hungry enough—right? No. He'd rather starve than eat something other than a hot dog. He wouldn't even eat the bun.

So he ate hot dogs for every meal.

My dad would grill them up every morning for breakfast and every night for dinner. For lunch we either got my mom to make him one or he skipped lunch altogether.

Except for one time.

She had a headache and wouldn't get out of bed, and Jared kept asking for a hot dog. I tried to give him microwavable soy sausage Alex's mom had given us instead, but he wouldn't take it, so I tried to cook one myself.

I got as far as lighting the coals before I set my hand on fire.

Third-degree burns—I used to have some scarring on the side of my pinkie and on the palm of that hand from where they were the worst. Then Ben healed me.

I thought nothing could be more painful than setting my hand on fire.

I was wrong.

Traveling through a wormhole to another universe hurts a thousand times worse. It burns like nothing I've felt before. Even worse than dying. I'm being suffocated by steam; it feels like my skin is being pulled apart.

My fingernails are melting—I can feel it.

I have fire instead of blood running through my veins.

I'm going to explode.

And then something pricks me, right in my chest, and the force of it makes me gasp for air. Ben and Barclay are leaning over me, and I'm flat on my back on a carpeted floor, staring at a white ceiling fan.

"Just keep breathing," Barclay says to me. "You'll cool off in a minute." Then he disappears from view.

My breath is desperate, more like panting, like I've suddenly developed asthma, but he's right, I'm already cooling off. I'm hot—sweating—but I'm not burning up anymore. I lift my left hand and look at my fingernails. My skin is red—like a bad sunburn—but everything looks intact.

Ben reaches for my right wrist—the one that's broken—and I flinch away.

"I'm just going to heal it for you," he says.

"No." I shake my head. "My skin."

"I said don't touch her!" Barclay yells from somewhere else. "Her skin is sensitive from the radiation. You could end up hurting her worse, even killing her."

Ben pulls his hand back, but he still hovers over me, and when his head eclipses the light from the ceiling, silhouetting him, I have a sense of déjà vu. It makes me wonder what cataclysmic events will come next.

"I'm right here if you need me," Ben whispers.

I nod, still trying to get my breathing under control.

"The good news is he knows it's not me," Ben says. "The bad news is someone opened another unstable portal, and it triggered more earthquakes. The worst one was in San Diego, but each portal causes shifts beneath the earth, and it's—"

Barclay is there again, cutting Ben off. He picks up my head and slips a weird braided wire necklace over it before lowering me back to the floor. "It's made from hydrochloradneum; it'll help."

Then he disappears, but I can still hear him. "You shouldn't do that."

"What do you mean?" Ben asks.

"It's not natural. The hydrochloradneum must have altered your genetic makeup, but people aren't meant to have abilities like that, and I doubt you really know what you're doing. You shouldn't mess with things you don't understand. You have no idea what it could do to you as you get older."

And then he's back. "How's your skin?"

"It's okay, I think." I hold my arm toward him, and there don't seem to be any adverse effects. I don't feel like a live wire anymore.

"Good," Barclay says, then sticks me with another shot. This one makes me feel like I'm dead. It travels from my wrist up my arm and into my chest, then everything goes black.

I dream of buildings collapsing and imploding. Cities turning into rubble in huge clouds of debris. A slew of tornadoes have taken out downtown Chicago. Earthquakes have leveled areas of Dallas and Las Vegas. A tsunami blankets New York City. Another one rises up and crashes against the Gulf Coast, and New Orleans is completely sunk. A third tackles the California coast. And then there are the wildfires—and they're everywhere. They spring up in different spots, but they seem to be sweeping the nation in all directions, and there's no one to fight them, so they just burn.

Millions of people are dead.

Millions more are missing.

The hospitals still standing are bursting with those who are injured.

People are looting or trying to evacuate the major cities.

Chaos reigns everywhere.

And then I dream of similar images for every major country all over the world.

When I wake up, I'm on a leather couch with a blanket around me, and Ben is sitting perpendicular to me, unconsciously petting my hair. My right wrist is splinted and wrapped with something a little better than an Ace bandage.

"I had the worst dream," I say, shivering a little and trying to sit up.

"Be careful," Ben says, helping me. "You were under a strong sedative."

I wonder if all IA operatives have a cache of drugs.

I look around. The furniture looks a little like something out of *Modern Home & Living* magazine—everything is sleek blacks and whites. The wall in front of me is covered with a few big frames showing digital backlit pictures of Barclay shaking hands with people who are presumably important. The light is bright, but I don't see any lamps—like it's all ambient.

Next to me is something that looks like a giant iPad, and when I touch it, it flares to life and a computerized voice asks me who I would like to call.

I look at Ben. "Where are we?"

"Taylor calls it Prima. We're at his home Earth."

I watch as his gaze lifts above me, like he's looking through me. Only I realize he's looking at something behind me, and when I turn around I see why.

The wall behind me is all windows—floor-to-ceiling windows—that look out over a city, like we're in one of the highest floors of a high-rise. Entranced, I stand up and move toward the window. At first glance, the sky looks gray, but when I look closer I realize it's iridescent. I can see shimmering shades of purple, blue, and pink depending on which angle I'm looking from. The gray is smog, hovering like a thick blanket of storm clouds.

A sliver of sun peeks through for a second and flickers off the crystal skyscrapers, making them look like ice castles or flowing liquid creations—the buildings are something out of an *Alice in Wonderland*-esque LSD trip.

Leaning my forehead against the window, I try to look down, but I can barely see through the fog—I can't see the streets, but I can see what looks like a huge brown square in front of me with a few patches of green. It looks a little like what Central Park would look like if all the grass had died. . . .

I turn to Ben. "Is this New York?"

"They call it New Prima here. It's the capital," he says. "But yeah, you can see the Empire State Building—or the New Prima equivalent—from the window in his bathroom."

Holy. Shit.

I can't believe it. I mean, I can—I did. I believed in other universes because I had to in order to swallow Ben's story. But I was so wrapped up in trying to stop the countdown, I didn't really have a chance to think about what *other universes* really means.

I wonder if this is what Ben's world looks like, or if his looks more like mine. I'm about to ask, and I turn to him. But there's something about the look on his face. There's no hint of a smile anywhere—no hint of relief that we're alive, that Barclay knows it's not Ben opening the portals.

"I had the creepiest dreams," I say, because I'm hoping talking about them will make him tell me what's wrong—and allow me to expunge them from my memory.

Only it doesn't.

Because Ben whispers, "Those weren't dreams," when I'm not even halfway finished. He looks at the wall where the TV is.

It's the largest TV I've ever seen. It takes up almost the entire wall, and it's so thin, it looks like it actually could *be* the wall. It's split into twelve squares, each of them showing a different newscast. But all the newscasts are showing the same thing. They're all showing footage of natural disasters and cities collapsing.

Buildings collapsing and imploding. Cities turning into rubble in huge clouds of debris. Being swallowed by the earth, blanketed by tsunamis, or eaten up by wildfires.

Ben says something, but I either don't hear it or my ears shut down and refuse to interpret the sounds. For a second I wonder what he could possibly say at a time like this.

But that wonder only lasts for a split second.

Because deep down, I know.

We're watching the collapse of two worlds. And one of them is mine.

PART THREE

Remember me when I am gone away,

Gone far away into the silent land;

When you can no more hold me by the hand.

—Christina Rossetti

01:01:26:07

W hat we're seeing is Wave Function Collapse in action.

My legs give out and I drop to the floor where I am and stare up at the television wall under the weight of that realization—everyone I know is dying right now—and I can't breathe. I feel like I'm sinking, like I'm underwater and weighted down, like everything is just collapsing in around me, pushing me down, and I'll never be able to get back up again—so why even try.

Ben is there, holding me and whispering and running his hands through my hair. But it doesn't matter—he still feels too far away.

When Barclay comes back from wherever he was, he sees us and says, "Stop worrying, I've gotten everything sorted out."

"Oh, like you can fix this," I say.

He stares at me for a second and then shakes his head. "You're not seeing Wave Function Collapse," he says. "Trust me, we wouldn't have reporters there showing it, if it was."

"What are we seeing, then?" Ben asks.

"Symptoms of the upcoming collision. It's brought back not-quite-live from reporters authorized for interverse travel in emergencies."

"You have reporters on my Earth?"

Barclay looks at me. His face says, *Of course we do*, but he doesn't elaborate. Instead he turns to Ben. "When they actually collide and collapse, there won't be anything to see. They'll cease to exist."

I don't know how he can treat this so calmly—even though I've surfaced, I still feel a little catatonic. What do we do now?

"What universe is this other one?" Ben asks, his face tight.

Barclay stares at him for a second before saying, "Yours."

"Mine?" His voice is breathless. "What do you mean?"

"You opened portals to your world; the instability is pulling both your universes together," Barclay says. "I thought I explained all this."

I reach out and grab Ben's hand, and squeeze. I know what he's thinking and feeling. Because it's the same thing I'm thinking and feeling—like I'm not sure whether I should just lie down and die or try to fight against the fact that all my insides feel like they've been torn out.

"Your ability to open *unstable* portals somehow allowed you to choose which portal to open," Barclay says. "You just didn't know it."

I get up because I can't sit still anymore. None of the stories about the apocalypse ever tell you how crazy you'll feel when you're watching it unfold. I've even had the thought that if we can't prevent the end of the world, I wish it would just hurry up and get here already.

Barclay explains how he brought us here against the rules, but his commanding officer has cleared him. After he showers, he's taking us to the IA building, where Ben will be taken into custody and charged for his crimes and I will be questioned.

I hear him, but I don't really listen. Instead I stare at the changing digital pictures on the wall, and wonder what kind of world this is where people can be so nonchalant about the loss of life. If this is what technological advancement got them, I don't want any part of it.

As soon as he disappears into the bathroom, I turn to Ben. "I don't like this plan."

"Good," Ben says with a half smile. "I have a different one."

"A good one?" I ask with a laugh, and in spite of everything, it feels good to know I still can.

"I think so." He nods, pulling a quantum charger and something that looks like a syringe from his pocket. "I swiped this from Barclay's closet while you were sleeping. I think I've figured out how it works. Every universe has coordinates based on where it is in comparison to Prima. It looks like you punch in the coordinates for the universe, plus the latitude and longitude for where we want to end up, and then it opens a portal."

For a second, I'm worried that his plan is to go home—to his home.

"I haven't entirely figured out all the coordinates yet, but I copied down the coordinates we came from." He gestures to the necklace. "I think between that and the injection you had yesterday, you'll be able to go through like I can, without it burning."

"You think?"

"If it doesn't work, I palmed one of the syringes, and I'll inject you with it as soon as we're through." He takes a deep breath. "I don't like it any more than you do, but I have to do this. You can stay here if you'd rather, but I have to go back for Elijah and Reid."

"I'm going with you."

He nods, and then looks down and away, and I can tell from his face something I don't want to hear is coming. "I know who's doing it."

My face feels cold, and I'm afraid to say the words out loud, as if that might make it untrue. "Opening the portals? You know?"

Ben shushes me and nods. "I've spent hours going over it in my head. I was wrong when I told Barclay no one else knows the science. Both Reid and Elijah know the science, and I don't want to think either of them would have opened a portal without me, but I know how bad Elijah wants to go home. And he was the one who first opened one with me. I don't know who else it could be."

I don't know Elijah like Ben does, but I still don't want him to have done this—and not just for Ben's sake. Elijah bothers me, and I think he's a jerk, but I was actually starting to not mind him that much, and I was willing to chalk his attitude up to the whole "I'm from an alternate universe" thing, because he was Ben's friend. But Ben's words make sense. I remember Alex saying something similar only a few days ago.

It doesn't physically hurt to find that he might have gone behind Ben's back to open the portals. I'm just mad.

"Let's go," I say, because we should be gone before Barclay gets out of the shower. Who knows how easy it is to track where one of these things can take us?

"You don't happen to know the latitude and longitude of your house?" Ben asks.

I shake my head, but you can bet I'll find out now.

Ben stands up and takes a deep breath. "Looks like we're headed back to mine."

"Hopefully not the basement."

He doesn't answer. He just presses some of the buttons, and that electrical sound—the sound of something powering up—is there. And then so is the portal.

I feel the cool air and smell rain and salt water first, but this time, before I step through, I really look at it. It's circular and at least seven feet in diameter, maybe more. And it really does look like we're about to step into a vertical pool of tar.

Which is why this time, when I take Ben's hand and we go through it, I hold my breath.

01:01:10:01

It occurs to me when I'm on the ground in Ben's driveway that we should figure out how to properly land if we plan on making interverse travel a habit.

If Elijah is the one opening the portals, it also occurs to me that he might have done more than just that. The portals are connected to the bodies and the UIED—they're connected to my dad's investigation. The one he was working on when he was killed. It's possible whoever is responsible for opening the portals is also responsible for my father's death.

I shake the thought from my head. I know I'm jumping to conclusions. Elijah might be the most likely suspect I have, but that doesn't mean it was him. I can't exactly see him killing someone.

Or can I?

I have seen how determined he is to get back to his world. He didn't care that Ben's portals had killed people.

What if my dad somehow got in the way of Elijah getting home? My heart beats in my ears, and I realize at this point, I'm probably far too traumatized by everything to trust my thoughts.

It's not until I stand up and see Ben's house—*correction:* where Ben's house used to be—that it occurs to me that I have no idea where Jared is.

Light-headed and short of breath, I bend at the waist and gasp. I can't believe I could have forgotten him. I look for Ben, who's pushing himself up off the ground. "We have to find Jared before we do anything else," I say, and I can't keep the hysteria from my voice. "We have to find him."

"Absolutely," Ben says. "Try your house first?"

I nod. Jared could be anywhere. He could be dead in a gutter or trapped under a building. As soon as I find him, I'm never going to let him out of my sight.

Ben manages to get my Jeep started, even though the engine is sputtering and it refuses to move faster than twenty miles an hour. Not that we'd be able to go much faster than that anyway—Ben has to navigate around debris and fallen trees, then we have to turn around and go a different way when the bottom of the hill past Park Village Road is flooded. And then we're derailed again because part of the 56 has collapsed. My eyes water as we drive.

And in the car we're silent. It's just the sputtering of the engine, my increasingly hysterical breathing, and Ben's occasional calm reassurances: "We'll find him," "It's okay," and "Try not to worry."

Because everywhere I look, civilization as I knew it is wrecked. The devastation is widespread and almost indescribable, as if San Diego got hit by every natural disaster imaginable all at once. Cars are overturned and discarded—in some places they're piled on one another at odd angles. Houses are missing, toppled, or burned, and yards are scorched, flooded, or buried under debris.

From far away, neighborhoods look like a discarded children's playground, like toys that someone just bulldozed over and left carelessly tossed aside. Up close, I feel like I've just stepped into a T. S. Eliot poem brought to life.

The debris is everywhere—pieces of wood and chunks of concrete are what I seem to notice first, but it's the flecks of color that demand my attention. The discarded red baseball hat—where's the person who was wearing it? The well-loved doll with bright golden-blond hair—where's the child who loved it?

When we finally get to my neighborhood, there's an overturned car and what's left of a house in the way, so we get out and walk.

A couple of times, Ben reaches out to steady me or help when I have to climb over something that doesn't belong in the middle of my street. At one point a cluster of downed palm trees is blocking our path and we have to climb over them. After I slide off one tree trunk, I curse and kick it as hard as I can, even though I know it's hardly productive.

"Here," Ben says before I start trying to get over it again. He puts his hand on the trunk, and the bark turns to flakes of sawdust. It starts at one center point—where Ben's hand is—and a hole spreads outward in a circle. When it's big enough for us to climb through, he pulls his hand back. He's sweating and breathing hard, but we don't say anything.

We keep walking.

Despite whatever we saw on Barclay's TV, I didn't expect what I'm seeing now.

Life will never go back to normal after this.

And then I see my house, and I have to stop walking. Involuntarily, like they have lives of their own, my hands clap over my mouth and I drop to my knees in the middle of my street.

Because *correction*: I see where my house should be.

It's been leveled. It's just gone.

My entire yard and driveway are a pile of debris. Discarded bricks and rubble surround two of the walls from what used to be my living room, like they're part of a grotesque life-size dollhouse.

Alex's house is sunken in next to where my house should be—it looks like his house imploded and mine blew away.

I don't realize I'm crying until Ben pulls me back to my feet and wipes my eyes. "Jared wouldn't have been at the house," he's saying. "No one was home."

I nod, but I'm paralyzed. I don't know where to go.

"Do you want to see if anything is salvageable?" Ben asks. But he's more optimistic than I am if he thinks there's anything anyone could salvage from that wreckage. "Okay, then let's go to the school. Remember when they turned it into an evacuation shelter a couple years ago when we had those wildfires? He might be there."

He doesn't say what I'm worried about, though. Ben was right—no one was at my house. But Jared was at school. What if we get there and it's gone too?

What if Jared is dead?

I'm suddenly too weak. I reach out a hand to grab on to something. I can't stand up anymore. Not while I've got that thought, and Ben has to help turn me around and carry/drag me to the curb so I can sit down. Stars are clouding my vision, and I'm dangerously close to losing my mind.

I can't be sure how long I'm on the curb, sitting with my head between my knees, but Ben leaves me to walk to the wreckage of Alex's house to see if anyone's there, and he picks through some of the debris where my house should be.

My street looks and feels like a ghost town. Like people just up and fled and took every sign and sound of life with them. It's eerily quiet—no sounds of traffic, people, even birds. And it's darker than it should be, like the sun decided it just couldn't bear witness to this. But the worst is the smell. I didn't notice it at first because it's far away, but the air has a permanent edge to it—the scent of burning.

Ben comes back with a navy hooded sweatshirt that was my dad's. It's dirty and it smells a little mildewed, but it's dry.

"It's going to get cold," he says. "You should definitely have this."

I take a deep breath and grab it as I stand up. "Let's go to Eastview."

We're climbing through the fallen trees when I see the driver's-side door of the Jeep is wide open and someone is rustling around in there. "Hey!" I call, not stopping to think that this person could be capable of violence now that civilization has literally crumbled.

But he raises his head and goes, "Thank God, I've been looking everywhere for you."

Struz.

I jump down from the trunk of the tree and run toward him. He's the first thing I've seen that looks the same as it did before. He's still gangly and too tall and thin, wearing a suit with a bulletproof vest instead of the jacket. And I know he'll know what I need to do.

"Where's Jared? Is he okay?"

400

"Calm down," Struz says. "Jared's fine. What happened to your wrist?"

I want to collapse with relief, but I stay on my feet.

"It's broken. Where is he?"

"How'd you break it?" he asks.

"I fell," I say. "Where's Jared?"

Struz sighs and rubs his hair. "He's in the hospital wing at the Federal Building. He's fine, but he broke his ankle during the earthquake. He's a little bitter about it, but he'll be in better spirits once he's not so worried about you."

"Why is he worried about me?"

Struz looks over my shoulder at Ben. "Do you believe this chick? J, you didn't go to school. You were at home when he left. Have you seen your house?"

"Oh my God, I didn't even think of that. I wasn't there either." I wonder when the fact that this is actually real will sink in.

"Yeah, I have some questions about that, but let's save them for the car. We've had a lot of trouble with looters, and it's not safe to just be standing out here in the open." He guides me toward a TrailBlazer—it's not the one he used to drive, and I wonder what happened to that one, as he opens the passenger door.

"Struz, this is Ben Michaels," I say as I get inside. "He's coming with us."

Struz nods and shuts my door.

When we're all inside and Struz is driving us down to the Federal Building, he asks what the hell I was doing cutting school, anyway—not that he's mad. And he of course wants to know about the cryptic message I left him before it all happened and where I've been since the quake.

"You're not going to believe me at first," I say. "So you need to trust me, and you need to hear me out until the end."

He glances at me out of the corner of his eye, like he thinks I'm being dramatic.

"I've never been more serious."

"Okay," Struz says. "I'm listening."

And I—finally—tell him everything. I start at the beginning for me—getting hit by the truck and coming back to life. And I keep going, up until the point where he found us headed toward the school. It's abbreviated, but I don't leave anything out.

When I finish, we're sitting in the parking lot of the Federal Building, and Struz is staring at me. I half expect him to ask what drugs I'm on.

I pull the wire necklace off and hand it to him. "I don't entirely know what this is. But I know it's made from a chemical compound called hydrochloradneum and it doesn't exist here. And it apparently neutralizes radiation or something. I'm sure you have people who can test it."

"Well, we used to," Struz says, taking it from me. "I'm not sure what we have now, but I'll have someone check it out." He turns the necklace over in his hands, as if he's expecting it to whisper the answers to him.

When it doesn't, he looks up at me again. "You're right, I don't entirely believe you, because I'm having trouble wrapping my head around it. But at the same time a lot of it makes sense, and I've got the same feeling I get when I know I've just broken a case."

"So where does that leave us?"

"I have no idea, but let's go see Jared, and let me try to think about what questions I should have," he says, then turns around to look at Ben. "You're with me, by the way."

Ben gives Struz a nod, and now that I've gotten it all out, I'm ready to see Jared, try to get in touch with Alex, and then go find Elijah and Reid.

Which is when I realize I forgot to even think about my mom.

"Do you know where Alex and my mom are?" I ask Struz.

"Alex is at Qualcomm. We've got it set up as an evacuation shelter," he says. "And I don't know where your mom is yet. Scripps sustained some damage, but it's still up and running, and she should have been there."

"But she's not?" I ask.

He shakes his head. "I've got her listed as missing, but J, you were my priority."

My eyes burn, but I understand, so I nod and turn back to the Federal Building and keep walking. I have the strangest image of my mother walking into the ocean like Edna Pontellier at the end of *The Awakening*.

The advantage to having an in with the FBI is that the bones in Jared's leg are set and he's being taken care of in a hospital that isn't overcrowded.

The Federal Building looks like any other office building in downtown San Diego—it's nondescript. But tonight it's more abuzz with life than anywhere else I've been. It's still standing, for one thing, and it looks virtually untouched by the chaos. And a backup generator steadily hums, making the dimly lit building seem like it's alive.

As we walk into the lobby, Struz ushers us through security— the metal detectors are down, and a security guard tries to stop us, but Struz flashes his ID and says, "They're with me," and that's the end of the discussion.

"Ben, we're going to need to sit you down and get all the information about what was in Eric Brandt's hotel room," Struz says. "And we're going to have to call in Elijah and Reid."

"You're going to do all that?" I ask, wondering whether he's going to tell everyone else what I told him—and if this is going to take time we don't have.

Struz ignores me—he's in a zone. But it doesn't matter. Ben glances at me and says, "Whatever you need."

He squeezes my hand, and I squeeze back even though I'm not sure when he took my hand to begin with. I turn to him and take in his face. While my own is probably wearing every emotion I've experienced over the last several days, Ben's dark eyes seem to lack focus, and the lines of his face are blank. It's an emotionless mask, similar to the one I've seen him wearing at school for the past however many years. But I recognize it for what it is now. He's thinking—not about the scene in front of him, but about something more pressing. Right now, I'd wager everything I have that he's thinking about Elijah.

The elevators are down, so we take the stairs, and as soon as we open the door to the stairwell, I'm tempted to run up them two at a time if I have to. I have to see with my own eyes that Jared is okay.

"The hospital is on the third floor," Struz says, as if he can read my mind. "It's pretty crowded, so stick with me and I'll make sure you can get in to see him."

We're halfway to the second floor, when the second-floor door opens and a guy in his twenties comes through the door. He bounds down two steps before he sees Struz, then pauses and stands up straighter. "Sir! You're back," he says. "The fires in Imperial Beach have been put out, and we've gotten the satellite phone lines up."

"Good, see if we can get ahold of someone in Washington or New York," Struz says. "And send the emergency responders from Imperial Beach to Poway."

"Already done," the guy says.

Struz nods—a silent dismissal—then the guy is running past

us and we're still heading to the third floor.

When we open the door to the hospital level, the strong odors of antiseptic and bleach assault me. It's crowded with people in scrubs and white coats, but also with people in civilian clothes. I spot Deirdre almost immediately, standing with a doctor, and she moves toward us.

I'm about to ask why an analyst is treating Struz like he's the big boss, when I figure it out myself. He *is* the big boss. My dad is gone, and the Bureau hasn't had the time to transfer anyone else in yet. And they're not going to have the resources or the manpower to do it now.

"Coronado," Deirdre says. "The whole base is underwater. It's as if the island just sank."

"Fuck," Struz says, shaking his head.

"That's not the worst of it," Deirdre adds. "Rady Children's Hospital still doesn't have power back up, and they're over capacity. They're treating people in the parking lot, but a big aftershock could take out the left wing, since the foundation is already shot."

I look at Struz, who's running a hand through his already messed-up blond hair—and I have to push the emotions back. If someone has to replace my dad, it should be Struz. I'm proud of him.

"That would be a disaster," he says. "Can you coordinate with San Diego PD and see if they can get anyone who's not critical evacuated and sent to Petco Park?"

"Petco's already full," Deirdre says.

Struz touches his chin and then says, "What about the Lakeside Rodeo grounds? We could set up a new evac site with medical there. It'll be out of the way for some people, but—"

"I'll talk to Red Cross and see what I can do," Deirdre says, and then she's turning around.

"Dee," Struz adds. "I need an APB out on Barclay. In fact, I need everything we know about him, and not just what's in his file. Everything."

I watch Deirdre's face. Her eyes widen slightly with surprise, and she frowns. "I haven't seen Barclay in a few days, I don't even know if—"

"I do," Struz says. "Call a meeting with everyone in fifteen minutes."

"Of course," Deirdre says, then Struz's hand is on my back and he's guiding Ben and me down the hallway again.

When I open the door to the room Jared is sharing with four other people, he's the first person I see. He's lying in the hospital bed, a bored look on his face, his left leg in a cast from toes to calf. I'm so relieved, I burst out laughing.

"Oh my God, you look like half a mummy," I say as I move to his bed.

He smiles for a second and opens his mouth, but apparently he changes his mind about being happy to see me. Instead he folds his arms across his chest and says, "Where have you been? Struz looked everywhere for you, and no one knew where you were."

I sit down on the edge of his bed. "I know, I'm sorry. I was with Ben. We've been looking for you."

Jared leans around me to look at Ben, who's standing behind me. He waves awkwardly, because I know he's been itching to get away since Struz first picked us up—we're wasting time.

I can't believe the world might still end in less than a day, and I'm having *this* moment. The one where my little brother is appraising the guy I'm in love with. It makes me want to get away too.

I run a hand through Jared's hair, but he ducks away.

"How's your leg?" I ask, because I know he isn't about to admit he was afraid in front of some other guy. "What happened to it?"

"I was in the locker room, getting ready for ENS, and the lockers came down." Jared glances at Ben. "They just got me at a bad angle."

"How long did they say you'll have to wear the cast?"

"Six weeks." And by the way he says it, I can tell it's the last thing he wanted to hear.

"Six weeks will pass in no time." Hopefully.

"Do you remember at Disney, when we rode the new Pirates of the Caribbean ride and you got soaking wet?" Jared asks.

"It was just a few days ago, dude." I smile. "Of course I remember."

Jared yawns and leans back against his pillow. "Good. Because I want to do that again, as soon as my leg is better."

I don't know if Disneyland is even remotely still standing—somehow I doubt it. But I don't tell Jared that. Instead I just say, "Deal." Hopefully I'll have time to figure that all out later.

"**S**lipping that leash was harder than I expected," Ben says when we're finally on our way to Qualcomm.

I can't help but smile at him despite everything going on right now.

Struz wouldn't let us out of his sight. He drove us to Scripps to look for my mother—and for Elijah. But my mother was gone, like Struz had said, and Elijah had been discharged. When we got back to the Federal Building, Ben and I needed to get out of there. We were keeping track of the countdown, and we had less than twenty-four hours.

But it wasn't that easy to just leave. Despite how busy he was, Struz made sure he didn't leave us alone. Until reports of wildfires came in, and Struz called another meeting. Agents and analysts were all too busy to babysit, and we managed to grab his TrailBlazer from the parking lot. Of course I feel guilty about leaving, but we have to move fast. We can't wait for bureaucracy to catch up.

"What's our plan?" I ask. Because I'm annoyed at how many of my decisions seem to be based on my reactions to things as they happen rather than on planning. I feel underprepared for everything.

"First we find Alex," Ben says, and I'm glad he doesn't seem offended by my abruptness. "We need to see if he knows anything about where Eli could be."

"You think he could be at home?" For a minute, I wonder how he could open portals in the hospital, but then I remember he can open them anywhere. He just has that ability.

Ben shakes his head. "No way. Even if it's still around, he got along with his foster family even worse than I did with mine."

"Your foster mom didn't seem bad when I met her," I say, hoping he won't take that the wrong way.

"No, she's not, it's . . . Janelle, I have a family. They're just not here, and it's hard not to resent people trying to jump in and be your parents, especially when you can't tell them who you really are. There's always a wall between me and them. Plus, I have Elijah and Reid. We're each other's family."

Neither of us mentions that it's an even bigger betrayal if one of them has gone behind Ben's back and been opening the portals despite the danger.

"There are a couple places Eli might go if he was well enough to be released from the hospital," Ben adds. "We'll find him."

I look out the window. The sidewalks and even full lanes of the highway have cracked and turned into small trenches.

It's not just Qualcomm that's an evac shelter, I realize as we pull up to the south entrance. The whole parking lot is an evac shelter as well. Cars are lined up on the side of the road haphazardly, as if people ditched their vehicles and ran for the stadium—and maybe they did. Even with the FBI vehicle, the security guard at the entrance won't let us drive into the entrance. Ben double-parks nearby, and I say a silent prayer that the TrailBlazer is still there when we come back. I'd like to return it to Struz, if we can.

The parking lot is full of makeshift tents and families with their pets, and I walk close to Ben with my head down. It's cruel and selfish, but I just can't afford the distraction of more heartache. These people might not know it, but this isn't over. We're down to our last day, and the end of the world is still coming if we can't stop it.

Inside, I look up and the first person I recognize is Kate. She's standing with both of her parents, surrounded by a ridiculous amount of designer luggage.

Three years ago it looked like we might get evacuated for a wildfire, so my dad made us pack up the car with things we wanted to save. But our car was filled with things like my mom's meds, blankets, photo albums, and a change of clothes for each of us. In other words, necessities and irreplaceables. Somehow I doubt Kate's Louis Vuitton luggage is full of anything other than clothes or her shoe collection. And how useful are those stilettos going to be ever again?

I look away before Kate has a chance to spot me, because as much as I hate her I'm still glad she's not dead.

"Here, let's go this way," Ben says as he pulls me toward one of the check-in points.

There are people everywhere, waiting in line with presumably whatever's left of their lives, and unless I can find Alex by aimlessly wandering—which would take forever—we need to stand in line like everyone else.

"I'll get in line if you want to look around for a second," Ben says. "Just don't go far."

411

I nod, though I don't want to go too far anyway. There's an irrational comfort in maintaining close proximity. But I also know he's not just asking about Alex at the check-in. He's going to ask about Reid and Elijah. And the more I think about it, the more I'm getting used to the idea that Elijah is the one opening portals. After all, the whole reason he was interested in Eric Brandt, back when we were calling him Suspect Zero, was because he wanted to know if Brandt could help him get home.

I keep the thought to myself, because even if Ben has acknowledged it might be Elijah—even if he knows it deep down—he doesn't want it to be true. And he still cares about him. They've been through something together I can't even fathom.

But someone is opening portals, and we have to stop them. Barclay wasn't wrong about that.

Someone's already set up a wall where people can post pictures and notes about people who are missing, and I find myself standing in front of it. My eyes wander over the smiling faces in the photographs: young, old, black, white, Asian. These people are all loved—and missed—by someone. My throat constricts as I wonder what percentage of them are dead.

More heartbreaking, though, are the hastily scribbled Post-it notes or the drawings on ripped spiral notebook paper. There's a certain desperation to those.

"Did you need paper and a pen to write something?" a weary but familiar voice asks the woman scanning the board next to me. A sense of relief that is becoming ever more familiar washes over me.

I wait until she and the woman are finished before saying her name. "Cecily."

She looks up at the sound of my voice, and her red-rimmed eyes widen when she recognizes me. Then she launches herself in my direction, her arms latching onto me.

"Oh my God, J, everyone thought you were dead! Your house . . . and you weren't in school . . . and no one knew where you were!" she says, and she keeps talking, but as she starts to cry it's clear I'm not going to be able to understand much more.

"Cecily," I say with a smile as I push her away from me and try to force her to look at me. "Take a breath."

She nods and tries—to no avail—to get control of herself. But at least I know she heard me.

I think she says something again about how she thought I was dead.

"Cecily, have you seen Alex at all? Ben and I—"

"Oh my God, Alex!" Cecily says with wide eyes. "He doesn't know? Oh, you have to go see him. Come on!"

She starts pulling me toward the stadium ramp, and I'm genuinely caught off guard by how strong she is. "Ben!" I shout, pulling back and digging in my heels. "Hold up, Cee."

And then through a wall of people I see Ben burst out, scanning for me. I wave, and I can see his body relax when he realizes I'm with Cecily.

I hold my hand out for him and then he's there, his fingers curling around mine. Cecily looks from me to Ben and back to me again, wide-eyed and mouthing the word "oh" before her whole face morphs into the happy girl I know with the infectious smile. She even giggles as we run after her up the ramp.

I'm at least glad something hasn't changed.

We find Alex in the nosebleed section, eating a hot dog and reading *Outliers*.

"Seriously?" I ask, ready to tease him—and a little relieved I still can. "You're still doing homework?" But as I get closer, I realize he's not reading *Outliers*. His eyes are red, and the tracks of his tears are visible on his face through the dust and sweat caked to his skin. The book is just sitting open on his lap, like he doesn't know what else to do, and that hot dog has probably sat untouched for a while.

When I put my hand on his shoulder, he looks up, and for a second, it's like he doesn't even recognize me. He just stares.

And then something clears in his eyes, and he grabs my arm and pulls me into him for a hug. It's awkward and uncomfortable the way I'm leaning over him, but I don't care. I feel the way his body shakes, and I know he's crying.

As I hold him, Cecily chatters on about how she found us and how Alex has been helping her all day with getting people situated. Her uncle apparently works for Qualcomm and is in charge of turning it into an evac shelter. When her walkie-talkie summons her and she has to head back downstairs, I glance toward Ben, who smiles and says, "Cecily, I'll help you for a second." Then he turns to me. "I'll get the car and pull it around front. See you down there."

When they're gone, I pull back. "Where's your family?" I ask Alex, because really there's no way to tiptoe around it.

"I don't know," he says. "They're both officially listed as missing. My mom wasn't at the house during the quake, which is a blessing since she definitely would have died, but I'm not sure where she was. If she's around, though, we can count on her finding me."

I don't doubt it. "And your dad?"

He just shakes his head. "His office building came down, and the department was on the thirtieth floor. But they don't know if he was there."

"I'm so sorry, Alex," I whisper, giving him another hug. "And I'm so sorry about the things I said to you. I didn't mean them."

He squeezes me tight enough it hurts. "I should have believed you."

"It's crazy. Of course you didn't believe me." I shake my head and smile.

Alex wipes his eyes with the heel of his hand. "You saw Jared and Struz?"

"They're fine." I'm still a little disconcerted about the book and the hot dog. "What about you? Are you okay?"

"I'll be okay," Alex says, even though he's not convincing at all. "I was worried your faces were melting off somewhere."

"Thanks for that image," I say, and like a girl, I burst into tears.

"Stop," Alex says. "I'll start crying too."

I roll my eyes. "Please, I think all of us have cried more in the past week than probably ever in our lives. Let's own that."

Alex doesn't laugh like I want him to.

Because it needs to be said and because the best way for us to cope with this is to make sure we're still around tomorrow, I add, "This wasn't Wave Function Collapse; this is just the beginning."

And then I recount everything that Ben and I went through with Barclay.

When I'm done, Alex takes a deep breath. "So we've still got to find out who's opening the portals and stop them."

And then he says, "I know who killed your father," right as I say, "I think I know who's opening the portals."

My heart pounds in my ears and I wonder if I heard him right.

"What?" I ask, my voice breathless.

He was shot three times. Once in the arm and twice in the chest.

My eyes sting just remembering it. I look at Alex straight-on, ready to know who it was.

"It was Reid," Alex says.

That's not the name I expected to hear. "How? How do you know?"

Time pauses. I see Alex's face, and I know from the confidence and the conviction behind his words that he's dead sure.

My heart aches for Ben—because I get it, Reid and Elijah are his family, and you don't want to think the people close to you are capable of that—but I think of my dad and the fact that he died without drawing his gun, and I don't care who Reid is to Ben.

Because he's not going home now. He's going to rot in a jail cell in this universe.

Alex just nods. "After the quake, I left school and went back to my house and then to Scripps to check on Elijah, since you told me he was there. He told me where he'd be when he got out, then he told me a couple other things, and it all started to click."

"What do you mean?"

"There's a house in Park Village that backs up against the canyons," Alex says. "It's for sale. Elijah's been crashing there some nights when he's sick of his foster family. Reid too. Elijah laughed about Reid hiding a bunch of Ben's science stuff there."

Alex turns and looks at me. "And that set of numbers in your father's wallet?"

I hold my breath.

"It's the address."

Biting the inside of my cheek, I try to get a grip. This is still circumstantial. We have to talk to Elijah and Reid. We have to tell the authorities what's going on—I should call Struz. But I don't. Instead I think about the fact that someone shot my dad when he hadn't even pulled his gun, and I look at Alex and say, "Let's go."

00:21:47:19

When we get down the stairs and are on our way to the south entrance to meet Ben, Alex grabs my hand. "Wait."

I turn to look at him, to ask what he forgot, hoping he hasn't had a change of heart. I'm sure he's about to say we should call Struz—that we shouldn't race off into the night like heroes.

But he doesn't.

Instead he says, "You're my best friend, J. Even though you get dramatic sometimes, and even though we fight when you're crazy, *and* even though I know you stole my Optimus Prime action figure when we were in kindergarten. You're the best person in my life."

"I know, Alex. You're mine," I say, my throat tight and eyes watery. "Why are you getting all sentimental on me?"

"The world might end tomorrow."

"Alex, this isn't some lame-ass action movie," I say, even though he's right. I just can't handle more crying right now. "No good-bye monologues necessary."

"Is it wrong I'm hoping we'll get at least one diabolical monologue from a bad guy?" he says, and starts walking again.

I'm not sure I want a monologue, but I do want answers.

I don't say that, though, because I see Ben in the TrailBlazer, and there's a more important point in all this. If the world ends tomorrow, I really need Alex to know, "I did *not* steal your Optimus Prime action figure, by the way. You totally left it somewhere and your mother probably confiscated it. You know she hated that cartoon."

As we drive, Alex relates to Ben the same things he told me.

"No way," Ben says when Alex suggests Reid killed my dad. He looks at me. "There's just no way Reid could do that. Elijah might be opening the portals, but there's no way either of them could ever kill anybody."

I don't disagree with him, but I don't agree with him either. Elijah and Reid never seemed all that broken up about the dead bodies they were pulling through the portals—that was Ben.

Ben shakes his head. "There's just no way," he says again.

This time, I notice Alex also isn't saying anything.

"Have you ever been to 3278 Park Village?" I ask him.

Ben shakes his head. "Elijah only found the house a few months ago, and I didn't have a car. Plus, I was usually working when he and Reid hung out there."

I'm secretly relieved to hear it.

"That's where Elijah will be?" Ben asks, his voice thick. "Well, let's talk to him."

"How will we find Reid?" Alex asks.

Ben shakes his head. "We won't. If we have Eli, Reid will find us."

A weird anxious anticipation has me on the edge of my seat when I spot 3278 Park Village Road. It's a modest house that looks similar to the rest of them—or it did when they were all standing. Now the porch has collapsed and the house has a droopy look to it, as if the foundation is off balance. But it's doing better than most of the other houses in the development. It's still inhabitable.

The irony of that is hardly lost on me.

When we pull into the driveway, the house is dark inside, and I worry that Elijah isn't here, until I remember electricity is out all over the city and of course it's dark inside.

I put my hand on Ben's arm. "You okay?"

He nods and shuts off the car, and the three of us get out silently and in unison. I've promised to let Ben do the confronting if Elijah is actually here. I'm not going to jump to conclusions.

Ben knocks on the front door, and Alex adjusts the strap of his backpack.

"Why didn't you leave that in the car?" I whisper, but he just shrugs and ignores me.

I think he's suffering from the same giddy excitement I am—and I think he feels weird and guilty about that like I do. It's perverse, this whole taking pleasure in taking someone down. But I don't think about it too hard—because if I'm not feeling *this*, I'll have to think too hard about everything that's happened.

Ben knocks again.

"What if he's not here?" I ask.

Without looking at me, Ben says softly, "We'll find him."

"More than half the city is destroyed," Alex says. "This house is practically the only thing still standing. Where else would he be?"

I'm about to say something else—about Alex and the smart mouth he's got on him post–natural disaster—but the front door swings open and Elijah is standing there in ripped jeans and a ratty plaid flannel.

"Thank fucking God," he says, clasping Ben in a tight hug.

"You're not going to get rid of me that easy," Ben says as they break the embrace. "Can we come in?"

"Hell yeah," Elijah says, opening the door wider. "Trechter, thanks for bringing my boy back."

Alex nods, and I almost ask him when he became such a tough guy.

"Tenner," Elijah says as I pass him. "Sight for sore eyes, as always. Where were you keeping him?"

I don't say anything because I agreed to let Ben do the talking, even though I want to say something like, *I just traveled through a portal to another universe, you asshole.* But Elijah's staring at me, so I look at Ben, who's apparently just done a military-style sweep of the first floor of the house. "Is Reid here?" he asks.

Elijah shakes his head. "I mean, he was, but who knows where the hell he slunk off to now. What the fuck do you want with Reid?" And I see in his face the moment where he starts to break down an assessment of the situation. "Wait, what the fuck do you want with Reid?" he says again.

"Someone *here* has been opening portals," Ben says. "And the only people who know the science are you and Reid."

"I told you, my dad's got to be looking for us, that—"

"Eli, I know it's either you or Reid. Just please tell me you didn't kill Janelle's dad too."

Elijah shakes his head. "No way—no, I've had enough of this fucking girl," he says. "She isn't one of us. Why would you believe her over me?"

"Eli—"

"No, never mind, don't even answer that," he says. "I can't believe this shit."

"Elijah," Alex says. "Janelle's dad was coming here, to this house, the day he was killed."

"And his body was dumped in that canyon," I add.

Elijah shakes his head, but the words don't come out.

"Was it you?" Ben asks. "Please, Eli, you're my best friend. Were you opening the portals?"

Elijah shakes his head, but instead of looking at Ben, he looks at me. "Reid, his foster parents, their backyard is next door to the house where all those people melted from radiation."

"What?" I remember them looking at each other when they pulled into the neighborhood.

"I thought for sure that was my dad trying to open a portal on his side," Elijah says.

"I told you, it's Reid. This isn't a coincidence."

I suck in a breath. I should have looked for that—but that's how it fits. Barclay said the portals Ben was opening up were too big and therefore unstable. That's why they were bringing things or people through. If Reid opened a huge portal, something that would encompass that whole house, and then lost control of it . . . he'd certainly think twice about opening a portal in his backyard.

"Sit down," Ben says, and then catches him up to speed.

Or starts to, because he's explaining Barclay and the IA when the front door opens and Reid walks in.

And Alex pulls my father's gun from his backpack and points it at Reid.

00:20:42:58

I want to ask him where the hell he got it, but my heart is pounding and my attention is on Reid, who's frozen like a deer in headlights in the doorway.

"Whoa, killer," Elijah says, standing up. "We can fucking talk about this."

But when Alex's eyes flick to Elijah, Reid takes off.

And because I apparently have a death wish, I take off after him.

The sun has long gone down, but Reid's wearing a white T-shirt and I'm close enough to him that he's not hard to follow.

I run faster than I've ever run in my whole life. I'm flying—hurtling over shrubbery and debris, I don't feel any tightness in my muscles or any exhaustion in my lungs. I just go.

I can hear Ben and Elijah calling after Reid and me, but they might as well have stayed in the house—I don't hear a word they're saying. And I don't care.

As I gain on him, I can hear Reid's panting breaths, and I have a moment to wonder if this is what a wild animal feels like when it's about to pounce on its prey, and then I hurl myself forward, grabbing on to that white shirt and tackling him to the ground.

"You son of a bitch, did you do it?" I punch him in the face, and I can feel his nose start to bleed. "Did you kill him?"

I manage to kick him in the balls before Ben catches up with us. He pulls me off Reid and looks down. "Stay there," he says, then turns to me. "Janelle, stop."

And I realize I'm still shouting the questions at Reid, and I swallow them back.

"Did you?" Ben demands. "Did you kill her dad?"

"It was an accident!" Reid screams back.

00:20:41:04

My dad loved *Star Wars*. He even had a Stormtrooper costume he used to wear on Halloween when Jared and I wanted him to go trick-or-treating.

One Halloween, when I was six and Jared was three, he wasn't going to make it home in time to take us trick-or-treating, and he made some junior analyst come to our house, put on the Stormtrooper costume, and pretend to be him. Only no one could quite pull it off like my dad could. Even Jared saw through it.

When I was ten, *Revenge of the Sith* came out, and my dad got us tickets to the midnight release. He also got us Jedi robes and fake lightsabers and wanted us all to go to the movie in costume. But I was just old enough to realize how lame that would look to other people, and I refused. I wore jeans and a T-shirt, crossed my arms, and refused to sit in the same row as the two Jedi I came with.

My dad had been so excited for that night, and I refused to participate in it because I was embarrassed of what people might think of me. People I didn't even know.

I never apologized to him for that. I never told him how later when I thought back to that night, how cool I thought it was that he had done that for us.

And now—because of Reid—I'll never be able to.

00:20:41:03

"He was shot three times—that's not an accident." I move toward Reid, but strong hands pull me back—Elijah's.

And then a light shines in Reid's bloody face, and Alex is next to us, flashlight in hand.

"Nice fucking shot, Tenner," Elijah says.

"I need to know what happened."

"Tell her," Ben says.

"It was an accident," Reid repeats.

"We'll be the fucking judge of that—what the hell were you thinking, opening up more portals when you didn't know what you were doing?" Elijah says. "Answer the fucking girl."

I jerk out of Elijah's arms. "What happened?"

"Ben was close to a breakthrough. We were this close to getting home, and then because of a couple missteps, he wouldn't keep trying."

"A couple missteps?" Ben yells. "Two people were dead!"

"I don't care about them," Reid yells back. "I want to go home, and Eli does too!"

"Yeah, I fucking want to go home," Elijah says. "I also want

430

to make it without getting burned up."

Reid shakes his head. "I put my hand through one night when I opened a portal by myself, and nothing happened. I didn't get burned up. The three of us can go through them fine."

Elijah looks at Ben, who nods.

But I don't care about this part. "What happened with my dad?"

"He figured it out," Reid says. "Not the portals, but he figured out I was involved. I talked to him when the portal took out the house. They were my neighbors, and he was questioning everyone, but he kept asking me the same questions again and again."

My eyes sting. My dad could almost always tell when someone was lying—he'd obviously known Reid had more to say.

"And then he must have followed me out here. He couldn't figure out what I was doing, but he knew I was involved somehow."

I'm so proud of my dad, my heart feels like it might burst. That he could have realized Reid had something to do with this after one conversation. I put a hand to my chest and shake my head. "So how did you accidentally end up shooting him?"

Ben gives Reid a kick. "Tell her."

"I started carrying my foster father's gun around when I was opening the portals in case something came through that wasn't dead."

"Shit," Elijah mutters.

"He surprised me. I was in the middle of trying to get a portal open, and he just walked in like he owned the place," Reid says. "The portal opened, and I couldn't let him see it. So I pulled the gun and I shot him. I didn't know it was your dad until later!"

I feel sick. Because that doesn't sound accidental at all.

"And then you just kept right on going?" Ben asks. "Even after the earthquakes and when we were chasing Eric Brandt around."

"You fucking got me shot for no reason," Elijah adds.

I hold out a hand to steady myself and hear Alex say, "It's okay, I got him," and then Ben is there, steadying me, as I lean over and vomit into the dirt.

It's while I'm bent over, puking up the food I ate today with Ben holding my hair, that I hear the electronic sound a TV makes when you turn it on or off in a quiet room. A cool rush of air hits the back of my neck, and my body shivers.

Elijah says, "Holy fucking shit," Alex grunts, and for a minute I don't see it. It's dark and it's hard to see too far in the distance. But to my left there's a perfect circle of landscape that seems to be missing. In its place is a nothingness, a black hole. I see it because it ripples like it's liquid—and because Barclay and Eric Brandt in full tactical gear are coming through. They both have guns trained on us, and Eric Brandt shouts, "Get on the ground, hands behind your head!"

Elijah steps toward him and Barclay yells, "Right now!"

Then I hear the gunshot.

And I turn in time to see that Reid and Alex both have their hands on my father's gun, and blood is pouring from a hole in Alex's neck.

00:20:40:13

I throw myself at Alex.

My hands go to the hole in his neck, and I press down to try to stop the bleeding. They're coated in his blood within half a second. I'm screaming for someone to help me, but Eric has his gun on Elijah and Ben, and Barclay has his on Reid.

"It's Reid!" I scream, because I can't deal with Ben getting shot too.

Reid looks at me, then raises his gun toward Barclay.

And there isn't even a split second of hesitation.

Barclay shoots him in the head.

Eric has Elijah and Ben on the ground with their hands over their heads. Underneath my own hands, I can feel Alex choking on the blood in his throat. I look over my shoulder and see Barclay checking Reid's vitals.

"He's dead!" I scream to Barclay. "Help me!"

Blood comes out of Alex's mouth, and I try to look him in the eyes and will him to stay with me, but they're already glassy and unfocused.

"Please, Alex, I need you!"

I can tell the exact moment he's gone, though. I just know.

Barclay is kneeling next to me, adding his hands to mine, trying to apply pressure to the wound. And I'm suddenly so cold, my whole body is shaking.

But I refuse to give up.

"Ben! Barclay, please, I need Ben!"

Barclay turns and shouts something to Eric. Something about Reid.

"It was Reid opening the portals!" I shout. I need Ben to help me. "Please, Barclay!"

I can't breathe. I can't believe this is happening. After everything. How could I be so stupid as to let Alex come with us? I should never have let him run around and play FBI with me in the first place.

Ben scrambles in next to me, and I grab his hands and thrust them into the blood where the bullet went. "Heal him, please." I'm crying.

"I will," he says.

And I feel Ben's hands start to warm up and heat underneath mine, and that heat seeps into Alex's skin, and then Elijah is kneeling down across from us, lending his hands to Alex's neck too, and I pull back since my hands aren't going to do anything but get in the way.

Before my eyes, the skin reknits itself together until there is no bullet hole.

But Alex doesn't wake up.

"What's wrong? Why isn't it working?"

"He's lost too much blood!" Elijah says.

"Here," Ben says as he pushes me out of his way and puts his hand on Alex's chest. He pours whatever he can into Alex's chest—to restart his heart. Alex's body jerks, and then Ben and Elijah are doing CPR.

"Please, please, Alex," I plead over and over again. But nothing happens. He doesn't open his eyes or take a breath.

Until Barclay is pulling me back.

"Tenner, he's already long gone," he says, and then he shakes my shoulders. "Janelle, they can't bring him back."

I look up into Barclay's blue eyes, and I must be delusional because I think he's actually trying to be nice to me. "People aren't supposed to have those kinds of powers," he says. "We're not supposed to be able to bring people back from the dead. You have to let him go."

"I'm supposed to be dead," I say.

Barclay at least doesn't lie to me. "But you're not."

"But why?" I whisper.

"Maybe you weren't ready to let go, maybe Ben didn't get to Alex in time," Barclay says. "It doesn't really matter, does it?"

And then someone is pushing Barclay out of the way and pulling me into their arms. "I'm so sorry, baby. I fixed what I could, but it was too late." I sag into Ben, breathing in his smell and letting him take my weight as my legs give out beneath me.

Until we're on the ground, holding on to each other, sticky with Alex's blood, and Elijah puts a hand on my shoulder. "I'm sorry, Janelle. I fucking liked him."

00:20:37:40

The IA finally has enough of my hysteria, and Barclay pulls me to my feet. Then he turns to Ben. "I'm not kidding about your abilities," he says. "Besides the fact that every time you use them, you fuck around with your body's chemical makeup, there are people out there who think no one should have that kind of power, and you'd be smart to not advertise, if you know what I mean."

I don't really know what that means, other than the fact that Barclay thinks Ben might be putting himself in danger.

"Got it." Ben stands and pulls me into him again.

"And no more opening portals," Barclay says, lowering his voice and glancing at Brandt. "At all. If anyone in IA finds out you were involved more than you let on . . ."

Ben nods.

"Once we're home, I have no reason to ever fucking leave," Elijah adds.

"Taylor, get the body," Brandt says before he approaches us. And he looks specifically at me. "Earth 19402 will be closed to interverse travel for at least six months after we leave to allow it to restabilize in its new position. But after that, as long as there's no unauthorized travel or unstable portal openings, you should gradually but steadily move away from Wave Function Collapse."

"And you're not going to release the Oppenheimer on us?" I ask.

"No, I'll disable it. As long as no one else opens any more portals, your universe should restabilize on its own," he says, and then he looks at Ben and Elijah. "This will get you home. It'll be open for four minutes exactly, and then it'll shut forever. Within the next few days, someone from IA will come by to debrief you on exactly what happened here, for the report."

And he points a quantum charger at open space, and a portal opens.

Then he turns, and without another word, he goes back through the portal he and Barclay appeared from.

I turn to Barclay. "You're taking the Oppenheimer with you, right?" Because I don't want that thing stuck here.

He nods.

"How did you find us?" I ask.

"There's a tracking device in every quantum charger," he says. "It took me a while to figure out how to turn it on." He doesn't say they made it in time, because Alex is dead, but he grabs Reid's body, looks at Ben, and says, "Don't fuck this up. Get through the portal. It's your only chance to get home."

Then he looks at me. "Take care of yourself," he says, and then right before he steps through his portal, he adds, "And good job."

Then he's gone, and the portal closes behind him.

And the countdown is over.

When Barclay is gone, Ben hugs me to him and tells me again he's sorry about Alex. He's crying too—his whole body shakes as he wraps it around mine. I swallow down the lump in my throat and wipe the burning tears from my eyes.

"It's not your fault," I say, even though it hurts. Because it's not his fault—and I know that—but I still don't understand why he could bring *me* back from the dead and not Alex.

"Guys, are you fucking seeing this?" Elijah says.

But I don't need to see the portal. *I feel it.* The air changes, the temperature drops a fraction of a degree, a breeze that seems to say *storm* picks up, a shot of electricity moves through the ground under my feet, and I can smell it—wet, never-ending, open.

I shiver.

Not just because it's cold.

I'm afraid to look at Ben, so I look at Elijah first. His mouth ajar, his eyes wide, he's leaning toward the portal. The front of his body has an eerie glow to it, as if the portal itself is reflecting off him, beckoning him to come forward, like it's waiting to reclaim him.

438

He turns, his eyes looking past me as if I'm not even here, a slow smile spreading wide. "We did it," he whispers. "We really fucking did it!"

And Elijah suddenly throws his head back and his arms out to the sides, and a laugh between elation and hysteria peals from his mouth, swallowing up the eerie silence.

And my throat constricts. My eyes burn. I try to swallow back the rising tide of emotions. I'm alive when I should be dead. My father is dead. Alex is dead. We just prevented the end of the world. We stalled Wave Function Collapse. We opened the portal they need to get them back home. It's all too much—and I don't know what I'm supposed to feel.

It doesn't matter that I knew this part was coming—I *hoped* for it, for Ben. I can't swallow. Instead I fight the urge to gag.

I turn to Ben. Only he's not looking at the portal, and he's not looking at Elijah. He's looking right at me.

Those deep-set eyes that look like they could tell stories for days, and that wavy brown hair that feels soft between my fingers. I try to memorize the angles of his jaw and the lines of his lips, because I know.

I know this might be the last time I ever see him.

Breath fills my lungs, my throat relaxes, and I can't help but smile. Because I can see what he's thinking as clearly as if he had spoken.

He doesn't want to leave—he doesn't want to go home.

He's going to choose me instead.

Ben lifts his hand toward me, and as my heart flutters, Elijah catapults himself in front of me, throwing his arms around Ben and tackling him to the ground.

"We're going home!" Elijah laughs. "We're finally fucking

going home. My parents—your brother! I've imagined what they'll say when they see us every fucking day we've been gone."

The reminder hits me like a punch to the gut. Seven years Ben's been away from his family. Seven years he's been in and out of foster homes. What kind of person would I be if I asked him to stay here?

If I let him stay.

I would never leave Jared—or even Struz—behind. What kind of regrets will Ben have if he chooses me over his family— his former life? How much resentment will he have toward me if I let him?

Elijah jumps up again and pulls Ben to his feet. "Ready?" he says, and I never thought I'd look at Elijah Palma and see an unbridled enthusiasm and a lightness in his step that reminds me of my brother.

"Eli," Ben whispers, a finality in his voice.

And despite the fact that my heart is hammering uncontrollably in my body, I know I need to take care of this.

"I'm not—"

I cut in. "Yes, you are."

Ben's eyes pivot to mine, and Elijah looks back at me, remembering my existence with surprise.

"Janelle . . ."

"Don't." My voice breaks, even though I'm desperately trying to hold it together. "You said it yourself. You don't belong here," I add, squeezing the words through the tightness in my throat. "You need to go home."

But my traitorous heart comes to life enough to scream that it still loves him. Because no matter what those other parts of me think, the part that decided that it loved Ben Michaels still

440

does. And it doesn't want to let him go without some kind of fight.

Ben pushes past Elijah and pulls me into his arms in a motion so swift that I can't follow it—not through the tears clouding my vision. But as his body curls around me, the irony that we just *fit* so perfectly together, like the contours of our bodies have molded together to maximize the points of connection, is hardly lost on me. He squeezes me against him—hard. Almost to the point that it hurts.

When he presses his mouth to my ear and his breath whispers into my hair, for a minute I'm delusional. *"I belong with you."* I want him to say it so badly that I imagine he does.

"Come on," Elijah says. "We've got less than a minute."

Ben pulls away, and I see Elijah standing at the portal.

Elijah looks back over his shoulder, as if he's daring Ben *not* to follow him. And then his eyes meet mine, and he nods. It's the closest to some form of acceptance and understanding that will ever pass between us. I get that, and offer one of his head nods right back at him.

He looks back at Ben, his eyes offering an unspoken threat. And then he moves through the portal, disappearing into the inky blackness.

Elijah Palma no longer exists on this Earth.

My chest feels like it's collapsing inward. I open my mouth, but I can't inhale.

Ben looks at me.

As his hand reaches out to cup my face, I can see that he's crying.

And suddenly, if I don't kiss him one last time, I will never forgive myself.

Our lips collide—lips, tongues, teeth all come together. His hands grip me so hard, I know I'll bruise, and I try to drink down the very essence of him through this kiss—try to memorize every moment we spent together.

I want to go back and freeze that moment, that first day in APEL where he asked how I'd want someone to propose to me, that moment when I leaned into him, my lips almost touching his ear, the smell of his shampoo in my nose, the way his breath caught in my ears while I whispered, *Fucking marry me.*

I'm going to miss more moments like that—physics labs and English debates like the ones we already had. Motorcycle-riding lessons, lunches in the library, talking about books, watching superhero movies or playing video games with Jared—moments we should have had together, but won't.

Ben pulls back, both of us gasping for air.

He takes two steps back. Closer to the portal.

I can't stop myself. "Ben," I call. And I'm not even embarrassed about how helpless my voice sounds.

Don't go.

"I'll come back for you." He takes another step back. "I promise."

Stay.

"Janelle Tenner," he says. "I will always fucking love you."

And then he takes one more step back. Into the portal. And blackness swallows him whole.

And then the portal closes. The last traces of Ben have left the world completely.

I sink down next to Alex's body and think of everything I've lost since Ben brought me back from the dead. I would have thought my eyes would be dry by now, that my ability to cry would be cut off—there should be a limit to tears.

But I lay my hand on Alex's forehead and remember the time I was nine and told his mother it was me who ruined her gardenias in the front yard, even though it had been Alex digging them up in a fit of rage because she'd forbidden him to play soccer. And I cry all over again, like I've never cried for anything in my life.

I remember the way Alex smiled when he came into first period in seventh grade after this crazy rainstorm had ended, with squeaking sneakers and wet socks that sloshed as he walked, leaving small puddles of water in each spot where his feet touched the floor. His black hair stood on end, and when our teacher asked if he needed a towel or a change of clothes from the nurse, he just shook his head. He ended up with the flu and couldn't audition for the school play like his mom had wanted him to.

I remember the field trip we took to Big Bear, when we both saw snow and experienced real winter for the first time. With soaked fuzzy mittens and red noses that burned, Alex and I were the only two people who didn't go skiing that first day. Instead we knelt over clumps of snow lumped by our feet, pushing them together until we had a snowman. We made snow angels and pelted each other with snowballs until we couldn't feel our faces.

And I remember how I felt after I woke up in that car freshman year, knowing my friendship with Kate was broken—irreparably. And knowing the only person I could go to was Alex.

When my tears have finally stopped, Alex's forehead has gone cold, and I make a mental note of exactly where we are so Struz can get someone out here for his body and we can bury him. If we don't find his mom, we can bury Alex in my mother's plot, right next to my dad.

I think both Alex and my dad would like that.

It starts raining when sunlight peeks over the horizon, and as the water hits my face and my hair, I try to imagine it washing all the heartache and loss away. I tilt my face to the sky, the rain mixing with Alex's blood and my tears.

I think of the way Ben looked when I saw him—really saw him—for the first time, when he brought me back to life. Looming over me with the sun behind him. I think of the first time we kissed on Sunset Cliffs, and I think of the way he looked when he said, *I'll come back for you.*

I don't know if he will, if he'll be able to, or if it would even make sense. If we belong to two different worlds, how could we ever be together?

But even if I never see him again, he's given me more than I could ever give back. I have so much to live for—Jared, Struz, this universe. There's so much for us to do—to rebuild.

Ben Michaels gave me my life back. He gave me a second chance.

I stand there until I'm soaked through, shivering, and numb from the cold. Until my eyes have put their tears to rest.

And I look around the canyon and the devastation that is now North San Diego County.

But I'm alive.

I'm alive.

More alive than I was before any of this happened.

Life is a fragile thing. Apparently the whole world is fragile too.

But it'll beat on.

Because it has to.

ACKNOWLEDGMENTS

This book owes its allegiance to an array of people. My mother, with her eternal patience and happiness. My sister, and her everlasting desire to challenge herself. My tenth grade English teacher, Mrs. Hall, and the love of literature she passed on to me.

Brooks, who introduced me to a writing workshop and encouraged me to do more than let my pages sit in a document on my computer. My amazing friends, who read overnight and took me to lunch at Cafeteria—Meredith and the Sara(h)s, you're amazing.

Everyone at Balzer + Bray and HarperCollins, who believed in Janelle and Ben and their story. Especially my editor, Kristin Daly Rens, who took what was essentially the skeleton of a novel and showed me how to make it whole, and Sara Sargent, whose excitement made me slightly less nervous about seeing my words out in the world.

My agent, Janet Reid, whose expertise and advice was—and continues to be—invaluable, and for refusing to let time goblins get the best of her.

And Dan . . . for *getting* it. All the texts, all the emails, all the late-night, last-minute phone calls. For the reliability and dealing with crazy. For letting his brilliance rub off. For. Every. Thing.

Turn the page for more amazing teen books
from HarperCollins . . .

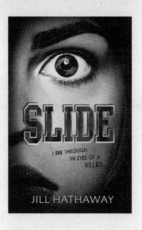

Vee Bell hates having narcolepsy.

But collapsing at schools is nowhere near as bad as the truth. When Vee passes out she slides randomly into other people's heads and ends up seeing through their eyes. Then Vee finds herself in the head of a killer, standing over the body of a cheerleader.

When another cheerleader turns up dead, everyone is a suspect. Struggling to understand her terrifying and unwanted 'gift', Vee is tangled in a web of secrets, lies and danger. . .

The dark, twisting scene looked almost the same as it did in each
of my horrible dreams.
Almost.
Because this time I wasn't the one drowning.
He was.

The only thing Amelia knows for sure is that she's dead and
trapped alone in a nightmarish existence. But everything
changes when she finds Joshua drowning in her river. As a
ghost, she can do nothing but *will* him to live. Yet in an
unforgettable moment of connection, she helps him survive.

But even as Amelia and Joshua struggle to keep their bond
hidden from the living, a frightening spirit will do anything in
his power to drag Amelia back into the ghost world. . . forever.

The human race is all but extinct, wiped out by a killer virus
released by genetically engineered soldiers, Partials.

Sixteen-year-old Kira is a trapped on Long Island. Her
community clings to survival, but what hope can they have
when no baby survives for more than three days?

Kira is determined to make a difference, to find a cure. Her
best friend is pregnant and Kira cannot let that baby die.
Time is running out – finding the cure means capturing a
Partial. . .